... of the Darkyn

Stay the Night

"Truly transfixing!"   —*Romantic Times*

"The best Darkyn novel to date." —*The Romance Reader*

Twilight Fall

"The pace is fast and the characters strong . . . whets the appetite for more."   —Monsters and Critics

"Flawed characters are Viehl's forte, and when you mix in rapidly paced plotting, the story shines with intense and dangerous emotions . . . one highly satisfying read!"
                    —*Romantic Times*

"[An] intelligent and breathtaking addition to the incomparable Darkyn series."   —Fresh Fiction

"Viehl scripts an excellent story in *Twilight Fall*."
                    —Paranormal Romance

"An electrifying addition to this top-notch series . . . a definite must-read."   —Romance Junkies

"A really good series . . . excellent."   —*Affaire de Coeur*

Evermore

"[F]ull of exciting twists and turns. . . . Viehl tells a self-contained, page-turning story of medieval vampires."
                    —*Publishers Weekly*

continued . . .

"Dual cases of unexpressed love have kept two potential mates dancing around each other. Add in guilt and remorse and this is a recipe for emotional disaster. Thankfully, Viehl knows just how to liven things up: by adding danger, treachery and betrayal to the mix. Things never run smoothly in the Darkyn world!" —*Romantic Times*

"Lynn Viehl sure knows how to tell a hell of a story."
—Romance Reviews Today

"[O]ne of my favorites, if not *the* favorite, Darkyn book to date." —Romance Reader at Heart

"[A]nother highly satisfying chapter in the Darkyn saga."
—Vampire Genre

Night Lost

"Viehl continues to weave an intricate web of intrigue in this contribution to the amazing series. . . . I became completely engrossed in this compelling story. Lynn Viehl had me hooked from the first page . . . exceptional. . . . I definitely recommend this marvelous book."
—Romance Junkies

"Fast-paced and fully packed. [Viehl] does an excellent job of world building and provides characters who continue to be explored book by book. You won't regret spending time in this darkly dangerous and romantic world!"
—*Romantic Times*

"Fans of the series will agree that Lynn Viehl is at the top of her game." —Alternative Worlds

OTHER NOVELS BY LYNN VIEHL

Kyndred Series

Shadowlight

Darkyn Series

If Angels Burn
Private Demon
Dark Need
Night Lost
Evermore
Twilight Fall
Master of Shadows
Stay the Night

DREAMVEIL

A NOVEL OF THE KYNDRED

———

Lynn Viehl

AN ONYX BOOK

ONYX
Published by New American Library, a division of
Penguin Group (USA) Inc., 375 Hudson Street,
New York, New York 10014, USA
Penguin Group (Canada), 90 Eglinton Avenue East, Suite 700, Toronto,
Ontario M4P 2Y3, Canada (a division of Pearson Penguin Canada Inc.)
Penguin Books Ltd., 80 Strand, London WC2R 0RL, England
Penguin Ireland, 25 St. Stephen's Green, Dublin 2,
Ireland (a division of Penguin Books Ltd.)
Penguin Group (Australia), 250 Camberwell Road, Camberwell, Victoria 3124,
Australia (a division of Pearson Australia Group Pty. Ltd.)
Penguin Books India Pvt. Ltd., 11 Community Centre, Panchsheel Park,
New Delhi - 110 017, India
Penguin Group (NZ), 67 Apollo Drive, Rosedale, North Shore 0632,
New Zealand (a division of Pearson New Zealand Ltd.)
Penguin Books (South Africa) (Pty.) Ltd., 24 Sturdee Avenue,
Rosebank, Johannesburg 2196, South Africa

Penguin Books Ltd., Registered Offices:
80 Strand, London WC2R 0RL, England

First published by Onyx, an imprint of New American Library,
a division of Penguin Group (USA) Inc.

First Printing, June 2010
10   9   8   7   6   5   4   3   2   1

For the greatest chef
I've ever known and loved—
my dad, Tony.

re·com·bi·nant (rē-kŏm´bə-nənt)
1. An organism or cell in which genetic recombination has taken place.
2. Material produced by genetic engineering.[1]

Literally hundreds of millions of experiments . . . have been carried out in the last 30 years without incident. No documented hazard to public health has been attributable to the applications of recombinant DNA technology. Moreover, the concern of some that moving DNA among species would breach customary breeding barriers and have profound effects on natural evolutionary processes has substantially disappeared as the science revealed that such exchanges occur in nature.

—Paul Berg, 1980 Nobel Laureate in Chemistry[2]

---

[1] The American Heritage® Dictionary of the English Language, Fourth Edition. Copyright © 2009 by Houghton Mifflin Company. Published by Houghton Mifflin Company. All rights reserved.

[2] "Asilomar and Recombinant DNA," August 26, 2004 (http://nobel prize.org/nobel_prizes/chemistry/articles/berg/)

PART ONE

Chez Soi

OCFS-7065A

(10/1998)

NEW YORK STATE

OFFICE OF CHILDREN AND FAMILY SER-VICES

AGENCY REPORTING FORM FOR ABAN-DONMENT OF UNIDENTIFIED CHILDREN/ TRANSFER TO PROTECTIVE CARE

Case type: Protective

Was SCR called? No

Was an SCR report registered? No

MPR? None—unknown

Date of Abandonment: September 29, 1998

CIN#: To be assigned

Date of Birth: Unknown; estimated 1987–1988

Sex: Female

Race: Caucasian

Name of Child: Unknown (temporarily designated YJF)

Agency or individual having legal custody: Unknown

Address: YJF picked up by police at undisclosed location on Lower East Side

List any witnesses: None

Physical description: Height 4'8", weight 51 pounds; cropped dark brown hair, dark brown eyes, pale skin.

Distinguishing marks: Child has permanent animal tattoos on both inner forearms.

Describe the details and circumstance regarding child's abandonment:

Police responded to complaint from local merchant of unsupervised child digging through trash, found and took YJF into custody. YJF transferred to DCS case worker Patterson and transported to hospital for standard medical evaluation (see attached ER assessment and admissions forms).

Attending physician reported YJF in fair physical condition, with minor bruises and lacerations to the extremities, signs of malnutrition, mild hypothermia, and moderate dehydration. Blood work negative for HIV, Hep-B, toxins. Admitted for 24-hour observation and treatment; discharged into DCS custody on September 30, 1998.

Interview: YJF appears lucid and cognitive, responds appropriately to verbal prompts, speaks English without an accent. Claims near-total memory impairment (unsubstantiated). Eats very well.

Shows no obvious signs of mental or physical impairment other than those previously mentioned.

Reason(s) for Placement into Protective Custody:
YJF shows aversion to physical contact of any kind; measured severely underweight (>2%) for height/age on CDC 2 to 20 years: Girls Weight-for-age grid. Observed by CW hiding food in clothing. Based on behavior, CW believes child has been neglected and/or starved for some time prior to abandonment.

Additional comments to supplement the above information or to clarify the child's situation, condition, prognosis, etc.: YJF attempted to bargain with CW several times to gain unsupervised access to building exits; may be runaway risk.

Recommendations: Transfer to foster care and follow up with psych evaluation and pediatric exam in one week.

Signed
> W. J. Patterson Sr.
> Senior Case Worker
> Department of Children's Services
> New York City
> New York

August 18, 1998
Manhattan, New York

"Lah-nah."

The slam of the door down the hall told Lana that her foster father was home. The thick, uneven tone of his voice warned her that he was drunk again. The thud of his footsteps, uneven and heavy, made it clear that he was coming to get her.

If he found her awake, he'd make her do it again.

"Hide in the closet," a voice whispered from beneath her bed.

"No." Lana's hands shook as she pulled the quilt up to her neck and held it there. She was ready for him. "Be quiet. Don't say anything." A movement made her turn her head, and she saw the dim smear of Jimmy's small face in the darkness. His brown eyes looked like holes burned through a bedsheet, reminding her that she wasn't the only one who was scared. "It'll be okay, Jimmy."

She jumped as the bedroom door flung open and hit the inside wall. Bits of plaster fell from the edges of an old hole made a little larger by the impact of the doorknob; it crackled as it pelted the floor.

Backlit by the hallway lights, her dad cast a wide, block-shaped shadow across Lana's bed. He stood there for a minute, wavering, taking another drink from the bottle he carried before he let it drop to the floor. As he came across the carpet the soles of his shoes scraped against the plush fibers.

Don't shake. Don't move. Don't touch him.

Lana felt his wide, damp palm press against her forehead, and pretended to stir rather than flinch. The hardest part was keeping her breathing slow and steady, as if she was really asleep, while she fought the other feelings. They crawled under her skin like bugs, itching to get out and do their work.

Touch him touch him touch him touch him tou—

"Lanie. Baby." Whiskey-soaked breath puffed against her face. "You 'wake?"

Lana mumbled something and turned over on her side, clutching the stuffed bear she slept with against her pounding heart. She could feel her dad swaying over her, watching her, deciding what he would do. It depended on how drunk he was. Some nights he'd remember how it was before, when her mom was alive and they were a real family, and he'd leave her alone. Other nights . . .

But that was her fault. She'd been afraid; she'd lost control. If she hadn't, he would never have found out.

"Tomorrow night, baby." Damp lips pressed against her ear before his rough voice crooned, "You'll be a good girl and do it again for Daddy, won't you?"

Bile inched up her throat. If he kissed her mouth, she would puke in his face. But he couldn't reach her mouth, not without losing his precarious balance and falling on top of her, so he straightened, shuffling back a step.

"Tomorrow night," he repeated.

Lana waited and listened as her dad shuffled from the room and the door banged shut. She heard the faint sounds of keys being pulled out and the creak of another door as it opened and closed. She didn't open her eyes until she heard the very last sound, the bell, and then she eased out of her bed and tiptoed over to put her ear to the door. Only after several minutes of silence did she know it was safe.

Jimmy sat up from his hiding place as she went to the closet and took out the backpack hidden behind the boxes of shoes. Her hands shook too much to unbutton her pajama top, so she pulled it over her head, revealing the T-shirt she wore beneath it.

"You can't run away," Jimmy said, careful to keep his voice low. "He'll call them. They'll find you. They'll make you come back."

"No." She opened a bureau drawer and grabbed a handful of socks. They didn't know about what she could do; he would never tell them. "I'm not ever coming back." She'd stolen a little money every week from the cash box kept in the kitchen, and while forty dollars and sixty-eight cents wouldn't take her far, it would have to be enough.

She couldn't do it again. Not ever.

"What about me?" Jimmy's voice climbed a panicky octave. "You can't leave me behind. He'll know that I helped you."

Her dad had a terrible temper, but while her mom had been alive he'd managed to keep it under control. He'd even been like a father to Lana, in a distant, indifferent way. She knew the only reason her parents had adopted her was that they couldn't have kids of their own, and her mother had wanted a little girl to love. Then things had changed, and her mom had stopped sleeping and started reading the Bible all day, carrying it with her everywhere, ignoring Lana and her dad until that last terrible night.

The slashing knife. *You hellspawn.* The fiery pain punching into her back. *You demon.* Every word screamed.

Lana's dad had never been the same after the funeral. He wouldn't talk to the police or anyone. He locked himself in her mom's room and drank. Whenever he came out, it was only to get more whiskey. Lana tried to speak to him and he hit her, knocking her into a wall.

You did this. She was right about you.

"He's gonna be really mad," Jimmy was saying.

"Call your mom after I leave and tell her that my dad hit you," Lana told him as she shoved some underwear into her pack. "Show her those bruises on your back you got from falling out of the tree. She'll believe you."

Jimmy's mother, who shared custody of him with his father, had already complained to her ex-husband about Lana's dad and how much he frightened Jimmy. The last time she'd come by on an unannounced visit she'd found Lana's dad sleeping on the floor in the hall with a mostly empty bottle of Jack Daniel's, and she'd warned Jimmy's father that she would go back to court and have the judge give her full custody. Jimmy had heard everything.

"But what if he comes to get me before my mom gets here?" Jimmy persisted. "He'll kill me."

"He won't." Lana shouldered her backpack and went over to kneel by the bed. Before she could say a single word Jimmy had her in a stranglehold hug.

"I don't want you to go."

She rubbed her hand carefully over his sore back. He'd been a good friend to her. "It'll be okay, Jimmy. You like living with your mom better anyway."

"My mom would help you, Lana." He pulled back, running his sleeve under his nose and blinking fiercely. "Maybe you could come and live with us. We could ask her. She likes you."

"My dad would find out, and you know what he would do to her." Lana gently removed his clinging arms from around her neck, and looked into his tear-filled eyes. "I've got to go now." She kissed his forehead. "Don't be afraid. Just hide until your mom comes."

She left Jimmy sobbing soundlessly into the side of her bed, and slipped out of the bedroom. After listening once more, she crossed the hall and crept out to the stairwell. She could see the front door from there, and the new locks her dad had installed a month ago, which required a key to open from either side. Fortunately everyone in the house had a copy, and Jimmy had been able to slip his father's from his key ring and bring it to her.

Lana clutched it in her fist as she moved toward the stairs. In a few minutes she'd be downstairs and out the door, and she'd be free. No more sleepless nights, no more hiding from her dad, no more fear. No more Lana, either.

She'd already picked out her new name, thanks to an old movie and a map of North Carolina. She didn't know how exactly yet, but she was going to find her real parents and call them. When she told them what had happened to her, they'd be sorry and come and get her right away. They had to.

A low chuckle behind her made Lana freeze.

"I knew you were faking it," her dad said against the back of her neck.

As Lana swung around, she saw Jimmy standing just behind her father. He was holding his baseball bat.

"You let her go."

Her father turned, his fist rising, and then Jimmy swung the bat, knocking it into the side of his head with a solid thunk. Lana bit back a scream as her father reeled into the wall and slid down it to sit on the floor, his head sagging against one shoulder.

Jimmy lowered the bat and looked at her as tears streaked his face. "Now you can get away. Go. Hurry."

Chapter 1

Five years hadn't altered much of Rowan Dietrich or New York City. The kid who had carried everything she owned in a backpack when she had left for Georgia still owned little more than the clothes on her back. She'd found friends, people who were as damaged and screwed up as she was, but the two most important had really been searching for each other, and now they were together and complete. They would have gladly gone on being her surrogate family, but she'd wanted more than that, more than they could ever give. Leaving them behind hurt, but Rowan knew she'd done the right thing.

If destiny did exist, she thought as she removed her helmet, being alone seemed to be hers.

November had iced the roads with slush and frozen puddles, and forced her to keep her speed minimal as she retreated to the alleys. A few hours earlier she might have smelled what passed as a festive fragrance here: roasted nuts hawked by sidewalk vendors too fat or too poor to care about standing out in the cold. After midnight, the vendors trudged home while the dampness of the river crept east. The unlovely, clammy fumes of the Hudson blended with the perennial sour reek of car exhaust, garbage, and decades of grime exuded by the streets. Not even Pittsburgh, one of the dirtiest cities Rowan had ever seen, stank like New York.

Something small with patchy fur and a long tail skittered

across the road ahead of her. It might have been a very small, ratty-looking cat, or a very large, catty-looking rat.

This was a stupid idea.

Sometimes she'd smelled as vile as the streets, back when she'd been a homeless runaway. Living in the bowels of the greatest city on earth didn't include regular bathroom privileges or ample opportunities to keep up her personal hygiene. No matter how often she'd washed, she'd soaked up the acrid, sour odor of the city until she thought she'd never be clean again. Sometimes it had been so bad she'd wondered if every night the city lifted some giant invisible leg and pissed on her while she slept.

Really stupid.

As for the sights, the Big Apple appeared exactly as she remembered it, a soulless gray and black labyrinth of concrete and steel, as cold in electric light as in the wells of shadow, as indifferent to her as she'd be to an ant. As she hooked her helmet to the lock she'd installed at the back of her seat, she wondered why the passing years hadn't shrunk the city into something smaller and less intimidating. Surely any minute she'd start feeling at least a twinge of fond nostalgia for the place where she'd spent the worst times of her young life.

It wasn't happening. She'd come back home unwanted and alone, and the city still didn't care. Realizing nothing had changed didn't chill her; resentment boiled in her chest.

Screw the Apple.

Her life had been polluted long enough by rage and fear of the things that had happened to her in this place without her permission. She'd come here to free herself of the past and finally face her fear. She would not be beaten into the pavement again by it.

Well? What's it going to be?

She hadn't been thinking about doing this when she'd left the interstate. She'd taken the exit thinking she'd just drive to the river, stop there, and have a look at the city from one of the docks. She'd reminded herself of all the excellent reasons why she had to stay on the Jersey side of the Hudson, and then she was driving through the Lincoln Tunnel and uptown into the theater district, her visor up, her eyes searching. For what, she didn't know. She'd left nothing behind but her innocence and two graves.

Three, she corrected herself as some cold part of her brain did the math. *The sisters are dead, and the old man is, too. There's no one left who knows who or where or what I am.*

In a few hours the Upper West Side would be choked with people and traffic, but in the predawn hours Rowan saw only a few cabs and patrol cars on the road, and some delivery trucks parked with their flashers on as they were being unloaded. Seeing the crates of produce and flowers being stacked on the hand trucks and wheeled into the groceries and restaurants made her stomach twist. When she'd been desperate, she'd stolen food off the back of some delivery trucks; seeing all that unguarded bounty still made her feel hungry—and ashamed.

Quickly she rode past a couple of pricey restaurants she didn't recognize. The leather bomber jacket that had kept her warm during the long, icy ride now felt smothering.

Welcome home, Rowan. Here, have a little panic attack to go along with your sniveling. A garbage truck passed her, splashing her left leg with gray slush. *And fuck you.*

At the next traffic light she stopped, braced her boots against the road, unzipped, and stripped. As she tied the jacket by the sleeves around her waist, she saw that sweat had soaked the two shirts she wore beneath it. A faint blue glow showed around the edges of her sleeves, and the skin of her inner arms crawled. If anyone had touched her in that moment, she wouldn't have been able to control herself.

Something was wrong, and the cause wasn't her ugly memories of the city. She scanned the surrounding area until she spotted a small group of Latino kids tagging a building under construction across the street. Stylized letters spelled out *Neva B Tha Same* in jailhouse jumpsuit orange and radiation-warning yellow. Other, equally artistic graffiti riddled the bare cinderblock walls around them.

On her side of the road there was no graffiti. Not a single tag, gang sign, or rap sentiment anywhere on the brick walls between the barred windows and grate-covered doors, all of which belonged to some upscale place. White letters on the dark brown canopy over the main entrance spelled out a single name in elegant script: *D'Anges.*

Angelic? For the angels? Rowan wasn't sure. Outside the terms used in gourmet cookbooks and magazines, her French sucked.

Red light turned to green, but she didn't ride on, and the sound of her engine finally drew the attention of the graffiti artists to her presence. The boys turned en masse to hoot, whistle, and call out sexual invitations while palming their crotches.

The ultimate thug accolade. Relaxing a little, Rowan studied them. She knew from experience that teenage boys were often the most dangerous predators walking the streets, but something told her this bunch were mostly gab and grab.

"Sí 'mana." The oldest boy, resplendent in his oversize football jersey and carpenter jeans, sauntered over. "I like your ride."

Rowan checked his hands, which were grimy and speckled across the knuckles with yellow back-spray, but otherwise empty. No knives, no guns, no bricks, no tricks. "Thanks."

"Muy melaza." His eyes ate up her bike before squinting at her. "You take me around the block?"

So he could dump her ass and deliver her machine to his cousin's chop shop? "Another time, maybe."

"Coño." He glanced back to smirk at the encouraging catcalls from his friends, and then shuffled closer. "So what you waiting here for? You need directions or something, *mami*?"

She noticed he bypassed ogling her tits to check out her ignition. *So that's the plan.* "Do I *look* lost to you, *hijo*?"

"Mira." Beautiful white teeth flashed against his dark face. "Maybe I take you somewhere, huh?"

As he reached to snatch her keys, she caught his wrist and jerked him closer. He wasn't expecting that, but she needed his body to block her from his friends' view. The leather sleeves encasing her forearms rippled as she looked into his eyes and saw the tiny reflection of her own face blur and change.

Inside Rowan's belly, a burst of heat solidified and began to expand. At the same time a stream of images and words poured into her mind. Ruthlessly she searched through them until she found what she needed. "You're being a bad boy, Juanito."

"¡Alábalo que vive!" The boy's eyes flew wide, until she could see the whites all around the dark irises. "Rosamada? *Es tu?*"

"Sí." She didn't know enough Spanish to command him in that language, but now that all he saw was the face of the girl he loved, he probably wouldn't notice. "It's too late for you to be out, 'Nito. Say good-bye to your friends and go home now."

Juanito nodded, tugging something from his neck and dropping it into her lap. "For you. You wear it for me, Rosa."

Rowan had to root between her thighs until she felt the metal links and retrieved the heavy chain. A gleaming, solid-silver crucifix hung from it. "Why are you giving me your ice?"

He looked past her. *"Enero."* Without another word, he turned and trotted back to his friends.

Once upon a time Rowan had been a Catholic, so the cross didn't give her the creeps. Seeing Juanito and his friends make the sign of the cross and kiss their thumb knuckles before they scattered did. She looked over her shoulder, but didn't see anyone or anything but the dark windows of the restaurant.

What the hell had spooked them?

Rowan grabbed her helmet and pulled it back on.

Enough was enough. In another day or two she'd reach Boston, where she'd been promised a good job and a cheap apartment. She'd never been there before, but she was ready to make a fresh start. If it didn't work out, she'd hit the road again and move on. There was always another place, another job, another chance.

All she had to do first was break a promise. The one she'd sworn she never would.

The threadbare, moth-eaten blanket of winter night, which covered little and protected nothing, had effectively emptied out the alleys. When temperatures dropped, the usual residents deserted their dismal crate and cardboard-box niches. Sleeping outside when the mercury sank below twenty was an automatic sentence of death by hypothermia, so like the rats and strays, the homeless retreated to the relative safety of the subway tunnels, abandoned cars and condemned buildings, where the cold couldn't kill them.

Two minutes before she laid down her bike, Rowan felt better about her bizarre impulse to come home one last time. There was no one to see her, and nothing to get in her way. She'd cruise through her old haunts on the way to the cemetery, then ride up through the Bronx and head north before the sun rose.

She rounded a corner and turned down the alley behind it when something hit her from behind. Her bike lurched forward, and she looked back, expecting to see a car that had crowded too close.

The street behind her stood empty.

Rowan glanced down at her tank, which she'd just filled up in Pittsburgh. If she'd gotten some bad gas it would have acted up long before now. The bike wasn't at fault; she'd felt the impact. Something had hit her.

Cold sweat popped out on the back of her neck as she accelerated, the thrum of the engine muted by the pounding in her ears.

He knows I'm here, the terrified kid in her head whispered. *The old man. He's coming after me.*

Fear-blind as she was, Rowan never saw what blew out her front tire. One moment she was speeding through the shadows and the next she was clinging to the grips as the bike went into a wild skid. Dimly she heard something else blow as the bike tilted, and then she was sliding sideways, the world turning on its head and the front end of a car rushing at her face.

In the instant before the crash, Rowan remembered why she'd promised herself that she would never come back to the city. She'd always feared that if she ever returned to New York, she'd die here.

And now she would.

"So I do not salt the eggplant or the zucchini," Bernard said, "or cook in separate pots. Chef, this is America, not Nice. Everything here, it is quick. No one could tell a difference."

Jean-Marc Dansant turned away from his sous-chef, mainly to keep from throttling him. "I could tell."

"The fat woman no complain, or send it back. She no care." Bernard threw out his hands in his favorite gesture, a combination of frustration and helplessness. "It was fine. The best. . . ." He paused as he groped for the correct English, but failed. "The best *courgettes à la niçoise* I make."

"*Naturellement.*" He removed his white jacket and tossed it in the laundry bin. "The problem, Bernard, is that she ordered *ratatouille.*"

"*Je m'en fiche.*" His sous-chef stalked out the back door. A few moments later the sound of squealing brakes and crashing metal came from the alley.

Dansant didn't feel alarmed by the noise. No doubt his sous-chef had knocked over the garbage bins with his car again. Bernard in a temper was nothing if not predictable. After inspecting the immaculate kitchen for the last time, Dansant shut off the light switches and went out into the alley to survey the mess.

He expected the smell of garbage, and the sight of it spread from one side of the alley to the other. He did not

expect to see a motorcycle lying on the ground in front
of Bernard's Volvo, or his sous-chef standing over a tall,
skinny boy whose leather garments appeared badly scuffed.
Then the biker removed his helmet, and under a mop of di-
sheveled dark curls was revealed the thin, furious face of a
dark-eyed, pale young woman.

In profile she was all angular bone and creamy white
skin; the stately line of her nose at odds with the decadent
contours of her mouth and the stubborn set of her jaw.

"Bernard." He spoke sharply to cut off the sous-chef's
stream of obscenities in their native language.

His voice drew the girl's attention for a moment, and he
saw that her lashes were like her hair, black, thick and curly.
They framed eyes that seemed too dark to be so bright. She
stiffened as if bracing herself for more trouble, and then
saw his face. Whatever she saw made her body change, and
she shifted on her feet, moving as if she meant to come to
him.

Dansant understood; the feelings rising inside him made
nothing in that moment more important than going to her.
"Did you knock her down?" he asked Bernard without
looking at him.

"*Non*. She crash into my car." He stabbed a finger at the
motorcycle. "Look at the bumper, the grille. They are ruin."
He turned his finger on the girl. "You pay for this."

Bernard had to repeat his demand for payment twice
more before the girl heard him and turned to face him.
"The hell I will. You shouldn't be parked out here in the
dark. It's illegal and dangerous."

Hearing her speak made Dansant's situation worse.
The girl's low voice had a faint rasp to it, and brushed
against his ears like silk cord. Silk, yes, that would suit her
more than her boyish leather. He imagined wrapping her
in yards of scarlet and gold, weaving it around the length
of her torso, coiling it along her long limbs, knotting it
so that her hands were bound to his, and everywhere he
touched her she would feel twice, on her body and against
her slim fingers. . . .

Never had he thought such things about a woman, Dansant thought, appalled. Not even with those he planned to seduce.

How could she do this to him, this girl? She'd barely glanced at him, and he was ready to grab her and drag her inside and lay her out on the closest flat surface.

He breathed in deeply, hoping the stench of the alley would clear his head, but smelled a familiar, coppery scent. At last he saw more than her eyes, her face. Her gloves were in shreds, and both of her knees showed, scratched and bloodied, through tears in her trousers.

Here she was hurt, in pain, and all he'd thought of was having her for his pleasure. He was no better than the idiot berating her.

"I work here," Bernard was telling her. "I park here every night. Bah." He pulled out his wallet and offered her an insurance card. "You give me yours."

"I'm not responsible. Someone hit me from behind." The girl ignored the card, hobbled slowly to where the motorcycle lay beside the car and crouched down. She ran her hand over one misshapen tire, then the other. "Damn it, they're both blown."

"Miss. *Miss.*" When she didn't respond, Bernard stalked over to her. "We call the insurance; let them say who pay."

She bent over to look under the car. "I don't have any."

His sous-chef did the same. "What do you say?"

"Insurance." She stood, bracing one hand against the hood of the Volvo to steady herself. "I don't carry any on my bike."

"So now *I* must pay for everything. Such convenience for you." Bernard straightened and took out his mobile. "I call police now."

"Wait a minute." She gave Bernard her full attention. "There's no need to get the police involved. We can work this out between the two of us."

She tried to sound more amicable, but for the first time Dansant caught a glimpse of fear in her eyes, and moved quickly over to stand beside her.

"I am French," Bernard informed her before Dansant could say a word. "No stupid. I know your game. You crash into my car on purpose, force me give you money."

"No, Bernard," Dansant told him. "Clearly it was an accident." And if the man didn't soon shut up, Dansant was almost certain he was going to beat him senseless.

His sous-chef folded his arms. "She is scumming me."

"Scamming," she corrected. "And no, I'm not doing that. Look, this was an accident, that's all. Why don't we just call it even and walk away?"

"You ruin my car. You have no insurance. You are no walking away." Bernard began to dial.

"*Écrase.*" Dansant took out his wallet, eyed the car, and removed a handful of hundreds, which he put in the sous-chef's soft hand. "This will pay for the damages, plus two weeks' pay."

"Chef." Bernard frowned at the money. "I do not need my pay tonight."

"Yes, you do. You're fired. *Adieu*, Bernard." Dansant turned to the girl, who stared at him with visible disbelief. Over Bernard's sputtering, he said, "You are hurt, but I can help you. Come with me."

"I'll be fine, thanks." She seemed genuinely unconcerned about her injuries. "Who are you?"

"Jean-Marc Dansant. I own this restaurant. Come, mademoiselle." He took her arm, and when she pulled back he gestured at her knees. "Look, there, you are bleeding. I have a first-aid kit inside."

"My name is Rowan." She turned her head. "My bike—"

"It cannot be taken, not as it is now," he assured her.

Rowan stared at the hand on her arm and then into his eyes. "Why are you doing this? You don't know me."

She is afraid—of me?

"*Oui.*" He didn't have the words to tell her, not yet. Not when he didn't understand what was pulling him to her. Whatever it was, he could not let it vanish into the night.

He released her as he tried to think of something to say. "It is the kindness of a stranger, yes?"

"Not something I usually depend on." Rowan looked down at herself and sighed. "But I do need to clean up."

He clenched his teeth as images of his hands undressing her and washing her filled his mind. "Then come inside with me, please." He offered her his hand this time, and after a long, silent moment, she took it.

"Jamais dans ma vie," Bernard called after them as Dansant guided her through the kitchen door and into the restaurant. "You be sorry you fire me. I am best sous-chef in—"

Fortunately the heavy steel door cut off the rest of what he shouted.

"Wait, please." Dansant left her by the long prep table and retrieved the first-aid kit from the dry storage room. When he returned she had stripped off her jacket and the shreds of her gloves, and was washing her hands at the rinsing sink beside the industrial dishwasher. Under a black T-shirt she wore a long-sleeved white thermal shirt, the cuffs of which were stained red with blood.

For the first time he realized how very tall she was—only an inch or two shorter than he was—and how perfectly her long body would fit to his. He'd never made love to a woman who matched him physically. Nor would he if he left her standing and bleeding in his kitchen while he indulged in such fantasies.

"Let me see," he said as he put the kit on the sideboard.

"They're not too bad. My gloves took the worst of it." She showed him her grazed, reddened palms before looking down. "My knees are a mess, though."

Dansant pulled an empty crate over by the table. "Sit here."

She didn't move. "Thanks, but I think I can do this by myself."

Dansant removed some gauze pads and a small bottle of peroxide from the kit. "You are still shaken, *ma mûre.*"

She limped over to the crate and perched on it. "So are you usually this kind to strangers?" Before he could answer, she added, "I'm not going to sue, if that's what you're worried about."

That she thought of herself as a stranger to him was perplexing. From the moment he'd seen her face, he'd known her. Not who she was, or why she had come to him now, but everything that mattered between a man and a woman. All he had to do was be patient, and wait for her to give herself over to him. Then he would show her that they were meant to be together.

Doesn't she feel it?

"I do not worry about this." He knelt before her to inspect the damage to her knees. "There is debris in the wounds. From the ground." He would need scissors to cut away her trouser legs. "I must remove it."

As soon as he put his hand on her leg, Rowan stiffened. "I don't think so."

He glanced up. "You do not like to be touched."

"Oh, sometimes I like it fine." She stared at his mouth before lifting her eyes to his, and he saw a glimmer of heat and longing. "It's the stranger part I have trouble with."

"So do I." More than he could ever tell her. "Perhaps just for tonight, we should think we are friends."

"Friends." She seemed amused by this, but leaned back on her elbows. "All right, Dansant. Do whatever you want."

Chapter 2

Rowan wasn't sure how she went from thinking her life was over while laying down her bike in a dark alley to sitting on a crate in a restaurant kitchen and watching the top of Jean-Marc Dansant's head. She had an excellent vantage point, however, as he knelt in front of her, one hand wrapped around her calf while he examined the ugly wounds on her knees.

Why couldn't we do this when I'm not torn up and bleeding?

His black hair, long enough to merit a ponytail, had begun to escape the band at the back of his neck, and strands of it fell around his face in poetic disarray. She spent a long time looking at his hair, concentrating on it as if it were the most important thing in the world. Only when her eyes began to burn did she remember to blink, and then she fell right back into staring.

After some time had passed, Rowan shook off her uncharacteristic fascination with his mop. As she did, she felt a peculiar disorientation, as if time had stopped while she'd forgotten where she was, and what she was doing.

What's wrong with me?

Evidently she'd hit her head harder than she'd thought during the crash, and it had turned her into a semizombie. She knew what she should have been thinking of: what to do next, how to get out of this, this restaurant, this accident, this city—this whole mess. Someone had hit her from behind. She'd come close to smearing herself like a bug all over the grille of a Volvo. She'd survived, only to strand herself in the last place on earth she wanted to be stranded.

Idiot that she was, she'd also let Dansant—a bona fide stranger—pay for the damage she'd caused, and then had followed him inside his restaurant. Now she was letting him touch her, take care of her, like they were best friends. Sitting there and doing nothing, like it was nothing. Like she couldn't think for herself anymore.

But she *was* thinking now, just one thing, over and over. *God, he's so damn pretty.*

It seemed Dansant had come into the world with all the luxury upgrades: golden, flawless skin, strong jaw, stunning mouth, perfect nose, sculpted cheekbones, heavenly blue eyes, smooth arched brows. Rowan had never thought much of handsome men—too in love with their own reflections, most of them—but Dansant seemed almost too beautiful to be human, much less a regular guy. She kept trying to find a flaw somewhere; something that would make him seem less celestial.

She didn't seem to care that she wasn't succeeding. Maybe it was those angel eyes of his, she thought as she breathed in.

His eyes were as morning-sky blue as his hair was midnight black, which was the only peculiarity. Men with Dansant's dark coloring usually came with all-matching accessories. From where she sat she could smell flowers, spices, and heat, but couldn't decide if it was coming from his hair, his body, or the restaurant's kitchen. Or all three. The floral fragrance seemed hauntingly familiar, too, although the exact name of it eluded her.

If that's what he's using as aftershave, he's been shopping in the wrong cologne department. That could also be why it didn't offend Rowan's nose like other guy cologne, although it seemed to be everywhere: on him, in the air, all around her—even on *her* clothes.

She couldn't remember ever seeing this restaurant, even

when she'd lived in New York, but for the first time since crossing the river, she felt as if she'd come home. In fact, she couldn't remember feeling as comfortable and protected as she did in this moment.

"Ow." Fresh pain shot through her throbbing thigh, abruptly sending the alarming amount of happy bullshit she was thinking straight out of her head. "Fuck, that hurt."

He glanced up, something she was sure he hadn't done once since she'd given him permission to have his way with her skinned knees.

Was that disapproval she saw? Probably; she had a mouth like a truck driver's. "Sorry about the language."

"*Vous êtes tout excusé.* That one, it was deep." He showed her a nasty-looking, bloody splinter before pitching it into the trash can beside them and going back to work.

Jacqueminot. That was what she was smelling. It had seemed so familiar because the woman who had saved her life had grown it in her garden. It might explain why she felt so at ease with Dansant; the scent brought back memories of the only place she had ever considered her home.

"Do you live near here?" he asked as he dampened a square of gauze with some water from a brown bottle.

"No, I don't"—she took in a sharp breath as he began cleaning the blood from her knee—"live in the city," she said as she exhaled. A burning, fizzing sensation spread over her abrasion, which began to bubble with pink foam. "I guess that's not water," she said, gritting her teeth to hold back another *Fuck*-prefaced protest.

"Peroxide, to kill germs." He showed her the label on the bottle. "The ground in the alley is filthy."

"Right." And if he kept talking, soon she might not feel any pain.

Not only was Angel Eyes the most physically beautiful man she'd ever met; he also had without a doubt the best voice she'd ever heard: rich, deep, dark and sweet—a double shot of espresso with a honey chaser. Hearing it made her bones melt. Part of it had to be the way he spoke English, with that low, liquid French accent spilling over every word; it felt like being kissed on the ears. She could close her eyes and listen to him read his grocery list, and probably get off by the time he reached the dry goods. . . .

Something here was seriously wrong. Twenty minutes ago she'd almost smeared herself all over a Volvo and had come within a phone call of mixing it up with the cops. Was she scared? Was she rethinking her declaration of independence? Was she even figuring out where she was going to sleep tonight?

No. She was thinking about banging the gorgeous Good Samaritan.

Jesus Christ. She had to get the hell out of here.

"Hey, uh, you don't have to do this. I'm sure I'll be okay." When that didn't get a response, she tried, "It's pretty late. Isn't there someone waiting for you at home?"

"My partner sleeps until dawn." He turned away to look for something in the kit. "Why are you here so late, Rowan? Do you visit someone?"

"Yes," she lied without hesitation, and pushed herself down from the crate. "Thanks for helping me out. If you'll give me your address, I'll send you the money as soon as—"

"Ça ne va pas, non?" He caught her hips between his palms. "You cannot go."

That grab went over the line for her, and she clamped her hands over his, intending to shove him away. Shifting her weight caused another jolt of pain to radiate from her knee, forcing her to instead hold on to him.

"Be still," he murmured.

It was the damnedest thing. Those two words chased off the pain and brought back that sense of safety and well-being, just as she'd felt before when he was cleaning her up. It confused her; she was hurt and that always made her angry. But trying to push him off suddenly didn't make sense, either; it wasn't as if he was trying to grab her ass or anything. Why was she acting like such a bitch? "It's okay; I'm fine."

"Your motorcycle," he reminded her as he stood up,

sliding his fingers through hers as casually as if they were on a date. "It needs some repair, *oui*?"

"It needs a lot of repair." She thought about the contents of her wallet; making the trip from Savannah had left it pretty thin. What cash she had wouldn't replace the tires, much less fix the damage to the chassis or whatever the crash might have done to the engine. She used to have a street map of the city in her head, but she'd replaced it with mental diagrams of Atlanta and Savannah and Albany. "Is there a bus stop near here that I can walk to that will take me to the Port Authority?"

"There is," he said. "But you cannot push the bike there or put it on the bus."

This would be the second set of wheels she'd abandoned in as many months, and she wouldn't have anything but her feet or public transportation to help her get around Boston. Still, she had no other option.

"I'm not taking it with me." She freed her hands from his, and stuffed them in her pockets to keep from reaching for him again. At the same time her head seemed to clear. "If you call in a complaint about the bike to the cops, they'll send someone to tow it away."

"There is something better to do," he assured her. "You can stay. Work for me. Until your bike is fixed."

"Work here? At the restaurant?" Rowan couldn't understand why he was offering her a job, until she remembered him paying off Bernard. *He thinks I'm going to stiff him.* "Listen, I *will* get you your money back, Dansant. There's a job waiting there for me in Boston, and I start as soon as I get there." Honesty made her add, "It might take me a couple of months to earn enough to cover what you gave Bernard, but I'm good for it. I promise."

"So? You are here now. I have a job for you." He spread his hands. "You stay, work, pay me back."

"Exactly what kind of job are we talking here?" She glanced at the industrial-size dishwasher in the far corner of the kitchen. "You want me to do dishes? A little cliché, don't you think?"

"You, a *plongeur*? Never." He began replacing the supplies in the first-aid kit. "I think you would be very good as *un tournant*, a . . . kitchen helper?"

She knew what a *tournant* was; little more than a glorified drudge who ran between stations to fetch and carry for the line cooks, and handled the dirty work no one else wanted to do, like cleaning out the grease traps and scraping plates. It was supposed to be like an internship, to give an aspiring chef a chance to see a professional kitchen staff in action, and learn how things worked on the line. But that didn't change the fact that *tournants* were minimum-wage gophers who spent hours up to their elbows in trash and shit.

Rowan might never have gone to culinary school, but she was better than that. "Thanks, but I'll pass."

"It is work, Rowan." He put his hands on her shoulders. "You have family here, or Boston? Friends? Someone to help you?"

She would have lied to him again, but by the time she'd completed the thought the "no" had already left her lips.

"Do you have any friends?"

She had friends, plenty of them, but the thought of asking them for help didn't appeal to her in the slightest. Matthias and Jessa were living on his farm in Tennessee, but at the moment she felt as if she'd rather walk to Boston on foot than call Matt and ask him for money. She hadn't exactly faced up to Jessa or explained why she'd deceived her, either, and she was in no hurry to have that conversation. Drew, the closest friend she had after Matt and Jessa, had moved on himself, all the way out to California.

No, she thought, dismissing the last shred of doubt. Her life was her own now; she had to deal with this mess herself.

"Rowan?" he persisted.

She shook her head. "There's no one I can ask for help."

He slid his hands down her arms before letting go. "Except me."

If he kept smiling and touching her like that she was going to climb the wall or jump him.

"It's sweet of you to offer me a job, Dansant, but even if I took it I'd still need a place to live." Seeing his blank look, she added, "This is Manhattan, my man. I'm broke, and minimum wage won't cover the rent for closet space around here."

"Of course." His expression cleared. "You will live here."

She couldn't help the laugh. "Uh, as comfortable as the floor looks, I think ceramic tile would be bad for my back. Or are you planning to let me use one of your storage rooms?" He was staring at her again, and she brought her hand to her nose. "Is there something on my face?"

"Yes. No." Dansant shook his head a little. "I am sorry. I do not mean live here in the restaurant." He gestured toward the ceiling. "Upstairs, there are two flats. One is empty."

Maybe he didn't understand the concept of *I'm broke.* "And what does the landlord want for rent?"

"Nothing."

Her brows rose. "There's no such thing as a free apartment, pal."

"There is when I am the landlord." He smiled briefly. "My partner and I own the entire building."

"Nice." She glanced up to keep from drooling over his teeth, which were of course as dazzling white and perfect as the rest of him. "You'd let me stay there for free, when you could rent out the apartment to someone who could pay?" The way he kept touching her, maybe he meant to handle rent another way. "You thinking of taking it out in trade?"

He was staring at her face again. "What is this trade?"

"You know." She let her gaze drift down the length of him, pausing to study the excellent fit of his khakis to his strong thighs and lean hips before looking into his eyes again. "You give me an apartment; I give you what you want. Trade."

"What do you think I want, Rowan?" He didn't sound

offended or angry; now there was something like pity in his eyes.

She'd spent years in bars hustling pool tables and getting hit on by beer-soaked Romeos; she'd heard every come-on in existence. She had few illusions about her looks. The only reason a guy hit on her was because he was plastered or desperate.

But Dansant wasn't drunk, and if he was hard up for a woman she'd eat her helmet. As spectacular as his looks were, he was also kind and gentle, and had tended to her as if she were some stray kitten he'd found in the alley. She had no right to think he wanted her to pay the rent on her back; he hadn't made one move on her. She looked at his hands again, and saw how immaculate and well shaped they were. The evocative scent of jacqueminot warmed her lungs, as if she was standing in some unseen garden. One where she could happily spend the rest of her days.

He'd definitely been shopping in the wrong cologne department. . . . *Isn't there someone waiting for you at home?* So beautiful and clean and perfectly groomed, Dansant was, right down to his manicured fingernails. *My partner sleeps to dawn.*

Oh, hell. Suddenly it all made sense. *He's gay.*

"Nothing. I was wrong." She ducked her head. "Sorry." And she was, for herself and all her sisters in the world who would never have a chance with the man. "You're sure about this?" Still a little heartbroken, she glanced up. "I mean, giving me a job, letting me stay here?"

"Oui."

He'd said only one of the apartments was empty. "Do you live in the other one?"

He shook his head. "The man who lives there is a mechanic. I think he will know how to repair your motorcycle."

A job, a place to live, and a neighbor who could fix her bike. That was a hell of a lot more than she had waiting for her in Boston.

"Well, you may be crazy, Dansant, but I'm not. All

right." She grinned at him. "You've got yourself a new tenant *tournant*."

The special analysis lab in the Atlanta headquarters of
GenHance, Inc., had been given many names since being
built. Administration identified it as "the clean room." The
few technicians cleared for limited, supervised access quietly referred to it as "the pressure cooker."

The janitorial staff, who were not permitted inside,
called it "Area 51."

In reality the room was an enormous, two-thousand-
square-foot sealed, sterile space, with its own air lock, power
grid, security system, and complex, multifiltered air supply.
Until they submitted to a full-body scan, no one who was
authorized access could enter the room. Each day security
personnel performed similar, intensive scans on the surgical steel walls, floors, and equipment inside the lab.

Nothing was brought into the room that was not first
thoroughly inspected.

The official explanation was that the stringent measures
were to protect the delicate materials involved in ongoing
genetic experiments. In reality the measures were taken to
protect the reason behind those experiments, and to assure
that no activity or conversation held inside the clean room
was monitored or recorded.

Lately, GenHance chairman Jonah Genaro had been
spending a great deal of time in the clean room, but he had
no choice. A month ago he'd discovered a traitor on his
staff, one who had been passing along information on Gen-
Hance's most sensitive projects to the company's primary
targets, the Kyndred. He was taking no more chances.

"I'm sorry, sir," Dr. Elliot Kirchner told Genaro after
he finished relating the details of his latest test trials, and
handed off the file to his assistant, Nella Hoff. "Results con-
sistently show that neuroblockers will not mute or nullify
the negative effects."

Genaro regarded the two scientists for a long moment.
Kirchner, a tall, gray-haired man with the graceless build of

a long-legged bird, looked like an ostrich beside his petite, slightly built assistant.

"Whoever injects the transerum will experience significant, cascading cerebral destabilization," Kirchner continued. "The breakdown of behavioral inhibitors and impulse control will occur within twenty-four to forty-eight hours."

As they had all witnessed when Bradford Lawson, a GenHance executive wounded during a botched attempt to capture a particularly valuable Kyndred, had stolen and injected himself with the transerum. "Is the damage reversible?"

Kirchner shook his head. "The transerum doesn't damage the brain, sir. It alters it."

"Permanently," Hoff added, nodding enough to make the bell of auburn hair around her face bob.

As chairman of one of the largest and most profitable biotech research corporations in the world, Jonah Genaro was accustomed to success. Under his direction GenHance, Inc., was actively researching therapeutic treatments for dozens of genetic abnormalities and disorders. His company was also widely considered the global leader in groundbreaking genetic research procedures, medical applications, and other important developments in the biotech industry.

Genaro had spent a great deal of time and money to create and maintain that illusion, to ensure that no one learned of the real work going on behind GenHance's humanitarian facade: using Kyndred DNA to create a serum that would genetically enhance humans and turn them into living weapons. He would not accept that the work of the past eleven years—indeed, of his entire existence—had all been for nothing.

Nella Hoff's delicate floral perfume didn't quite cover the odor of her sweat, and Genaro noted the woman's nervous hand movements and damp temples before he addressed the chief geneticist. "What will it take to deal with this destabilization issue?"

Kirchner frowned. "We've explored every possible modification, sir, without success. As it is now, the transe-rum cannot be used on humans without serious consequences."

"Unacceptable." Before the geneticist could reply, he added, "Lest you forget, there are hundreds of human beings in the world who have already been successfully enhanced. The Kyndred were genetically altered and given extraordinary abilities. They still lead normal lives. None of them has gone insane."

"That we know of," Hoff broke in. As both men regarded her, the skin around her nose tightened, but she plowed on. "I'm sorry, Mr. Genaro, but Dr. Kirchner is right. The transerum can't be fixed unless we re-create the original experiment. The process used to enhance them was lost along with the geneticists who created them. The records were destroyed. There are no living witnesses. Where we are now, we're dead in the water."

Genaro glanced at Kirchner, whose expression remained remote. "The Kyndred are alive."

"They're idiots," Nella insisted. "Most of them probably still don't even realize that they were deliberately enhanced."

"Dr. Hoff is correct. I've reviewed all of the transcripts from the interrogations of the Kyndred we've captured alive," Kirchner admitted. "It's obvious that they were altered in utero or in early infancy. They have no real recollection of the experiments, only fragmented memories and nightmares from childhood. They can't provide any useful information."

Genaro wasn't interested in the childhood tragedies of the Kyndred. "Then what is the next step, Dr. Kirchner?"

His geneticist began to speak, but once more Nella interrupted. "I believe I've discovered the solution, sir." She lowered her voice a notch. "While Dr. Kirchner was testing the neuroblockers, I decided to take the initiative with another approach. I accessed the bioarchives, retrieved a Kyndred sample, and used it with an organic human specimen in the neurosequencer."

"What?" Kirchner's face darkened. "You took a sample and wasted it on a cadaver brain?"

"Only a recovered partial sample," Nella snapped back, ire sparkling in her pretty green eyes. "We never recovered a full cell spread from the female. It was useless to us."

Now Genaro cut off Kirchner's furious response. "What were the results, Dr. Hoff?"

She produced a confident smile. "Introducing the Kyndred cells to the cadaver brain stabilized the serum. I recorded the simulation. If I may show you, sir?" When he inclined his head, Nella went to a terminal and pulled up a video file to play onscreen. "This is the neurosequencing of the specimen after being injected with the transerum. As you can see here"—she traced a bright yellow, branching light—"the destabilization process is well advanced. At this point I introduced DNA recovered from the female's single tissue sample." The web of yellow light began to shrink and in a few seconds disappeared altogether. "The specimen stabilized completely after thirty minutes, at which time the female's DNA became dormant."

Genaro had her run the simulation a second time before he asked, "Do you know why?"

"I have a theory about this particular female, sir," the assistant said, all eagerness now. "It's related to her specific enhancement. She's the most powerful Kyndred we've identified to date. Her ability physically transforms both matter and energy. That makes her what I like to think of as a dominant."

Kirchner made a disgusted sound. "First you help yourself to the bioarchives, and now you think you can categorize them?"

"With you wasting time on testing conventional inhibitors, someone had to," Hoff replied before turning back to address Genaro. "Sir, I can provide you with a detailed analysis of my experiment. All indications are that a full cell spread from this female subject will control the destabilization process during the enhancement stage. This is the breakthrough we needed."

"So it would seem." Genaro studied her damp face, and wondered why such an attractive woman would choose re-search science as her success vehicle. *Perhaps she hasn't.* "Dr. Hoff, why did you not first obtain permission from Dr. Kirchner for this experiment?"

"With all due respect, sir, Dr. Kirchner is not interested in anyone's opinion but his own. I knew he would treat my theory with utter contempt, and refuse to allow me to run the simulation." She folded her arms. "Conducting the ex-periment without his knowledge was the only way."

Genaro nodded slowly. "Very well. Make copies of the simulation, and I want to see a complete analysis of the ex-periment as soon as possible, including all pertinent notes and research."

"I'll have it on your desk before the close of business today, sir." Without looking at Kirchner, Nella left the lab.

Genaro waited until the doors of the air lock resealed before he spoke to his geneticist. "Your assistant is a very ambitious woman, Elliot. She wants your job, I suspect, so she can have complete access to the project materials."

"You think she's a spy?"

Genaro shrugged. "Has she offered you anything out of the ordinary?"

"Sex, a month after I hired her. I thought I had dealt with it." Kirchner rubbed his forehead. "I apologize, Mr. Genaro. It won't happen again."

"Don't have her terminated." When Kirchner gave him a surprised look, he added, "She did solve the problem with the transerum. I think that in itself deserves some reward."

Kirchner frowned. "What exactly did you have in mind, sir?"

"Once we recover the female Kyndred with the domi-nant DNA and use it to stabilize the transerum, we will need a fresh cadaver brain." Genaro eyed the simulation loop still playing on the screen. "Dr. Hoff's should serve adequately."

Chapter 3

Taire took one last peek through the hole she'd wiped in the ice-covered windowpane, and watched Dansant lead Rowan toward the stairwell by the back storage room. She relaxed the fingers she'd knotted into tight fists, and rested her forehead against the glass. Her breath melted some of the thin frost, which slid down the window like the tears on her face.

Rowan was banged up from the accident, but not too badly. Taire had overheard everything else. She was taking the job Dansant had offered. She was staying.

It had worked.

Taire wiped her face and nose on her sleeve before she moved away, taking care to stay in the shadows. No one was on the streets now, and she was only three blocks from her place, but she wouldn't risk being seen. Not now, when she was so close to getting some real answers.

She's older, and she's on her own. She lifted her cold, curled fingers to her mouth and blew on them. *She has the marks. She has to know something.*

An hour ago Taire had been idly watching some kids tagging a building when Rowan had stopped her bike at the traffic light. The first thing she'd spotted was the jacket tied around Rowan's waist, which in the freezing cold made no sense. Then one of the homeboys had gone over to sweet-talk her and then tried to grab her keys, and she'd grabbed him back. When the edge of Rowan's sleeve slid down, and the edge of a black tattoo appeared, Taire had straightened.

Then something strange had happened.

Taire couldn't see Rowan's face, but she got a good look at the weird blue glow that had appeared under both of her sleeves. She'd heard the tone of the boy's voice when he'd called her some Spanish name. Cold as it was, Taire had also picked up the faintest scent of something tart and fruity and—for want of a better word—ticklish. Complex and alien, it was coming from Rowan.

She had breathed in deeply to break down the other girl's scent into its components. It smelled of grapefruit, oak, apple, pears, and mint. Then it came back to her, that New Year's Eve, when one young nanny had smuggled a bottle of champagne out of the wine cellar and up to the nursery to have her own private celebration. She'd let little Taire take a sip from the clear, flat-bottomed cuvée.

Rowan—a biker chick—smelled like that. Like Cristal.

Taire stopped across the street from her place and waited, turning her head to watch both sides of the street. The old hotel had been closed for several years, but the owner had hung onto the property until his death last year. Taire had found the place after reading about the owner's heirs suing each other over rights to and disposition of the property, as the land the hotel was built on was worth millions to the city's space-hungry real estate developers. Until the case was settled, and ownership established—something that would take years, according to the paper—the hotel would continue to stand, empty and useless, slowly decaying behind the graffiti-covered plywood nailed over its doors and windows.

It wasn't as bad as some of the places Taire had slept. Once she'd spent a weekend hiding in the corner of a warehouse in the meat-packing district, and the stink of old blood and raw meat had made her so sick she'd puked up everything she'd tried to eat. She knew better than to try sleeping in Central Park, but she'd nodded off out of exhaustion one afternoon while sitting on a bench, only to wake up in the dark to find some old boozer groping through her jacket pockets for money.

He hadn't even been embarrassed over getting caught. *Ain't you got nothing you can gimme, little girl?*

Taire tried never to think about him, but sometimes she woke up smelling rotten breath laced with cheap wine, and seeing those bloodshot eyes bulging out as if they were going to pop out of his dirty, scabby old face.

It wasn't my fault. I was so tired.

Once she felt sure no one was watching, Taire closed her eyes. A moment later she darted across the street and climbed through the narrow gap in the boards, pausing only to secure them again before moving toward the old reception desk.

The city had cut off water and power to the building long before Taire had moved in, so the interior was as frigid as the outside, and the boards and sheets of plywood blocked out any light from the street. She'd bruised and scraped her hands and face falling over things more than once, but eventually she'd memorized every inch of the place, until she could walk freely in the dark. Now she moved confidently through the labyrinth of dry-rotting furniture in the lobby, sure of every step, leaving puffs of her breath to hang in the frozen air.

To keep anyone from discovering her presence she'd been careful to disturb nothing, leaving the cobweb-laced drapes drawn open and the front desk to collect nothing but layer upon layer of dust and dead insects. Rats had been a problem for a while, until she'd found all the holes they'd been using to get in and sealed them from inside, where the repairs couldn't be seen, using some drywall patches and filler that she'd taken from a supply shed at a construction site.

Every time she stole something, guilt ate at her stomach. She wasn't a thief. But taking something that didn't belong to her was better than waking up to find some of her hair gone, gnawed off to line a rat's winter nest.

Since the elevators no longer functioned, Taire used the

service stairs to go up to her room on the fifth floor. Along the way she checked each step for new footprints or signs that someone else had moved in. An abandoned building was an open invitation to anyone left out in the cold, and the plywood boards were getting old now. This winter was going to be a bad one; she could almost smell in the wind the coming snowstorms. If squatters broke in she couldn't fight them; she'd have to go and start looking for another place.

She thought of the faint blue glow that had appeared so briefly under Rowan's sleeves. *Or maybe I won't have to.*

The door to the room she used was locked like all the others, but she'd filched one of the master keys from the manager's desk and used it to let herself in. It was the smallest on the fifth floor, and contained only a single twin bed covered with a cheap brown and green paisley spread, an empty metal television stand (the heirs had gotten to the TV sets before the case went to court), and a cramped shower and toilet. The inch of water left in the toilet had frozen.

Taire had chosen the room not because of the bed, which she never used, but for the closet tucked away behind the door. The small room adjoined another, larger suite, and the closet between them could be opened from both sides. If someone came in unexpectedly, she could take her things and slip out into the adjoining suite without opening the interior door or being seen.

She went into the bathroom and stepped into the tub, tugging down her jeans before she crouched down low and emptied her bladder into the drain. It had taken some practice before she'd learned how to pee that way without splashing herself with her own urine. When she was finished she stepped out and poured down the drain a little bleach from the small jug she kept hidden behind the toilet. The smell from her urine abruptly disappeared.

Out in the room, she shrugged off her jacket and hung it on the closet rail before looking down at the sagging black garbage bag that contained her spare clothes and shoes.

She'd spread the extra blanket she'd found on the closet shelf over a mound of sheets and cushions she'd removed from some rooms on another floor to make a bed for herself. Because the closet was only three feet wide she had to sleep curled up like a shrimp, with her feet braced against the inside of the door, but the cramped quarters made her feel safer than if she had been sleeping out in the open.

At first it was like curling up in a refrigerator, but it didn't take too long for her to warm up in the small space. The three blankets she'd taken from other rooms trapped her body heat and kept her from freezing even on the coldest nights.

She didn't bother to remove her shoes as she settled in, covered up, and clenched her teeth to keep them from chattering. She began to warm up a little, but then her stomach started to growl. After a few minutes of listening to it, she took half a protein cereal bar from her jeans pocket. The foil wrapper crackled as she unfolded it and held the torn end to her nose. Although it was stale now, the white chocolate, toasted rice, and dried strawberries still made her mouth water. It was the last of her food stash, and she knew she should save it for tomorrow, but she was too cold and hungry now to sleep.

Her eyes stung as she nibbled at it, chewing every bite slowly to make it last as long as possible. This time a year ago she would have been asleep in her own bed, warm and cozy, her belly full. She'd never realized how lucky she'd been to have so much; she'd taken it all for granted. Back then she'd wasted enough food in one week to live on now for a month or two. Then it was gone, as if it had never been.

No more mistakes.

Taire reached under one of the pillows, took out the flashlight she'd found in a utility closet downstairs, and turned it on as she removed a folded paper from the plastic bag holding her belongings. The paper, a glossy, professionally printed flyer, had the photo of a young girl in the center along with a detailed description. Anyone who had information leading to the recovery of Alana King, the flyer promised, would be given a reward of five hundred thousand dollars. All they had to do was call the toll-free number printed on the flyer.

Taire crumpled the stiff paper in her fingers, and then smoothed it out and refolded it neatly before putting it back in her bag. She was convinced that Rowan could help her, but asking for that help would be almost as bad as making the call to the hotline for Alana King. She didn't know Rowan. The biker chick might not want to help her. She might even turn Taire over to the cops.

She was so close that it didn't seem fair that so many things could go wrong now. But they could, and just like the last time, one wrong decision would destroy everything. She had to be very careful, or she'd blow her last chance to make things right with her father. If she didn't fix this, he would never let her come home again. He wouldn't send her to the room. This time he'd make sure she never had a place to live or someone to love.

This time, he'd kill her.

It'll be all right. Taire tucked a cold hand under her cheek and closed her eyes, imagining herself back in her old bed, surrounded by white eyelet lace curtains and clean linens, falling asleep while watching the snow fall outside. *Rowan's here now, and she'll make everything fine again. She'll help me get back home.*

"So when are you gonna come stop by the office in person for your messages, Sean?" Rita the answering service operator asked. " 'Cause I'll tell ya, we got a pool going on you now."

"Yeah?" Sean Meriden spotted a parking spot opening up in front of a deli and slid his Mustang Cobra into it a few seconds before a suit in a silver Beemer could. "How much?"

"Hundred ten bucks so far." She popped her gum. "Whoever guesses right where you land on the *Lost* stud scale takes the pot."

He grinned at the Beemer's blaring horn as the driver gunned his high-priced engine and moved on. "Do I want to know what the *Lost* stud scale is?"

"*Lost*, like the TV show, you know? We made a scale of one to ten for the guys on the show," Rita advised him. "Ten being Josh Holloway, and one being that googly-eyed guy who plays Ben."

The things women did to entertain themselves. "Who's five?"

"Desmond." She sighed. "He's not bad to look at, but that freaking Scottish accent and the way he's always like calling every guy 'brotha' gets on everyone's nerves."

"I think I'll let the pot build up a little more." Meriden climbed out, locked up, and fed the meter some coins while he enjoyed the gawkers. His red and white sports car might have been an antique, but it still drew the envious eye of every middle-aged man on the street. Women, on the other hand, paid more attention to Meriden. "Any other calls come in?"

"Couple." Paper shuffled on the other end of the line. "Mr. Dansant called just before midnight. Said to tell you that he moved someone into the other apartment. Didn't leave a phone number or ask for a call back."

"No." Meriden's smile faded. "He wouldn't."

"The last call came in about an hour before the day shift started. This guy said he was Gerald King of King Properties in Manhattan"—she snickered—"and that he needed to talk to you about doing a job for him. Left the number for his private line; I texted it to you."

He didn't have to think about the name; in Manhattan it was as well known as Donald Trump's. "He's not Gerald King."

"That's what I told my supervisor when I picked up your overnight messages. She said maybe it was an alias for some other important guy who needs you." Rita chuckled. "You get the weirdest messages sometimes, Sean."

"Goes with the job, sweetheart." He looked down the block until he located a phone booth. "I'll check in with you around noon. Page me on the mobile if you get in something urgent."

"I've got twenty bucks on nine," Rita confided. "You gotta be a Matthew Fox. Big guy, scruffy, tattoos, beat all to hell, but a born hero. I could tell first time I talked to you." She disconnected before he could reply.

Meriden looked down at the inside of his right forearm. The tat in the center of his arm, a taijitu formed from the body of a snakelike dragon, had been rendered in scarlet ink that some people mistook at first glance for blood or a bad burn.

A born hero. If only Rita knew.

Meriden pulled up the text with King's number as he made his way to the phone booth. He never called clients from his mobile; that would give them the ability to call him at any hour or even track his whereabouts. His answering service covered calls to the number on his business cards, and any callbacks he had to make he did from a public phone.

He dialed the number from the text and waited for an answer.

The line connected on the third ring to a soft, dry male voice. "Hello."

"This is Sean Meriden. Gerald King left this number with my service, asked me to call about a job."

"Yes, I made that call, Mr. Meriden. I presume you know who I am?"

"Gerald King died five years ago," Sean pointed out. "It was in all the papers. He your dad, or is this your idea of a clever alias?"

"There was an attempt made on my life five years ago," King said. "To prevent another, I have since allowed the general public to believe the first was successful."

King had been a complete recluse before he'd died— or had faked his death—so his story was almost plausible. "Are the police involved in your charade, or this job you want done?" Meriden avoided butting heads with the NYPD whenever possible.

"Not at all. I prefer working with independent contractors. Excuse me for a moment." He continued speaking for a minute, but he must have covered the receiver, because Meriden couldn't make out more than the muffled sound of his voice. Then he said, "I would like to hire you to find my daughter Alana, Mr. Meriden. I haven't seen her since she ran away from home, but according to the latest information I've been given, she was seen in Manhattan yesterday."

Meriden felt oddly relieved. "I'm sorry, Mr. King, but I don't work missing persons cases. I'm strictly bond jumpers and parole violators."

"When you find Alana and bring her home, I will pay you five hundred thousand dollars," King said as if he hadn't heard him. "In cash, if you prefer."

He rubbed his forehead. "It doesn't matter if you pay me in gold coins, sir. My answer is still the same. I don't do runaways."

"I believe I can persuade you to change your mind."

Meriden checked his watch; he had only seven hours left before he'd have to call it a day. "I believe we're done, Mr. King."

"Not yet," the old man said. "Would you turn around for a moment, please?"

Surprised by the request, he looked over his shoulder, and then turned. A heavyset man in a parka stood a few feet behind him. He was making short work of a pastrami sandwich half wrapped in greasy deli paper. When Meriden met his gaze, he scowled.

"You gonna be all day, pal?" the fat man asked. "I'm freezing my ass off here."

"Watch," he heard King say over the line.

Meriden heard a hiss, and the man waiting to use the phone flinched and clapped a hand to the back of his head. His eyes widened as his hand, now wet with blood, slid away. The half-eaten sandwich hit the icy sidewalk a moment before the fat man's knees did, and then disappeared

under the heavy body as the man toppled sideways and
didn't move again.

As a passing woman stopped and screamed, Meriden
saw the neat bullet hole at the base of the man's skull.

"I can arrange the same thing to happen to you," King
said softly. "At any time, in any place. As with that unfortunate gentleman on the sidewalk, there would be no warn-
ing at all."

"All right." He heard sirens approaching. "What do you
want?"

"As I said, I want you to find Alana—"

As flashing lights appeared at the end of the next block,
Meriden hung up the phone and wove his way through the
gathering crowd around the body until he broke free of
bodies. He pulled his car out of the parking space a few
moments before the patrol cars arrived, and used the mo-
mentary traffic disruption to make a U-turn and drive away
from the murder scene.

He watched his rearview to see if he was being followed
while taking several unnecessary turns. Once he felt safe,
he went directly to the garage. He left the Mustang parked
in the bay, let himself out onto the roof, and stood watching
the street for an hour.

Gerald King was crazy, of that he was convinced. But if
he went to the cops with this story, they'd lock him up as
a suspect or send him over to Bellevue. The last thing he
needed was to spend a night in a holding cell or on a psych
ward. He could hear the sound of the phone in the garage
office below ringing, and his gut told him it was King.

Meriden climbed down the back fire escape stairwell
and went on foot to D'Anges, where he used his key to get
inside and head up to his apartment. Fortunately he kept
very little in the way of personal possessions, so it would
take him only a few minutes to pack up. Then he saw the
stack of money and note left on his kitchen table.

Dansant had left the note, which Meriden read then
swore. The bike in the alley belonged to Dansant's new girl-

friend, and he wanted Meriden to fix it. His fucking lordship had taken on another damsel in distress. Well, this time he'd have to walk away from his new charity case. They had to get out of the city now, before King tracked them down.

Meriden was just closing his suitcase when the phone rang. No one had the number here, not even the girls at the answering service. The phone, like the apartment and the restaurant, belonged to Dansant. He considered tossing it through the window before he picked up the receiver and held it to his ear.

"I'm disappointed in you, Mr. Meriden," King's dry voice said. "Perhaps one demonstration was not adequate. Shall I arrange another?"

"You'll kill me whenever you like, King," he said. "Whether I take the job or not. So have your shooter do me now, because I'll burn in hell before I work for you."

"An interesting response—not at all what I'd expected. I myself don't believe in hell." He paused. "It seems you have a new neighbor. I think you'll find the surveillance photos of her with your landlord to be most interesting. An envelope should be delivered to you within the next minute."

Meriden dropped the phone and went to the door, yanking it open. A kid wearing white ear buds and holding a plain brown envelope stood stooped over, and looked up in surprise.

"Hi. I'm supposed to stick this under the door." He handed the envelope to Meriden, who grabbed the front of his ratty T-shirt. "Whoa." He held up his hands. "I don't know what it is. Some guy down the street paid me fifty bucks to deliver it, okay?"

"Yeah." Meriden released him, shoved a five into the kid's hand, and shut the door. He opened the envelope and took out a short stack of five-by-seven photos and a file folder. The pictures showed a sequential series of shots of a tall dark man leading a tall pale girl into the kitchen and treating her scraped knees. The condition of her clothes looked as if she'd slid across dirty concrete. He shuffled through the photos, studying them. Whoever the girl was, Dansant was definitely interested in her. One of the pictures showed him kneeling and looking up at her as if she were an angel.

Meriden went back and picked up the phone. "You get your rocks off peeping through windows, old man?"

King didn't respond to the insult. "According to the sous-chef your landlord fired last night, her name is Rowan Dietrich. It seems Mr. Dansant paid for the damages she caused before he tended to her injuries and let her into the apartment across from yours. A great kindness on his part."

The stupid bastard. "Neither of them have anything to •
do with me, King. I just live here."

"Perhaps you have no history with Ms. Dietrich, but you and Jean-Marc Dansant are quite another matter." King made a thoughtful sound. "The two of you met in Paris and traveled all over Europe together before coming to the States. He helped you finance your garage, while you supervised renovations for his restaurant. I don't know how you were able to arrange his U.S. citizenship, but it was granted in a third of the time it usually takes."

He thought they were friends. Meriden began to laugh.

"You think this is funny?" For the first time the old man sounded angry.

"Go ahead and shoot Dansant," Meriden told him. "You'll be doing me a personal favor."

"What about Ms. Dietrich?"

He looked at the image of the battered girl. He had no interest in Dansant's strays, but something about her eyes made his gut knot. "I don't know her. She's his problem, not mine."

"Not the words of a born hero, Mr. Meriden," King chided. "Rita Gonzalez would be so disappointed."

He'd been monitoring the mobile, somehow. "Fuck you."

The old man chuckled. "Given the charm of her voice, I was surprised to discover that Rita is a rather plain, plump

woman of multiracial background. Too young to be a single
mother of three, of course, but her kind always seems to
breed indiscriminately. She walks fifteen blocks to work
each day to save on subway fares. Her mother is already
raising four grandchildren in a one-room flat, so I don't
imagine three more will be welcome."

The information on Rita made it clear that King had
been investigating him for some time. "You're bluffing."

"I've just received the background information on Ms.
Dietrich." King drank something. "It seems she was recently
involved in some very unpleasant business in Atlanta. She's
wanted on multiple assault charges, vandalism, and various
computer crimes. One of the corporations she defrauded is
offering a sizable reward for her apprehension and return
for prosecution."

Meriden said nothing.

"I can arrange to have both Rita and Ms. Dietrich picked
up today," the old man continued. "Some of my employees
are former convicts, you understand, and prefer to indulge
some of their personal vices before they carry out their
specific orders—"

"Enough." He closed his eyes. "I'll do it."

"I thought you might." King's voice turned crisp. "The
file in the envelope contains all the information you need
to locate my daughter. Once you have her, you will bring
her to me directly." He gave Meriden the address of one of
the last privately owned mansions in Manhattan. "One last
thing I should mention. Your movements and your communications will be under constant surveillance. Any attempt
on your part to involve the authorities in any capacity will
result in the immediate execution of someone you know,
starting with Ms. Gonzalez."

Meriden opened the file and saw a stack of neatly typed
pages, along with the photo of a young blond girl about
nine years old. The kid was smiling, but her dark blue eyes
looked frightened. "I suppose now you'll give me some sort
of impossible deadline to do this."

"Not at all," the old man said. "I understand these sorts

of investigations do take some time. I will give you three weeks to locate my daughter and bring her home."

"Why three?" Meriden asked. "Why not one, or five, or twelve?"

"Because I only have three weeks to live, Mr. Meriden," King said calmly. "And, unless you find Alana, so do you."

Chapter 4

The town of Halagan, California, didn't appear on most maps, and was barely large enough to rate a Welcome sign. The only paved road was Main Street, which curled through Halagan's official business district, a cluster of old wood-sided buildings, one or two that dated back to the Gold Rush days, when miners came down out of the hills to buy flour, salt pork, and, if they'd panned enough that month, an hour with one of the tired whores at one of the town's five taverns.

A few weeks ago Andrew Riordan had stopped here for gas, caught a glimpse of a for-rent sign in the window of a boardinghouse, and decided it was as good a place as any to hole up in.

His landlady, an older woman who bred horses on a ranch a few miles outside of town, had not asked for his phony references or much in the way of a deposit.

"Rent's due on the first of the month, utilities included," she told him briskly. "You pay for your phone calls per week. No kids or pets, no loud music, no cooking, and if you have a girlfriend by, she needs to leave before breakfast."

"Fair enough." He handed over his cash deposit. "Who else lives in the house?"

"Besides my good-for-nothing nephew?" Her mouth twisted. "A geologist doing some survey mapping up in the hills, one of the elementary school teachers in the middle of a nasty divorce, and Mr. Cantwell, who is collecting government disability while he tries to finish his first novel."

Drew winced. "What's his disability?"

"I believe he has a terminal case of lazy-ass, don't-want-to-work syndrome." She tucked his money into a bank deposit envelope and met his gaze. "My brother-in-law is a county sheriff, and he's going to run your name, your driver's license number, and your tags. If he shouldn't, tell me now, and I'll return your deposit and you can keep going."

"I'm clean."

"Good." She handed him a business card. "Any problems, you can reach me at either number anytime. Just be warned, you call after midnight, the place had better be burning down around you."

Drew chuckled and shook her hand.

The room he'd rented had several bonuses: It was clean, comfortably furnished without being crowded or fussy, and the windows gave him an excellent view of both sides of Main Street. The tiny bathroom offered only a shower, but the water was hot, plentiful, and had the crystal-clear, faintly mineral taste of the mountain reservoir from where it originated.

Drew didn't unpack for the first week as he looked around and made himself known to the townspeople. A few eyed the new beard he'd grown, and one of the waitresses at the local diner claimed he looked just like that red-haired actor during his *NYPD Blue* days, but other than that he passed inspection.

His cover story was as new as his beard; he was David White, a native of Los Angeles and graduate student who was spending his winter holidays on the road to see a little of the state while he figured out his thesis. It was just specific enough to explain his joblessness and the temporary nature of his residence, and vague enough to keep anyone from running more than a cursory background check. Even if someone did, Drew's hacking abilities combined with a little help from his friends had insured that every detail would hold up. David White was registered as a graduate student at his college, had last resided in a small apartment off campus, and had inherited a small but tidy sum of money from a deceased uncle that was financing his mini-sabbatical. His taxes were paid, his student loans were up-to-date, and even his car was registered to the nonexistent David White.

He had bought his phone in L.A. from a store that specialized in the latest preservation of privacy gear, and while it looked like an ordinary cordless, it encrypted its own signal and could detect a trace within five seconds of activation. His computer, salvaged from the house in Savannah that had served as a base of operations for him and his friends, also boasted enough safeguards to rival those of the Pentagon.

Drew liked living in Halagan well enough, although he'd have to move on by the time the new year arrived. After several years of working undercover at GenHance, Inc., he had been exposed as a spy and had barely escaped being captured, killed, and dissected. Although outwardly he appeared to be nothing more than an ordinary, somewhat geeky computer nerd, Drew's DNA was something more than human, and had made him part of a secret new order of superhumans that had named themselves the Takyn.

Like his other friends, Drew had been genetically altered as an orphaned child by scientists working outside the law. No one knew exactly what they had intended, but their experiments had resulted in children with powerful, unique, and sometimes frightening psychic abilities. After an accident destroyed the main experimental facility and killed most of the geneticists working on the project, the surviving children's memories had been suppressed or erased before they were placed for adoption and scattered throughout the country. Neither the children nor their new families had any idea of what had been done to alter them.

Their Takyn abilities remained dormant for the most part throughout their childhood, although some of the children showed minor, precursory abilities. As a boy Drew had always been able to sense the presence of copper, usually in the form of pennies on the ground. He was so good at finding the coins, some of his friends in the old neighborhood had used him like a metal detector. Then when he was nine, Drew had gone swimming in a nearby lake with some friends, swallowed some water after being dunked, and had contracted an amoebic infection that had caused his temperature to spike at one hundred and six degrees.

Later his mother had told him that the doctors had prepared her and his dad for the worst. "They said you had lesions on your brain, and if you did come out of it you might never be able to talk or understand or take care of yourself again."

Drew had stunned his parents and doctors by not only surviving, but coming out of the lethal sickness completely well. Aside from a nagging headache, he'd apparently suffered no ill effects at all from the infection. Until his father woke him up one night to his mother's shrieking and water flooding across the floor of his room.

"The bathroom pipes burst," his dad had told him, shouting to be heard over his mother. "Come and help your mom."

Drew got out of bed and followed his dad, but something tugged at him and he changed direction. The pipes in his house were old, and as he went down the hall of his one-story home he ran his hand along the wall, tracing the path of the pipe he couldn't see but could somehow feel.

"Andrew."

"Hang on, Mom," he called back in an absent tone. He moved his hand over the wall as he sought out the weak spot in the pipes, and then found it. He could feel through the wall the ragged edges of the split in the metal and how they curled out like a tattered flower. His dad was going to have to get the plumber to knock a hole in the wall to get at the pipe.

Unless . . .

The headache he'd had since returning from the hospital disappeared, and in its place came another feeling, a sizzling warmth that gathered behind his eyes. It traveled down into his shoulder and through his arm, moving like warm water, and seemed to pour through his hand into the wall. The water rushing across his feet began to slow, and then stopped.

"Thank God, your father finally got the water turned off. Oh, look at you," his mother said behind him. "You're soaked to the skin."

His dad came up the stairs from the basement. "The shut-off valve is too rusted to turn, Bridget. I'd better call ..." He stopped and looked at the floor. "What happened?"

Drew turned and smiled at his father. "I fixed it, Dad."

Ron Riordan stared at his son before he burst out laughing. "And how did you do that, boy? With a prayer to the patron saint of piping?"

"No, with my headache." Drew grimaced as he glanced down at his pajamas, which were sodden to the knees. "Can I change into my Transformers, Mom?"

Bridget looked at the wall and then sighed. "Sure, darling. But you bring those wet things into the laundry room."

As Drew trotted back to his bedroom, he heard his mother say, "Broken pipes don't go and mend themselves, Ronnie."

"Something got stuck in it, I imagine. I'm calling Crowley. He'll have something he can use to loosen up that gee-dee shutoff valve."

The next day Mr. Crowley, the neighborhood plumber, came early to inspect the damage. Drew had to go to school, and didn't give any more thought to the broken pipe until he found his father waiting for him outside the school gate.

"Dad." Drew couldn't remember his father ever coming to school to pick him up. Ron drove a bus, and didn't get home until after six every night. "What are you doing here?"

"I took the day off, son. Boys." Ron nodded to the two

friends Drew usually walked home with. "Come on. Your mother's waiting in the car for us."

Drew wondered if he was in trouble, especially when he saw his mother's face. She looked as if she'd been crying. "Did I do something wrong, Daddy?"

"No, son." Ron rested a hand on his shoulder. "Your mother and me and you, we just need to have a little talk."

His father drove them to the park where Drew sometimes played ball with his friends. The bleachers were deserted today, however, and as they went to sit by the dugout he began to see that his parents weren't just upset; they were frightened.

"Mom?"

Bridget sat down and took his hands in hers. "Last night, Andy, when you were touching the wall, what did you do?"

"I fixed the pipe." He searched his parents' faces. "Didn't I?"

"Mr. Crowley cut a hole in the wall to look at it. The pipe did break there. At least . . ." Bridget stopped and looked helplessly at Ron.

His father crouched down beside him. "How did you fix the pipe, boy?"

"I felt it through the wall," Drew said, trying to put the strange feelings into words. "The metal. I could feel where it was broken. Then my head got hot, and the heat went down my arm and into the wall. It made the pipe go back together."

"You felt the metal."

Drew nodded. "It feels funny. Like . . ." He paused to search for the right comparison. "Christmas morning."

"Does it now?" Ron fished a handful of change out of his pocket and put it in Drew's hand. "Can you show me with this what you did to the metal?"

Drew frowned at the coins. He couldn't feel the dimes or the nickels or quarters. "Not with all of them." He picked out five pennies and handed the rest back to Ron. Then he concentrated, bringing back the warm feeling in his head as he held his hand open.

The pennies began to dance a little, which made him smile, and then he made them stand on end and roll in a circle. He spun the pennies faster, pouring more of the heat into them, and they began to stretch and melt into each other.

"Dear God in Heaven," he heard his mother whisper.

Drew felt proud. He made the pennies join together into a solid ring, and then pulled back some of the heat so it wouldn't burn his hand. When the copper stopped spinning, it was a perfect circle, the same size as the pretty bracelets his mom liked to wear.

It was cool to see what he couldn't last night, not with the wall in the way. He looked up at his dad. "That's what I did, kind of. Is it okay?"

His mom's fingers trembled as she took the bracelet. "It's only a little warm." She handed it to Ron, and then covered her face and began to sob.

"Mom?" Drew threw his arms around her. "I'm sorry. I won't do it again."

"No, darling. It's all right. You didn't do anything wrong." She choked back her sobs and wiped her face quickly before she rubbed her hands over his arms. "It was just . . . a surprise, sweetheart. But a good one."

Drew wasn't so sure about that. The only time he'd seen his mother cry that hard was the day he'd woken up in the hospital.

"Andrew." His father looked stern now. "Does anyone else know you can do this thing? Have you told your friends at school?"

"No, sir. Just you and Mom."

"Good." His gruff voice sounded less strained now. "Now listen to me, boy. We can't be telling people outside our family about this, ah, thing you do."

He almost asked why, and then he considered what he could do. No one that he knew could make metal dance. Well, there was Magneto in the *X-Men* comics, but he was a villain. Drew could never be a bad guy. He squinted up at his father. "I'm kind of like a superhero, aren't I? That's why we have to keep it secret?"

His parents exchanged another long look before his father said, "Yes, Andrew. That's why."

Bridget squeezed his hands in hers. "You have to be careful with this, darling. Being able to make the metal dance is fun, I'm sure, but metal can be hard and sharp, and you could hurt yourself. Your friends, your teachers, or even me and your dad. Do you understand me?"

On some level Drew knew that metal would never hurt him, but his mother was right—he might accidentally burn someone when he made it hot, or cut them when he made it into different shapes. "Yes, ma'am."

She kissed his forehead. "Now I think we need to go to Haskin's Ice Cream Shop and have some hot fudge sundaes. I know I do, very badly."

From that day on, Drew never had cause to regret revealing his ability to his parents. It didn't change their feelings toward him, and if anything made them all closer. Over the years his father worked with him on learning the extent of his ability and what he could do with it, and in the process taught Drew more about copper, its properties and uses, than the average metallurgist knew.

Although she didn't tell him until he'd graduated college, from that day on his mother quietly began trying to find his birth records and through them his biological parents. She and Ron had adopted him as a baby through a placement program run by their church, but there were almost no records of Drew's birth aside from a hastily written police report about an older, unidentified man bringing him to an emergency room shortly after his birth and abandoning him there.

"It's as if you just appeared out of nowhere," Bridget said sadly. "Your mother was probably his daughter or granddaughter, and gave birth at home. At least he took you where you'd be safe and cared for."

Thanks to the love of his parents, Drew had always lived

comfortably with his ability. Even after learning of how he and the other Takyn had been meddled with, knowing what some of the other Takyn could do made him feel as if he'd gotten the kind end of the DNA swizzle stick. One of his oldest friends among the Takyn, a man he knew as Paracelsus, was plagued with visions of the past, often so real that more than once they had almost destroyed his mind. His newest friend, Jessa Bellamy, could see the darkest secrets in anyone's soul just by touching them.

And then there was Rowan.

As he thought of her, Drew settled down at his computer to pull up the tracking program he'd initiated on Rowan. She didn't know that before they had parted ways in Savannah, he had planted a GPS locator on her bike. Matthias, a former Roman soldier who had survived two thousand years of accidental burial in ice, and the oldest of the Takyn, hadn't asked him to do it, but at the time Drew had thought it would be a good idea to keep tabs on Miss Independence. When he told Matthias about it, the older man had agreed it was a smart move.

Drew had followed her progress as she rode from Savannah toward Boston, where she had found a job working for another of their Takyn friends. The signal told him only where she was, not what she was doing, but it comforted Drew to know. Rowan might be tough as nails, but she was also young and on her own—and hurting.

Jessa had confirmed his suspicions. "I think Rowan left us because she was in love with Matthias. It would have been hard for her to stay and watch me with him, especially now with the baby coming."

"How is Maximus Junior?" Drew asked.

"At the moment, trying to kick a hole through my spleen," she said wryly. "But that's better than the morning sickness. Listen, Drew, I know Rowan is proud and needs to go it alone and all, but she's still so young. If she calls you—"

"I'll talk to her," he assured her. "Don't worry. With some time and distance, I'm sure she'll get over it."

Tonight he expected her to be through New York City and well into Connecticut, but the signal track still showed her at the border between New Jersey and New York City.

"What are you doing, stopping for an egg cream?" he murmured as he zoomed in and watched the tiny bright light move across the Hudson. "You should have moved out here with me, girl. I'd have taught you to surf." Just as soon as he learned.

Drew picked up his cordless and dialed the number to Matthias's farm in Tennessee. Jessa answered, and after exchanging pleasantries put Matthias on the phone.

"Are you well?" was the older man's first question.

"Well and truly bored. I haven't been able to hack through GenHance's new security measures. I think I taught my staff a little too well," he said, referring to his old job working as chief of the technical department. "Any word from Rowan?"

"She has not called us. You?"

"No, but I'm looking at her right now. She's screwing around somewhere in New York City." He frowned as the signal fluttered, and then winked out. "Shit." He attacked the keyboard, trying to boost the signal. No light. "She just disappeared off the radar."

"What does that mean?"

"It means the locator isn't putting out a signal anymore. Maybe she found it and tossed it in the river. I'd better give her a call. Hold on." Drew picked up his disposable mobile phone, dialed Rowan's number, and put it on speaker.

"This is not me," Rowan's voice said. "This is computerized bullshit pretending to be me. Leave a name and number at the tone, or this is all you'll ever listen to."

"Ro, it's David. Give me a call back right away." He switched off the mobile and spoke into the cordless. "Her phone is going straight to voice mail."

"She may be angry about finding the locator."

"Yeah." Drew frowned at the screen map. "That's probably it. I'll wait for her to call."

*   *   *

Rowan never slept well the first night in a new place, but for once her periodic insomnia didn't keep her watching infomercials until dawn. She didn't even bother to turn on the small television in the apartment Dansant was letting her use, but went into the bedroom, unfolded the long black futon, and flopped down on it to judge the fit. Most day-beds and singles were too short for her long frame, but this one was an oversized full with a decent mattress. The last thing she remembered doing was looking up at the beaded honey pine ceiling, and thinking it was a lot newer than the oak and cherry checkerwork parquet floor.

Then nothing. Just sweet, endless, dreamless sleep.

She opened her eyes to the same ceiling, and lay there for a time, letting the sunlight from the three old casement windows play over her. From the strength and position of the sun she judged it to be early afternoon, which meant she'd slept six or seven hours straight. She had plenty of time before her first shift started at six.

Rowan knew how lucky she was. *I could be in a hospital right now, scaring the shit out of some doctors.*

Her knees throbbed a little, but from the slight pulling and stiffness she felt when she bent them she knew they were already heavily scabbed over. Tomorrow the scabs would fall off and the lacerations would be gone. Another bonus from the mad scientists who had fucked with her genes when she was a kid; she never got sick and she healed almost as fast as she got hurt.

She rolled over, hugging her pillow as she lazily re-played bits and pieces of her conversation last night with Dansant.

You're really going to let me stay here? She'd come out of the large bedroom into the spacious front room, which combined a large sitting room with a breakfast/dining area that opened out onto a private terrace. The furnishings were basic—a futon, side table and lamp in the bedroom, and a loveseat, armchair and kitchen set in the front, but everything was clean and in good condition. There was also a closet stocked with fresh, neatly folded linens and towels.

You could get three, four thousand a month for this place, easy.

Not everyone wishes to live above a restaurant, Rowan. You must also share the bath with the other tenant.

She'd already taken a peek at the big full bath situated between the two apartments. Someone had recently updated the plumbing with European-style fixtures, and paved every inch of it but the ceiling in quarried stone tiles the color of old honey spilled on polished slate. Rowan could easily imagine spending several hours soaking in the big beautiful claw-footed tub. *The lock on the door works, right?*

Oui.

After that Dansant had handed her the keys, smiled, and left her to it. Total access, complete trust.

The man was a saint. The man was insane.

Hunger drove Rowan out of bed, and after rummaging through the stuff she'd taken from her bike panniers, she found an unopened bag of her favorite trail mix. An investigation of the tiny kitchenette's cabinets and drawers produced a clean mug and a spoon. She ran the hot water tap until it was scalding—as she'd figured, the restaurant's water heater was set to an inferno temperature—and using some gratis packets she'd swiped from the last motel she'd stayed at, mixed up a cup of coffee.

Now all I need is a big half-naked guy to feed me grapes and fan me, and I'll know I'm in heaven.

Carrying her improvised breakfast out onto the terrace felt completely natural, as did sitting in the wicker patio chair and watching the tail end of city lunch hour gridlock. Her neighbor's apartment was on the opposite side of the building, so if he had a terrace it overlooked the alley. She even had the better view.

That it was all a little too good to be true didn't bother her. Rowan felt safe, and she hadn't felt that way since leaving Savannah. Her normal alarms and alerts simply weren't going off. Dansant was a decent guy who had shown her nothing but kindness and compassion. Whatever strings came along with this minor miracle, it seemed for now she was going to enjoy it.

The nuts, raisins, and chocolate in her trail mix quieted the snarling beast that lived in her belly, but she'd need to shop before she started work tonight to stock up on some supplies. Dansant had told her he made a traditional family meal every night for the staff, and she was welcome to use whatever she wanted from the pantry, but she was already taking advantage of him. She had enough cash to cover the basics, and from the wages they'd agreed on she'd have another thirty or forty dollars to spend on food every week. As long as she didn't splurge, that should cover her needs.

Dansant had promised her that Meriden, the guy who lived in the other apartment, wouldn't charge much to work on her bike, but Rowan had a feeling that was going to be a much bigger expense. Even if Meriden could get them discounted, new tires alone were going to run at least three hundred bucks.

She calculated her expenses, along with repaying Dansant for what he'd given Bernard and what she roughly estimated the bike repairs would be. If she had no other unexpected expenses, she should be able to earn enough for everything by the end of January at the latest.

Looks like I'm spending Christmas in New York. She'd dreaded the thought of getting through the holidays alone and friendless in Boston. Here maybe she'd be allowed to share a little of the festivities with Dansant and his crew.

Since the sisters who had taken her in and looked after her had died, she hadn't spent Christmas with anyone. Matt had never celebrated the holidays, and she hadn't tried to change that because he had already been coping with an entire world of changes that had come about in the two thousand years since he'd served as a soldier in the Roman army. Rowan had explained Christmas to him once, and he'd been appalled.

"I know of this man," he said. "Iesus Nazarenus. He caused much unrest in Judea. Many were killed in the riots. But his people did not call him Jesus or Christ. He was known among his own kind as Y'hoshua."

Even now, Rowan giggled over the thought of the Son of God being called the ancient equivalent of Joshua. If not for the Romans and how they translated Hebrew into Latin, they might be celebrating Joshmas. Still grinning, she swallowed the rest of her sugary coffee before raiding her pack again for fresh clothes and her bathroom stuff.

As Rowan took a towel from the closet she wondered when Meriden used the shared bath. Dansant had told her only that her neighbor worked days; she hoped he preferred to shower in the morning or evening. Working in a busy kitchen all night was a messy business, and she knew from experience that she'd need to bathe before she went to bed. But if it caused problems, she could give herself a quick bath inside her apartment. As long as she had running water and a sink, she never had to go to bed sweaty or smelly.

Rowan bundled her things together and let herself out of the apartment, locking the door behind her. She heard footsteps behind her and smiled as she turned.

"I thought you said you didn't—" She stopped as soon as she saw the size of the man coming out of the opposite apartment. Definitely too tall and broad to be her new boss. "Oh, sorry. I thought you were someone else."

He closed the door and pocketed a bunch of keys before facing her.

"You must be Meriden." She held out her free hand. "I'm Rowan, your new neighbor." When he ignored the gesture, she dropped her arm. He might think he was insulting her, but she was suddenly, irrationally glad she didn't have to touch him. And for the life of her she couldn't remember if Dansant had told her his first name. "You *are* Mr. Meriden, right?"

"Just Meriden." The dark landing kept his face in shadow, but from the pitch of his rumbling baritone he didn't sound like he was smiling. "Didn't waste any time moving in, did you?"

Suspicious, but this was New York, and she would be living ten feet from his door. "I don't have much stuff." Although she understood the need for his being cautious, she couldn't help adding on in her head, *Are you always this much of a jerk?*

He reached past her head and switched on a light.

In the dark Meriden resembled a distant linebacker, big but anonymous. Illuminated by the overhead light, he looked like a pissed-off gladiator who ate linebackers for an afternoon snack, and used girls like Rowan as a toothpick.

I have every right to be here, she reminded herself, straightening her shoulders. *This is Dansant's place. Not his.*

Meriden wasn't at all handsome like her new boss, thank God. Everything about him reminded her of forged metals, from the quarter inch of white-blond hair covering his scalp to the dark gold stubble darkening his jaw and chin. His summer tan hadn't completely faded from his fair skin, but she suspected he'd look just as scary with a winter-pale hide. Life or luck had hammered and beaten his features into a collection of hard edges and dented planes, lending him a rough-hewn look more suited to less-civilized times. He would have made an excellent gladiator, too; beneath his slanted brows dark eyes watched her with unnerving stillness.

If he were about to die, Rowan thought, *he wouldn't salute anyone. He'd already be chopping someone to pieces.*

The stretched white A-line undershirt tried to cover some of Meriden's chest, but the standard male dimensions it had been manufactured to fit simply didn't apply to Meriden's Olympian build. He hadn't pumped up; he'd grown out, somehow creating layer upon layer of heroic, sculpted muscle that belonged in some arena where barbarians were butchered and tigers were wrestled.

Living with Matthias, Rowan had grown accustomed to being around a man whose body had been developed to optimum levels. Matt had merely maintained what a lifetime of battle experience had shaped, but he had become her standard, the mental yardstick with which she measured all other men and found them lacking.

Her next-door neighbor wasn't Matthias. He was bigger, wider, harder, and—if all that brute muscle wasn't false advertising—as strong as if not stronger than her old friend.

"Seen enough?" he asked. "Or should I drop my pants?"

Rowan should have snapped back with something equally insulting, but she had been staring at him like a love-struck kid. She glanced down at Meriden's faded jeans, which sported an impressive amount of smears, spots, and stains. The seam edges had frayed into a short white fringe, and a split ran across the lower part of his left thigh.

"I don't know," she said honestly as she glanced up into his dark-hearted eyes. "I'm not sure my heart can take any more."

He didn't laugh. Such a specimen of rugged masculinity in its most intense form never came equipped with a sense of humor, of course. That would mean there was a God and He liked her.

"Look, I took a spill last night in the alley," she said quickly. "My bike needs new front and rear tires and some repair work. Dansant told me that you're a mechanic. Maybe you could look at the damage and give me an estimate?"

The way he was glaring down at her made her think he was going to refuse, but then he surprised her again. "I've got another job to do. It'll have to wait 'til next week."

She nodded, feeling a little relieved that she'd have some time to build up her cash supply. "Are you okay with me making payments for the repairs?"

"Talk to Dansant."

"I can put down about a hundred—"

He shook his head. "He'll pay me. You pay him."

Rowan let it go. "Okay. The only other thing is working out the bathroom arrangements." She gestured at the door between their apartments. "Is there any specific time you need it to shower, shave, whatever?" He didn't reply. "I'd like to use it after my shift, around two a.m., and whenever I get up in the morning, probably around ten or eleven. That okay with you?"

He kept silent, kept watching her.

Patience had never been one of her virtues. "It's a yes or no question, Meriden. A simple head movement should cover it."

"I don't care what the fuck you do, Cupcake." He bent his head so she could see directly into his eyes. Now they were diamond hard and demon black, as if he were an icy volcano ready to blow. "Just stay out of my way."

"My pleasure." The sting of *Cupcake* made her add an insulting amount of wattage to her smile. "Soon as you get the hell out of mine, Farm Boy."

Meriden took a step to the side, creating just enough space for her to edge past him without causing physical contact. Rowan ignored the heat of his huge body, and how it warmed the suddenly oversensitive skin of her cheek and throat, but the smell of him, as cool and dark as a midnight tide, filled her head. She refused to fiddle with the bathroom door or glance back at him. She wasn't some kid for him to scare into scurrying away.

Cupcake my ass.

She managed a casual "See you around" before she stepped inside and carefully closed the door behind her. Which was a good thing, because somehow in spite of her fury her knees were liquefying and she was trembling all over.

Rowan listened, but she didn't pick up his steps moving away or hitting the stairs. He was still standing there on the other side, waiting for something. Her heart bounced in her throat as she groped behind her for the locking latch, and twisted it.

After a long moment, heavy footsteps moved across the landing and down the stairs. A few seconds later the back kitchen door opened and slammed shut.

He was gone, and she was sliding down the door until she sat on the floor in a muddled, jittery mess. Rowan hugged her legs with her arms and pressed her forehead to her knees, willing herself to calm down. So Meriden was an oversized, bad-tempered jackass; at least she knew that up front. He worked days; she would be working nights. All she needed to do was learn his schedule and avoid him whenever he was coming or going.

Then she'd work on figuring out why it wasn't terror that was making her shake like this.

Chapter 5

Dansant came to open the restaurant after sunset, but instead of posting the menu for the night he went directly to the back stairs to see if Rowan had come down yet. She was already in the kitchen, walking around and inspecting everything.

For a moment he watched her, unsure if he would have the same unsettling reaction as last night.

He had intended only to see to her wounds and assure himself that she did not need to be taken to the hospital. That much he would swear to. But as soon as he had closed the door, the scent of her enfolded him, sinking into him and going straight to his head.

Dansant had controlled himself until she had uttered those words: *All right, Dansant. Do whatever you want.*

Rowan remembered nothing of what had happened next, of course. Later, after he had regained his control, he had taken the memories from her as easily as he had brought her under his influence.

Rowan. Look at me. Look.

Your eyes—something . . . wrong . . .

Her own had widened as she resisted him for a moment, and then her lashes drifted down, framing the faint reflection of shining turquoise from his own.

Now the same longing and hunger besieged him as soon as he breathed in her scent, but while it was as intense as before, he seemed to have a better grip on his self-control now.

Dansant also felt a terrible weight lift from his heart, as if some part of him had been convinced she would be gone before he came here, before he could touch her again. But she had stayed. She must have slept well, too, for her color was better and her eyes brighter, although she still moved with some residual stiffness. Her head turned as she became aware of his presence and she smiled, although that seemed carefully measured as well; just so much of a welcome and no more.

She must feel the same as I, he thought. *But if she does, she does not wish me to know it any more than I want her to remember what I did to her.* "*Bonsoir*, Rowan."

"Hey, boss." She had dressed simply in jeans and a T-shirt, and had tied a blue bandanna around her dark curls.

She appeared younger tonight, barely more than an adolescent, which helped steady him. Compared to him she was a child, one who needed a friend more than a lover. He would keep reminding himself of that. "You look as if you slept well."

"I did," she agreed.

Last night he had not wasted time with polite inquiries or any sort of finesse. As soon as Rowan's defenses had fallen he had stood and placed his hands on either side of her face. She smiled blindly up at him, her lips parted, her soft skin warm against his palms.

He had watched her eyes as he slid his fingers into her hair, angling her face so that the overhead lights bathed every inch of her. She was a midnight jewel, this girl, alabaster moon-skinned and onyx star-eyed.

Her mouth, soft and gentle and unguarded, had drawn him down. As their lips met, her breath whispered out of her, a silent sigh that he covered and drank in.

"Ready to put me to work?"

Her voice brought him back to the present. Glad to have something to do other than remember what he had done to her, Dansant took a white bib apron from the stacks shelved above the sink and gave it to her.

"I will show you the setup of the kitchen, the stations,

and how we do things before the others arrive," he told her. "We begin preparations at seven and seat at nine."

"What's the seventy-seven for?" she asked as she tied on the apron, looking down at the small embroidered patch on the left side of the bib.

"It is the restaurant's logo," he told her. "The street number for our building is seventy-seven."

"To remind people where you are. Smart. You could have called the restaurant 77, too. Everyone remembers digi-named places, like 17 Murray, or 2 West at the Ritz-Carlton."

He thought of the true meaning of the number. "I prefer D'Anges."

"For a French restaurant, that doesn't hurt, either." She smoothed down the tapered pockets below the waist ties.

He watched her hands as he recalled the taste of her. Her mouth had been especially luscious, rich and sweet, like brandied pears. His first taste of her had led to a second, and a third, and then to an endless, mindless kiss that tore into him, deep and savage as a jagged blade.

"Dansant?" When he looked at her, she asked, "Why do you seat so late?"

Late? Last night he had lifted her from the crate and held her against him, all his to do with as he pleased. Now he had to chat with her as if none of it had happened. "We seat late to, ah, discourage the before-timers."

"Sorry?"

He'd been so wrapped up in his recollections that he'd forgotten the term in English. "It is like capons. No, not them." Just when he thought he could speak her language well enough, he stumbled over something like this. "Older people who arrive at opening and expect special pricing."

Her smile flashed. "Early birds."

"Oui." He turned his head so he wouldn't stare at her mouth.

Last night he had been intent on that, hers and his. In the thrall of pleasure he had forgotten that he had brought her inside to care for her, but it had never been like that for him. He had come to this country and lived this life not of his choosing because there had been nothing left of him or for him. That he woke every night and found he was still alive, still able to live, seemed a miracle each time he opened his eyes.

After learning what had happened to him in France, he had never dared dream of more.

Now this woman had crashed into his life, and she was looking at him with no knowledge or understanding of what he was, or what he would never again be.

"No early birds," she said. "Check."

He had to move away from her, so strong was the compulsion to touch her. He had to get on with it, this charade of employing her.

"The work begins here," Dansant told her as he led her out to the back entry door. "Everything we do in the kitchen is by design—*la marche en avant*."

Rowan frowned. "We're moving backward out of the kitchen, not forward."

She had managed to surprise him again. "You understand French?"

"I can read it, not speak it." She sounded defensive now. "I've . . . worked in a couple restaurants, and picked up some stuff from books, mostly kitchen and cooking terms. It sure doesn't sound the same as it looks on paper."

"But you have a natural ear for it, I think." Dansant decided to test her. "I will say the French for each place in the kitchen, and you will tell me what it is in English and what you know of it." He gestured at the door. *"Entrée, réception des matières."*

"Entrance and receiving," she translated. "Where everything comes through and is delivered."

He nodded and moved to the right into the main storage room. *"Stockage à sec."*

"Dry storage, where you put the dry goods." She made a face. "I cheated. I looked at the shelves and guessed."

From there he introduced her to the three *chambres froids* used to store meat, frozen goods, and fruits and vegetables; the *légumerie* where the vegetables were washed; and the *plonge* sinks and equipment on the opposite side of the section for cleaning pots and dishes. She correctly identified each one and even began echoing the words he said in French under her breath.

It pleased him that she wanted to improve her understanding of his language. Years of living in New York had taught him that few Americans were willing to make such an effort.

"Why is everything sectioned off this way?" Rowan asked after he had brought her back into the front of the kitchen. "Wouldn't it be easier to do all the prep work in one area, have the storage units together?"

"Using *la marche en avant*, the staff assure that work is done in the correct order," he explained, "with no clean foods coming near the unclean things like garbage and soiled dishes."

Her expression cleared. "Okay. So everything moves clockwise until it's plated and ready to be served: delivery, initial prep, storage, hot and cold prep, plating, then service." She waited until he nodded. "Trash and bus bins are brought through the side door and go down that way to the sinks and the compactor, away from the food."

He smiled at how quickly she comprehended what had taken the French three hundred years to perfect. "You must have worked at many restaurants."

"To be honest, only a bakery shop—Emmanuel's Pâtisserie," she amended. "We had a couple of tables out in front for coffee, cakes, sandwiches, that kind of thing. Manny ran his kitchen the same way you do."

"Then he was French, or taught by a Frenchman." Dansant escorted her to the center *cuisine* island, where the bulk of the cooking was done, and explained the layout of the equipment. "Here we have cooktops and stoves on this side, rotisseries and broilers on the other. The *brigade de cuisine* work mainly here, but the *garde-manger*, *rôtisseur*, *saucier*, and *pâtissier* all have their own *mise en place* at their stations where they ready the food for final cooking.

When the orders begin they will go through their provisions quickly and call for what they need from cold or dry storage. That is when you will collect it for them, and perhaps assist or plate for them."

"Sounds good."

"Later, after we have our family meal, you will help clean and sanitize the kitchen surfaces." He saw her palm as she tucked back a curl that had strayed from the edge of her bandanna, and caught her wrist without thinking. "What is this?"

"It's a hand." She sounded puzzled. "I come equipped with two of them."

So she did. Last night both of her palms had been grazed, but not deeply enough to mar her fair skin. Now he saw no trace of them.

"They weren't as scratched up as I thought," she said quickly, as if she had read his thoughts. "It was mostly blood from my knees. I must have grabbed them right after I crashed."

She was lying now. "How are your knees?"

"Sore." She checked the chunky watch she wore, deftly removing her hand from his in the process. "Who takes care of cleaning up the restaurant tables and stuff out front?"

"The front of the house," he corrected. "A cleaning crew comes two days each week. The waiters and service manager see to the rest before they finish their shift."

"So all we have to worry about is keeping the kitchen clean."

"Everyone tends to their own stations. The rest we do together." He regarded her steadily, trying to see what else he had missed last night. She had the unmarked, translucent skin of a child, and he saw no lines or other indications of her age. "How old are you, Rowan?"

"Twenty-one. Completely legal." She didn't like him asking. "What, you want to see my ID?"

Dansant wondered if it would be genuine. He had not intruded on her mind last night more than was absolutely necessary—he had violated her enough by holding and kissing her—but certainly she was young. Perhaps she spoke the truth, and was nothing more than what she appeared, but now doubt brought with it one possible explanation for what had compelled him to touch her. "Where is your family?"

"I told you last night, I don't have any."

He had to be sure. "No parents, brothers, sisters?"

"None." Her tone grew bitter. "I was abandoned at birth, and raised in foster care. No one has ever claimed me as their daughter or sister or third cousin twice removed, but then, they probably would have gone to jail for child abandonment if they had." She turned away from him.

Dansant felt like an ogre for pressing her, but from the scant details she had given him he would have to know more. Silently he decided to have Meriden perform a discreet background check on his newest employee as soon as possible. "I did not ask to be rude, Rowan. *Je suis désolé.*" His staff would soon be arriving, and he had yet to post the menu for the night. "How is your handwriting?"

"Readable, but nothing fancy."

"Then it is a thousand times better than mine." He took down the big blackboard and handed her a piece of chalk. "We offer a small menu each night, five *plats principals* with *hors d'oeuvres* and desserts that suit them. We list the main courses on the board in French and English."

She held the chalk above the board. "Fire away."

"Loup de mer rôti aux herbes," he told her as he moved to stand beside her and watch.

"Roasted sea wolf?" Her grin reappeared. "Is that with or without the fur?"

"Roasted sea *bass,*" he corrected, "with herbs only."

"Then why not just call it bass?"

"It would be confusing." He loved to see her smile. "In French, bass is *un instrument de musique.*"

"It is in English, too," she assured him, "and we never get confused."

He pointed at the board. *"Loup de mer,* if you please."

Dansant gave her the rest of the menu, throughout which

she joked and even constructed a kind of story. His *poulet demi-deuil* was not a chicken with a truffle-stuffed skin, but a depressed widowed hen; the *filet de boeuf au vin* had done something unspeakable to the hen's *coq*, probably by stewing him in the *petits pois aux morilles*, or dropping him in with the cabbage and potatoes to make *trinxat*.

"The poor chick," Rowan sighed as she finished writing the last item on the board in English. "She loses her guy to a side of beef, stuffs herself with high-priced 'shrooms, and then ends up roasting for it." She chuckled as she gave him a sideways glance. "Ain't love grand?"

Dansant's amusement faded. Love was not grand; it was tragedy, it was horror. For him, there could never be love.

Last night, when Rowan had been in his arms, she had murmured something against his mouth, and another voice woke inside his head.

This life was never yours. Neither is she.

In dousing his need, that voice had been as effective as a fire hose. Dansant had groaned as he pushed Rowan from him, holding her arm only to keep her from collapsing. Commanding her made her pliant but also temporarily stripped her of her power of mind and will; she would do nothing but respond willingly to his desires. Even in that she had no choice, and once more Dansant was reminded of the monster that he was beneath his civilized veneer, that he could do this to a being as helpless as she.

"Before I kissed you," he said to her, "did you want me? Give me your truth, Rowan."

She nodded slowly, and then shook her head.

It seemed she shared his confusion. "Do you have a lover or husband?" Another shake of her head. At least he had not trespassed on another man's claim. "You will remember nothing of this. As before, you will feel safe and at ease with me. You will trust me as you do a friend." He couldn't help adding, "More so than any of your other friends."

He'd taken his hands from her, and knelt before her, and after releasing her from his control had tended to her injuries. She would never remember the kissing or the touching.

Or how close she had come to being stripped and dragged to the floor and fucked until she screamed for him.

"Dansant?" A slim hand waved in front of his face. "You keep zoning out on me."

"Forgive me." Not for the first time he wished he could erase his own memories. "Talk of love . . . it is not always so grand."

"*You* got burned?" Her chin dropped. "Come on."

"It was a friend," he lied. "He lost his beloved one, and it sent him into hell. I did what I could; I tried to bring him back to life, but he . . . he suffers still." Part of it was true. They had both suffered, each in their own way, after discovering what had been and never would be again.

Her eyes became distant. "That's why they call it true love, I guess." A rumble came from the alley, and she put down the chalk. "Sounds like the first delivery is here. I'll get it."

As Rowan went to the back door, Dansant looked up the shadowy flight of stairs, almost expecting to see Meriden there, waiting, listening. He could almost see his black eyes, staring at him, knowing everything, despising him for what he had done to Rowan. Hating him for what he was, wanting to kill him.

It was a pity, Dansant thought, that he was already dead.

"Whadayawanmista?"

Meriden glanced at the menu board over the counter. "Large black coffee and a bow tie."

The tired-eyed girl nodded, cracking her gum as she punched the picture keys on her register. "Three-oh-seven."

He handed her four bucks. "Keep the change."

She worked up a smile for him. "Thanks." After she'd poured and handed him his coffee, she went to the doughnut racks. "Oh, crap. Mister, the bow ties aren't out yet."

Which was why he'd ordered one. "I'll be sitting over there." He nodded to a corner table.

"Yeah, okay." She turned to the next customer. "Whada-yawanlady?"

Meriden sat down and sampled the coffee, which was drinkable, and took out his notepad and the photo of Alana King. When the counter girl walked over with his bow tie wrapped in a two-sided bag, she saw the photo.

"That your daughter? She's cute."

"No, this is a girl I'm looking for." He checked the counter, which was clear. "She was seen here getting some coffee."

"Kid that age?" She folded over her bottom lip. "I don't think so. I'd remember selling coffee to a little one."

"She's older now. About sixteen."

The counter girl glanced back before she sat down across from him. "Is this that missing kid? I talked to a couple detectives about her." She gave him a suspicious look. "You a cop, too?"

"Private investigator." He showed her his identification and license. "I'm working for her father."

"Runaway, huh?" She grimaced. "The cops don't care much about missing kids unless they're real young. So what do you want to know?"

"According to a witness who saw her here, you waited on her. She bought a small coffee, and you gave her a muffin." He saw the uneasiness in her eyes. "It's okay, I'm not going to say anything to your manager. I just wanted to know why."

"If it's the girl I think you mean, she's a street kid. You know, living out there." She grimaced. "I'm not supposed to give out stuff, but it's hard, you know, when they look at stuff on the racks, and they pay in nickels and pennies, and you know they ain't got enough to get something else." She looked down at the table as if she was ashamed. "My ma, she says they can go to a soup kitchen or a church any time, but I can't help it. I mean, a muffin, come on, it's not a big thing. And she buys something every time she comes in."

"She's been here more than once."

The counter girl nodded. "She comes in regular, late at night. Maybe a couple times a month."

"Is there anything else about her you can tell me?" When she shrugged, he added, "Does she always leave in the same direction?"

"I'm sorry, I just don't look after they leave the counter."

"If you remember anything else"—he slid one of his business cards across the table—"give me a call. Anytime."

"Sure." Her expression turned dubious.

"One more thing." He slid a ten across the table. "A muffin *is* something, and you're a good person."

"Yeah." She offered him a genuine smile. "I just wish it was enough." She pocketed the ten and went back to work.

Meriden worked the area for the rest of the morning, questioning the merchants with businesses around the coffee shop, and making no headway on the case. He grabbed a sandwich before he went to the garage, where he intended to put in a couple of hours before he called it a day.

Rowan Dietrich's bike sat at the back of his bay, delivered there by a tow-truck driver who owed him a favor. He resented it like everything else Dansant stuck him with, but the sooner he got it repaired, the sooner the girl would be on her way.

He didn't like her living in his back pocket, but he had to admit she had a sweet ride. He'd spent a lot of time biking when he'd lived overseas, both for convenience and to save money. A motorcycle didn't require as much fuel, which was outrageously expensive over there, and it could be parked almost anywhere. He suddenly realized why he disliked the bike so much. It was a Ducati.

Nathan had loved Italian racing bikes.

Although his own years in Europe were just a blur of anger and confusion now, Meriden could clearly remember a few things about Nathan. The rest he'd put together after some careful, painstaking research. He'd been sent to Rome to study, but he'd left there after a year to hitchhike his way across a half-dozen countries, paying his way by picking up work as a cook. He'd met Gisele at her father's restaurant, and it had been all over for Nathan the moment she smiled at him. She felt the same, for she had been the one to convince old Giusti to take him on as an apprentice.

Meriden knew Nathan had fallen for her, hard, and had gambled everything to have her. They'd had only a year together, but from all accounts they'd been incredibly happy. If the dark men hadn't come for Nathan, he'd still be there, cooking beside Gisele's father.

When he'd learned the details of what had happened to the Giustis, Meriden had gone back to Nice to make sure Nathan was dead. He'd bribed a hospital employee in Nice to obtain copies of the medical records. Nathan had been horribly burned in the accident that had killed his wife, and despite attempts to resuscitate him, had died that night in the hospital. His death certificate had been signed by the attending physician.

The facts were undeniable. Irrefutable. Inescapable.

Pain spiked through Meriden's skull. Thinking of those days gave him a migraine; if he didn't stop he'd end up locked in a dark room. He'd accepted what had happened to Nathan, how he had died, and the bizarre aftereffects that had brought Sean together with Dansant in France. One accident, one horrific, tragic choice, and three lives had been changed forever. Sometimes he wondered what Nathan would think of him and Dansant. If he would be as accepting, or if he'd want them dead, too.

If he had known what would happen, Sean thought, would he have still run into the flames?

Despite his and Dansant's efforts to discover the truth about Nathan's past, and if there was any possibility of it affecting them in some way, there were still countless, troubling gaps in the man's personal history. Nathan had gone to Rome, but then he had disappeared for almost a year. There were no records of when he had left Italy or how he had traveled to France; it was as if he'd simply rematerialized there. He'd been running from something, or he wouldn't have gone to the trouble of forging his papers and creating an entirely new identity for himself. He'd done an excellent job of becoming someone else, but the dark men had still caught up with him. Why they would wipe out an entire family simply to get their hands on an expat who liked to cook made no sense to Sean, but few things about Nathan did.

"Hey, Sean." Eugene, one of his regular customers, strode in through the shop door. "Where you been, you lazy bastard?"

"Job across town." Sean stood up and shook hands. "What can I do for you?"

"I need to order some parts." He bent sideways to look at the bike. "Is that a Ducati Monster?" He whistled. "Tires are fucked. What'd the owner do, get spiked?"

Eugene had a couple of motorcycles he was perennially working on, and Sean didn't mind asking for a consult. "Collision in an alley. You ever seen two tires blow at the same time?"

"If they were spiked, yeah. Or maybe some shitty retreads." Eugene crouched down to finger the split in the rear tire. "This don't look right. See how the rubber is peeling outward? This bitch blew fast and hard." He stood up and walked over to look at the front tire. "Same here."

"Overfilled?"

"If you filled 'em with cement or something." He scratched his head. "This is some fucking weird shit happening here, my brother."

"I'm putting two new tires on it." Sean made a mental note to order them from his supplier. "Come in the office and I'll write your parts."

Eugene glanced back a few times as they crossed the bay. "Hey, can I have the old tires off that bike?"

"For what? Bookends?"

"I want to show 'em to a friend of mine," Eugene said. "He's got a junkyard, and collects spooky shit. He's got this eight-track he pulled out of a wrecked van that went over a bridge, killed a bunch of kids back in the seventies. It's got a tape stuck in it, but when you turn it on it only plays 'Free Bird.' Creeps me out."

Sean chuckled. "Sure, you can have 'em if you haul 'em."

"Excellent." Eugene took a crumpled piece of paper out of his pocket. "Okay, let's talk carburetors."

The view from Gerald King's bedroom window never changed. From his position on the top floor of one of the last freestanding mansions in Manhattan, he could see the streets below, the river beyond, and in the distance a vague smear of New Jersey skyline against the twilight sky.

During the spring and summer he seldom looked out, indifferent to the city's myriad celebrations of warmer temperatures and better business. Only when the fall began leeching the green from the trees and the people from the streets did he come to admire the view. As winter finally arrived with its bitter winds and gray snows, the city became like the landscape of his soul: empty, desolate, an ancient Titan chained for eternity to the rocks of existence, feeding on poison daily just to stay alive.

If he had been a man who prayed, he would have made a single request of God—that he be given a second chance at life with the only thing he had ever loved. And she was here, in the city, perhaps even now just around the corner. Just out of his sight.

What was she doing? Walking the streets? Watching faces? Looking for his? After all this time, did she still think of him? Or had she made herself forget him?

She could do that, and more. With her powers she could make dreams come true. He had seen it with his own eyes; touched the proof of it with his own hands. And now she was out there, lost and alone, hiding herself among the herd of common humanity, who should have been gathering around to fall on their knees to worship her like the goddess she was.

The knowledge that she lived made him feel young again. It also made him aware of every tick of the clock on his mantel, every shadow shifted by the passage of the sun.

"Mr. King."

Gerald kept his staff on a ruthless schedule designed to keep his contact with them to a bare minimum. The interruption now, however, could not be avoided—not when he was so close to finding her. "What is it?"

"You have an electronic message from Atlanta, sir." The communications technician remained standing just beyond the threshold. "The transmission came through flagged as urgent and encrypted for eyes-only."

That meant only King could open the message. "Upload it to my system and then destroy the original transmission."

"Yes, sir." The technician withdrew.

No one had access to King's private computer array; he kept it completely isolated from the rest of the household terminals as well as the networks used by his various business interests. A subterminal system allowed one-way communication between the household system by accepting uploads, which were then vigorously screened and sanitized before a second upload to the private mainframe. Nothing on King's system could be downloaded or copied; any attempt to do so would initiate a terminus protocol that would destroy King's computer as well as every computer that had ever uploaded anything to the subterminal.

It took time for the subterminal to scan, study, and clean the upload before it was forwarded. King used the time to engage his privacy measures, which isolated and secured his living space from the rest of the house and generated an electronic signal that would scramble any listening device within five hundred yards.

He glanced at his terminal, where the words *upload completed* appeared. "Open most recent encrypted file, password silence-one-one-two-seven-one-nine-five-six-rebirth."

The terminal's voice recognition software responded not only to the spoken code but to King's voice itself, which it instantly compared with the voice print kept on file. Because the voice matched, it accepted the code; if anyone else had tried to use it the result would have been initiation of the terminus protocol.

"Audio file opened," the system's computerized voice told him. "Hold, replay, save, or delete?"

"Replay."

A moment later, a familiar voice came through the system's speakers. "Mr. King, the partial DNA sample taken from the female prime has been used to resolve the problem with the transerum. Mr. Genaro is now aware of the value of the female and has determined that she is presently in New York City."

Pain lanced through his head and for a moment split his vision in two before he reached for his phone.

King had obtained much of his communications equipment from various agencies involved in high-tech surveillance and other covert operations. The satellite phone he used to place the call was one of only three in existence; it could not be monitored and any call he made on it could not be traced to the line he called or back to his residence.

The voice that answered was as void of emotion as its owner. "Yes, Mr. King."

He had to unclench his teeth in order to speak. "How did Genaro find out she's in the city?"

"I've been unable to determine that, sir," his operative said, "but I believe he's using some unconventional means to locate them."

Them. As if King cared about anyone but her. But if Genaro had developed some new technology that could track her . . . "What could he use?"

"Theoretically speaking, a government spy satellite could be programmed to search for them. They all have unique energy signatures that register off the grid. But I don't think he has enough information gathered to correctly identify a targeted individual." The operative paused. "He may be using one of them to locate the others. We've yet to identify a remote viewer, but it's certainly not beyond the scope of their abilities."

King closed his eyes, forcing the pain back. "You told me he was killing everyone he captured in order to harvest their DNA."

"That is what we've been told," his operative agreed, "and what the records show."

The chairman of GenHance had many secrets; it would be nothing for him to deceive even his most trusted employees. "What action is being taken?"

"A team of trackers has been dispatched to recover her," was the reply. "They will arrive within the next twelve hours."

Genaro's efficiency and decisiveness remained unchanged, but this time he was sending his men into King's territory. "Send complete profiles and photographs for each member of the team."

"They're being transmitted to you as we speak."

King heard a faint rushing sound in his ears, as if sand was pouring out of them. "Has Genaro tested the modified transerum on a living human subject yet?"

"No, sir."

Genaro's uncharacteristic hesitancy gave King a slight advantage, one he would use to eradicate his wealthy rival in Atlanta. "Continue monitoring the situation. When the transerum is tested, report back to me at once."

"Yes, sir."

King ended the call and left his bedroom, moving through a short passage and through a door no one but he was allowed to enter. Inside the smaller room the air was much cooler and drier, but still scented with the faintest trace of lily-of-the valley.

He went, as he always did, to her pristine bed, where snow-white Belgian lace cascaded from a gracefully arched canopy to veil the cream linens. They lay pushed aside, as if someone had just risen from the bed. The right pillow still held a slight indentation, and draped on the end of the mattress lay a long robe of pale pink satin.

He reached out a shaking hand, reverently touching the depression in the pillow as he thought of the many nights he had come to this bed and found the ultimate pleasure in her arms. She had been so sweet and trusting, and while she had never truly understood his passion, she had accepted it. Her love had indulged his every desire, giving him all that he had asked of her, refusing him nothing.

That selflessness, that unstinting generosity—that was true love.

King turned slowly toward the painting hanging on the south wall. He had commissioned her portrait just before she had come to him, and the world-renowned artist had captured every nuance of her being: the pale gold of her hair, the exquisite whiteness of her skin. Her eyes, large and beautifully blue, looked down at him, shining from within. All the love she had brought into his life he saw in her gentle smile, her thin hands.

He could not bear to look upon her for more than a few moments; so great was his grief that he turned and moved to her little vanity table. The dainty pearl necklace that she had set out to wear that day curled beside the ivory brush and hand mirror she had used that last night. Some strands of her hair remained caught in the bristles of the brush, and when he brought it to his face he could smell her sweetness and goodness.

Carefully he set down the brush exactly where it had been in the thick layer of dust that he never noticed. When he glanced in the curved mirror, he saw only his own eyes, dark with the pain he bore, wet with the tears he refused to shed.

"Soon we'll be together again, Alana," he murmured. "Very soon, my love."

PART TWO

Chasse

MISSING PERSON/RUNAWAY REPORT

Manhattan Police Department

100 Centre Street

New York, NY 10013

Case #: J5720

Incident Location: King Estate, 371 Riverside Drive, Manhattan (at 109th St.)

Date: September 29, 2008

Missing Person Information

Name: Alana King

DOB: 11-7-92

Age at Disappearance: 16 years

Race: W **Sex:** F **Height:** 5'4" **Weight:** 105 lbs.

Hair color: Blond **Hair Style/Length:** Straight, shoulder-length **Eye Color:** Blue **Complexion:** Fair **Build:** Thin

Medical, Mental, and Physical Condition: Physically frail; mentally incapacitated and medication-dependent (See attached psychiatric profile)

Prior Medical History: Various surgeries to correct birth defects (See attached medical records)

Birthmarks/Other Identifying Marks: Tattoos on both inner forearms (See attached photo)

Piercings: None

Teeth: (See attached dental records)

Clothing worn at time of disappearance: Blue jeans, white T-shirt, brown cloth jacket, brown wool skullcap, brown scarf

Jewelry: None

Employer/Work/School: None/None/Home Tutored

Circumstances of the Disappearance: On the evening of September 28, 2008, the estate security system was deactivated due to equipment failure. During the failure Ms. King left the premises without alerting parent or household staff and did not return.

Known reasons for disappearance of minor: Father reports that daughter is mentally incapacitated and under close psychiatric care but may have stopped taking antipsychotic medications.

Please describe any additional information that may be helpful to assist in locating the missing person: A $100K reward is being offered by Gerald King (father) for information leading to the recovery of minor.

In authorizing this missing persons/runaway report, the parent(s) hereby agree(s) that MPD will be notified as soon as the missing person/runaway has returned home or is found. (Initialed by parent)

Signature of Investigating Officer

Det. W. J. Patterson Jr.

Chapter 6

The kitchen staff began to arrive for work at D'Anges while Rowan was sorting out and shelving the dry goods that had been delivered. As they came in, each one of the line cooks eyed her apron and then her face, but no one came over to her, said hello, or otherwise acknowledged her presence. Instead they went to their stations around the kitchen and began preparing for their shift, talking to each other in low tones and occasionally giving her a quick look.

She didn't scowl back at them, but she didn't bother to paste a friendly look on her face, either. She knew enough about chefs and cooks from reading books about them and the service industry to recognize that as a new hire she had yet to prove herself, and until she did she would be treated as an unwelcome outsider.

Rowan also saw that she was the only woman in the kitchen—Dansant's staff was apparently all male—which obviously wouldn't help matters.

The shortest guy on the crew finally came over to speak with her. He was a burly, balding Italian who looked like he busted kneecaps on his days off. "You got a name, kid?"

She placed the last bag of rye flour on the shelf. "Rowan Dietrich."

"I'm Lonzo." He didn't offer a hand, but turned and started pointing to the others. "That's Manny, George, Vince, and Lou. Dishwasher's Enrique, but he don't speak English

too good. Bernard's the sous-chef, but he's late again." He
gave her the once-over. "Why'd Dansant hire you?"

She didn't think saying *I crashed my bike into his sous-
chef's Volvo* would go over well. "I needed the job."

"He walk you through the place, show you the stations?"
When she nodded, he did the same. "All right, Trick, you're
my *tournant* tonight. Do what I tell you, don't fuck up, and
we'll see how it goes."

It was not the warmest reception in the world, but it was
a fair one, and she'd rather be called Trick than *kid* any day.
"Thank you, Chef."

Rowan expected some form of initiation or other trial by
fire, and wasn't disappointed when Lonzo took her to a big,
sunken table at the back of the kitchen, handed her a six-
inch flexible blade with a slight curve, and got her started on
her first task. That was where Dansant found her thirty minutes later, up to her elbows in fish innards and slime as she
worked her way through gutting and cleaning fifty pounds
of striped bass.

"What are you doing?"

She finished trimming a fin before she spared him a
glance. "You need me to explain this procedure to you,
Chef?"

He made an impatient sound. "I meant, why are you doing this?"

"Easy. Your idiot supplier doesn't clean them." She
made a slit in the carcass's belly skin, extending it from the
anus to the gills. "Also, if I don't do this, Lonzo will kick my
skinny ass."

Dansant scowled. "He will do no such thing."

She turned her head toward the front of the kitchen.
"Hey, Chef," she yelled, "what'll you do if I stop cleaning
this fish?"

"I'll kick your skinny ass," Lonzo shouted back.

"See?" Rowan reached inside the carcass, felt for the
spot where the guts were all connected at the base of the
head, and stripped out the lot. "Why doesn't your supplier
clean these guys out first?"

"He purchases them from a fish farm, and brings them into the city in tanks. That way he can keep them alive until it is time to deliver," Dansant told her. "I prefer to have them cleaned by my cooks."

"Farmed, tanked fish." She shook her head, amused.

He didn't go, but watched her scrape out the bass's liver and slice away the remains of its swim bladder. "You have done this before tonight."

"No," she admitted. "But I'm good with knives, and you guys only have to show me how to do something once for me to get it." She also sensed their conversation had drawn the attention of the other chefs, which made her shoulders itch. She didn't want to be seen as receiving any kind of coddling or special treatment from Dansant. That would turn the staff's wariness and suspicions into resentment and contempt. "Is there something else you need me to do, Chef?"

"Yes." He studied her face. "Add some ice to the bath"—he nodded toward the basin of water in which she'd placed the cleaned fish—"or the warmth of the water will leech out the flavor."

Relieved, Rowan nodded and quick-scrubbed her hands at the sink before grabbing a scoop and hurrying to the ice machine.

A second after she had dropped the last fish into the ice water, Lonzo called her over to one of the prep tables, where a basket of brown, wrinkly morels and a huge colander of bright green pea pods sat beside a smaller, cloth-swaddled wooden box.

"After we do the chicken you're gonna shell those peas," he told her as he began unwrapping the box. She picked up the colander to take it to the rinsing table as he lifted the lid to reveal a dozen ugly black lumps nested like charred eggs in what appeared to be an airtight inner container. He caught her staring and took out one of the largest to hold it in front of her face. "You know what this is?"

She tried not to breathe in the intoxicating fragrance, but it was too close to her nose to resist. It smelled of the earth and rain, with just the slightest hint of hazelnuts. "It's a truffle."

"It's a Périgord black truffle." He turned it over in his hand as gently as if he were holding a newborn baby chick. "Twenty years ago you could only get these from Europe. The French exported them, but it would take a week or better, and what they sent was too small or old." Lonzo made a nasty sound. "Greedy bastards kept all the best ones for themselves."

She'd read about these rarest and most prized of cooking fungi in books, but at prices that rose as high as sixteen hundred dollars a pound, she'd never had the money to buy even a dinky one. "Are they really that good?"

"They're the reason I go to the church on Sunday," Lonzo said flatly, "and thank God that He loves us so much." He removed a very thin, honed knife from the roll of black cloth beside the cutting board. "Now we got *trufflieres* that grow them right here, in America. Things go right, in a few years we're gonna have all the black diamonds we want," he added, using the fungus's extravagant nickname.

"You want me to wash the diamonds?" Rowan asked, and watched Lonzo yank the truffle back as if she had tried to spit on it. Dansant came over to the station and selected three more of the black tubers out of the box. "Or maybe I could just watch." She was curious to see her new boss at work.

"You ain't got time." Lonzo stepped between them and dumped into her arms several perforated plastic bags containing fresh rosemary, thyme, and mint. "Rinse the herbs, check them for black spots, and then take them to George's station."

Over Lonzo's shoulder, Dansant gave her a wink. Suppressing a chuckle, Rowan took the bags back to the rinsing sink.

Although she stayed busy, Rowan was able to turn slightly and observe Dansant working with Lonzo. After delicately wiping clean his precious truffles, the *gardemanger* handed them to Dansant, who sliced them into perfectly even, wafer-thin rounds while Lonzo began lining up several untrussed chickens to one side of the cutting board. Once he had sliced enough rounds, Dansant loosened the skin of one chicken from the neck opening all the way across the breast, and then did the same for the legs.

Rowan caught herself holding her breath as Dansant began deftly slipping one at a time the thin rounds of sliced truffle under the skin. His long, elegant fingers worked them in place, until most of each thigh and the breast were covered with the aromatic fungus. Once he had finished, he used kitchen string to bind the ends of the legs before crisscrossing it over the breast and under the back.

By the time Rowan had delivered the cleaned herbs to George's station, Lonzo called her over to tell her to carry the truffled chickens, now plastic-wrapped, back to the meat refrigerator.

"Shouldn't these go over to the *rôtisseur*?" she asked as she stood holding the tray while Lonzo unloaded them onto the shelves.

"Vince will roast them tomorrow night." For every package of chicken he put into the fridge, he took out another and placed it on the tray. Then Manny yelled for him, and he cursed under his breath before trotting off.

"The truffles must have a day to infuse the meat with their magic," Dansant said right behind her, making her nearly drop the heavy tray. He came around and supported it from the other side. "These are the chickens we stuffed last night." He peeled away some of the wrap and pulled back the breast skin, enough for her to see how the truffle had darkened the meat.

"*Poulet demi-deuil* must be real popular," she said, looking up at him. Tonight all the lights were on in the kitchen, and made his eyes look so dazzling a blue that Rowan almost let the tray slip a second time. "To make it every night. Do you? Put it on the menu every night?" In some corner of her head she knew she was babbling, but she couldn't stop looking at him. Gay or not, he seemed to become more beautiful to her with every slam of her heart in her chest.

"It is a house specialty." He moved his hands around
the edge of the tray until his fingers slid over hers. "Tell me
what you are thinking."

"Why should I do that?" she heard herself ask in a
strange, hollow voice.

He bent his head until his breath cooled her damp scalp.
"Why shouldn't you, *ma mûre*?"

"*Trick.*" Lonzo's bellow jerked her back to herself just
as she felt her eyes sting. "You go deaf or something? Vince
is waiting for the tray. Bring it over, now."

"Right away, Chef." She ducked her head, ashamed for
making such a transparent ass out of herself in front of the
rest of the staff, and hurried off.

Taire heard the guys in the kitchen calling her Trick, and
smirked a little. If Rowan thought they were doing it because they liked her, the trick was on her.

She went to her usual spot, a recessed doorway hidden
in the shadows, and sat down on the cold slate stoop. From
there she watched the comings and goings, although the
only person she saw was Rowan going on garbage runs.
She passed the time by counting the number of times the
other girl emerged from the back doorway carrying two
or three overstuffed black bags, which she trotted over to
the restaurant's fenced-in Dumpster. At first she tossed
them in like they were filled with feathers, but as the night
stretched out, her tossing became heaving and a couple
of times she groaned and rubbed her arm before trudging
back in.

Taire felt a twinge of sympathy. The guys in the kitchen
weren't as nice as the Frenchman, and they didn't like
women. Sometimes on other nights she had listened to a
couple of them joking while they stood out in the alley on
a smoke break. They considered women good for only two
things: folding napkins and fucking. No doubt they were
going to make Rowan suffer as much as they could. Men
loved it when women cried and quit.

Father hadn't been as crude or mean, but what he had

expected of her had been just as harsh. *If it were easy, my dear, anyone would do.*

She pushed her father from her thoughts and looked down each side of the alley. Sometimes bums came to rifle through the garbage bags. There would be plenty of scraps in them, good food from unfinished meals, and even the stink from the older garbage under them didn't drive off the bums. No matter how hungry she was, Taire knew better than to rummage around a Dumpster. If Rowan or one of the guys from the restaurant didn't catch her, the rats that were already gnawing their way into the bags would.

Rowan made another run, and this time Taire had to press her arms around her waist to muffle the gurgle of her stomach. Being hungry sucked—and she was always hungry—but sitting there and breathing in the delicious scents that came rolling out along with Rowan made it worse.

It was Taire's own fault; she'd had all day to sneak out and get more food for her stash. She had enough change for a coffee, and the girl at the doughnut place where Taire usually went almost always slipped her a muffin or something for free. But thinking and dreaming and worrying had led to planning, and she'd paced her room all afternoon while she worked it out different ways in her head and then immediately shot down each one: *I could write her a letter* (but all she had was hotel stationery). *I could call her on the restaurant's phone* (but the call might be traced). *I could ask one of the kids to give her a message* (and the same kid could go to the cops). *I could break into her apartment upstairs* (but she didn't know how to pick locks, and anything else she might try would look like a burglary).

All that, and still no plan. She was too afraid to do anything, and would be until she knew for sure she wouldn't be caught.

Taire didn't know what Rowan could do, or what she might do to her after she told her. Rowan had to be stronger; not even crashing her bike had really hurt her. And what if she was just as scared as Taire was? She might attack her.

Her head whirled a little as she pushed herself up. Her hunger burned in her, worse than it ever had been; if she wasn't careful she might pass out and be found. They'd call the police, or an ambulance. They'd take her to a hospital or a shelter. They'd find out who she was, and then they'd kill her.

Or worse, they wouldn't.

The back door flung open, but Taire didn't realize she was standing in the light until Rowan turned and looked directly at her. She staggered back into the shadows, but it was too late.

"Hey." Rowan set down the garbage bags by the curb and squinted at her. "Who's there?"

In her head Taire was running away, but her legs shook too much for that. She crouched down and huddled over, holding her breath, hoping the other girl would think she was only seeing things.

"Hey, kid." Rowan took a few steps toward her. "You need some help?"

Taire felt the slate under her heels shift, and pressed her lips together to keep from shrieking. *Yes! Help me! Save me! No! Stay away!*

"Wait a second, okay?" Rowan went back into the kitchen.

Now was her chance to get up and out of here. Taire made it as far as the next door when she heard a familiar trotting step and glanced over her shoulder.

Rowan stopped a few feet away. "It's all right, kid." In her hands was a large black plastic container with a clear top. "You hungry?"

Taire could smell it now. Roasted chicken, herbs, potatoes, onions. Something more exotic and savory. She turned around, staring at the container—it was stuffed with food—and the red and silver can in Rowan's other hand.

A Coke. She'd brought her food and a Coke. For nothing.

Rowan didn't come at her, but held out her arms, putting the container and the can as far out as she could. "It's for you." When Taire didn't move, she crouched and carefully put it on the ground, then stood and moved back. "Take it."

Taire shuffled forward, keeping one eye on the food and the other on Rowan. Anticipation was making her feel sick now, her belly shrinking in on itself, her chest tight, her throat a vise. At the same time the smell of it had her mouth watering so bad she was practically drooling. She hadn't eaten real food in weeks.

Jesus. She hadn't had a Coke since she'd left home.

"Go on," Rowan urged.

Taire snatched the container and the soda up from the ground. The alley tilted, and she choked back a liquid sound as her stomach heaved. She had to say something, but all she could do was hold the food tight against her so no one would take it back. It was hers now. Rowan had put it on the ground. That made it hers.

"So, what's your name?" Rowan asked, still peering as if trying to see her face.

Terror forced Taire to trip backward, spinning and clutching the container as she fled. She dodged around the corner and cut through two more streets, not looking back or hearing anything but the ferocious slam of her heart in her ears.

Finally she found a spot between two parked cars, slipped into it and crouched down. She had to hold her breath and press the cold soda can against one ear before the pounding ebbed and she could hear again.

Nothing. No running footsteps, no calling voice. Taire waited to be sure, but after several minutes she knew Rowan hadn't followed her.

She set down the soda can carefully before she tore off the top of the container and grabbed a small whole potato speckled with flecks of herbs. She shoved the entire thing in her mouth, her eyes leaking thin tears as the alien sensation of having her mouth full nearly choked her.

Slow down slow down slow down.

Taire took the potato out of her mouth and instead held it like an apple so she could take a small bite. The taste was silky and buttery and flavored with thyme and rosemary, and she wanted to gobble the whole thing again. It took all her willpower to hold back and nibble away at it in small bites.

The chicken was even better. She lifted a golden-brown drumstick from the container and smelled it before sinking her teeth into the fragrant, juicy meat. Something soft and dark and thin under the skin came with it, and expanded in a dark, rich cloud of flavor inside her mouth. The taste was so warm and wonderful she moaned.

Oh God that's so good.

If she didn't stop stuffing her face so fast it was all going to come back up, Taire knew, from the shock of so much rich, solid food on the bottomless pit of her belly. Because she had no way to keep it she'd have to eat everything tonight, but it didn't have to be here or all at once. She could spend the rest of the night savoring the meal.

She couldn't wait for a taste of the Coke, though, and tapped the top of the soda can before she opened it and took a little sip. It was so cold and sweet it made her teeth ache, and a little slopped over the edge as her hand shook. As she sipped at the spillage from the rim, she tasted a trace of something else that wasn't as sweet, something tart and dry that took her back to the night before, when she'd watched Rowan take on the young tagger. When she'd seen the blue glow beneath the other girl's sleeve. She hadn't remembered every detail before, maybe because it had been another shock, like eating this food, to have so much within reach after having lived with nothing for so long. . . .

I'm the Coke and she's the Cristal.

Taire laughed as soundlessly as she cried.

Chapter 7

After her first night working at D'Anges, Rowan dragged herself upstairs, stripped to the skin as she staggered to her futon, and fell face-first onto the cushions. She was asleep as soon as she closed her eyes, and stayed that way until her stomach and her bladder combined forces to drive her out of bed.

Bathroom. Food. Bathroom first.

She trudged naked in that direction, then stopped and remembered the shared facilities. "God damn it." She pulled on a T-shirt and a pair of jeans before unlocking the door.

The landing was empty, no light showed under the edge of Meriden's door, and the bathroom door stood slightly open, so she figured she was alone.

She found out she was wrong as soon as she walked inside.

Sean Meriden, dressed only in a pair of jeans, stood over the sink. He used his razor to remove a strip of white foam from his mostly shaved face before he eyed her in the cabinet mirror. He smelled of soap and menthol and heat, and there were tiny beads of water scattered over the short gilded stubble covering his scalp and the smooth muscles of his back. The pale light from the small window illuminated them, making him look as if he'd been crystallized.

"Morning." Normally she would take a moment to admire all the bare, sparkling man in her face, but if she didn't soon pee her first task of the day would be mopping up a puddle. "You almost done?"

He didn't say a word. She waited, but he simply finished shaving and cleaned his razor under the tap.

"Okay." She did an about-face to head downstairs. The kitchen had a small half-bathroom for the line cooks to use; that would have to do. Maybe she'd grab something from the pantry; she was so hungry Meriden's massive biceps was starting to look tasty.

"It's five thirty."

She turned around, surprised and confused. "Huh?"

He dried off the bottom of his face with a hand towel, and then looked in the mirror and touched a small bloody spot on his jaw where he'd cut himself shaving. "You said you wanted the bathroom at two and between ten and eleven." He pressed an edge of the towel over the cut. "It's five thirty."

Well, at least he'd listened to her yesterday. And what the hell was she doing up so early? She hadn't finished work until well after Dansant had left at midnight. "Uh, right. I didn't look at the time. Sorry." Something occurred to her, and she swung back around. "You do mean it's five thirty in the morning, right?"

He shook his head slowly.

"Son of a bitch." She'd slept through the entire night and day, and she had only thirty minutes before her next shift began. "You're not planning to do anything like soak in the tub for the next hour, are you?"

He grinned, and it was a beautiful, evil thing to behold. "I might."

"Leave some room for me, then." She turned and dashed downstairs.

Once she'd eliminated the risk of puddle making, Rowan ran to the pantry and quickly scanned the shelves. She needed lots of calories she could eat fast, and appropriated several bars of dark sweet baking chocolate and a can of condensed milk. She paused long enough to open and empty the thickened milk into a glass with ice, and then rushed back upstairs.

Meriden wasn't in the bathroom, so she detoured to get her soap and a towel before running in to turn on the shower and strip. At the same time, she tore open one of the bars of chocolate and crammed half of it into her mouth, chewing in between gulps of the cooled milk.

In the shower she ate the rest of the chocolate bar from one hand while she used the other to soap herself from head to toe before she rinsed off. Just as she was wiping the water from her eyes and reached for the tap, she heard the door open.

Shit, she'd forgotten to lock it. "Almost done," she called out desperately.

Meriden cast a big shadow on the other side of the curtain. "How did you blow both tires on the bike?"

This was not the conversation she wanted to have while she was standing naked and dripping wet with a paper-thin piece of opaque plastic between them. "I don't know. Something hit me from behind."

"They're fucked."

So was she. "Okay."

"I ordered new." He made it sound as if he'd paid for them in blood.

"Thanks." Could she reach for her towel without flashing him? Probably not. "Let me get dressed and then we'll go over—"

"Don't bother." His voice sounded odd. "I'm outta here." And then he was.

Rowan peeked around the edge of the curtain to be sure, then stepped out and dried off with two swipes. Her damp body made it harder to get back into her clothes, but she was nothing if not determined.

Once she'd covered everything she didn't want him ogling, she stepped out onto the landing. Meriden wasn't there, so she knocked on his door and waited, rubbing the towel over her wet curls. He didn't answer.

"Snotty bastard." She stomped back into the bathroom, collected her stuff and went into her apartment. She had meant to go shopping today for supplies, but she'd blown that. She ate the rest of the chocolate she'd filched from the pantry to quiet her belly and chugged the last of the iced condensed milk, wishing for coffee but not daring to spare the time to make it. By the time her watch read 5:55 p.m., she had made herself presentable and went downstairs.

Lonzo was waiting for her. "You're late."

Maybe Dansant hadn't told him what her working hours were. "I start at six."

"If you're not fifteen minutes early," he told her with a stab of his finger at the wall clock, "you're late."

From the depth of his scowl Lonzo was clearly in a bad mood. "I'm sorry, Chef. It won't happen again." She glanced around. "Did you see Meriden—uh, the other tenant who lives upstairs—come down and leave?"

"What am I, your fucking doorman?" He made a rude gesture. "We got a truck waiting outside and five *meez* to restock. Get your ass out there and start unloading."

Rowan started for the back door.

"Trick." When she turned, Lonzo tossed an apron at her. "This is your uniform. I see you outta uniform again, you're cleaning squid for a week."

She'd probably be cleaning squid for a week anyway. "Understood, Chef."

The delivery truck's driver was only slightly less annoyed with her than Lonzo, but Rowan kept her mouth shut, her head down, and unloaded the boxes marked for D'Anges. By the time she stowed the last one inside, another truck rolled up. While she was unloading that one, the line cooks started arriving. No one offered to help, but Rowan knew better than to ask. Vince, the *rôtisseur*, stayed outside the back door to smoke a cigarette and watch.

Of all the line cooks, Vince was the one Rowan liked least. He was a few inches shorter than her and about a hundred pounds heavier, with wiry strawberry-blond hair and a pudgy face. Rosacea bloomed like heat rash on his chin and cheeks, and a network of broken capillaries around his nostrils attested to a serious drinking problem. He had light brown eyes nested in the puffy bags and deep wrinkles of a much older man. He'd visited the kitchen john several times the night before, and from the used-ashtray smell of his whites she guessed he'd gone in to sneak a smoke.

Vince had a wheezing, high-pitched voice like a washed-up boxer who had gotten punched in the nose and throat too many times, and when he spoke to her it was mainly in the direction of her tits. "You enjoying the new job, baby?"

"Love it." Rowan counted the boxes before she checked the driver's invoice and signed off on it. She bent to pick up a box, and straightened into a cloud of smoke. He'd shifted a little so he could blow it in her face, but she'd be damned if she'd let out a single cough. "Those things will kill you."

"That or the whiskey," he agreed. He squinted again at her chest, his lips pursed as if he were judging it for a boobs contest. "Danz gave you a place upstairs, I heard."

She started to carry the box inside, but he barred the door with one beefy arm. The box dragged at her arms, and if she ducked under she'd drop it. "Yeah. He did."

"You getting lonely up there, by yourself?" He showed her his crooked, nicotine-yellowed teeth. "Maybe you want a little company later?"

Telling him she was a lesbian would probably just turn him on. "I got company, thanks."

"Oh, yeah? Who? Not Danz," he said, answering himself. "He don't exactly go for the ladies, know what I mean?"

"Guy across the hall does." She leaned into his envelope of smoke. "About six-six, two-fifty, works on bikes and cars. You know him?"

Vince cleared his throat. "The Irishman. Sure, I seen that guy." He tried to curl his lip. "Not really your type, baby."

"Yeah, well, you shouldn't listen to your girlfriends." She let her gaze drift down and then back up. "Size *does* matter."

He dropped his arm, and she carried the box in. Lonzo

was standing just inside, but now he wasn't glowering. He was looking at her as if she'd just grown another head.

Here we go, Rowan thought, kissing her job good-bye.

"Vince," he yelled, not looking away from her face. "Drop that butt and start getting them boxes in here."

All Vince said in return was a remarkably meek "Yes, Chef."

Meriden stopped at the first pay phone he found and called the number Gerald King had given him to use to make his daily report.

"I went to the coffee shop where Alana was spotted," he told the old man as soon as he answered. "The girl who served her thought she might be in trouble. From her general description of your daughter it sounds as if she's living on the street."

"That girl is not my daughter," King told him. "She is remembering the wrong person. Go back and question her again."

"The girl she served matches Alana's physical description—"

"So does every blond, blue-eyed girl in the city," the old man snapped. "Alana is not living on the street. Nor would she go out or wander around the streets during the day."

"Why? Is she a werewolf?"

King produced a dry, hacking laugh. "No, Mr. Meriden, she is most certainly not. Didn't you read the file I provided for you? Wherever she is, Alana will need constant access to food. Check the grocery stores, the delis, the hot dog stands, and anywhere one can buy food cheaply and quickly."

He frowned. "You didn't tell me your daughter has an eating disorder."

"She doesn't. Alana has an unusual metabolism combined with a digestive problem," King said. "She has to eat many times a day or she begins rapidly losing weight."

This might be the lead he needed. "Is she on any medication for it?"

"No. Her condition is untreatable." King covered a cough before he added, "Is there anything else?"

"I need to interview the man who called in the sighting," Meriden told him. "He may have noticed more than he told you."

"The transcripts from his interview are also in the file," King said. "He told me everything he remembered."

"I'd rather interview him again and be sure."

The old man sighed. "Alas, that is no longer possible. Mr. Sengali is deceased."

"You killed him?" Meriden's skin crawled. "Are you crazy? He was the only person who's seen your daughter in a year."

"Mr. Sengali neglected to tell me that he had a weak heart. After questioning, he had a heart attack and died of natural causes." King's tone hardened. "That needn't concern you, Mr. Meriden. You have a young, strong heart, and three weeks to ensure that it will keep beating long after our business is concluded." He hung up.

Meriden slammed the receiver down, cracking the plastic earpiece in the process. "You stupid shit son of a bitch."

The last rays of the sun filtered through the maze of Manhattan's skyscrapers and glittered on the icy waters of the Hudson. He should have gone back to his apartment, but Meriden drove instead to a new building, and swiped a plastic security card at the gate to the underground garage. He parked his car in the empty space marked PH-1 and used a key to enter the elevator.

The condominium had been built to provide accommodations for the city's up-and-coming power brokers, and was as high-tech and sterile as their offices in the financial district. As the lift whisked him up to the top floor, he clenched his keys in his fist, not feeling the sharp edges cutting into his palm.

King was being too open and unguarded; he'd already given him enough information to destroy the old man's life. At first Meriden thought it was because King was dying, but now he wasn't so sure. Whatever happened to King in three weeks, whether Meriden found Alana or not, the old man now couldn't afford to let him live.

Dansant owned the top two floors of the building, but only used the apartment with the best view of the Upper West Side. Meriden used another key to let himself in. Dansant knew Meriden had duped all of his keys and cards without asking, but he had never altered his codes or changed the locks. As he walked into the spacious front room, he felt a surge of envy and hatred that hadn't diminished since the first time he'd seen the place.

Rather than compartmentalize the three-thousand-square-foot apartment into separate rooms, Dansant's army of interior designers had knocked down most of the walls and replaced them with floor-to-ceiling panels of clear and translucent glass. The effect allowed anyone standing in any corner of the apartment to see most of the interior simply by turning their head. Enormous sheets of smooth, camel-colored limestone covered the floors, and the twelve-foot exterior walls were painted a matte cream that had been faintly textured to absorb light rather than reflect it. The effect was something like standing in a cloud.

Unconventional furnishings and fabrics graced each room, from the imported ivory silk carpets from China to the low-slung sofas and chairs designed to flow like ribbons fluttering in the wind. The only colors used were muted earth and sky tones, which faded away into the cloudlike walls as if they were in the process of disappearing into them.

Meriden despised clutter, and he might have warmed to the place himself if not for the dozens of portraits hung on the walls, each one a slam of color to the eye.

He had no idea who the people were that Dansant painted, but they pissed him off every time he looked at one of their faces. The oil paintings, which showed both men and women standing surrounded by mists or shadows, were dark and composed of thousands of short, broad strokes, more like sketches than paintings. Framed in precious woods and polished steel, each one was illuminated by an incandescent spotlight in the ceiling, which emphasized the rich jewellike colors and compelling movements of the brushstrokes.

The men were handsome and the women gorgeous, but there was something wrong with all of them.

Despite the heavy hand Dansant used with his paint, he managed to draw out disturbing details from each portrait: lethal chrome eyes, a twisted angelic smile, a slash of scar. One of the youngest subjects in the paintings, a tall, dark-haired kid with glowing purple eyes, looked at times like a feminine boy and at others a boyish girl. Another portrait showed a man whose hair and skin were covered with green shadows that echoed the eerie color of his emerald eyes.

The one he really hated most was the one he'd christened the Bitch Madonna, a portrait of a woman dressed in white, the only one of his subjects that Dansant had painted in profile. She stood half-turned toward something, the shape of another figure cloaked in the shadows around her, but instead of looking at her mystery companion she eyed Meriden like he was a swatch of slime under a microscope. Her nose was too beaky and her eyes too sharp for her to be called pretty, but the colors the Frenchman had used for her made her shimmer with life, from the red lights spiraling through her long chestnut curls to the golden warmth of her skin.

She radiated light like high noon on a summer day, but something about her made him think of thunderstorms at midnight.

D'Anges's executive chef rarely spent more than a few hours in the place, and didn't stock anything for himself in the brushed-steel fridge or glass-fronted cabinets. Meriden never knew when he was going to end up here, so he kept a stock of his own supplies. He took out a cold beer before he pulled back the silver drapes and stepped out onto the teak floor of the narrow balcony that wrapped around the entire floor. From the west side he could watch the sky, which he often did, counting the minutes until the night crept over the city.

Meriden lifted his beer in the direction of King's mansion. *Cheers, you evil motherfucker.*

The Frenchman would be late to the restaurant tonight, Meriden thought with some satisfaction, so by the time he got there that long, cool woman he'd hired would be too busy working to flirt with him. He guessed Rowan Dietrich was already half in love with Dansant; there wasn't a woman alive who could resist him. Let Dansant have her, too. Meriden wasn't interested in a skinny kid with eyes like permanent bruises and a subconscious death wish.

All right, he admitted to himself, she was something to see, all long legs and racing curves. Meriden usually preferred his ladies blond and built, with bodies he could really sink into and play with, but the slinky little black cat had the kind of speed and grace that aroused something else in him.

If a man had an itch, she'd definitely scratch.

When she'd run downstairs, he'd wanted to follow, to chase her down. He scowled at his own thoughts, not sure why he'd felt that. She thought she was tough, you could see it in the set of her shoulders and the curl of her hands. The way she had of tilting her head to bring up her chin and look down her nose when she was pissed, should have annoyed him. Instead, it tickled the shit out of him. So did her sense of humor, so sharp it came equipped with teeth and claws.

He shouldn't have walked back into the bathroom earlier; he'd known from the sound of the shower she was in there washing up. And if he was going to be honest, that was exactly why he'd gone back in. She'd never know how close he'd come to yanking back the curtain and joining her. He'd have been happy to scrub her back, her front, and any other parts that needed some close, personal attention.

He couldn't remember the last time he'd gotten laid; maybe that was why he'd gotten a hard-on that still hadn't subsided. There were half a dozen women he could call for something easy and quick, and still he didn't want a damn one of them.

Talking to Rowan had been a mistake. He could have found out what her deal was through Dansant. Now he was screwed. He wasn't living ten feet away from her without touching her. Not now that he knew what she smelled like when she stripped down to her skin.

Sure, break into her apartment tonight and wake her up by fucking her brains out. Of course she'll come to thinking that you're her dream prince.

Meriden felt the last glimmer of sunlight touch his face before he drank the rest of his beer and went back inside. He looked at all the silent fixtures, the understated elegance and clean lines, knowing that—like Rowan—it would never be his. He threw the bottle across the room, watching it smash against the frame around the Bitch Madonna.

The last dregs of his beer ran down the portrait's face like amber tears. Another of Dansant's victims, no doubt, not that Meriden would ever know for sure. The Frenchman kept his secrets. Still, after all these years together, he had a pretty good idea of how it would go.

Dansant hadn't hired Rowan or given her the apartment out of the goodness of his heart. He wanted her, and he intended to keep her where he could have her and make regular use of her. When he got bored, he'd employ his mojo, wipe her memory and send her on her way.

He went into the bedroom to stand beside the bed. "You can have any woman in Manhattan," he muttered as the light from outside disappeared. "Any woman in the fucking world. Just leave this one alone. She didn't ask for this shit. She didn't ask for you. You hear me?"

No one answered.

Chapter 8

Not for the first time in his new life, Dansant woke to the smell of beer and rage.

He knew the cause of it. Meriden had sometimes indulged his penchant for breaking and entering as well as ale and anger in years past, although since coming to America he had calmed down considerably and had worked hard to make their arrangements comfortable. Dansant never fooled himself into believing Sean was happy, but he had assumed the younger man had made his peace with their situation.

What has gone wrong now?

He tracked the scent from his bedroom through the empty apartment to one of his paintings, beneath which lay scattered broken brown glass. A chip in the frame and the splatter of beer across the canvas testified to what had happened.

He knelt and collected the glass in his hand, disposing of it in the kitchen before he went back to carefully clean the surface of the portrait. The narrow, clever face of the chestnut-haired woman seemed to soften with sympathy.

Would you feel sorry for me, chérie? he wondered as he blotted dry her features. *Or would you side yourself with him?*

He despised the circumstances that had brought him and Meriden together, and forced their dependence on each other, but when it came to a resolution, he was as helpless to change it as his partner was. Perhaps more so, for he had done nothing by design to harm Sean or intrude on his life, and had in fact been dragged into this uncomfortable partnership with no choice at all. Yet he had never blamed Nathan for what he had done, not when he had come to understand the reasons behind it. Without the terrible choice Nathan had made, Dansant would be nothing but a collection of tubes and samples in a laboratory; where what remained of his body would have been used to change others into becoming something like what he had been.

But without Dansant's intervention, Sean Meriden might never have had a life, either. Then Nathan's heroic act would have resulted in nothing more than a nameless corpse rotting in a potter's grave.

A pity Sean never remembered that.

Dansant didn't know why Meriden had come to the apartment, but the hour was late, and he had to move quickly to prepare for the night's work. He showered and dressed before he called down for a taxi.

Downstairs the doorman, a silent but watchful ex-Marine who had lost an arm in Afghanistan, greeted him with a smile. "Evening, Mr. Dansant. Your cab's waiting."

"*Merci*, Jason." As he put on his coat, he glanced outside. "No new snowfalls?"

"No, sir. Should stay clear and cold until midnight, and then some snow flurries are coming in from the east." Jason opened the door and escorted him to the curb. "My fiancée went crazy when I told her you invited us to your next chef's table. We couldn't even get reservations at your restaurant until next summer or fall, I think."

Dansant's chef's table, a private, invitation-only free dinner he held once a week at D'Anges, had become legend among the city's fine dining patrons. Many food critics, famous gourmands, and several chefs from competing restaurants had tried repeatedly to angle for an invitation, only to be summarily turned down. None of them was aware that Dansant had very specific criteria for who joined him at his table.

"She's been shopping for a dress all week." The doorman sounded proud and embarrassed. "Any hints I should drop on what she should wear so she doesn't, ah, look out of place?"

"I am sure anything she chooses will be charming." Dansant had seen the young woman in question, who was a pretty redhead with milk-white skin, who often picked up Jason after work. "If she cannot decide, there is in her closet perhaps the little black dress, *oui*?"

"Oh, yeah, about twenty of them," Jason said drily. "With matching shoes."

"I will tell you a secret," Dansant said as Jason opened the taxi door for him. "All American women love the little black dress because it is the classic, and they all look good in it. And they know this."

The younger man frowned. "So why is she always asking me what she should wear?"

Dansant grinned. "Because, *mon ami*, she does not wear for her sake."

At the restaurant, he found his brigade at work prepping their equipment and stations for opening. Lonzo had posted the menu he had left with him last night, and the wait staff were already arriving. The only person he didn't see in the kitchen was Rowan, although he smelled her scent in several places.

"We got a beautiful shipment of mussels in," his *garde-manger* told him as he chopped garlic into impossibly thin slices before scooping them into a bowl of parsley and tarragon. "I thought we'd add *moules farcies gratinées* to the appetizers tonight."

Lonzo never altered the menu without speaking to him, but Dansant had learned to trust his choices. The herbed garlic would complement the freshness of the mussels. "*Très bien*. Where is Rowan?"

"She's in the storeroom, chopping figs for the duck breast." Lonzo glanced quickly at Vince, who was giving his roasting racks painstaking attention. "Thought that would keep her outta everyone's hair while we prep." He lowered his voice. "She's still getting her line legs. I figured she could use a break."

"*Merci*, Lonzo." Dansant went on to inspect the other stations and speak with his cooks about the menu. Only after he made his rounds of the brigade did he go back to the storeroom and step inside.

Lonzo had set up one of the rolling chopping blocks, beside which Rowan sat on a high stool. She had a sack of purple-red figs wedged between her thighs and she was chopping them lengthwise with slightly more force than the fruit required while she muttered under her breath.

He caught the words "ass" and "Boston." "Are you ready to leave me so soon?"

Rowan glanced at him. "That's not a question you want to ask me right now, Chef."

"I see." He thought of how oddly Lonzo and Vince had behaved. "Someone put a move on you." Then he saw the strip of rag wrapped around her left hand and seized her wrist, neatly avoiding the blade in her other hand as she jerked. "What is this?"

"Nothing. Just a little accident." She tried to pull her hand back, but he kept a firm hold and untied the makeshift bandage.

Several thin, dark pink burns ran diagonally across her palm. "Who did this?"

"I did."

She was a very good liar. "How, please?"

"It was an accident. I picked up the wrong roasting rack." She put down the knife, drew her hand away, and rewrapped the burn. "I'll be fine."

Dansant swung around, intent on finding his *rôtisseur* and introducing Vince's face to several other wrong racks.

"Oh, no." Rowan caught his arm. "You go out there and rumble with Vince, and the rest of the crew will serve me for dinner."

He gripped her wrist. "He did this deliberately."

"Of course he did. He's a nasty man with a big ego and a small dick. Unfortunately I brought this to his attention, and I paid for it." She shrugged. "Don't worry about it. Lonzo already balanced the books. He took care of it," she added when he frowned over the unfamiliar expression.

"Did he." Dansant knew his burly *garde-manger* ruled the kitchen like Napoleon had France, but he had seen Vince looking remarkably well with no burns on any visible part of his body. "Perhaps *I* do not consider them balanced yet."

"You will when you see Vince get started on cleaning the new delivery of squid." She folded her arms. "Something I'm planning on enjoying immensely, so please, don't fuck that up for me."

He didn't want to let it end there, but the satisfaction in her tone told him she considered the matter settled. "You are very forgiving."

"I'm a woman working with seven men," she countered. "This is a fraternity, not a sorority. I have to do this their way, or every one of them will shut me out and consider it their God-given duty to make my life hell for the next couple weeks."

A couple of weeks. She was already thinking of when she would leave him. "I will think of something else for you to do."

"I suck at waiting tables," she advised him. "The cleaning crew aren't going to share their turf. Enrique might let me scrape dishes and scrub pots for him, but he doesn't even let Lonzo near the washer."

She had a point. "You can work in the office."

"The phone rings—maybe—once every four hours. I've seen your files. The CIA isn't that color-coded or organized. Lonzo has to interview all the applicants for Bernard's job." She watched his eyes. "I'm not a wimp, Jean-Marc. I didn't break down and cry over a little burn, and I didn't say a word to anyone. If Lonzo hadn't been watching me so close no one would have even known what happened. The guys will remember stuff like that."

"I didn't bring you here for you to be hurt," he muttered.

"You didn't bring me here," she said softly. "I crashed the party, remember?"

He put his hand to her cheek. She looked thinner under the harsh fluorescent lights, and there were shadowed crescents under her eyes. "You wouldn't tell me what you were thinking last night." He drew her closer, bringing her under his influence as easily as he had unwrapped her hand. "Tell me now."

"I was thinking about you."

"You were." She made a low affirmative sound in reply. "Is it too much for you? Working in the kitchen?"

"No. I'm learning a lot." She yawned a little. "Just tired. Too much sleep. Didn't get my coffee. I love watching you work."

He felt a little better, and bent his head until only a breath separated their mouths. "Are you afraid of me?"

"No."

He knew better than to ask while she was like this, but he couldn't resist. "What were you thinking about me last night?"

"I was thinking I wanted to kiss you." Her expression turned to confusion. "But I can't do that."

If only she knew how much she affected him, how delicious the heat of her body was against his, the way her scent intoxicated him. In the state he was in, he feared at any moment he would go down on his knees and beg her to have him. "Why not?"

"Because . . . you don't want me to." She exhaled the words.

He couldn't stop himself then, not with the taste of her breath in his mouth. He kissed first her top lip and then the bottom before coaxing them apart with the tip of his tongue. She must have tasted one of the figs earlier; a faint sweetness of it lingered in her mouth. No, it wasn't fruit, it was . . . chocolate? He sucked on the tip of her tongue, and she did the same to his. The show of desire loosened something inside him. He slid his hands under her arms and lifted her up onto the chopping block.

Rowan made a low sound in her throat as he stepped between her thighs and wrapped an arm around her hips. He couldn't get enough of her mouth, and he would have had a lot more of her if the storeroom door had been locked.

"Chef?" he heard Lonzo call.

Dansant wrenched his mouth from Rowan's to answer, "Just a moment." *Mon Dieu.* His hands were shaking; he could hardly speak. "Rowan. You will forget we did this— you will forget everything that has troubled you."

"Forget." Her pupils, dilated almost to the rims of her irises, contracted slightly. "Yes."

"Good." He closed his eyes and held her head against his for a moment. "Are you afraid of Vince?"

"That scumbag?" She made a contemptuous sound. "No."

He held her close for another moment. "You will come to me if you are afraid, or if you need anything. Only to me. Do you understand me?"

"I understand."

He hated to release her, but he couldn't keep her like this, not when Lonzo or one of the others could walk in at any moment. "You will come back to yourself now."

She stepped back and blinked several times. "Whoa. Déjà vu." She looked up at him. "I didn't faint again, did I?"

"No. You were a little dizzy. You will take the rest of the night off." She shook her head. "Rowan." She appeared unmoved. "Tomorrow, then."

"I work five nights on, and have one night off," she said. "Just like the rest of the crew."

Her resistance puzzled him. A moment ago she would have stripped naked and lay at his feet if he had asked it of her. Now she was behaving as if he had. "I want to do something for you. To make up for what Vince did."

"You've already done plenty." She drew his hand away from her face and sat back on the stool. "But if you want to give me a little bonus, I'd love to watch you make the reduction with these figs for the duck."

Dansant knew the power of his influence. He could compel others with it, and alter their memories, but he could not plant desires in their minds. She would not have asked for his kiss or responded to it if she had not wanted it. Now she spoke to him as if they were nothing more than pleasant but distant acquaintances.

I felt her need and her delight. She wants me as much as I hunger for her.

She was waiting for him to answer her. "Very well. Finish splitting those figs while I collect the wine and the herbs for the reduction."

Rowan nodded, but when she tried to sit down on the stool she stood again and groped at the back of her jeans. She produced a squashed fig and frowned at it. "Hmmm. How did that get back there?"

Even after the ugly incident with Vince and the weird moments in the storeroom with Dansant, Rowan decided her new job wasn't half bad. The second night was just as tough as the first, but her body quickly adjusted to the unfamiliar physical demands, and by the third night she got into the rhythm of the line, trotting back and forth between the stations and carrying out dozens of small tasks for the cooks.

Vince's cruel trick of asking her to pick up a red-hot roasting rack was not repeated, and her silence on the matter seemed to earn her a measure of respect from the other cooks. Lonzo never said anything about it, but after everyone watched Vince plow through a hundred pounds of squid at the gutting table, he didn't have to. In return, Rowan made sure the *garde-manger* never had to wait for anything he called for.

Gradually she began noticing each chef's work and how he went about it, and while she picked up a few new tricks, after a week she felt sure she could outcook most of the men on the line. She didn't mind her menial status, however, because for all the fetching and carrying she did, she spent at least an hour every night watching Dansant cook.

No one could best the executive chef at anything, she

decided. He used his knives like a surgeon, slicing and chopping and filleting with frightening speed and pinpoint accuracy. He also had a nose that could pick up anything from a bit of rotten basil leaf to a neglected tray of crème brûlée about to blacken under the broiler. Not even Lonzo, who had amazing hands and a psychic's intuition when it came to cooking times, could keep up.

New York's cutthroat fine dining scene had not changed a great deal from what Rowan had seen during her years of hanging around restaurants, but it did surprise her to discover just how successful D'Anges was. Not a single night went by that they didn't have a full house or did less than a hundred and fifty meals. She'd already peeked in at the dining room when it was at full capacity, and seen a lot of happy, relaxed faces around the tables. Although the interior looked exactly the same as that of any fine dining establishment, the atmosphere was as warm, intimate, and relaxing as Dansant's amazing cuisine was delicious.

It all seemed to her a little too good to be true.

She learned that patrons had to make reservations months in advance just to get in the door, and a place at the chef's table—Dansant's once-weekly event where he dined with a group of patrons in a private room—had become one of the most coveted spots in the city. Dansant made the rounds of the dining room every night, and sometimes Rowan saw how the women gushed all over him. It made her stomach turn a little.

She could admit she was a little jealous over how her entire gender seemed to sparkle around her boss. She could also feel sorry for them. If her secret love for Matthias had taught her anything, it was that wanting the unattainable is as stupid as expecting to have a chance at it, and where Dansant was concerned an unrequited, juvenile crush was all she could ever hope for.

Rowan worried that her interest might annoy her boss, but Dansant seemed happy to have her hovering at his side, and readily explained everything he was doing as he worked. He also insisted she taste practically every dish he prepared, and as she sipped and chewed and savored he tested her knowledge of the ingredients. That was how she learned that there were three types of snails used for *escargots*, and the American wine she knew as Chablis was an insult to its own name.

"The *escargots* we use for cooking are called *coureurs*, or runners, in spring," Dansant explained, "and *voilés*, or veiled ones, in summer."

"What do you call them in winter?" she asked with a straight face. "Popsicles?"

"*Operculées*, the covered ones. You see?" Dansant showed her a snail shell, and traced his finger around the membrane that sealed the open end. "This they do when they go to sleep during the cold months, and because of it they have more moisture than the snails we use in spring and summer. This makes them the best for all dishes."

Rowan was still trying to get used to the fact that D'Anges's chefs kept their supply of snails alive until they were ready to cook them. Although the current stock were hibernating away under a generous layer of grape leaves in a tank kept in the storeroom, it made her shudder to think of them crawling around the work stations while the chefs worked. She was also convinced that while she was not picky about food, and would never turn down a gourmet meal, she wasn't going to be able to make herself eat *escargots* no matter how moist they were or when they were cooked.

Dansant didn't seem insulted when she refused to taste his snail concoction, although he smiled as he tossed the morsel to a grateful Enrique. "You Americans are afraid to eat snail, but you will stand in line for hours to eat raw fish."

"Sushi doesn't crawl," Rowan told him. "It swims."

Dansant accompanied her down to his wine cellar when he needed her to retrieve a bottle of Chablis for a sauce he was reinventing. When she protested that she could find a bottle of wine on her own, he corrected her. "To you Americans Chablis is something you pick up at the convenience store. They sell it by the gallon for a few dollars, do they not?"

"They do," she admitted. "But I'm guessing the Chablis you use doesn't come in a screw-top jug."

"*Non.* It does not." He led her down the cellar stairs, turned on the overhead lights, and took her to a high rack filled with dusty bottles. "This is the Chablis we use." He selected one bottle and wiped it off carefully with a towel. "There are tasting glasses there." He nodded toward a row of small, upside-down goblets. "Take one."

"I don't really drink."

"You are not drinking. You are tasting." When she took down the glass, he continued. "French Chablis is made entirely from Chardonnay grapes. There is only one town in France that produces it, the town of Chablis in Burgundy."

He took a corkscrew from a nail on the rack and carefully uncorked the bottle, then poured a small amount into her glass.

"In the old times the vintners would ferment and age their Chablis in special barrels made of oak. Now most of them follow modern ways and use vats made of stainless steel." He urged the glass up to her nose. "Close your eyes. What do you smell?"

"Wine." She chuckled, and then sniffed. "Uh, grapes. Alcohol. And . . . vanilla."

"That is the influence of the oak barrels. At the modern vineyards they say the steel vats make for a purer wine, but I will not buy from them. By its nature Chablis is dry and very flinty, and it needs to age in the oak for balancing." He pressed the edge of the glass against her bottom lip. "Now taste."

Rowan took a sip, and instead of the sweet vanilla flavor she was expecting from the scent, the wine filled her mouth with a cool, sharp-edged taste that reminded her of biting into a green apple.

"Your American winemakers blend together weak wines that are barely a month old and call it Chablis," Dansant said. "The best French Chablis is not sold until it has aged at least twenty years."

She opened her eyes after she swallowed. "Oh, shit. Was I supposed to spit it back in the glass?"

He grinned like a boy. "I will not tell anyone if you will not."

Dansant was as demanding as he was charming. He would return any delivery that wasn't up to his standards, which were apparently much higher than those of other chefs around the city. As a result Lonzo often fielded irate phone calls from their vendors. He also expected the kitchen to be kept scrupulously clean, and once they had finished cleaning up after the last meal of the night, he personally checked the equipment and stations. If he found something not to his liking, he didn't call over Enrique to handle a second cleanup, but made the chef responsible for the area do it while Dansant stood and watched.

In return the line cooks gave Dansant the kind of deference and respect men usually reserved for successful professional athletes. More than once Rowan caught one of the cooks watching Dansant work before turning away and shaking their head as if in disbelief. Enrique especially worshipped the executive chef, and while the dishwasher mainly kept to his corner of the kitchen, he watched Dansant like a hawk. The chef never even had to call for a clean pot or utensil; the dishwasher always seemed to anticipate his needs and brought it over as soon as Dansant had his ingredients assembled.

Rowan had already resigned herself to silently lusting after her handsome, charming boss for the duration of her employment. It wasn't his fault he was born to make some other man very happy, although at times she wondered if his partner really appreciated how lucky he was. Whoever he was, Dansant's boyfriend never showed up once at the restaurant, not even to pick him up after work. Rowan knew the cost of keeping a car in the city was outrageous, and the cab Dansant called every night to take him home was probably much cheaper, but it didn't seem right that the guy never once bothered to stop in. None of the line cooks ever said a word about Dansant's domestic situation, much to Rowan's annoyance.

She did wish her boss could give her next-door neighbor a couple of private lessons on how to get along with people. Since she'd moved in she'd seen Meriden several times, usually in passing on the stairs. She always said hello, but he either ignored her or grunted something too low for her to hear. She figured he had a bad case of insomnia, as he usually arrived home an hour before her shift ended at one a.m. and left for work early in the morning before she woke up. Once she'd gotten up at dawn to use the bathroom and found him on the way out.

After her second week working at D'Anges, Rowan left a note for Meriden under his door, asking him to stop by and let her know about the status of her bike. When he didn't, she tried knocking on his door when she knew he was home, but he didn't answer. Other than staking out the bathroom, she wasn't sure what to do.

Rather than bother Dansant about Meriden, she asked Lonzo one night if he knew where Meriden worked.

"He's got a garage couple blocks from here. He the one working on your bike?" When she nodded, he waved her over to the office, where he flipped the Rolodex to M and jotted down an address on a sheet of notepaper. "Here's the address and phone. I'd pay him a visit, see how the work's going."

"Thanks." She folded the paper and slipped it into her pocket. "I think I will."

Chapter 9

Meriden's garage had no sign above the one open bay, and only a rust-edged metal door with a small meshed-glass window leading to what Rowan assumed was the office. Since she didn't hear any work sounds coming from the bay, she guessed he was in there, but decided to have a look around first. It wouldn't hurt to see what kind of setup he had, considering how she was trusting him to do right by her ride.

Inside, the garage was surprisingly spacious, framed by walls covered from floor to ceiling with Masonite pegboards hung with tools. The cement floor was painted the same shade of gray as the office door, and had the usual dark puddlelike shadows made by oil and fuel leaks, but it looked as if it was swept and mopped regularly.

The tools Meriden kept on his walls were grouped by type and arranged by size. Several workbenches, fashioned out of double sheets of half-inch plywood nailed to floor frames handmade of precisely cut two-by-fours, held screw and small part bins. On one she saw an a/c compressor that had been taken apart and was being reassembled. She smelled oil, grease, solvent, and the citrus tang of waterless hand cleaner.

Her bike sat parked between the bay's two lifts, between a garnet-red compact car missing a hubcap and a dark blue pickup in need of a new paint job.

"What do you want?" Meriden said, his baritone booming through the bay.

Rowan turned and nearly smacked her face into his chest. "Shit." She took a step back. "Ah, hi. I thought I'd drop in and see how it's going."

"It's going." Meriden wiped his dirty hands on an equally grimy red shop rag before sticking it in the back pocket of his jeans. He'd unbuttoned his work shirt, and grease spots splotched the front of the white wife beater he wore under it. "Don't you have some overpriced carrots to peel?"

"Today's my day off." Rowan went around him to her bike, and crouched down to check the tires, which he hadn't yet replaced. "Did you figure out what blew my tires?"

"Yeah. Stupidity." He retreated back into his office.

Rowan didn't run after him, but took a minute to inspect the work he'd already done and give herself time to cool down. That she wanted to knock him upside the head with an impact wrench didn't bother her; she'd bet money Meriden had the same effect on everyone. It was the set of his jaw when he'd looked at her, the glitter in his black-hearted eyes, the way his mouth had flattened. He didn't like her any more than she liked him, but obviously, there was something else going on under that thick skull. All that seething antagonism might have fooled someone else, but not Rowan. Meriden didn't know that she had the equivalent of a PhD in pissing off people.

She rose and went around the pickup to the inside door leading to the office. At first glance it appeared as tidy as the garage, so she focused on the man standing behind the desk. He was shuffling invoices between two stacks while drinking from a coffee mug that had seen better days. He didn't look at her, but Rowan saw the set of his shoulders shift and the muscles in his arms bunch.

No use dancing around it, not with Meriden. "Have you got some kind of problem with me?"

"I'm waiting on some parts." He took one pile of invoices and carelessly stuffed them into an accordion file. "Your bike will ready in a week or two. Bye."

"You didn't answer me." She went over to the desk. "What have I done to you that's got your boxers in such a knot?"

He finally eyed her. "You'll want to stay out of my pants, Cupcake."

"See, that's where you're screwing up." Rowan sat in the customer chair and folded her hands behind her head. "Always making it sexual. I haven't come on to you. Most I've done is play the good neighbor. How you doing, nice day, that's it. Not what you'd call a green light to test-drive my box of condoms, is it?"

He dropped the rest of the paperwork and came around the desk to stand over her. "You've got a mouth on you."

"Mouth, tits, ass. Brain." Rowan gazed up at him. "Just because they're female doesn't mean they work any less than yours." She cocked her head to one side. "Oh, wait. You do have a brain in there, right? Or is that space just packed with more brawn?"

He looked away from her. "You know where the door is."

"You know something? I didn't start this shit. You're the one who's been treating me like you wouldn't wipe your feet on my face." She was crazy for standing up and leaning into him, but if she backed down now he'd stomp right over her forever. "Well, here I am, Big Guy. You want to unload on me, be my guest. Just do it now and get it the fuck over with, because I am *done* tiptoeing around your hostile ass."

He regarded her for a long moment. "You tiptoe?"

"Like I've been dropped in the middle of a fucking minefield," she assured him. "Every time I have to pee, I feel like I should be calling SWAT for backup."

His mouth tightened, and for a minute she thought he was going to let her have it. Then a rumbling sound came from his chest, and she realized he was laughing—or trying to. And she was laughing right along with him, laughing until tears sprang in her eyes and she had to fall back down on the chair and clutch her aching sides.

"It's not funny," he told her, still chuckling.

"Oh, yeah? You should try listening through a door with your legs and eyes crossed." She covered her mouth to smother the last of the giggles, and then wiped her eyes with the heel of her hand. "God, I needed that."

"Yeah," he agreed softly. "So did I."

She glanced up. He looked less menacing without the usual scowl; his eyes almost looked warm and friendly. "So are we Sean and Rowan now, or back to Farm Boy and Cupcake?"

"Rowan." He tested her name as if it belonged to a foreign language. "I've got a lot on my plate. Sorry for taking it out on you."

"So buy me a beer sometime. *Sean*." She cuffed his arm in a friendly gesture. "And thanks for working on my bike. I know it wasn't your idea."

His expression changed, became more reserved. "You doing all right, working at the restaurant?"

"It's good. I'm learning a lot from Dansant." She didn't like the way he was looking at her now. "I probably should head back."

He leaned over, grabbing the armrests and trapping her between him and the chair. "You said it's your day off."

"I've got things to do."

"So?"

He straightened. "So come on." He grabbed his jacket and shrugged into it. "I'll buy you that beer."

Maybe we should have stayed Farm Boy and Cupcake. Rowan got up and followed him out.

The bar Meriden took her to was small, dark, and un-apologetically Irish. The smell of beer and whiskey blended with that of a couple decades of cheap frying oil and ex-haled cigarette smoke to give it a dank, sour ambience. Not one of the half-dozen men parked on the bar stools looked a day under fifty. The bartender, an impassive-looking thug with smudged blue anchors tattooed on his biceps, greeted Sean with a jerk of his chin.

"Let me guess," she said as she parked herself next to him at the end of the bar. "You're a regular."

"Don't insult my watering hole." He held up two fingers, and the bartender brought them two bottles of dark ale. "Thanks, Clancy." Sean exchanged a ten for them, and then lifted his bottle to her. "Happy days, Cupcake."

"Back at you." She took a swallow, nodded over the agreeably bitter, yeasty taste, and examined the label, which sported the name of an unfamiliar local brewer. "Nice. I was expecting Guinness."

"I'm not that fucking Irish." He checked the football game on the overhead television and then glanced at the pool table behind the bar.

"You up for a game?"

He regarded her. "You're not going to do that girl thing where you act like you've never played before and then proceed to wipe up the floor with my ass."

She smiled serenely. "I never do the girl thing."

He snorted and picked up his beer. "I bet."

Rowan waived her feminine right to break, and watched as Meriden nearly cleared the table in less than five minutes. Only a bump in the table's aged surface spoiled his fourth bank shot.

"You're good." She chalked the cue she selected and walked around the table, assessing the lousy shots he'd left her. "I think I'm in real trouble here. Care to make a friendly wager?"

He folded his arms. "I told you about the girl thing."

She laughed and set up for her first shot, and then went to work. Meriden was good, but she was better, and by the time she sank the eight he had dropped his arms and was watching her along with every other guy in the bar.

Clancy came out from behind the bar and joined Sean as they studied the pathetic remains of the game. "Look at it this way, lad," the bartender said, clapping him on the shoulder. "At least we own the world." Shaking his head, he retreated.

Rowan managed to keep her face straight as she parked the end of her cue on the floor. "Good game. Want to go for two out of three?"

"My rep's shredded enough, thanks." Sean took her cue and returned it to the rack. "Come on. Finish your beer, and I'll buy you a victory hot dog."

Meriden led her from the bar to a corner pushcart, where a talkative Chinese man with a beautiful Bronx accent built them two dogs on toasty home-baked rolls.

"Best thing for a cold day, huh? All beef, all the best," he assured Rowan. "You want onion, sauerkraut? No? Ah, your boyfriend not care, sweetheart."

"Let me check." She turned to Sean. "Boyfriend, you care?"

"Wait," he told the hot dog man, then bent over and kissed Rowan fast and hard on the mouth. "Okay, she can have them now."

The vendor grinned so wide his merry dark eyes became crescents. "You see? I always right."

Rowan licked her lips, which stung a little. "The things I do for a little sauerkraut."

They walked over to Central Park, found a bench and sat to watch the after-work joggers huffing along the running paths. Rowan devoured her hot dog in a few bites and washed it down with the Coke he'd bought her. "I guess you're not a fan of French cuisine."

"I'm too big to be picky." He sat back, bracketing the back of the bench with his long arms. "You work in a lot of kitchens before this?"

"I kept house for a couple of ladies, worked in a bakery. Took care of . . . an older guy." She frowned as she realized she hadn't thought of Matthias in days. "How'd you end up a mechanic?"

"I flunked the rocket scientist test."

"Yeah, that one sucked." She felt his hand against the back of her neck, not grabbing or stroking, just resting there. "You do a good business?"

"I do okay."

She shouldn't ask this, but she couldn't resist. "You seeing anyone?"

"I've been spending my quality time with your bike." He tugged at one of her curls. "You asking because you're interested, or because I kissed you?"

"Now *you're* doing the girl thing." She turned her head and caught him watching her. "What?"

He stroked his thumb across her cheek. "Right now, with the sun on your face, you look about fifteen."

"I'm over twenty-one." Probably. She'd never know for sure. "Want to card me?"

His mouth hitched. "I'm thirty-two."

That surprised her. "I figured you were late twenties, tops. What else are you hiding from me?"

"No wife, no girlfriend, no kids, no transmittable medical problems." He ran his thumb along the outside of her bottom lip. "I hit Clancy's maybe once or twice a month, and yeah, when I can afford it, I like French food just fine. But I'm more a pizza and beer guy."

"Want to be my baby daddy?" When he slid closer, she went still. "Uh, kidding."

He smiled a little, pressing his thumb down to part her lips. "We could get together sometime, Cupcake. Practice making one."

Rowan barely felt the cold now. "You're moving pretty fast. I think I'm getting friction burns on my face."

Whatever she said, it acted like a pail of icy water. Meriden jerked away from her, and abruptly got to his feet.

"Sean?"

"I have to get back to the shop." He turned and looked over her head. "You know where you are, how to get to your place from here?" When she nodded, he shoved his hands in his jacket pockets. "All right. See you around."

"What did I say?" Confused, Rowan watched him stride off. "What the hell did I say?"

"Good evening, Mr. Taske." The manager of the club stopped by his table for his customary fawning session. The faint flush on his cheeks betrayed his nerves. "It's very good to see you back."

What he meant was that he hadn't been able to charge anything to Taske's account at the club since August. Since Taske was their wealthiest member, this was a cause for alarm.

"I was out of town for a few weeks." In reality he had spent the last two months roaming the American Midwest, trying to locate more Takyn breeding centers, but he saw no reason to share that information. "Business."

The manager's head bobbed. "May I do anything to make your evening more enjoyable?"

"I thought it odd that I received no messages from the club while I was away," Taske said. "My lockbox is also empty."

One of the privileges of belonging to the outrageously expensive private club was having access to the private offices and receptionist services. It afforded Taske an extra measure of privacy, a way for his Takyn friends to contact him at once without compromising his identity, and a reasonably effective buffer between him and the men who would not hesitate to kill him, cut him to pieces, and sell him like spare parts out of a chop shop.

The manager seemed dismayed not to have an explanation for him. "I'm not aware that any messages came in for you, sir, but I'll check on that at once." He hurried off.

Taske's waiter, a well-educated Brit who had relocated to the States to make his fortune, arrived with his dinner.

"Onglet aux échalottes et aux frites," he said, his accent as perfect as the drape of the snowy napkin folded over the sleeve of his uniform jacket.

"Only you can make steak and french fries sound elegant, Morehouse," Taske said.

"We must endeavor to earn our four-star rating, sir," the waiter returned smoothly. He straightened, and then stepped back a discreet distance as a young woman in a black mink coat sauntered up to Taske's table.

"Samuel, I thought that was you." She brought her

face down to kiss the air beside his right cheek. "Where have you been? Harrison has been beside himself with worry."

Taske glanced past her to the Urnharts' table, where the Honorable Harrison Urnhart the Third was dozing over a half-finished bowl of soup. "So I see."

"You should have mentioned you were leaving the country." Mimi shifted slightly to block his view of her octogenarian spouse, and to allow the front of her mink to reveal a little more of her sequin-encrusted gown, and the generous amount of flesh trying to escape it. "We might have tagged along with you. So where did you go? Paris? Geneva?"

"Here and there." He tried to imagine her tramping alongside him through the backstreets of St. Paul and Detroit, or spending the night curled up on an air mattress in the back of his cargo van. At least the mink would have kept her warm. "Do give your husband my best wishes."

Mimi understood she was being dismissed, but she hadn't married the seventeenth richest man in the United States by being easily discouraged. "Why don't you join us? I know Harrison would love to hear all about your trip."

"Perhaps another time. Morehouse." The waiter appeared at his side. "Would you arrange a bottle of wine from the private stock for Mrs. Urnhart and her husband?"

"Of course, Mr. Taske." Morehouse regarded Mimi. "Madam, may I show you and your husband the reserve list?"

"Oh, very well." She pouted one last time before she led the waiter back to her table. When they arrived, her elderly husband woke with a start, listened to her and Morehouse for a moment, and then spoke sharply to Mimi. She flounced down in her chair and began sullenly stabbing her salad with her fork.

Several of the other men dining alone in the vicinity of Taske's table silently raised their glasses to him. In the club, that was the equivalent of a standing ovation.

Morehouse soon returned. "Mr. Urnhart sends his sincere appreciation for the wine and your patience, sir. May I refresh your orange juice?"

"No, thank you." Taske knew his food and beverage choices often bewildered waiters, who were accustomed to far more sophisticated orders from the champagne and caviar set. He also doubted any other club member wore leather gloves to eat, or brought their own drinking glasses and utensils. But Morehouse, who had served British gentry since leaving school, never blinked an eyelash, no matter how bizarre Taske's requests seemed. "An evening paper would be—" He stopped as the waiter gently set a brand-new copy of the *Times* at his elbow. "I see you've anticipated me again. I'm becoming dreadfully predictable, aren't I?"

"Not in the least, sir," Morehouse assured him. "I believe the last time you visited, you asked for *USA Today*."

Along with his exquisite manners, the waiter had a subtle sense of humor that was lost on most of the club's members. "Morehouse, you do know that eventually I'm going to try to lure you away from this place," Taske warned him.

The waiter cast a discreet eye around them before he replied. "You have but to say the word, Mr. Taske, and I will type up my notice immediately."

"Consider the word said." Samuel grinned at Morehouse's delighted expression and turned his attention to his meal. Mimi remained sulking at her husband's side, but halfway through his *onglet*, the manager reappeared. Now he was visibly perspiring, which was never a good sign.

"I do beg your pardon, Mr. Taske." The manager drew out a handkerchief, mopped his forehead, and tried to smile. "It seems several of your messages were accidentally placed in another club member's lockbox. The mistake was only just now discovered by myself and the administrative office manager—"

Taske no longer had the time or patience to listen to his babbling. "How many is several?"

"Fourteen, sir." He drew a long envelope out of his jacket and placed it on the table as if it were leaking nitro. "On behalf of the management and the entire staff, I deeply apologize for the delay in delivering them to you. I will personally assure that this never, ever happens—"

"Be quiet." Taske opened the envelope and quickly sorted through the slips inside. They were all from the same contact. "I'll need an office, a computer with Internet access, and a secured landline." He rose, using his cane as a brace. "Now."

As the manager led him across the club's dining room and through a maze of halls to the row of business offices, Taske checked the dates of the messages. Vulcan had been trying to contact him every day for the last two weeks. Then he noticed the fine notes at the bottom of three slips that indicated the number of repeated calls with the same message and the times. Over the last three days Vulcan had phoned to leave the same message every four hours.

The manager ushered him into a large office with an impressive-looking computer array and a neatly appointed desk. He hurried around to switch on the computer before dodging out of Taske's way.

"Is there anything else I can do, sir?"

He glanced up. "Go."

"Yes, sir." The man actually bowed a little. "Thank you, sir."

Taske removed his gloves—wearing leather while typing on a keyboard made him clumsy—and sat down. The computer appeared to be new, but from the minute traces of dust and matter lodged between the keys he knew it had been used. He focused, composing his thoughts before he placed his hands on the keyboard.

Colors, shapes, and motion flashed behind his eyes, trying to get past his mental barriers to form themselves into images. It had taken him years of meditation and self-discipline to learn how to block them from his thoughts, and even now it did not always work. But fortunately the keyboard had been recently manufactured, and had not had the time to acquire too many impressions. The older and more used an object was, the harder it was to keep its entire history out of his head.

Once the unrealized visions faded, he was free to use the keyboard without impairment. He brought up the Internet server and logged on to the account he maintained under the name of an ancient alchemist.

He hadn't thought to check his e-mail while he'd been away, and more than three hundred new messages appeared on the inbox screen. A third of them were from Vulcan, and to save time he opened the most recent.

Subject: Aphrodite Lost
Date: 10/30/09 4:34:40 P.M. Eastern Daylight Time
From: Vulcan@takyn.com
To: Paracelsus
Only three things matter to us. The goddess Aphrodite prays for lost loves and no other divine contact means anything. Since this is the 14th through 16th prayers we call on Saint David to bring White magic back a.s.a.p.
  Live Long and Prosper.
  Your lucky Lotto numbers are: 62 7 64 35 25 20.

The code was simple, and determined by the numerical sequence of words in the second and third sentences of the e-mail. Taske read it again, this time picking out every third word: *Aphrodite lost no contact since the 16th call David White a.s.a.p.* The Lotto numbers provided the telephone number, and from the area code, it appeared David White was currently somewhere in northern California.

The news was distressing to Taske. Aphrodite was one of his oldest friends among the Takyn; the first he had discovered through the Internet. Over the years she had helped him in innumerable ways, especially in finding disciplines to help him control and refine his ability. Like him, she wrestled with a powerful talent that had scarred her emotionally, and while she had never discussed it in detail, he knew enough to guess that she was one of the few Takyn who could shape-shift.

Vulcan would not have requested him to call unless the situation was urgent, so Taske didn't bother returning the e-mail. After putting on his gloves, he took a small device from his jacket and attached it between the desk phone's base and the line leading to the wall jack. After switching it on, he picked up the receiver and dialed the Lotto numbers.

A voice answered in the middle of the first ring. "White."

Although they had never spoken over the phone, Taske felt an immediate sense of recognition. They all shared a nameless connection that made them aware of one another in such strange ways. "It's Paracelsus. I just received your message. Has there been any word?"

"Nothing yet. Is your line secure?"

"Yes. Tell me everything."

Quickly the man he knew as Vulcan related the details of Aphrodite's disappearance. The last time she had e-mailed Taske, she had told him that she was relocating to Boston, and would be out of touch for a week. Now she had gone missing for two.

"Why was she in New York City?" he asked when Vulcan had finished.

"I don't know," Vulcan admitted. "Maybe she wanted to see her adoptive family. I know she was raised there."

Taske recalled one late-night IM session, during which Aphrodite had been unusually forthcoming about her youth. "She would never go back to them voluntarily; she'd live on the streets first. GenHance?"

"I've been trying to hack into their database, but I haven't found a way in yet. Our watchers in Atlanta say no new acquisitions have been delivered since we lost Savannah." He hesitated. "She left Matthias, and not on entirely good terms. She's nursing a broken heart."

He sighed. "Aren't we all."

"What I mean is, it's possible that she wanted to go off the grid, break all contact with us."

"Not Aphrodite," Taske said firmly. "Have you checked the hospitals?"

"I'm monitoring them daily." Vulcan sounded bleak. "No one matching her description has been admitted."

That decided matters for him. "I'll drive down to the city tonight. E-mail me the map with her last known position, a description of her motorcycle, and any photographs of her you may have."

Vulcan uttered a dry chuckle. "And here I thought I'd have to talk you into going." His voice grew serious. "Whatever has happened to her, we need to get her back."

Taske looked at his gloved hand. "My friend, I won't stop searching for her until we do."

Chapter 10

Nella Hoff waited until Elliot Kirchner was engrossed in the view from his microscope before she let herself out of the secured analysis lab. Since she'd embarrassed him in front of Jonah Genaro, she'd been expecting some kind of chauvinistic backlash, probably in the form of making her into his personal gofer, but the chief geneticist's attitude toward her remained seemingly unchanged. That disappointed her, because if he had been angry she might have used that to push him into a sexual encounter. Men loved to fuck women they despised; it was their favorite way of settling accounts and exerting dominance.

Nella understood because she felt the same way about men. Nothing turned her on more than cutting some self-important prick down to size between her thighs.

Since Kirchner wasn't providing her with any new opportunities to get what she wanted, it was time for her to switch to her backup plan. After she visited the restroom to prepare, she took the elevator down to the security section.

"Good afternoon, Dr. Hoff," the receptionist greeted her. "How may I help you?"

"I need to speak with Mr. Delaporte, if he can spare a few moments," Nella said, glancing at the closed door of his office. "It's in regard to some security measures in the lab."

"Just a moment." The receptionist picked up her phone,

pressed an intercom button, and repeated what Nella had told her. Then she said, "Yes, sir. Thank you." She hung up and smiled as she collected her purse out of her desk drawer. "Go right in, Dr. Hoff."

Nella watched the receptionist leave, and then went to Delaporte's door. She took a moment to fluff her hair before she went in.

"Dr. Hoff." The chief of security stood up behind his desk. He indicated the chair across from him. "Please, have a seat."

Nella smiled her thanks as she sat in the chair, allowing her skirt to ride up over her knees as she positioned herself. She pretended not to notice in order to give Delaporte an excellent view of her legs up to mid-thigh, where her stockings ended and her garter belt straps began.

Don Delaporte was one of Jonah Genaro's most devoted sycophants, and normally Nella would never have trifled with him. He was overweight, mug-faced, and had the personality of a cardboard box. But on her first day at GenHance, when Kirchner had introduced her to him, she noticed a minor shift in his body language. The cues were subtle—slight tension in the shoulders, the droop of his eyelids, the not-too-firm grip he used for their handshake—but they told her he was attracted to her. Later, after some discreet chats with other female employees, she learned that the security chief had a thing for petite women—the smaller, the better.

"His last girlfriend was this little Asian girl," one of the secretaries from accounting told Nella over lunch. "We thought she was his stepdaughter or something until Dave over in distribution found out she was divorced and had a kid and everything. Do you know what she called him, even in front of other people?" She snickered. "Big Daddy Don."

A background check revealed more about Don Delaporte's predilection for tiny women. The security chief had spent a considerable amount of time of his younger days in the military, and after being discharged had graduated to mercenary work. While his military and civil records were spotless, some of his former colleagues had attested to his fondness for spending his off-duty hours with the very young prostitutes. When he had served in Thailand for a year, he had even installed a teenage whore in his household, telling the other men that she cooked and cleaned for him.

It seemed "Big Daddy Don" Delaporte liked women whose bodies reminded him of the good old days, when he could buy a night with a tweenie for twenty bucks.

It sickened Nella to think that the only reason the security chief was drawn to her was because of her girlish build, but it had given her an advantage with him that she might otherwise not have. Now that she had gotten nowhere with Kirchner, she would have to use it.

"I told your assistant a little white lie," Nella said, ducking her chin and twisting her fingers together in a nervous fashion. "I'm not here about the security of the lab. I need to report something I saw." She deftly altered the pitch of her voice so that it sounded younger, more uncertain. "Something I don't think I was supposed to see."

Delaporte flipped open a notebook and picked up his pen. "Go ahead."

"Do you have to write this down?" She grimaced. "I'm sorry. I'm very conflicted about this. You see, I've had some disagreements with the way Dr. Kirchner runs the analysis section. Reporting this, well, it might seem like sour grapes on my part."

"The chairman expects us to do the right thing for the project and the company," Delaporte told her in a distinctly paternal tone. "If you've seen something that in any way violates the rules or poses a threat to our security, you have to report it, Nella."

Now she was Nella instead of Dr. Hoff. Appealing to him like some adolescent twit was working.

"All right." She exhaled slowly, tremulously. "The other night I stayed late to monitor the simulations that were running. I could have checked them in the morning, of course, but with the project at such a crucial stage in development I feel I need to monitor everything closely. I don't want anything to go wrong."

He nodded his approval. "Go on."

"I wasn't aware of it at the time, but Dr. Kirchner was also working late in another part of the lab. I went to get a soda from the lounge and saw him come out of the specimen storage unit." She bit her lower lip and then released it slowly. "He had a mobile phone in his hand. He was talking into it to someone."

Delaporte's eyes narrowed. He knew about the new rule against bringing any mobile phones into the building; he had written the memo about it himself. "Do you know who he was speaking to?"

She shook her head. "As soon as I saw what he was doing, I stepped behind a cabinet. I don't know why, exactly. I think I was afraid. I've never been very good at confrontations." She produced a weak chuckle. "I couldn't make out much of what he was saying, but he mentioned the transerum and the dominant female Kyndred Mr. Genaro is searching for." She waited until he finished writing his notes and looked up at her. "I did hear one thing clearly. He said they would be arriving within twelve hours. Mr. Delaporte, he must have been talking about the team that was sent to New York to retrieve that girl."

Delaporte watched her until he realized he was staring, and then returned to his note taking. "Have you seen Dr. Kirchner use this unauthorized mobile phone since that night?"

"No," she conceded in a small, ashamed tone. "But if he were using it to pass sensitive information to a party outside the company, wouldn't he have it with him, or keep it someplace safe, like in his office? In the event something important came up and he had to make contact quickly?"

She'd pushed the girlishness a little too hard; Delaporte's gaze turned harder, less sympathetic. "I wouldn't know, Dr. Hoff. The only way to check would be to search him and his office. I couldn't do that without Mr. Genaro's approval. I doubt he would give it based solely on a verbal report from a single witness."

He would need more of an incentive to do something on his own, Nella thought, resigned to what would have to come next. She got up from her chair to walk over to the row of eight monitors showing ever-changing views of the interior of the building. "Can you check the security videos for that night? Maybe one of them shows him using the phone."

Delaporte joined her, and stood just a little too close for professional courtesy. "We don't use cameras in certain portions of the lab. There aren't any by the specimen storage unit."

Nella turned to him, making sure the front of her body brushed his before she put one hand on his chest. "I'm so worried about the project, Mr. Delaporte." She lowered her chin and continued in a strained whisper. "It's been so difficult for me. You don't know how cruel and vicious Dr. Kirchner has been. The things he says to me when we're alone." She thought of what would happen to her if she failed to get rid of Elliot, and lifted her face so that Delaporte would see the very real fear in her watery eyes. "I feel so powerless, and scared. I don't know what to do."

His arms came up to support her as she collapsed against him. After several wet sobs into his shoulder, she lifted her face to press her cheek against his, and breathed through her mouth so he would feel it against his ear.

"Nella." Delaporte's hands shifted, pressing her close instead of simply holding her. The front of his trousers were tented over his erection. "It's all right. You don't have to deal with this alone anymore."

"I knew I could depend on you." She turned her head to give him a kiss on his cheek, and then gasped as he turned his so that their mouths met. *"Mr. Delaporte."*

"Don." He pulled back and looked into her eyes. "Don't worry, baby. I'll take care of you." Then he kissed her again.

She deliberately stiffened before relaxing against him and opening to the wet, hard push of his tongue.

Nella faked the moans, the trembling, and the limpness as he moved her over to the couch. She had to keep her eyes closed to endure the groping and sucking that followed, and fantasized about her last lover to stay wet enough to be convincing. But when Delaporte mounted her she discovered the stout, homely looking man sported a beautiful cock the size of a small club, and what he did while he kept her pinned down and impaled on it was better than the efforts of her last five lovers.

"You're so big," she gasped out, not having to fake the tremors of shock she felt every time he thrust. When he finally seated himself to the hairy root, she cried out. "Oh, no. No, please, I can't take it, I can't." She thrashed her head from side to side, whimpering as she pushed at his chest. "Please it's too big, please stop."

Her whining and pleading only spurred him on, as she suspected it would, and he began to grunt with satisfaction as he plowed into her. He was like a screwing machine, she thought, and perspired like a pig, but for some reason his endless, unimaginative pistoning of her and the smack of his sweat-slick body were getting her hot. Then with a genuine squeal of astonishment she had a gushing orgasm, and when she finished he pulled out and ejaculated into a handkerchief he had produced like a magician.

Nella would never admit it, but she wasn't entirely faking the tears she burst into a moment later.

Delaporte tucked in his shirt, zipped up his trousers, and disposed of the handkerchief before he came to kneel beside her. His big, hot hand on her exposed breast made Nella curl over toward him.

"I'm sorry if I hurt you," he said quietly. "But you knew what you were doing."

Nella shook her head, still trying to play the innocent. Her heart wasn't in it, however, and she fought a terrible urge to tell him the truth about her and Kirchner and everything she'd done. *Suicide*, she thought. *I might as well stick a gun in my mouth and pull the trigger.*

"Nella, look at me." He waited until she did. "You're going to leave early today. Go home, and get some rest."

"I can't leave." She sat up, pulling her blouse over her breasts. He'd left suck marks all over them, and seeing the dark pink love bites made her sex clench. She looked up at him. "What did you do to me?"

"I took good care of you, baby." He brushed her hair back from her face. "Just like I will when I come to your place tonight."

Nella pressed her lips together. Having sex with him in the office was a necessary task, but if he came to her apartment, he'd expect to stay. The prospect of being subjected to his battering ram of a penis for an entire night scared the hell out of her. It also thrilled her down to her heels.

I can work on him, she thought, not caring that she was lying to herself. *By tomorrow he'll do whatever I want.* "Do you really want to come over tonight?"

"Of course I do. You need me." He tipped her chin up so that she looked into his eyes before he gave her a firm kiss. "Now be a good girl and go home."

Nella straightened her clothes and after glancing one more time at Delaporte, slowly walked out. She went up to the lab to retrieve her purse before checking out.

On the ride back to her apartment, Nella used the mobile phone in her car to make a call. "I'll be out of touch until the morning," she told her employer. When he asked why, she answered honestly. "I have some personal business to attend to."

Being unceremoniously dumped in Central Park by Meriden left Rowan sitting with her jaw in her lap for all of five minutes. Whatever she'd said to chase him off, it had worked superbly. She could spend the rest of her day sulking over it—and on some level, probably would—or she could run her errands and enjoy what was left of her day off.

At her request, Dansant had paid her wages weekly in cash, but refused to take more than a quarter of what she'd earned as repayment for what he'd given Bernard. He also overpaid her, and when she'd tried to argue with him, had told her what he paid the others—more than twice the going wages for line cooks.

"Why aren't you bankrupt?" she demanded, aghast at the staggering sum he laid out for his employees.

"D'Anges does a good business," was all he would tell her.

Later that night she asked Lonzo about just how well the restaurant did every week.

"On average we do nine hundred, maybe a thousand," he said, referring to the number of meals served. "Customers tip well, too, so the waiters always clean up."

She did some rapid calculations in her head. "Holy Hannah. Nine hundred, every week? You sure?"

He glowered at her. "You think I can't count how many dinners I plate every night?"

"No, I just . . ." She shook her head. "That's unbelievable. This place isn't even that big. I mean, you'd have to sit every table every single night straight through from opening to close."

He puffed up a little. "In case you haven't noticed, kid, we do. That and we got the group room filled three, four times a week." His gaze turned speculative. "You're thinking how with the lousy economy, right? Maybe some other places are hurting, but it's never made a difference to us. People keep coming because they know at D'Anges they'll have the best meal they'll eat all year. That's why you won't see any prices on the menu, Trick. We don't need 'em. They don't give a shit what we charge 'em."

She glanced toward the back stairs. If Dansant was pulling in millions every year from the restaurant—which by her calculations he had to be, even after paying all of his employees and covering the cost of food—he probably didn't care that she was occupying an apartment he could have rented out.

"It wasn't like this in the beginning, though," she said to

Lonzo. "It couldn't have been. He would have had to make a name for the place."

"I was the first chef he hired," Lonzo told her. "We had a full house opening night, and since then there hasn't been an empty table in the place."

"It doesn't make sense."

"That's the other reason I keep going to church," the *garde-manger* said. "So I can thank God I didn't take that other job I was offered at the chophouse over on Columbus. They closed a year after we opened."

She decided to go to the public library, where she could use a free-access computer to do some research on her mysterious boss. There was something else she needed to do; she couldn't remember what it was but she was sure once she was online it would come to her.

On her way to the library Rowan passed a few shops she remembered from the old days: a secondhand clothes store where she'd traded a couple of shirts for a warm jacket, an old-fashioned candy store that still sold penny candy (the only kind she could afford back then), and a florist that specialized in exotic orchids. She was happy to see that all three were still in business, and even browsed around at the consignment shop for a while. She didn't precisely need the Mets baseball cap she bought, but it was only a couple of bucks and she was tired of wearing a bandanna at work.

She'd didn't think Stallworth's would still be in business, but when she came to the block where the old bookshop had been, the old black sign still hung from a bracket above the narrow door. With a grin she stepped inside.

The shop had originally served as a small printing press before the Civil War. While the original Mr. Stallworth had gone off to fight the Rebs, his wife and young son had kept the business going by buying and selling books. Losing a leg at Gettysburg had finally sent Stallworth back to civilian life, but by then the business had been doing so well he decided to abandon his racks of type and ink for the pleasures of the book trade.

Together with his son he renovated the shop, installing rows of cedar bookcases and building shelved tables to better display their growing collections. Mrs. Stallworth had already scandalized other neighborhood merchants by having some comfortable armchairs and settees brought from her home to the shop, but she convinced her husband that offering their patrons a place to sit and read would entice them to buy, as would the afternoon tea and cakes she offered for a modest price.

Over the decades the handmade tables had been replaced with modern display stands, and the antique furnishings had been traded for more durable seating arrangements, but many of the old books remained where they had been shelved, waiting patiently to be taken home by their next owner.

"I don't carry magazines," a cranky voice said from the back. "Or cigarettes, gum, or beverages. You can get them at the CVS around the corner."

"How about Patricia Briggs?" Rowan called back. "I could use a little magic in my life."

A wrinkled face framed by a helmet of salt-and-pepper spikes popped into view. "I know you." The old man wandered out, his arms filled with a stack of leather-bound Dickens volumes. He looked her up and down a few times. "Rosie. Rolanda. Roberta. No, that isn't it." He frowned, muttering to himself before triumph lit up his face. "Rowan."

"That's me." She grinned. "Your shop is still the coolest place in the city, Mr. Stallworth."

"If only more shared your opinion, my dear." He set down the books and came to give her a hug. "It's lovely to see you again." He stepped back with a new frown. "What are you doing in New York? I thought you'd gone off for good."

"I changed my mind. How's the book biz?"

"At the moment, it's all about the young vampires." He sighed. "One is either Team Edward or Team Jacob, it seems. But I live in hope that chick lit will enjoy a revival."

Rowan chatted with him for a few minutes, and admired wallet photos of his newest grandchildren. He was happy to learn that she was working at D'Anges, but not surprised.

"I still remember those ginger cookies you would bring for me from the bakery," he said. "You were so proud of them, and rightfully so. You ruined me for every other cookie on the market, young woman." His expression turned serious. "A few weeks after you left for the god-forsaken wilds of the South, some men came around the neighborhood. They were asking questions about a run-away girl. They said they were detectives but I did not get the impression they were working for the NYPD. And before you ask, no, I didn't tell them about you."

Rowan felt her stomach twist at this confirmation of her worst fears. "I appreciate that, Mr. Stallworth." She glanced at one of the display tables, featuring stacks of books for young adults with vampiric-sounding titles. "I am interested in finding some books about vampires, but not the Twilight knockoff stuff. I'd like to see whatever you have that's nonfiction. Older books."

"Stephen King old, or Bram Stoker old?"

"Stoker."

He waved for her to follow him into the back of the shop. Once there, he went to a locked, glass-fronted case and pulled out his keys.

"I had to install this after I caught a girl attempting to shoplift some of the newer volumes. I'm sure she intended to resell them across town; the poor child looked half-starved." He unlocked the case, opened the doors, and began pointing out shelves. "Early twentieth century, late nineteenth, early nineteenth, and so on. The oldest volume I have dates back to 1820, but I think it's utter rubbish so you can have that one half-price."

Rowan took in some of the titles. "Wow."

"One must strike while the trend is hot." He smiled and patted her shoulder. "I have some shelving to do, but call if you need me."

From the work she had done researching and compiling books for Matthias, Rowan had a good working knowledge of the subject matter. Most of the twentieth-century books were useless; they'd been inspired by Hollywood's conception of the vampire. But the older books were more interesting, and ranged from scholarly studies of historic vampirism to histories of blood-rite cultures. She selected several to flip through and began setting aside the ones that looked the most promising.

It was the circa 1820 book of "rubbish" that intrigued her more than any of the others, however. The author had been chronicling the Romantic period in English poetry, and had obtained several letters that had been exchanged by some of the big names of the era. Among them he noticed a series of unusual metaphors and oblique references to a gifted young poet who had died of consumption before his talent had been fully realized, and opinions on later reports that his grave had been robbed.

We have ascertained through the authorities in Rome that remains were found in the grave, one poet wrote, *but some of our friends were present at the exhumation, and they insist that the body was too fresh to belong to our friend. If he has indeed enjoyed the dark resurrection, would not the body in the grave be that of his first victim?*

Rowan suppressed a shudder, added the book to the stack she had assembled, and carried them to the front of the shop. Stallworth joined her there and after casting a jaundiced eye at her selection rang up her purchases.

"I never imagined you would develop a fascination for the dark kyn," he said as he bagged the books. "It's a lot of superstitious nonsense, you know."

"But interesting nonsense." She handed over the cash. "Have you read much about them?"

"As much as I ever care to. The idea that plague victims in the Dark Ages rose from mass graves as vampires has been around as long as the legends of monsters in Loch Ness and animal attacks that result in one growing fur under the full moon." He reached under the counter for a book and added it to the stack. "An advance reading copy of the new Patricia Briggs. No charge," he added as she pulled out more money. "I'd have never pegged you for a lover of shape-shifter fiction."

"She's the only one who gets it right," she murmured. She looked up quickly. "I mean, I love the way she writes it."

"Well, if you come 'round again, I'll introduce you to her new series about those of the moonstruck and fur persuasion." He reached across the counter to take her hand. "Do take care, my dear."

"I will. Thanks, Mr. Stallworth." She felt an unwelcome but all-too-familiar sensation that had nothing to do with fur or the moon. With an effort she controlled the sudden urge to change. "Say hi to your wife for me."

As she left the bookshop, Rowan felt an odd sensation, and looked over her shoulder. She didn't see any familiar faces among the people walking around the shops, but that combined with the passage she'd read from the old book and what Stallworth had told her gave her the creeps. She gave up on the plan to visit the library and began walking back to the restaurant.

The man she hadn't seen waited until she disappeared from view, and then walked up to the bookshop door and let himself in.

PART THREE

Trouvaille

September 29, 2008
Tanglewood Middle School
Biology Class
Mrs. Withers—Period Four

Total Makeover: How Recombinant DNA by Nonbacterial Introduction Might Make Us All Supermodels Someday

A Science Fair Project Proposal by Tiffany Angela Ephram

My biology project for the school science fair this year is about recombinant DNA, and how someday doctors might be able to use it so that anyone who wants to improve their looks can, even if they want a total body makeover so that they can become as beautiful as a supermodel.

Recombinant DNA is already made in three ways. They are Phage Introduction, Bacterial, and Non-Bacterial Transformation. The bacterial and phage processes require alteration of the original DNA with things like restriction enzymes and antibiotic markers. New DNA is introduced which is designed to repair the existing, altered DNA while resequencing it. I would research one of these methods, but after having strep throat four times this year my parents don't want me deliberately exposing myself to germs. For that reason I'm making my project about Non-Bacterial Introduction.

To make this type of rDNA (recombinant DNA) no germs are necessary. A doctor can give you a microinjection that adds new DNA to your preexisting DNA and the new genes take over and replace the sequences in your DNA that are not wanted anymore. Some scientists also invented a new process of introducing the new DNA with biolistics, or tiny particles of gold or tungsten that are coated with the new DNA, which is shot into the patient's body like a thousand tiny bullets. They call that high-velocity microprojectile bombardment, but it doesn't hurt the patient and delivers the new DNA in the same way the microinjection method does.

None of these methods work very well unless some other things happen at the same time. Once the rDNA is inside the patient, the preexisting DNA has to receive some signals from the body to convince it to accept the new genes. The signals are sent by expression vectors, and they have to understand and accept the new DNA before they'll send the signals for the body to do the same. Some scientists believe the body has to have a strong reason before it will accept the rDNA, such as a terminal disease or a lethal injury.

rDNA is becoming important to the human race because of its many valuable uses. For example, scientists are using it to grow crops that are more weather-resistant, and to manufacture medicines to help patients who have serious diseases like diabetes and hemophilia. A company called GenHance has been working on creating rDNA that will stop babies from being born with serious defects and life-threatening conditions. On the GenHance Web site they have an entire section about how rDNA should not be used for frivolous or unnecessary changes to human DNA, such as altering our outward appearance, but I think how people feel about themselves can be just as important as good health.

I've had to wear braces for two years now, and they're very uncomfortable. I can hardly eat anything I like. If I could use rDNA to change the genes that gave me crooked teeth, and replace them with genes for straight teeth, I wouldn't have to wear them until the middle of high school. I think it would also be much cheaper for my parents to pay for a single shot of rDNA instead of two years of visits to the orthodontist every nine weeks.

The reason I decided to use supermodels as part of my project is because almost every plain girl I know dreams about being beautiful. There are also some girls like my best friend Gemma who want to work as supermodels when they grow up. Gemma isn't very tall, and she has a large birthmark on her face. She's going to ask her mom if she can have laser surgery as a graduation present, but wouldn't it be better for her if a single injection could make her taller and take away her birthmark? If science can make our lives better, then why shouldn't Gemma have a chance to improve her appearance so she can follow her dream?

I plan to use a Photoshop program to demonstrate how rDNA might transform people's appearance for the better. I also plan to research the different types of particles that can be used to deliver the rDNA to the body and will show samples of the metals in my display.

I believe that rDNA can be used safely, not just to make sick people better, but to help people save time and money while trying to improve their appearance, and feel better about themselves. I'm really excited about this project, so I hope you will approve my proposal and let me show the world that GenHance is wrong.

Chapter 11

Taire woke from the nightmare of the dark room with a shriek, and as soon as she realized where she was she pressed a hand over her mouth to smother the sounds until they stopped. She lay still and listened until the silence reassured her that no one was outside the closet. No one had heard; no one knew she was here.

A few months ago she would have spent the next hour crying into her pillow, but she had neither the tears nor the time to wallow in her misery. The sun was setting—she could always feel it, even in here—and she had to get up and get moving.

One of the hardest things for her to do was one of the simplest tasks in life, one she'd never thought about before she'd left home: bathing. The hotel had no running water, and there was no place in the city that did that would allow a runaway to make use of their facilities. Using the sinks in one of the few public restrooms to wash more than her hands was too embarrassing; Taire had tried it once and some tourist woman had actually tried to take a picture of her. A few of the kids she'd met on the streets sometimes used public fountains for a quick soak in their clothes during the summer nights—occasionally getting themselves arrested in the process—but Taire couldn't risk it. After a month of being unable to wash herself properly, she'd started to bring her own water into the hotel, one bottle at a time.

Everyone drank bottled water these days, so it had been easy to scrounge enough bottles out of trash cans around the city. Every night she filled three of them at a public water fountain, tucked them in the pockets of her jacket, and carried them back to her place, where she stored them in a room on the first floor. Once she had collected twenty-one filled bottles, she had enough to bathe.

Taire uncapped the bottles and lined them up beside the tub in the first-floor room where she took her baths. After she cranked her flashlight and turned it on, she set it on the sink with the beam aimed at the tub. As she stripped off her clothes, the frigid air made her shiver, and the cold water in the bottles didn't help. She'd learned to keep them covered with a mound of towels to prevent them from freezing solid, but it didn't warm the water any.

She stepped into the tub and took the first bottle, pouring it slowly over her head while working her fingers through her hair. The water was so cold it made her gasp, but after the second bottle it wasn't as much of a shock to her skin. It took another two bottles to get her body wet, and then she went to work with a mini bottle of shampoo and a thin bar of soap she'd scrounged from one of the housekeeping carts. When she was completely soaped down, she began the laborious process of rinsing off, one bottle of water at a time.

The first time she'd tried it she hadn't brought enough water, and had been forced to walk around for another day with sticky hair before she'd collected enough bottles to rinse it clean. Now she had it down to a science, and by the time she used the last of her water she was soap and shampoo free.

She wrapped a hotel towel around her wet head and used another to dry off and rub some warmth back into her shivering limbs. Once dry, she changed into her cleanest set of clothes—doing her version of laundry required so much water that she only washed her clothes when she couldn't stand the smell of them anymore—and rubbed her hair briskly until it was a damp tangle.

The other drawback to bathing was that she had to wait

for an hour or so until her hair air-dried before she went outside. The temperatures in November rarely rose above freezing, and while she never got sick, going out with wet hair caused her to lose too much body heat, and her fingers and toes would go numb. Once she had wiped out the tub with the damp towels she'd used, and hid her empty water bottles on the top shelf of the room's closet, she carried the wet towels back to her room, where she folded and hung them on the bathroom rack to dry.

Taire liked to read, but searching the hotel rooms had only turned up a single book some guest had left behind. Since she couldn't afford to buy more she had to read that or the Gideon Bible in the nightstand. She settled into her closet, fished the book out of her clothes bag, cranked her flashlight for a few minutes, switched it on, and began to read chapter one.

There was no possibility of taking a walk that day. We had been wandering, indeed, in the leafless shrubbery an hour in the morning; but since dinner (Mrs. Reed, when there was no company, dined early) the cold winter wind had brought with it clouds so sombre, and a rain so penetrating, that further outdoor exercise was now out of the question.

I was glad of it: I never liked long walks, especially on chilly afternoons: dreadful to me was the coming home in the raw twilight, with nipped fingers and toes, and a heart saddened by the chidings of Bessie, the nurse, and humbled by the consciousness of my physical inferiority to Eliza, John, and Georgiana Reed.

Taire had mixed feelings about the book. It was depressing, filled with bad things that happened for no good reason, and the characters often made no sense. She also didn't think even back in those days that a ten-year-old girl talked that way. But she knew how the orphaned Jane felt, first being dumped on relatives who hadn't wanted her, and then being shipped off to that horrible school, where she was abused and the only friend she made ended up dying.

At least Jane had Helen Burns. Taire didn't have anyone. *And there are worse things than being plain.*

Father knew about Taire's physical inferiority, of course, but he had believed she could overcome her flaws. She'd always gone along with whatever he had wanted changed because she knew he was trying to make her a better person. It hadn't been easy; every year there had been another operation, sometimes two or three, and he would never come to see her until the bruising had disappeared. Then he would visit her in the golden room, and he would watch her and smile, nodding every time she did something right. He would be in such a good mood that he would pretend not to notice any of her mistakes.

You're doing well, child, was what he'd usually say. Once in a great while he would point out something specific and tell her *That's almost exactly as it should be.* Those were the best times with Father, when she had pleased him enough for him to mention it. Then she would have four or five or even as much as six months of freedom from the dark room.

It was the freedom that always spoiled things for her; Taire could see that now. She would get used to being able to move around the house, and have her meals downstairs, and go to the library whenever she wanted something to read. The servants would smile at her and do little things for her, like giving her a snack in the kitchen or letting her play with the grand piano in the music room. When Father was pleased, everyone was happy.

That was when Taire would forget, and do something that was not allowed, and even if no one had seen her do it, somehow Father always knew.

Her nanny would take her to him, and he would make her confess to whatever wrong she had done. Taire would cry as she admitted to the wrong, and beg him to forgive her, but Father would only nod to the nanny, who would lead her back to the dark room. It was small and dark and empty except for a toilet in the corner and a sleeping bag on the floor. It also had no windows, and when Taire was locked in she felt as if she had gone blind, and screamed and cried for hours. Only when she stopped making noise would someone push a tray of food and a cup of water through the slot in the door three times a day. Unless she pushed the tray and cup back through the slot, the servants wouldn't bring her anything else to eat or drink.

No one came to see her when she was staying in the dark room. Once a week they put something in her food that made her go to sleep, and when she woke she would be dizzy but clean and wearing new clothes.

Taire sometimes tried to count the meals to see how long Father kept her in the dark room, but she always lost count after two weeks. Every time he sent her there, it felt like forever.

Father never spoke of the time she spent there, and the servants pretended like the dark room didn't exist. When Taire was sent there, it was like *she* didn't exist. Sometimes, after she had been locked in for a while, she wondered if they would ever forget about her. Every food tray was a relief, something that brought her one meal closer to freedom.

Then came the wonderful day when the door would be unlocked, and her nanny would take her to the golden room, where she would give her a long bath, and wash her hair, and dress her in her prettiest clothes. It took some time for Taire's eyes to adjust to the light, and she was often stiff and sore from sleeping on the hard floor of the dark room. But the bath helped, and once her eyes adjusted to the light, she felt very peaceful.

Before her nanny took her down to the dining room, she would always tell her the same thing: *Show your father you can be good this time.* And Taire would be very good, for days and weeks and months, even when the doctors came, before freedom made her forget again and she had to stay in the dark room again.

Taire understood why she needed to be punished—Father wanted her to have time to think and remember how much he did for her, so she would control herself—but the last time she did something wrong everything had changed. She still wasn't sure what her mistake was, because she had been out of the dark room for only a few weeks, and she had been thinking all the time about what she was doing and not losing control. Then Father had come to her, had walked right into the golden room where they were always happy together, but he had shouted at her. Taire had never before seen her father so angry. She had never once heard him raise his voice to her or anyone.

"You worthless, stupid girl. Get up." When Taire had scrambled to her feet, Father had grabbed the clothes her nanny had laid out for her and flung them at her. "What are you waiting for? Get dressed."

In her terror she had fumbled, unable to make the buttons go in the holes, but all Father had done was drag her from the room with her clothes hanging open. One of his men stood waiting in the hall, and Father had pushed Taire at him.

"Take her," Father said, his voice harsh. "I don't care what you do, just get rid of her."

Taire had cried out, fighting the man's grip on her arms as she pleaded to stay. "Father, what did I do? Father, please, don't send me away. I'll be good."

He had strode away without looking back, and the man had taken her down the back stairs.

"Don't you give me any shit, kid," he said when she'd tried to pull free in the garage. He'd dragged her over to one of Father's cars, the one the men used at night.

Taire didn't realize he meant to put her inside until he opened the door. "I can't go with you." She'd never left the house. She wasn't allowed to, not even on the window balconies. "Let me go."

"We're gonna take a little ride out to the woods," the man said. "You'll like it. It's real pretty out there. You might see some deer." Then he licked his lips and stared at her front. "So be nice."

As he tried to push her into the car, his jacket fell open and Taire saw the holster and gun he wore. He was one of Father's guards. The only people they took away never came back.

Taire didn't want to think about what she had done then. She hadn't meant to; she hadn't even been thinking about it. She'd been a good girl and controlled it because that was the biggest mistake, something Father told her she could never do again or she would have to leave him forever.

When it stopped—when she stopped—she looked down and saw the dirt and blood all over her clothes. The man lay across the garage his body all wrong, his face smashed flat. Father's car was ruined, too.

She'd done this. All of this.

Taire heard men shouting on the other side of the door leading into the house, and backed away into the door leading to the street outside. She'd pressed the button to make it go up, but it was bent in the middle and stopped halfway, and she'd had to crawl under it.

She didn't remember much after that. She'd run from Father's house, following the sidewalks and banging into people. They'd yelled at her, and one woman had hit Taire with her purse. She hadn't stopped until she reached the big park and found a place to hide in the bushes. She'd crawled into them and stayed there for a long, long time.

Taire had never tried to go back alone. She knew what she had done was a terrible thing, and if she tried to see Father by herself he would send her away, or maybe even put her in the dark room and forget about her. She had to make up for what she had done to the man and his car, and the only way she knew was to bring him what he wanted most in the world.

He didn't think she knew anything about the time before she had come to live with him, but she had found the hidden journal when she had been playing in the golden room. She'd read it, every page of it, and learned all about the secrets he had been keeping. She'd always sensed she wasn't the first one in his heart, but the journal told her exactly who was. All she had to do was give back to Father what he had lost.

His beloved one.

Taire held the book against her heart, hugging it like a

bandage over the pain throbbing inside. His beloved one was the key to everything, and bringing her back was the only way for Taire to go home. When she did, then Father would be happy again. He'd know how much Taire loved him, and he would let her stay, and they would be a family. No one else could do this for him except Taire, because even Father didn't know what his beloved one looked like now.

Only Taire did.

Rowan got back to the restaurant an hour before opening, and hauled her purchases upstairs to put them away. Along with the books she'd bought at Stallworth's, she'd picked up some boxes of cereal, milk, eggs, bananas, some multigrain bread and a huge jar of peanut butter with which to make sandwiches. She also found some nutritional protein bars she liked that didn't taste like ground-up vitamins; they'd come in handy when she took her mid-shift break.

I'd better not let Dansant see the peanut butter, or he might fire me.

She showered, changed, and sat down to watch the evening news for as long as she could stay awake, which was about five minutes' worth. Sometime after midnight she woke to an infomercial for a set of vegetable peelers and shut it off. Her stomach persuaded her to have a banana before she went to bed, and then it wanted a peanut butter sandwich. By the time Rowan had quieted the beast she was wide-awake.

This is what I get for working nights.

She started reading one of her new books, a study on the blood rituals of ancient South American cultures. The author, an anthropologist who had spent several years working at a number of archaeological sites, had photographed a series of unusual carvings at one ancient temple that seemed to indicate vampirism had been introduced to one society about the time the Europeans began arriving in the New World. Rowan tried to focus, but even the ghastly description of how high priests had once drunk blood from

still-beating hearts they had carved out of the chests of living victims couldn't hold her attention.

Finally she slammed the book shut and shoved it away.
Meriden had really done a number on her head, and pretending like he hadn't was stupid.

What did I say that pissed him off? Something about
how fast he was moving. Maybe he'd expected her to fall
all over him instead. She'd spent the better part of the day
with him and the man was still a complete question mark.

She heard footsteps climbing the stairs, and got up and
walked over to the door to listen. Keys jangled, a lock
turned, and the door across from hers opened and closed.

So he was home for the night. She opened her door to
glance downstairs, and saw that the kitchen was empty and
dark. Everyone had left, and it was just her and her un-
friendly neighbor.

He's probably tired, she thought as she looked at his
door. *He'll want to shower and go to bed, and I should let
him. Whatever happened in the park is his problem, not
mine.*

She was tiptoeing around him again, this time in her
head.

Rowan stepped out onto the landing, and as soon as
she closed her door Meriden's opened. He didn't come
out, but propped an arm against the frame and looked at
her. If he'd worn a sign around his neck, Rowan imagined
it would have read, ABANDON HOPE, ALL YE WHO
FUCK WITH ME.

"SWAT is on their way," she said casually, "but they'll
probably get hung up in the late traffic over in the theater
district."

He turned away from her and went back inside his
apartment. He didn't bother to close the door, however,
and Rowan considered that the equivalent of an invitation
to follow him.

Meriden's apartment was slightly larger than hers, but
her view was better. From the look of the interior, which
was half-Spartan, half-machine-shop-leftovers, he'd had

the Army Corps of Engineers in to decorate the place. But the surfaces were clean and uncluttered, and there was the same sort of defined order she'd noticed at his garage.

He watched her look. "Curiosity satisfied?"

"Totally." She was going to burn in hell for all the lies she told. "You just get off work?"

"Yeah." He opened the fridge, took out two beers, and handed her one. "Sit down."

Her choices were the couch, which looked too comfortable, and a loveseat, which she didn't want to try out at all. She pulled out one of the chairs of his dining set, which looked like he'd stolen it from a hunting lodge, turned it around, and straddled the red-and-black plaid cushion.

Meriden didn't sit. He leaned, this time with his back against the kitchen counter.

Rowan figured she had the time it would take her to drink the beer before he kicked her out, which might be enough. "Today, in the park, what did I say to piss you off?"

He shook his head, drank a little, and looked at a crack in the floor tile.

The hostility wasn't there, but neither was the ease. Rowan's intimate knowledge of the male psyche could fill maybe half a thimble, but Meriden was using the nonverbal tough guy act to cover something else.

Something, she suspected, that had nothing at all to do with her. "If you want me to come in, Sean, you have to open more than a beer."

He shifted his weight, and just when she thought he was going to tell her to get out, he came over and sat beside her at the table.

"I lost someone close in a fire once," he said bluntly. "Long time ago. It screwed me up for a while." He thumbed an edge of the label on his beer. "Still does."

The rawness of his voice told her not to ask who or how. "I just walked away from the only guy I've ever loved," she heard herself say, just as abruptly. "He didn't know, and then he found someone else." She paused to take a drink. "My best friend, as it happens."

Sean frowned. "She know you loved him?" When Rowan shook her head, he let out his breath. "Shit. You *don't* do the girl thing."

She let a little of her bitterness show through in her smile. "Not even when I should."

They sat together in a companionable silence, during which Rowan wondered why she felt so comfortable with him. Old wounds and mutual states of general hostility toward the world aside, she knew almost zero about him, and he about her. After what he'd said about his past, she had no desire to commence excavations. Dansant knew him; maybe she could wheedle a little more information out of him.

"You said you liked working with the Frenchman," Sean said out of the blue. "So what's he like?"

That was a loaded question. "I don't know. Okay, I guess. What did you think when you met him?"

"I've never had the pleasure."

She blinked. "But he works downstairs, practically every night. You have to walk through the kitchen to get to the stairs."

"He's always gone by the time I get home from work." He studied her face. "You like him."

"He gave me a job and an apartment for nothing," she reminded him. "What's not to like?"

"I don't know." He sounded annoyed. "He's French."

Like that was an STD. "So in addition to being a bad-tempered jackass, you're also a bigot?"

He didn't like that. "Just answer the question."

"What's he like? Well, he's French"—she glared at him—"tall, dark, gorgeous, talented, wealthy, and kind." She thought for a moment. "In fact, if he liked women, he'd be perfect."

Meriden actually choked on his beer. "What?"

"He's gay." She watched him as he shot to his feet. "Let

me guess. You don't like gay men, either. Tell me something, Meriden. Is there anyone you *do* like?"

"He's not a fairy."

"Don't use stupid fucking slurs," she snapped. "He told me he lives with a guy. He called him his partner—"

Meriden suddenly laughed, but it wasn't a pleasant sound. "Yeah, he does. But the partner is straight."

Now she was lost again. "You said that you've never met Dansant."

"I know the partner." He picked up his beer, walked to the window, and braced a forearm against the upper frame. "So now that you know he's straight, you can do him."

"I can *do* him?" It was her turn to laugh. "Sure. I'll jump him behind the meat cooler right after my next shift."

"Have a good time." He sounded bored.

Rowan's confusion evaporated. There was no reason for her to stay and listen to his garbage. He'd done her a favor, telling her that Dansant was straight. Maybe. She still couldn't see how he'd come to that conclusion, especially if Dansant and his partner were being discreet.

Figuring she'd give it one more shot, she put down her beer, rose, and walked to stand beside him at the window. Below them, the streets were almost empty, with only a couple of late-nighters walking in pairs.

"Dansant's okay. He's a decent man, a wizard in the kitchen, and I like him a lot. The tall, dark, and gorgeous stuff still stands." She hesitated, trying to put into words how she felt. "He helped me when he didn't have to. I don't just owe him for bailing me out of a tough spot. He's kind of restored my faith in other people, and showed me that there are some decent ones out here."

He turned his head. "Are you going to fuck him?"

How like a man, to reduce it all to sex. "Aside from that being none of your goddamn business whatsoever? No."

"Why not?"

Now he sounded angry, which threw her off again. "In case you forgot, I do work for the man. Sleeping with your

boss is about as smart as stealing from him. Dansant's also
way out of my league."

"I'm not."

He was jealous. Rowan almost laughed out loud. *Jealous
over her.* "Then maybe I'm out of yours, Sean."

She'd never uttered a better exit line in her life, and as
she walked across the landing to her apartment, it worked
wonders for her battered pride. But as she dropped into
bed, Rowan realized something she hadn't before: The two
men in her life she was most attracted to had suddenly
become attainable. And if she had to pick between them,
she'd be in real trouble.

For now it seemed she wanted Sean as much as she
wanted Dansant.

Gay. She thought the Frenchman was gay. Jesus fucking
Christ.

Meriden grabbed his jacket, stomped downstairs, and
unlocked Dansant's office. After two arguments with Rowan in one day he was in the mood to trash the place, but
settled for grabbing a Sharpie out of a drawer and leaving a
few choice thoughts on the French fuck's desk blotter. And
oops, did his elbow knock over a nice neat pile of invoices
so that they scattered all over the floor? Apparently it did.

He couldn't go back upstairs until he cooled down, not
when all that stood between him and Rowan was a bunch
of stupid misunderstandings and a flimsy door. She was a
smart-mouthed, demanding bitch. And she was the hottest
damn woman he'd ever wanted to nail on the nearest flat
surface.

He drove down to the river, and parked where he could
watch the tugs. There were five phone numbers flashing in
the back of his head; all of them belonging to women who
would welcome him at their door no matter what hour he
knocked. He could make one phone call and be naked between a soft pair of thighs in fifteen minutes. He didn't owe
Rowan Dietrich a goddamn thing.

Want to be my baby daddy?

Meriden swore and put the car in gear, squealing his tires as he reversed and took off. He drove the streets around the coffee shop for an hour, looking for solitary kids who fit Alana's description. But the night was cold, and the only people on the street were the ones who were paid to be there.

He spotted a waste management truck parked at a corner, and pulled up behind them. The two men dumping cans in the back eyed him but didn't stop working.

"Talk to you for a sec?" Meriden called out to the bigger of the pair as he approached.

"Free country," the man replied. He sounded casual, but he held on to the empty can he'd carried from the curb, and his left hand dove into his jacket pocket, where Meriden was sure he'd tucked a handgun or a shiv.

"I'm a P.I.," he told him, taking out his credentials and holding them out until the man got a good look at them. "Have you seen a girl about sixteen years old, short, thin, blond curly hair, blue eyes?"

"Can't say I have. Runaway kid?"

Meriden nodded.

"I'm sorry for her folks. I got a daughter that age," he added for clarification. "I'd tear apart the city with my hands if she were living out here."

Meriden shared a grim smile with him. "You notice anyplace in the neighborhood where kids like to flop regularly?"

The man shook his head and turned to his partner. "Hey, Frankie, you said you saw some kid crawling out a boarded-up place last week when you were working Cleaver's route. Where was that?"

"Ah, shit." The smaller man's face scrunched as he thought. "Maybe over on Fifty-seventh. Not my route," he explained to Meriden. "I was filling in for another guy."

He handed both men a business card. "If you spot her and get a chance, give me a call. Her father just wants her home safe."

The men agreed, and then finished with their load and moved down the block.

Meriden drove over to Fifty-seventh Street, but two slow passes didn't turn up any buildings with boarded-over entrances. It was a weak lead, but there were only so many buildings in Manhattan that were not being used; any that were empty were slated for renovation or demolition. It made his belly knot to think of a kid like Alana King sleeping in a building that might one day be torn down around her. But at least there was a chance she was sleeping indoors, and he wouldn't find her body in some alley, frozen stiff from falling asleep on an icy night.

He also wondered why she had run. He knew from her file that she had some mental problems, but being Gerald King's daughter meant she would have lived a very privileged life. King was a sick, twisted fuck, but from the way he talked about Alana, Meriden had no doubt that he loved her. Enough to kill for her.

So why had she run to the streets? What had happened to set her off? And why hadn't she gone back home?

Meriden headed over to his garage. He hadn't yet performed his own background check on Alana King, and maybe it was time that he did.

Chapter 12

Dansant noticed the change in Rowan almost at once. Before she had been impersonally friendly toward him, treating him no differently than any of the other men when they worked together. She shared her smiles and jokes with him, but she paid more attention to his cooking than his person.

After so many years of effortlessly drawing women to him like hummingbirds in a flower garden, he found her lack of interest disturbing. Even more puzzling was knowing that she was not indifferent to him. Under his influence, she had responded passionately, beautifully to his touch, and that made her indifference even more of a paradox.

Since coming back to work after her second day off, however, Rowan's behavior toward him had changed. Now he felt her watching him constantly, not to observe his cooking but to study him. Her easy, friendly manner had been replaced by a silent, edgy tension that seemed to hum in the air between them whenever she drew close. She had also begun to avoid even the slightest physical contact with him.

Dansant waited patiently for her to come to him with whatever was causing her discomfort, but after a week passed with no change in her demeanor he realized she had no intention of confiding in him. Perhaps it was the atmosphere of the kitchen, or the presence of the other men, but whatever the cause he decided he would have to be the one to broach the subject.

The only time they were alone was when he called her into his office to pay her for the week, so when she came in he asked her to close the door and sit down.

"What's up, boss?" she asked as she perched on the edge of the chair.

He had debated for days whether to bring her under his influence again to compel the truth from her, but after recalling the explosive moments they'd shared in the storeroom he had decided against it.

"Tomorrow is your night off," he said. "Have you made any plans?"

"I've got to do some shopping, but that's all." She frowned. "Do you need me to work?"

"No, that is not why I asked." He produced a pair of tickets a grateful patron had given him after he had hosted her thirtieth anniversary dinner. "I am going to the opera tomorrow night, and I need an escort. I was wondering if you would accompany me."

She stared at him. "You want *me* to go to the opera with you?"

He smiled. "I would very much enjoy that, yes."

"I'm, uh, flattered, but I can't." She rose to her feet. "Thanks for asking, though."

"You said you had no plans," he reminded her.

"That's right." She stuffed her wages in her pocket. "I don't have opera clothes, either."

"I see." He had forgotten about the limitations of her wardrobe. "If you had them, would you go with me?"

"I don't think so." She looked bewildered. "I'm not what you'd call the opera type, and why are you asking me? Shouldn't you take your, ah, current love interest?"

"I am sorry to say there is no one interested in my love at present." He tried to look humble. "If you do not go with me, I must give these tickets to someone else."

"I'm sure Lonzo and his wife would love to go the opera," Rowan assured him. "He's always singing that song from the Boeing opera."

"La Bohème."

"Yeah, that one." She started for the door, but stopped when he said her name and turned around. "We can't go on dates, Dansant. Me being an employee and all, it would get messy."

He got up and came around the desk. "Do you want me to fire you?"

That startled a laugh out of her. "No."

"It will not be messy." He took her hands in his. "It will be you and me at the opera, and you will enjoy it, I promise." Her fingers were so tense they felt like twigs. "Please, say you will come with me. I will see to the clothes you need—"

"Oh, no," Rowan said. "You can't buy me clothes to go to the opera, not on top of everything else."

He was tired of her refusing him, especially such a small thing as a gown and a pair of shoes, but to snap at her would only stiffen her resolve. "I can leave the price tags attached and return them the next day, if you like."

She grinned up at him. "You liar. You'd never do that."

"Lonzo's wife does," he told her. "She even has a trick to keep from getting antiperspirant marks on the inside of the sleeves."

She thought for a moment. "All right, here's the deal: I'll go with you, but I buy the opera outfit."

"It is customary to wear an evening gown," he warned her.

"Oh, I can do a gown, don't worry." She sighed. "Just don't change your mind between now and tomorrow night, or you *will* be paying for the opera clothes."

They agreed to meet at the front of the restaurant, and the next night Dansant arrived in a taxi to wait for her to appear. Normally he wore his tux to the opera, but in deference to her budget he instead opted to wear one of his more conservative suits.

"Your girl going to be much longer, Mr. Dansant?" the cabbie asked, eyeing in the rearview mirror the line of cars behind them waiting for the valet spot where he had parked.

"She should be out momentarily." Dansant watched the front doors, and just as he began to worry that Rowan would not appear, a woman in a black gown walked out.

The dress was a beautiful column of brushed velvet with wide, V-shaped panels of sheer lace placed strategically at her throat, shoulders, and waist. As she stepped across the walk, he saw she wore black velvet platform shoes with black silk flowers blooming above her toes. Her hands and arms were covered by elbow-length black satin gloves. A pillbox hat and half veil covered dark, sultry eyes, while a full red mouth smiled at him as she approached the cab.

It was Rowan, her curls brushed back and tucked behind her ears, making her look as if she'd just stepped out of a film from the forties.

"Hi," she said as she climbed in. "You haven't been waiting long, have you?"

Dansant breathed in her scent as he took her gloved hand in his. "Not at all. You look . . . incredible."

"It's rented," she whispered. "All of it. Even the shoes. Don't scuff me or I have to pay a damage fee."

He found her ingenuity charming. "Is it a costume?"

She nodded. "There's a place down by the Met that rents out theatrical clothes for parties and auditions and things. Everyone will think I've gone retro."

The taxi dropped them off at Lincoln Center, where Dansant offered Rowan his arm before they walked inside. He enjoyed the wide-eyed attention she gave everything, from the enormous, exquisite chandeliers to the extravagantly dressed men and women who had come to attend the performance.

"I forgot to ask you what opera we're seeing," she said a little breathlessly as he guided her through the crowd.

"Madame Butterfly," he said. "Are you familiar with it?"

"No." She glanced at the cover of her program. "It's Japanese?"

"The story is set in Japan," he said, "and the main character, Cio-Cio San, is a Japanese woman who falls in love with an American. The opera is performed in Italian."

"Why?"

"It's traditional," he explained. "Puccini, the composer who wrote it, was Italian."

"Okay." She squared her shoulders. "Bring on the butterflies."

Dansant suppressed a chuckle as he escorted her to their seats, and showed her the Met titles screen, where an English translation of the opera would be displayed in sync with the performance. The massive gold curtain covering the stage rose a few minutes later, and the first act began.

Having seen Puccini's heart-render more times than he could count, Dansant waited until the lights dimmed before he turned his attention to Rowan. She watched the performance with full absorption, glancing now and then at the Met titles screen for a translation before returning her attention to the stage. During the intermission she asked him a dozen questions, which he found as delightful as her reactions to his explanations.

"So Pinkerton just goes off and leaves Butterfly with the baby?" Rowan frowned. "How could he do that when he knew she was pregnant?"

"He doesn't know yet," Dansant said.

"I don't believe this." She folded her arms. "She's gorgeous, and in love with him, and she just gave up everything to be with him, and he leaves? Just like that? He's a moron."

Her anger amused him. "It is a tragedy, Rowan, not a romance novel."

"Great." She sighed. "I'm going to cry at the end, aren't I?"

He took her hand in his. "I will be here to comfort you."

She gave him a narrow, sideways look, but by then the lights were dimming and the performance continued.

Dansant sensed the change in her toward the very end of the opera, when the soprano playing Cio-Cio San made her fateful decision and took up her father's sword. Rowan's entire body went rigid as the soprano crossed the stage, carrying the sword toward her young son.

"Is she going to kill him?" she whispered furiously.

Dansant leaned close to make a joke, and then saw her eyes. "No, *ma mûre*. The boy survives."

As soon as the opera drew to its unhappy conclusion, Rowan pulled her hand from his and got up.

"I have to get out of here." She didn't wait for his reply, but darted into the aisle and hurried off toward the lobby.

Dansant followed, but with the rest of the audience rising to go soon lost sight of her. He made his way impatiently through the throng to the lobby, where he looked at every woman in black, but didn't see Rowan.

"Michael?"

Dansant turned to find his arms filled with a chestnut-haired, petite beauty dressed in a stunning sapphire gown. She had her arms around his neck and her smiling, lovely mouth an inch from his before she froze.

The soft scent of lavender filled his head, making him smile down at her wide, burnished brown eyes. "I regret to say that I am not your Michael, madam." He put his hands on her forearms and felt the softness of her thin, pale caramel skin. "But I think he is a fortunate man."

"Oh, my God." She blinked twice before she laughed. "I don't believe it." She looked all over his face. "You could be his twin brother." Her gaze went to his brow. "Except for the hair." As if realizing for the first time what she was doing, she eased away and stepped back. "I'm so sorry, I really thought . . . what's your name?"

"Jean-Marc. *Enchanté*." He glanced around her, impatient to find Rowan. "Have you seen a tall dark-haired woman in a black velvet and lace dress?"

"Skinny as a rail, cute little hat?" The woman pointed to one of the exit doors. "She went out through there pretty fast." As he nodded and made to go around her, she put a hand on his arm. "I'm sorry, I don't mean to keep you, but are you related to anyone in France? Maybe a family named Cyprien?"

"*Non*, madam. I have no family. I was *un enfant trouvé*." He kissed the back of her hand. "If you will excuse me now, I must find my friend." He strode toward the back entrance.

Dr. Alexandra Keller watched the man stride out of the Met with mixed emotions. She had the feeling she had just made a terrible mistake, and not by trying to kiss a complete stranger.

Whoever he was, Jean-Marc moved quickly, and disappeared from sight a moment later, almost as fast as a Darkyn would. But despite his eerie resemblance to her lover, he didn't move like Michael Cyprien, and now that she thought about it his eyes had been a much lighter blue.

Michael Cyprien came to stand beside her. "*Chérie.* Is something the matter?"

Automatically she reached for his hand as she shook her head. "That was very weird." She glanced at him and felt a little embarrassed now. "I just grabbed a strange man and tried to kiss him."

"Oh?" His voice chilled a few degrees. "For any particular reason?"

"I thought he was you." She turned to him. "Michael, he looked just like you. Same height, same features, same blue eyes . . . same everything."

"It is said that we all have a twin somewhere in the world." He encircled her with his arm. "Come. Phillipe is waiting for us."

On the drive back to their suite at the Hilton, Alexandra brooded in silence about the odd encounter at the Met. She was able to picture Jean-Marc's face clearly, and there was something about it that nagged at her. She was so lost in her thoughts that Michael had to repeat her name three times before she gave him her attention.

"Sorry, what?"

"I asked if you enjoyed the performance."

"It pissed me off," she admitted. "Pinkerton was a jerk. The acoustics were amazing. That fat chick in the fuchsia dress sitting in front of us smelled like bacon. I think she had some in her purse. Michael, are you sure you're the only Cyprien left?"

"The last member of my human family died childless in the eighteenth century." He stroked her cheek. "I am not upset that you tried to kiss another man. I would be only if you had succeeded."

"What if you or someone in your family had a kid you didn't know about?" she persisted. "That was pretty common back in the day, right?" She made a rolling gesture. "You meet a pretty milkmaid, have a tumble in the straw, you go your way, she pops out a blue-eyed kid nine months later, and everyone thinks it's her husband's or whatever."

"Alexandra, I was a warrior-priest," he reminded her. "We did not make a habit of tumbling milkmaids. We were too busy slaying Saracens."

"But not everyone in your family worked for God back then." She searched his face. "I don't know what it is, but I swear, that man is somehow related to you."

"Why? Because we have the same color hair, the same physique? As much as I wish to think that I am unique among men, *chérie,* I fear I am not. I would think that there are many humans in the world with whom I share a resemblance."

"You don't understand. The guy was just too perfect. Like a replica. He didn't just look like you. He *was* you." She sat up straight. "Oh, shit. Phillipe," she called out to Cyprien's seneschal. "Turn the car around and go back to Lincoln Center."

Phillipe glanced in the rearview mirror, and when Cyprien nodded moved into a turn lane.

"It is unlikely that he will still be there, *chérie,*" Michael told her.

"Maybe we'll get lucky." She gripped the edge of the seat as she looked out through the windshield at the traffic blocking their way. "Come on, come on."

It took some time, but eventually they arrived back at the Met. As soon as Phillipe parked at the curb, Alexandra jumped out of the car and hurried toward the arched windows at the front of the opera house. There were some stragglers still coming out from the performance, but none of them proved to be Jean-Marc or his lady in black.

Cyprien caught up with her just as she began cursing under her breath. "Alex, what is it?"

She pressed her fingers to her mouth as she scanned the faces around her one last time. "It was his face, Michael."

"Yes, as you indicated, we seem to share the same one—"

"No, you don't." She turned to him and looked at his face, the face she had reconstructed out of a horrific mass of ruined flesh and bone after Michael Cyprien had been beaten and tortured. "I gave you that face, and while it's very close to the one you were born with, it isn't the same."

"What are you saying?"

"Do you remember that painting that you had Phillipe bring to me in New Orleans? The portrait of you on the horse on the battlefield, all the dead bodies everywhere?" When he nodded, she said, "That guy Jean-Marc isn't your twin. He's a twin of the guy in the painting. He looks exactly as you did before the Brethren fucked up your face."

Michael shrugged. "So he was my twin before I was tortured. What difference does it make?"

"He had a little mole riding his jaw here." She touched the corresponding spot on the side of his face. "Exactly where it was in the painting. You don't have it anymore because when I was rebuilding your jaw I had to put a skin graft there."

"I see." Michael grew thoughtful. "An interesting coincidence."

"I don't believe in coincidences," she told him. "When you were captured in Rome, you said that the Brethren beat on you for days before Phillipe got to you." When he nodded, she asked, "Did they do anything else? Did they bring in a doctor? Did he operate on you?"

"No. They only interrogated me; they . . ."

He trailed off and rubbed his hand across his face. "There was a day when a new man came to my cell. I could barely see him but his scent was different. He asked questions like the others, but not about the Darkyn or where they could be found. He wanted to know about my talent."

"Did you tell him anything?"

"No, *chérie*. As with the other interrogators, I told him nothing." He encircled her waist with his arm. "It is growing cold. We should return to the hotel."

"You're sure the man didn't operate on you."

He thought for a moment. "I was conscious the entire time he was with me. He did not touch me once. He gave up rather sooner than the others had, although I thought he meant to have me taken to the interrogation room. He asked the guard where it was. But then he left and I never saw or smelled him again. Forgive me, but that is all I remember."

"It's okay. I don't mean to remind you of that shit." She made a face. "Let's go back to the hotel and I'll make up for it."

Alex said no more about the matter until an hour before dawn, when she and Michael were soaking together in the massive tub in their suite. She was wonderfully exhausted after an extended bout of lovemaking, and happy that she'd agreed to come on this trip with her lover. New York City's operas might suck, but the shopping was fabulous, and she had spent a considerable amount of time acquiring better equipment for her lab. Although she was no longer seeking a cure for the Darkyn's blood-dependent immortality, she continued cataloging Kyn blood types and the strains of the pathogen that had infected them. One day she might be able to trace the origins of their condition back to the source of the infection, the progenote that had started it all back in the Dark Ages.

It was thinking about her work with the blood samples that made Alex catch her breath. She turned around, sloshing water over the side of the tub.

"Again, *chérie*?" Michael looked hopeful.

She kissed his mouth, but before he could take that to the next level, she eased away. "That man who came to see you in Rome, the strange one, did he ask you medical questions?"

"He sounded like you when you are working in the lab." He tugged her to him. "Do that again."

"Hold on, baby." She put her hands on his shoulders. "Why would the Brethren send a doctor to talk to you? They don't give prisoners medical treatment. And why would a doctor go to an interrogation room? Not to check the equipment, or to take a few practice swings with the copper pipes."

"I cannot say." His eyes narrowed. "He carried a case with him. I heard glass clinking together when he moved it."

She got up out of the tub and reached for their towels. "How much do you want to bet he was there to take DNA samples?"

"But he did not touch me, Alexandra."

"He didn't have to. There would have been bits of you left all over that torture chamber." She went out into their suite and grabbed some clothes from the selection Phillipe had hung in the armoire. "We've got to find this Jean-Marc guy," she said over her shoulder as Michael joined her. "All I need is a blood sample from him, and then we'll know if he's Kyndred or not."

Michael pulled on his trousers. "How do you propose we find him?"

"How many guys named Jean-Marc do you think bought tickets to the opera tonight?"

"Only one, I am sure. Alexandra, forgive me but I do not know how this man could have been made from my DNA."

She stopped dressing. "You need me to explain again the entire process of using vampire DNA to turn humans into Kyndred?"

"No, it is not that." He came over to her and began buttoning up her blouse. "I was taken in Rome six years ago. It was the only time I had ever been captured by the Brethren."

"And?"

"You and the other humans who were made Kyndred were experimented on when you were children," he reminded her. "For the man you met tonight to be my . . . progeny, he would have to have been a young child. No more than six years old."

"Shit." She threw down her jacket, disgusted with herself. "I hate this. I hate not knowing what they're doing, what they've done. . . ." She rubbed her forehead. "All right, so being Kyndred is off the table—for now," she added, glaring at him. "We still need to find him and see if he is the descendant of a Cyprien who wasn't busy slaying Saracens back in the day."

"But why?"

"That man could be walking around with your human DNA," she told him. "If I'm ever going to figure out how the pathogen works, I need to look at both sides of the equation. He may still carry in his body the immunities and genetic anomalies that allowed you to survive the initial infection."

"All right. He did not tell you his last name? Did you notice where he was sitting in the auditorium?" After she answered no to both questions, Michael went to the phone and placed a call to one of his human friends in the city, who called back a short time later.

Michael listened, thanked the caller, and hung up before turning to Alex. "None of the tickets sold for tonight's performance were purchased by a man with the Christian name Jean-Marc."

Alex swore as she dropped onto the sofa and covered her face with her hands. After she reined in her temper, she looked over her fingertips at Michael. "Can we run a check on guys named Jean-Marc in the city?"

"Of course we can." He sat down beside her. "It is not a common name, so it should only take a few months, perhaps a year, to interview each Jean-Marc living in the city. Assuming he resides here. Then we can check the Jean-Marcs living in New Jersey, and Washington, and work our way across the ocean to the Jean-Marcs living in France. I believe that will take more time."

She chuckled. "If I asked you'd do it, too, wouldn't you?"

Michael smiled and kissed her forehead. "You have but to say, *mon coeur*."

"This is where I say 'no, that's okay,' and I'll let it go."

"No." He glanced at the pale light coming through the windows, and drew her to her feet. "This is when you say 'I love you,' take off my clothes, and come to bed with me."

Surrendering to the inevitable and the pleasurable, Alexandra did just that. Just before they drifted off into the curious sleep of the Darkyn, she remembered something the man had said to her.

"Michael, what does *un enfant trouvé* mean?"

"It is a term used for children who are lost or abandoned, and cannot be returned to their family," he told her.

"Orphans?"

"No, that is not quite the same. An orphan's parents are dead, but the parents of *un enfant trouvé* are unknown." He held her close. "I think the word in English is foundling."

Chapter 13

Dansant tracked Rowan by her scent, and found her sitting on a bus stop bench some distance away from Lincoln Center. Anger followed his relief as he noticed a group of young men watching her from the opposite street corner, but it dissolved as soon as he saw the tears on her face.

"I should have listened to you," he said carefully as he sat down beside her. "When you said you were not the opera type."

"I'm not now, not after that." She fiddled with one of her gloves. "Sorry I ran out on you. I just felt like I couldn't breathe in that place."

He kept an eye on the group of teenagers watching them as he took out his mobile and called for a cab. "We will try Broadway next time."

She sat back against the hard slats of the bench. "There's going to be a next time?"

"Many, I hope." He took out his handkerchief, but instead of offering it to her went about drying her tears himself. Oddly, his fiercely independent Rowan didn't resist. "But no more tragedies. A comedy, perhaps. Neil Simon."

"Do you think Butterfly wanted to kill her kid, and just didn't have the spine to do it?" she asked him suddenly.

He considered her question even as he wondered what had provoked it. "She is a passionate character, and her love for Pinkerton drove her to suicide. But her mother's-love for her child would not have permitted her to harm the boy."

"Mother's-love." She made a contemptuous sound. "I wish I believed in that."

"Your mother must have had her reasons for abandoning you, Rowan. She may have been very young, or had no means to support you. She was probably very frightened."

"Let's say she wasn't young," Rowan countered. "And she had all the means in the world to support me. What if something else frightened her? Something about me. What if she thought I was evil?" She added, "What if she was right?"

"Do you remember your mother?"

"My birth mom?" She shook her head.

"Then how can you ask these questions?"

"Never mind." She stood and looked at each end of the street. "Where is that damn cab? Maybe we should walk back to the Met."

Dansant saw that the group of boys had now drifted from their corner across the street and were moving toward them. They moved casually enough, talking among themselves, but apparently with a definite purpose as they drew closer to the bus stop. "I think that would be wise."

Unfortunately the narrow tailoring of Rowan's gown didn't allow her to take her customary long strides, and halfway back to Lincoln Center the group of teenagers caught up with them. Several passed Dansant, and then stopped and turned, sandwiching him and Rowan in the middle of their group.

"You got a dollar, pop?" one standing in the middle asked.

"Nice threads," another one said, this time to Rowan. He reached out to touch her sleeve, and she shifted away. "Aw, she don't like me."

Dansant kept his gaze on the one in the middle. "Let us pass."

"Pass what? Go?" The boy grinned and held out a hand. "That'll cost you a wallet, pal."

Another boy came up behind Rowan and tucked his face over her shoulder. "You for sale, baby, or just for rent?"

"Patrol cars come by here every ten minutes after a performance," she informed the group at large. "Last one I saw was nine minutes ago."

"Yeah, well, those cops, they go for coffee at midnight," the one in the middle told her. "They won't be back on the beat for a half hour."

The one behind Rowan snickered. "Plenty of time for us to get to know each other." He grabbed at her chest from behind, and she drove her elbow into his ribs, whirling around at the same time. He roared with pain, grabbing his midsection with one arm before he lashed out at her with the other, punching her in the face. Her head snapped back, and she rocked on her feet, but stayed upright.

"Rowan." Dansant saw blood streaming from her nose, and felt the fury spread out inside him.

"I'm okay," she said, curling her fists and moving to stand with her back to his.

The other boys laughed, and Dansant removed his wallet, holding it out. When the leader of the group tried to take it, he grabbed his wrist with his other hand. "You and your friends don't want to harm us."

The boy's eyes darkened. "No, we don't want to do that."

He sent out his influence in a wide arc, encompassing the group. "You should forget about this and go back to your place on the corner."

"Yeah. We should." The boy's voice sounded dreamy. "Come on, guys."

The other boys followed their leader, and walked out into the street. They stopped only for a car whose driver hit the horn loud and long.

Dansant turned to Rowan, who was pressing her nose between her fingers. "Let me see." He cradled her face.

"I don't think it's broken." She held still as he used his handkerchief, this time to mop up the blood on her mouth and chin. "How did you do that? How did you make them go away like that?"

The blow to her face had prevented her from falling under his influence, or she might have gone with them. "I asked politely."

She took her hand from her face. "There were ten of them and two of us. Under the circumstances, asking politely doesn't work."

"It did tonight."

"Dansant, don't snow me. You hypnotized them or something. All of them." She rubbed her arms. "I could feel it."

He seized on what she had said as an explanation. "The power of suggestion can be quite effective, even on large groups." A cab stopped at the curb, and he put his arm around her. "Now I suggest we leave."

As before, Rowan refused to go to the hospital, dismissing her injury as minor. He considered taking her back to his apartment for the night, but his living situation would raise too many questions. He directed the cabdriver to the restaurant, where he paid him before he escorted Rowan inside.

"You don't have to stay with me," she told him as she went to the rinsing sink and splashed her face with cold water to remove the last traces of blood. "I've been popped in the nose plenty of times."

He felt a surge of relief as the scent of her blood vanished. "This is not how I envisioned the end of our evening together."

She dried her mouth with a paper towel. "Just what were you envisioning, Jean-Marc? A private tour of my apartment?"

If only he had the time. "I have already seen it."

"You know what I mean." She threw away the crumpled towel and removed her hat, shaking her curls loose around her face. "You took me to the opera, which I could never afford to do on my own. You chased off those kids, and probably saved me from being gang-raped. You've definitely earned it. I'm willing."

"You are angry and hurt, and I think I am leaving." He

went to her and kissed her brow. "Thank you for a mostly lovely evening."

"Wait." She put her hand on his arm. "I didn't mean that the way it sounded."

"Of course you didn't." He pulled her close, holding her as long as he dared before releasing her. "Good night, Rowan."

Dansant walked to the end of the block before he realized he had left his coat back at the restaurant. Not wishing to disturb his young tenant, he let himself in through the front of the building, where he heard some clattering from the kitchen.

Dansant went to the pickup window, through which he saw Rowan at Lonzo's station. She was dicing up a conglomeration of ingredients: zucchini, tomatoes, celery, carrots, new potatoes, garlic, parsley, and fresh thyme. Her hands flew, and her chopping blade made short work of the raw vegetables and herbs. Fascinated, he stood and watched her carry the board over to a deep skillet on one of the cooktop ranges. She took down a squeeze bottle of olive oil from Vince's speed rack, laced the bottom of the skillet with the golden liquid, and then swept the diced bits from the board into the pan. As she worked the pan, flipping the vegetables with expert rolls of her wrist, she added some scallops, chunks of bass, shrimp, and a squeeze of lemon.

She cooked so rapidly and proficiently that Dansant hardly knew what to make of it. This was not the bedraggled young woman he had hired out of sympathy; Rowan was an experienced chef. Quite experienced, judging by the delicious scent of the meal she was preparing.

"It's stir-fry, Dansant," he heard her say as she brought the pan over to the long table where they had their family meal every night. "My own recipe, if you want to risk it."

He went through the swinging doors and stood beside the table. She filled two shallow bowls and handed one to him. "How long have you been cooking?"

"Like this?" She tilted her head to consider the air above his. "I don't know. Five, six years."

He lifted the bowl to his face and breathed in before inspecting the contents. "I know this."

"When you made it," she said, "it was *pot-au-feu de fruits de mer.*"

"Which I stewed," he pointed out. "In a pot."

"I didn't feel like waiting." She retrieved a couple of spoons from the drying rack.

"Rowan, you cannot stir-fry *pot-au-feu.*"

"You said *au-feu* meant 'on the fire.' That made me think of trying it as a stir-fry." Her expression changed. "I only borrowed some of the leftover bass, and I bought the rest of the ingredients with my own money. You did say I could use the kitchen after closing."

He set the bowl down. "You did not add clams, mussels, or squid."

She shrugged. "I didn't have enough money for them. Maybe next time. Oh, and I didn't make any of that aïoli for that either. I don't like garlic in my mayonnaise or mayonnaise in my stir-fry. Chinese five-spice is more my style."

Dansant didn't know whether to applaud or shake her. "Why didn't you tell me you could cook like this?"

"Would you have believed me?" Before he could reply, she said, "Look, I'm not formally trained. I've read a lot of cookbooks, watched a lot of cooking shows on TV, and just . . . practiced. Kind of like Rachael Ray on a much, much smaller budget."

"You did not learn to do this from a cookbook."

"That's why I watch Food Network." She sat down. "This is not as good cold. I speak from experience."

He glanced at the wall clock, and saw that his time was almost up. "I cannot stay to share your meal. Rowan, when Lonzo comes in tonight, you will give him a message for me."

"Sure." She hunched her shoulders and took a sullen bite of her food. "What do you want me to tell him?"

He rested a hand on her shoulder. "I'm promoting you to sous-chef."

She stopped chewing, and then swallowed with difficulty. "You can't do that."

"I just did."

"On the basis of what? Watching me throw together one meal? You just said you can't stir-fry a stew." She made a dismissive gesture. "You're crazy."

He bent down. "One wolf recognizes another, Rowan. I always thought there was something familiar about you. Now I know what it is."

"You can't do this to me." She rested her forehead against her hand. "I just got these guys used to having me around the kitchen. They'll never go for it, not in a million years."

"They will do as they're told." He gestured toward her meal. "Eat. You're too thin as it is. I will handle the rest."

She stared at the bowl, and then him before she rose, carried the food over to the trash bin, and dumped it inside.

"Rowan."

"I don't need you to *handle* things for me," she said as she turned to face him. "I'm not a kid, I'm not your girlfriend, I'm your employee."

"And tomorrow night you will be my sous-chef, or you will find another place of employment," he snapped back. He immediately felt sorry for issuing the threat, but from the look on her face it was too late to apologize. "Unless you are too afraid. Then you may continue fetching and carrying for the cooks until your debt to me is repaid."

"You want a sous-chef?" She carried the dishes over to the washer and dropped them into the empty racks. "You got one." She went to the stairs and ran up them out of sight.

Dansant was weary of trying to fathom Rowan's moods while fighting back his own unfulfilled desires. Silently he climbed the stairs, but when he reached the door of her apartment he heard a low, soft sound coming from behind it. It took a moment for him to recognize it: She was weeping again.

Tonight a death scene from an opera had reduced her

to tears, but then she had been struck in the face and made to bleed and had not uttered so much as a whimper. Now after having a simple argument, she wept as if her heart were breaking. Dansant didn't understand her as much as he wanted to believe he did.

What woman took physical abuse without a murmur but ran away from fulfilling her own gifts?

He had no more time to wrestle with the puzzle that was Rowan. No matter how much he wanted her, he had to gather together all the pieces of her life in order to make sense of it and her. To do otherwise would be not only foolhardy, but dangerous for them both.

It tore at him to turn away from her door, and what he had to do next filled him with despair. But such was the price of his new life, and the hope that at last he had found the woman who might share it with him.

Meriden pulled on a pair of jeans and a flannel shirt before he stepped out of his apartment and stood outside Rowan's door. As soon as he heard her, he reached up to the top of the door frame, took down the spare key Dansant had left there, and let himself in.

She hadn't bothered to turn on any lights, so he followed the sound of crying to the source, curled up on the floor beneath the window.

"Rowan." He scooped her up in his arms, dodging her fist and carrying her back to the big armchair, where he sat down and held her on his lap, turning on the lamp beside the chair to get a look at her.

She was a mess.

"How did you get in?" she demanded, choking out the words. "Forget it. Just get out." She pushed at him. "Let go of me."

"Not happening, Cupcake." He held on, letting her struggle until she ran out of steam and went limp. She pressed her face into his shirt as she sobbed, shuddering now and then as she muttered broken, nonsensical phrases.

Meriden didn't waste his breath on words of comfort;

she was beyond that. Wherever she was, he'd be here when she came back. And gradually she calmed, enough to regain some control of her limbs and the convulsive clutching motions of her hands.

"If you say you're sorry," he told her when he heard her drag in a deep breath, "I will beat the living shit out of you."

"I'm not sorry."

"That's my girl." He tugged her head back so he could see her face. Her nose was more swollen than it should have been, and a small graze marred her right cheekbone. Something roared softly in his head. "Who hit you?"

"A kid with nasty hands." She probed her cheek and the bridge of her nose. "How bad do I look?"

"Like you went a round with Holyfield." He turned her face toward the light to check her eye, but it was clear. "So tell me about this kid."

"He has a couple of cracked ribs now, courtesy of my elbow." She met his gaze. "And I'm not sorry about that, either."

He nodded, feeling his rage ease back. "So what was all this about?" He thumbed some tear trails from her cheek. "Postknockout depression?"

"Maybe." She settled back against his chest and sighed. "You ever get into a street fight? A bad one?"

He thought of the time he'd gotten jumped outside Clancy's by a drunken Marine and four of his buddies. "Now and then."

"I didn't know how to fight the first time I ran away," she said. "I was just a little kid, and I only had a couple bucks to my name. I was looking around for someplace where I could buy some food, and these two junkies came out of nowhere. One held me from behind while the other one searched me, and even though they were sick and needed a fix they were so fucking strong, Sean. Desperate strong. They took all the money I had, and when I tried to go after them to get it back, they taught me just how easy ribs crack."

"What were you doing on the street that young?"

"Nowhere else to go. It doesn't matter. They picked me up a couple days later and put me back in foster care." She knuckled her eye and winced. "Have you seen that girl who's been hanging around the restaurant at night? About five-four, blond hair, real skinny?"

More than once he'd sensed someone out in the alley, but there wasn't a backstreet in New York that didn't host someone who didn't want to be seen. "I haven't seen her face, but I think I know who you mean."

"I've taken some food out to her a couple times, and tried to talk to her, but she always takes off." She plucked at one of the buttons on his shirt. "I think she's about sixteen, same age I was when I finally ditched the foster care system for good. I want to tell her I know how she feels, maybe help her find a safe place to stay, but she won't let me get near her. She grabs the food and runs."

"You're helping her by feeding her," he pointed out.

"It's not enough. Kid like that, she needs a home, a real bed, clean clothes, and someone to take care of her. Hell, if I thought I could get away with bringing her up here and having her stay with me, I would."

"And she'd probably knock you over the head and clean you out while you were unconscious," he predicted.

"I guess." She yawned. "You should go to bed."

She felt good against him, warm and soft, like a long, sleepy cat. "I should."

"But not with me," she murmured, closing her eyes. "I'm not sleeping with you, you know."

She was asleep a moment later.

Meriden sat and held her, content to wait until her breathing slowed and deepened before he lifted her and carried her carefully back to her bed.

She stirred briefly when he laid her out, but only flung an arm out before she went back to dreamland. Meriden considered curling up beside her for a couple of hours—he could think of some great ways to wake her up in the morning—but reluctantly decided against it. When he had sex with Rowan, which he fully intended to do sometime in the immediate future, he wanted her fully awake, completely willing, and one hundred percent aware of him and what they did to each other.

He pulled up the linens around her, but when he lifted her arm to tuck it under he saw something dark just above her wrist, too dark to be a bruise. He turned on the lamp beside the bed, angling the shade so the light didn't shine on her face, and then rolled back her sleeve.

An intricate, densely inked tat of a black dragon with red eyes stretched from just above her wrist to the inside of her elbow. He put her arm down and tugged the covers away from her to have a look at the other forearm, which sported a mirror image of the same dragon. The light caught something else, a faint patch of glowing blue, and when he checked the other tat he saw the same.

The black dragons weren't the first images tattooed on Rowan's arms. There was something else, an older tat, under each one.

She can't be, he thought, sitting down on the edge of the bed. His weight depressed the mattress, causing Rowan to roll over toward him. He stood up quickly, standing over her for a long moment before he reached into his pocket and took out his mobile phone. After snapping a photo of her face, he turned off the light and left.

He had no choice. He would have to run her.

He locked Rowan's door, pocketed the spare key, and returned to his apartment, where he took out the file on Alana King. Rereading the medical reports didn't convince him; the color of the tattoos on the girl's forearms was not listed. They were not described as dragons, either. Everyone had tattoos today; even little old ladies.

He also didn't believe that Rowan was only sixteen years old. She might have a young face, but her eyes belonged to someone older, a traveler who had maybe seen too much of the world already. She also had none of the awkwardness of an adolescent girl who had just gone through major body changes. A kid wouldn't be as at ease as Rowan was in her skin.

Still, there was a remote chance that he was wrong, and the girl he had to find to save his own life was sleeping across the hall.

He took the laptop out from his desk and booted it up, accessing a face-morphing program he'd gotten from a medical examiner in exchange for some bodywork on a Dodge Charger the examiner had been lovingly restoring. The program, which was not available commercially, was used by several agencies and organizations involved in missing persons cases. Any photo loaded into the program could be virtually aged to any point in that person's life, a technique used primarily to help identify children who had gone missing for several years.

Meriden uploaded the photo he'd taken of Rowan with his phone into the system, and pulled it up alongside the school photo of young Alana King. He saw no resemblance between the two faces, but entered the formula to age-progress Alana King's features to what they would look like at age sixteen. The little girl blossomed into a pretty teenager, but she still looked nothing like Rowan. He advanced the progression a few more years, and got a look at how Alana would appear as a grown woman, but struck out a third time.

She could have altered her coloring with hair dye and colored contacts, he thought, and removed the age progressions of Alana, restoring her photo to its original appearance. He then changed Rowan's hair color to blond and her eye color to blue, and had the program age-regress her one year at a time. Although Rowan grew younger and more childlike with each new regression, she still bore no resemblance to the other girl.

Whoever she was, Rowan Dietrich had never been Alana King.

Chapter 14

Delaporte drew Nella's arms from around his neck and got up, taking his pants from where he had draped them over the end of her bed. She had suffered from insomnia most of her life, she'd told him, but after a few hours in his arms she would fall into a deep, unmoving sleep that lasted until her alarm clock went off. Sometimes, she confessed wryly, she would even sleep through that.

After he checked the living room and kitchen, he unlocked the back sliding door and went out onto the small deck. Stepping outside to call in was an unnecessary precaution—she wouldn't rouse unless he shook her—but Delaporte didn't care to be anywhere near his girlfriend when he spoke to Genaro.

His girlfriend. He lit a cigarette, inhaling deeply. Nella Hoff had several PhDs, all of them in subjects he didn't understand and never would. He liked that she never referred to her education or his lack of it. It would have been much harder to be with her if she'd been a snob.

He dialed Genaro's private line, which Genaro answered at once.

"You're late," the chairman said. "What is your status?"

"I've completed a sweep of the apartment, but she isn't keeping anything here," he said. "The phone she planted on Kirchner was a throwaway paid for with cash, so there won't be any paper on it."

"What about her phones?"

"I've installed tracers in the landlines. I think she's keeping her mobile in her vehicle." He turned so he could watch the dark interior of the apartment through the window. "Unless there is something else you want, I'm finished here."

"I've just received a report from the New York branch," Genaro said. "Our team has disappeared."

He went still. "All of them?"

"Yes. New York will monitor the morgues, but I think it unlikely that King would leave any corpses to be found." Genaro sounded tired. "I would like to know how he identified the members of the team and their location."

So would Delaporte; he had personally trained the team, and several of the men on it had been his most dependable hunters. This changed everything. "Do you want me to finish here?"

"No. Until the female is found, Hoff still has some value." Genaro paused as if thinking. "We'll take her tomorrow in the lab. Kirchner will need your assistance. Report to my office first thing in the morning."

"Yes, sir." Delaporte ended the call.

Engaging in an affair with an enemy of the company had been distasteful to him, as had the role he had taken on—to appear to Nella Hoff as a potential blackmail target. He understood the psychology behind posing as a would-be pedophile in order to intrigue her, but he hadn't cared for having his background records salted with indications of a predilection he personally despised.

But the disgust he had expected to feel when he was with her had never manifested when they were together. It was true that he preferred women who had an open, mature attitude about sex, but something about Nella Hoff had made the role-playing less of a chore. He'd enjoyed her submissiveness, even if it had been self-serving.

The sex itself had been unnervingly erotic.

That part of his assignment had come to an end now. Tomorrow when Nella went into work, she would be drugged, removed discreetly from the lab, and installed in one of the "treatment" rooms, where he and Kirchner would begin a lengthy and painful interrogation. From what Genaro had said, Delaporte imagined he would be called upon to sexually abuse her. It was always more emotionally effective when the captive was subjected to repeated violations by a former lover.

He walked back to the bedroom to look at her one last time, so that he could remember her as she had been.

Delaporte registered that the bed was empty a moment before the lights snapped on and a gun barrel pressed against the base of his skull.

"You really should look inside the tampon boxes and under the trash can liners, Daddy," Nella said in a mocking, girlish voice. "You wouldn't believe how much you can hide in those little places."

"So it seems." He felt almost proud of her. "What are we going to do now, Nella?"

"You're not going to move, because I know the information in your records about your skills as a soldier and a mercenary wasn't complete bullshit," she said. "And as much as I'd like to pull this trigger, I need some information from you."

He smiled. "Then go ahead and pull the trigger."

She slid the gun around as she came to stand before him, until it rested under his chin. "Let's clear the air first. You're not a pedophile in the making, and I'm not a Daddy's girl."

"Does it matter now?"

"It does to me. You knew I'd look for the weakest link, and you set yourself up to resemble one." She watched his eyes, her own bright with nerves. "Where did I fuck up?"

"You were a little too heavy-handed with Kirchner," he told her, at the same time subtly changing his stance. "Also, offering him sex was a mistake. He's a celibate as well as a misogynist."

She grew thoughtful. "I didn't think the wife was window-dressing."

"She's an experienced bodyguard," he said. "So are the two women posing as his teenage daughters."

"You know, you're giving me a great deal of free, valuable information, Don." She pressed the barrel in a little harder. "I don't think it's because you like talking to your plants."

Her pun amused him. "I admire your resourcefulness."

"Oh, you admire my tits and my arse," she corrected, her voice changing from American to a working-class British accent. "He's called you off, then?"

He saw no point in lying to her. "He has."

"When am I to be taken?"

He gave her a wistful smile. "Now."

He took her down with a minimum amount of trouble, knocking the gun away before he pinned her to the floor under his bulk. The weapon didn't discharge, and Nella didn't make a sound. She tried every trick he knew to dislodge him, and a couple of moves that were new. Then she stopped and lay under him for a moment, panting hard.

"Do me now," she said, lifting her chin like an animal baring its throat. "Go on. It's this or I have to open a vein. You can tell that pisser Genaro I got the jump on you, and you just reacted too fast."

"No one gets the jump on me." Delaporte wrapped one big hand around her neck. "And I tell him only the truth."

"Ballocks." She wriggled. "Do you need a bit of theater again to get the job done? Should I do the death scene from *Othello*? 'Kill me tomorrow, let me live tonight.'"

Delaporte applied enough pressure to temporarily impede the flow of blood to Nella's brain, causing her to lose consciousness. He released his grip in time to keep from killing her, and then moved aside, sitting on the floor beside her.

Judging by the mistakes she'd made, Nella had not been in the field for very long. Nor had she been trained properly. Delaporte disliked seeing the waste of a good agent, even one that worked for the other side.

No, if he was honest, he hated the thought of seeing this

woman tortured and killed before her body was burned to ash in the lab's massive incinerator. She'd been exceptionally brave and, in her own fashion, honorable.

He stripped off her nightgown and tore it into strips, which he used to bind her ankles together. As he rolled her over onto her belly to tie her hands behind her, the light illuminated her back and he saw what appeared to be a loose flap of skin on her shoulder blade. On closer inspection it turned out to be a small circle of thin, flesh-colored latex that had been glued directly onto her skin with spirit gum.

Delaporte found the edge of the latex patch and peeled it back slowly. Beneath it was a black oval with the outlined profile of a very familiar face.

He took out his mobile and dialed a number he rarely called. "My lord," he said when his master's low, powerful voice answered. "We have another problem here in Atlanta."

Madame Butterfly stood over Rowan, her sword glittering like the madness in her eyes. "Hellspawn. I saw what you did. I saw." She brought down the sword.

Rowan rolled out of the way, and landed with a thump on a hard floor. Sunlight blinded her as she groaned and clutched her aching head.

Another one of the nightmares, and now it had opera in it.

She grabbed the edge of the futon, using it to pull herself up to grab her watch and check the time. It was either eight a.m. or eight p.m. She really needed to invest in an alarm clock.

It took a while for her to wake up, not that she didn't seriously consider crawling back under the covers and hiding there for the rest of her life. She drank two cups of coffee, one in the bathroom, where she saw what looked like the remains of a black eye instead of the beginnings of one. Hopefully her ability to heal quickly would get rid of most of it by the time she had to go to work.

As Dansant's new sous-chef, an evil, gleeful little voice

inside her head reminded her as she dressed. And wouldn't that promotion make her everyone's best friend.

On her way back and forth to wash up, she eyed Meriden's door. She remembered Sean coming in her apartment, the soggy cuddling session, and not much else. There were no signs he'd done anything while she'd slept in his lap except put her to bed, not that she thought he would have. She would have never pegged him as a guy who would offer his shoulder to cry on. The breaking and entering, now, that was more his style.

She had unfinished business with Sean Meriden, but it would have to wait until she figured out a way to deal with Dansant.

Rowan made a bowl of cereal and idly picked up one of her new books to read while she ate. This one was a memoir, written in the late nineteenth century by an ex-priest who had been sent to exorcise some people who thought they were vampires, and in the process had lost his faith and given up the cassock.

According to the introduction the ex-priest had penned the memoir while he was in his eighties, which meant he'd gone vampire-busting in the late eighteenth century. The preface, written by some snotty editor, also warned that the contents were largely considered by the literary community of the time to be creative nonfiction.

There was a lot of Latin terminology to plow through, Rowan discovered, and by her third bowl of cereal she was pretty sure she agreed with the editor. The ex-priest alternated between ranting about secret societies within the church and cursed souls who'd tried to attack him and drink his blood while he'd doused them with holy water and prayed over them.

She was just about to give it up when she got to a page listing what the author had discovered about the people he referred to as "truly damned by God":

They who are damned for eternity will be comely of appearance, the men strong and handsome, the women delicate and lovely. They exude the precious scent of God's gift of torment, that of flowers, but it is a lie to lure and trap their unsuspecting victims. They will partake of neither food nor drink but wine. When brought into the light of heaven they will shield their eyes and grow agitated; if left in shelter they will sleep without breath or movement. They have knowledge of the black arts and wield these against their victims, each with their own spell to create confusion of the senses and to enslave with but a few words. Few can resist their murmurings and touches. They fornicate freely and respect not the bonds of marriage or betrothal. Nothing may cut their flesh but copper, which burns them like fire. They heal from any wound, but thanks be to God may be dispatched back to Hell by beheading.

She read the passage three times before she understood why it riveted her: confusion of the senses . . . enslave with but a few words.

Last night Dansant had used a few words to stop them from being mugged. Those boys had had the perfect opportunity to roll them, and yet they had done exactly what he had told them to without a murmur. They'd acted like he'd turned them into zombies.

She began comparing what she knew about her boss with the ex-priest's crazy list. Strong and handsome, check. Smells like flowers, check. Never eats, never drinks anything but wine . . .

She skimmed through the rest of the book, looking for more lists, and stopped only when she saw the image of an old engraving of a Templar warrior sitting on a horse in the middle of a battlefield. It was a gory portrait, the ground around him littered with dead bodies.

The warrior-priest's face looked exactly like that of Jean-Marc Dansant.

"No. He can't be." Rowan slammed the book shut as she thought frantically. She'd worked beside Dansant for weeks, had watched him cook, and she couldn't remember a single time she had seen him taste the food. He never ate with her and the line cooks for the family meal; he would simply sit at the head of the table and drink a glass of wine.

Last night when she'd given him a bowl of her stir-fry, he'd smelled it, but he hadn't tasted it.

And in all the time she'd been here, she had never once seen him during the day.

"Oh, for Christ's sake, he's not a vampire." Saying it out loud didn't make her feel better. "He works nights. He said it was hypnosis. Maybe he wasn't hungry."

She opened the book and stared at the engraving again, absently touching her neck. The artist had done a lot of fine detail work; he'd added tiny lines for the eyelashes and the warrior's mustache, and a dot on his jawline in the exact same spot where Dansant had a tiny mole....

Oh, shit. Rowan got up and ran out to the bathroom.

She checked her throat, her arms, and then stripped down to her skin and did a full body check. She found no bite marks or any signs to indicate she'd been used as a blood bank.

Of course there aren't any marks, that slimy, malicious voice in her head purred as she got dressed. *You heal too fast.*

She didn't know what to do. It wasn't as if she could walk up to the executive chef and ask him if he was an immortal killer who fed on human blood. But she knew the dark kyn were a reality, and from the research she and Matthias had done, she knew they still existed in clusters all over the world, living apparently normal lives in order to hide in plain sight.

It wasn't a stretch to believe one of them had decided to open a French restaurant. *When you want to catch a mouse, you don't set out an empty trap. You bait it with something they can't resist.*

Speculating like this was ridiculous. What she needed was a computer, so she could run some basic checks on her boss. Looking into his background would doubtless provide logical explanations for all of his weirdness, and that would settle things.

Rowan went to the nearest branch of the New York Public Library, which was busy but fortunately provided public-access computers. She sat at an open terminal, put down the notepad she'd brought with her, and logged into her Internet account. A window with a blinking red border popped up to inform her that she had exceeded her e-mail account storage limits.

I haven't written an e-mail in weeks, she thought, annoyed as she entered her password for her inbox. *Must be SPAM.*

It wasn't SPAM. There were over four hundred new messages waiting to be read, and the senders column read like a Takyn roll call: Romulus, Jezebel, Vulcan, Paracelsus, Delilah, Zephyrus, Magdalene, Orion, Sapphira ...

Before Rowan could open the first e-mail, an IM screen popped onto the monitor. The sender was Paracelsus.

P: *He jests at scars*

She typed in the last words of the quote to confirm her identity: *that never felt a wound.*

P: *Where are you? Are you hurt?*

No, she wrote back. *I'm fine. I'm in New York.*

P: *I know. I've been turning it upside down looking for you.*

She chuckled. *You're still here?*

P: *Of course. I wasn't going to leave until I knew you were all right.*

I'm good. It wasn't exactly a lie. *Sorry I haven't been in touch.*

P: *You vanished off the face of the earth for weeks. We've been frantic, all of us.*

That explained the e-mail overload. But no one should have been worried; she always checked in. . . . Rowan frowned. She hadn't checked in, now that she thought about it. She'd completely forgotten about her friends.

I got tied up with personal business, she typed. *But I'm okay. Everyone else all right?*

P: *No. G. sent a team to New York to take a special girl. We thought they were after you. Then they disappeared. Another player in the game.*

Rowan sat back in her chair, trying to take it all in.

He couldn't have tracked me, she wrote back. *I dumped the bike. He doesn't have anything on me.*

P: *V. finally gained access to G.'s clubhouse. What little there is about the op says the target is a female with plenty of talent who escaped custody.*

That could be any of us girls. Yet even as she typed the reply, she remembered facing Genaro's goons in Price Park. Technically speaking, she and Vulcan had escaped custody, although she couldn't have left behind any DNA for them to mess with, not unless . . .

She had touched one of Genaro's hunters. She had needed the physical contact to shift into the woman he loved most, some blond bombshell named Rosie, and tap him for information. She must have shed some skin cells when she'd dreamveiled herself.

If G. and this other player are after me, she wrote to Paracelsus, *I should get out of Dodge now.*

P: *No, my dear, it's too dangerous. We have not yet identified this new player, and losing the team will have G. watching all points of exit. Stay where you are and keep your head down until V. and I can arrange safe passage.*

Safe passage meant creating a new identity for her and relocating her across the country. *So much for Rowan Dietrich*, she thought. On the IM screen, she typed *When should I contact you again?*

P: *Check in with me in a few days. I sent you my Lucky Lotto numbers. You should buy a ticket today.*

That translated into instructions for her to buy a throwaway mobile phone and call him on a number he'd e-mailed her. *Okay, I'll take care of that as soon as I leave here. My access is public, so would you pass the word around to everyone?*

P: *Consider it done. Be careful, my dear.*

Rowan closed the IM screen, checked Paracelsus's e-mail and jotted down the phone number disguised as Lotto numbers, and then wiped all traces of her session from the terminal.

At a nearby convenience store, Rowan picked up a

throwaway phone and a card for several hundred minutes' worth of air time. As she stood in line to pay for it, she thought of all the e-mails stacked in her inbox. She had never received so many, and the idea that evidently all of the Takyn were worried about her made her feel absurdly pleased.

Sometimes, especially after Matthias had brought Jessa back from Atlanta, she'd felt as if she'd become more of a liability than an asset to her boss. She should have remembered that she had other friends, good friends who cared about her and wanted her to be happy.

She should have remembered . . . "That son of a bitch."

The Puerto Rican man standing in front of her glanced back. "You talking to me, lady?"

"No. I mean my bastard of a boss." She dragged a hand over her head. "He's been messing with my head."

The man grimaced in sympathy. "Mine uses a stopwatch when I take lunch. I come back five minutes late, he docks my pay."

Rowan clenched her jaw. "Yeah, well, mine isn't going to dock me anymore."

Chapter 15

Dansant had Lonzo send Rowan on an errand to get her out of the kitchen, and then called each of the cooks into his office, where he had what the others thought was a private meeting to discuss their performance on the line. Using his influence over them, he instructed them to accept Rowan as the new sous-chef, and almost all of them did.

Only Lonzo, who had the strongest will of all the men, resisted briefly.

"She's just a kid," he told Dansant in an uncertain tone. "She ain't got the chops for it."

Dansant tried another approach. "Do you like Rowan, Lonzo?"

"Yeah, Trick's okay," he admitted reluctantly. "For a woman."

Dansant suspected that his *garde-manger*'s chauvinistic attitude toward the fair sex would never change. "She has learned a great deal from you."

Now the burly man's chest puffed out. "I've taught her a couple things, sure."

"Then you will agree that it is a credit to you that she has moved up to become the new sous-chef," Dansant told him. "That is why you will accept this, because it was your teaching that helped her."

"No shit?" His expression became filled with confusion, and began to clear. "I'm that good a teacher, huh?"

Dansant had suspected appealing to his chef's vanity

would be a way around his stubborn will. "Yes, you are. And you will watch over Rowan and assure that others are respectful of her. An insult to her is the same as an insult to you. Do you understand my instructions now?"

The last of the doubt faded from Lonzo's harsh features. "Yes, Chef."

It was rather comical, watching the reception the line cooks gave Rowan when she returned from the market with the Italian parsley Lonzo had sent her to buy. Vince cuffed her shoulder as he passed by her, and George asked her if she needed help setting up Bernard's old station to her liking. Manny gave her advice on how to stock her speed racks, and even Enrique watched her anxiously, so that when she needed a certain pan or dish he had it at her station before she could call for it.

Much to Dansant's disappointment, Rowan showed no reaction, although she flinched several times whenever he came near her. Unlike the enthusiasm she had shown on previous shifts, now she took no interest in his preparations, and left her station only to make a quick trip to the restroom halfway through the night.

Her cooking was as inventive and marvelous as Dansant had hoped. She remade his *cuisses de canard au chou*, using a dusky merlot instead of the traditional cognac, and cranberry jelly instead of tomato paste. The result did not greatly change the appearance of the dish, but subtly altered the aroma and emphasized the flavors. When Dansant made the first of his customary rounds of the dining area, his patrons raved over the dish.

"This reminds me of the duck we used to have at Thanksgiving every year," one delighted matron told him. "My grandmother used cabbage in her stuffing, and would glaze the bird with cranberries and burgundy."

"I thought Americans celebrated Thanksgiving with turkey," Dansant said.

The woman chuckled. "Not when their father goes duck hunting every November."

The kitchen remained busy for the rest of the night, and

Dansant decided to keep his distance from Rowan to let her enjoy her victory. It wasn't until after closing, when the line cooks congratulated her on their way out, that Rowan looked directly at him, her eyes filled with suspicion and dislike. He returned her gaze until the last cook had left, and watched her stalk toward the stairs.

"Rowan." He watched her come to a halt. "Don't go."

She spun around, her features tight, her eyes glittering. "Is there something else you wanted, Chef?"

"You have obviously had enough congratulations," he said, walking toward her. "I thought you would be pleased."

"I would be, if they were sincere." She closed the distance between them. "What did you do to them?"

"Do? Nothing."

"The same way you did nothing to those kids the night we went to the opera," she countered.

She thought he had hypnotized the line cooks. Well, it wasn't far from the truth. "I may have threatened to fire them all if they treated you badly."

"They're cooks. That would have made them behave worse." She planted her hands on her hips. "Have you ever done that to me? Hypnotized me, made me forget things?"

He didn't stop to wonder how she had come to such a conclusion. He also felt a fresh wave of shame for the times he had used his influence over her. "I have only tried to be your friend, Rowan."

"Friends don't fuck with other friends' minds, Dansant."

He could compel her now to forget all about this unfortunate discovery, and tomorrow night she would be back at his side and happy to be there. And he would be even more of a monster than he already was. "If I have said or done anything to upset you, I apologize."

She sat down on the bench by the table where the line cooks ate together. "I don't know what to believe from you anymore. You're making me think crazy things."

He wanted to tell her everything, but it was not yet time. He had to first regain her trust. "How can I convince you that I am sincere?"

She seized an apple from the bowl of fruit on the table and tossed it to him. "Take a bite of that."

He regarded the apple and then her. "Why?"

"Because if you're who I think you are, you won't. You can't."

He polished the apple on his sleeve and took a bite, and then another. Only when he had reduced it to a core did she sigh and prop her head in her hands.

"Do you want me to eat something else?" he asked. "A pear, perhaps? Some blueberries?"

"No," she said, her voice muffled by her hands. "I'm an idiot." She lifted her face. "And I'm sorry. My imagination has been in overdrive lately."

"It served you well tonight," he reminded her as he came to sit beside her. "Your cooking was very imaginative, and inventive. The patrons loved your duck."

She grimaced. "It's just food."

He took another apple from the bowl. "Food keeps us alive, but cooking, that is like life."

"That's basically the same thing."

"*Non.* Food comes to us new and untouched, as we are to the world when we are born," he told her. "Preparing it changes it, makes it a thing like us."

"So that crate of Italian parsley Lonzo sent me out for," she said, "that would be like a box full of newborns?"

He ignored her sarcasm. "We take food and shape it and blend it with other things to make it more than it is, better than it is. That is like childhood, when we first discover what will make us what we will be. Then it is tasted and tested and becomes more than it is, something wonderful and beautiful to see and touch and taste and smell. Something that can give comfort and pleasure as well as sustain life."

"Which makes us the same as cannibals. Yum."

"It is not the same, and you know," he chided. "What we

create, what we are, is consumed by hunger, but surrendering to it allows us to become a part of another living thing. That is when we truly come alive. As for food, if our passion has transformed it, has made it what it was meant to be, it can never be gone or forgotten. It becomes part of another life. It will live on in them forever. As we do."

She uttered a shaky laugh. "You make it sound like sex."

"Love," he corrected. "That is why it is so important to us, *oui*? Why it pleases us so much. When it is done correctly, cooking does not feed our pride or lust. It does not make us better or more noble. It is not meant for us at all. It is our gift to the world. A gift made from the purest, deepest love. The love we feel for others. The love we know in our dreams."

She rubbed her eyes with her fingers. "Yeah, well, some of us don't get that dream. Some of us are dumped here. Dirty and worthless. Unwanted and unloved. Just like garbage."

"You are wrong."

Dansant drew Rowan to her feet. "Close your eyes." When she tried to step away, he put his arm around her. "Let me show you what I mean. I *did* eat the apple for you."

So he had. Reluctantly she closed her eyes. "If you're going to feed me something to inspire me, it had better not be that tuna that came in yesterday. Lonzo said it smelled off." She felt something cool and wet against her bottom lip, and smelled warm, ripe peaches. "I've seen that movie *Nine and a Half Weeks*, too, so no jalapeños." But when she licked her lower lip, she tasted the smooth, decadent taste of heavy cream.

What the hell is he doing?

"If you open your eyes," he warned, "it will not work."

"All right." She waited.

The smell of peach darkened, became more complex. At the same time something brushed her top lip, dusting it with a sandy substance that her tongue discovered was crystals of brown sugar.

"Do not swallow yet," he whispered against her ear. "Only open your heart, and taste."

She knew the tiny dot of liquid he put at the corner of her mouth was vanilla extract from the intense smell, but another dot on the other side turned out to be almond. The two blended on her tongue with the sugar and the cream, making her hungrier for the peach slice he had to be waving around under her nose.

But when she opened her mouth to take a bite, he placed a fragment of something thin and crumbling on her tongue that tasted of butter and flour. Then something popped, and the juice of a blackberry dripped over the fragment.

His hands cradled her face. "Now us."

He put his mouth to hers, opening her to his tongue, which tasted of a peach that had been poached in a dark wine. Her head whirled as he kissed her, and all the flavors came together as their mouths melded.

Rowan wanted to jerk away, but the coolness of his tongue slid against the heat of her own, and kissing him back was suddenly everything, the world without end, all that she was pouring out from her mouth to his, a flood of hunger and satisfaction entwining and melting and becoming something more. She clutched at the softness of his white jacket, afraid she would drop into some dark and mindless place with him, and then terrified that she wouldn't, that he would end this and leave her alone and cold.

"Shhh." He lifted his mouth and kissed her temple, holding her, rocking her a little. "Do you see now, *ma mûre*? It begins with a single thing. A peach. A blackberry. A kiss. And then we make it more. We make it love."

She couldn't believe she was crying, but she was, all over his immaculate whites. The tears flooded her eyes and streamed down her cheeks, dashing the beautiful taste in her mouth with salt.

"You can't do this to me. Not now. Not when I don't know . . ." She would not mention her feelings for Sean. And there was no way in hell she would ever tell him that she'd suspected him of being a vampire—or that she felt just as strongly for him as she did Meriden. She ground her forehead into his shoulder. "I can't do this now."

"I know." His hand stroked over her curls. "But the time will come when you can. I hope it is with me, Rowan. I would very much like to be there." He kissed her forehead. "I must go now. I will see you tomorrow, *oui*?"

"Yeah." She managed a wan smile. "Have a good night."

After Dansant left in his cab, Rowan went upstairs to shower and get ready for bed. Although watching her boss eat normal human food had gone a long way toward reassuring her, she had a whole new set of problems. He was definitely interested in her; he would never have kissed her like that if he were gay.

She would not think about the kiss. If she did, she'd be up all night remembering it and savoring it and dissecting it, moment by moment. After all, it had been the best kiss of her life.

Hearing Meriden coming up the stairs helped clear her head. She pulled on her clothes before she stepped out to catch him on the landing.

"Hey."

"Hey yourself." He turned to unlock his door.

"Got a minute?"

He turned on her. "Are you going to cry all over me again?"

She winced. She had been going heavy on the waterworks lately, something Dansant seemed to have no problem with but she suspected Sean hated. "No. I just wanted to explain—"

"No explanation required, Cupcake." He went into his apartment and slammed the door in her face.

If that didn't decide things for her, nothing would. Meriden wasn't interested, and Dansant was. She could have the prince instead of the frog. And why was her hand reaching for his doorknob? She didn't give a damn what Sean thought of her, or why he'd shut her out—again—or whatever new bug had crawled up his ass. She'd just go in and make that clear to him, once and for all, so there were no future misunderstandings.

He was standing over his desk, flipping through a file. He didn't even bother to glance at her. "I told you, not tonight, honey. I've got a headache."

"You've got something." She leaned back against the door and folded her arms. "I'm going to say this, so you might as well listen."

He stopped flipping, and under his shirt his back muscles went rigid. "What?"

"You were decent to me last night, and I'm grateful. But I can't have you wandering in and out of my place whenever you like." As he looked at her, she held out her hand. "Give me the key."

"It's sitting on top of the frame over your door," he told her. "Go get it yourself."

She dropped her hand. "How did you know it was there?"

"I'm psychic," he snarled. "You done?"

"With you?" She showed him some teeth. "Absolutely."

He crossed the floor with a few strides. "Then why are you still here, Cupcake?"

She frowned at the third button on his shirt. "I don't know."

He took hold of the front of her shirt with his fist, tugging her up. "I do."

Somehow she went from standing to dangling, until he plastered her against him, pulled her head back by her hair, and took her mouth with his. His arm pulled her ass in so tight she could feel the hard edges of his belt buckle against her mons, and the way it rubbed against her as he carried her to the desk sent heat slamming through her.

She made the mistake of straining and wriggling, and then he was sweeping his arm across his desk to clear it and laying her out on her back. Before she could sit up he was on her, spinning her around as he buried his mouth against her throat, his teeth dragging over her skin and sending her right out of her skull.

"Fuck." He lifted off her, dropping into his big chair, and sliding her off onto his lap. "Come here."

Rowan got a grip on his shoulders as he situated her legs and then ran his broad hand over her left breast. The rough caress knocked the wind out of her, along with his name. "Sean."

"Shut up." He wound his fingers through her curls and held her, looking all over her face as he put his other hand to her breast again, his palm hard and rhythmic, a beast's paw kneading. "So fucking hot."

Yes, she was. He had her right where he wanted her, straddling his crotch, only her panties and his jeans keeping them apart, and from the length and stiffness of his erection she could think of nowhere else she'd rather be.

"Yeah," he breathed, his eyes closing a little as he rocked his hips into hers. "Like that. Right there." He used a handful of her shirt like a shop rag, dragging it up the damp line of her torso to expose her bra. Then he went at it with his teeth, jerking one edge out of the way so he could get at her, his mouth open and wet and sucking, teeth grazing, making stars burst inside her skull and sending a gush of wetness between her legs.

"Wait." The word barely made it through the vise of her throat, so she tried again. "Sean, wait."

He let her go, the release of the erotic suction making a soft pop. "No. Give me that mouth."

She put her hands against his hot face. "I kiss you, you turn me loose."

"No fucking way." He shoved her hips down on him. "You feel that?"

"Kind of hard to miss." She rested her forehead against his. "I know. Jesus. This is nuts." She sucked in a breath of terrified delight as the ridge of his cock bumped into the folds over her clit. "A kiss for now."

His eyes narrowed, and he shifted under her. "Where you gonna kiss me?"

Rowan's head spun as she saw herself sliding from his lap, opening his pants, and taking him out. Her mouth watered as she imagined gripping the hard shaft and putting her tongue to the bulb of his cockhead. She could feel his hands in her hair, holding her, guiding her as he pushed between her lips, gliding over her tongue as she sucked . . .

He knew what she was thinking. "You like that, don't you?" He dragged her hand down, pressed it over him.

"Oh, honey." She rubbed him, blind with her own lust. "I'd love it."

He pulled her close, whispered in her ear. "You gonna let me kiss you, too?" He licked the rim of her ear. "Because I want it. I want to kiss you and lick you. I'll eat you all night, Cupcake."

She was going to come, right like this, spread-eagled on his lap and shaking with need. And he knew it, because he started moving her back and forth, dragging her across him as his tongue did evil things to her ear, his breath harsh against it as he kept talking.

"I can feel it, all warm and wet for me, aren't you?" He pushed against her, stroking her harder. "Yeah, I'm gonna spread those long legs and hold you down and kiss that sweet little pussy. Can you feel my tongue inside you? Fucking you nice and slow, in and out, until you beg for my cock?"

"Stop," she groaned, but he only laughed and bit her earlobe, then pushed the tip of his tongue in her ear.

Rowan exploded, coming and coming again in waves that wouldn't stop, until she thought she would lose her mind, her body twisting and fighting his hard grip and then shuddering over and over, convulsing from the force of it, and on some level she felt his arms tighten and heard the wrenching sound of his groan as he jerked under her, his hips slamming up once, twice, three times.

"God damn it." He gathered her in and held her, his hands rough but reassuring as he stroked her arms and back. His chest heaved under her as if he couldn't get enough air into his lungs. "What the fuck was that?"

"I haven't a clue," she panted, still fighting for oxygen herself. "I think I'm bleeding from the ears."

"You're not. I already checked." He tucked her head against his neck and sat back, holding her that way as they both cooled down. After a long time, he said, "I haven't come in my pants since I was a kid."

"Me, I usually take mine off." She was too drained to lift her head. "I don't know what that was."

"You need a term?"

She offered up a weak chuckle. "No, I'm good." Slowly she began the process of untangling her limbs from his, until he stopped her. She lifted her head, surprised to see the regret on his face. "Sean, that was the best orgasm I've had in years. Maybe ever. So if you give me shit about it, I'm punching you in the face."

"Right." He lifted her off him and set her on her feet before he surveyed the dark stain covering the crotch of his work pants. "What do I get if I say I didn't mean to be so rough with you?"

"Kicked somewhere it hurts bad." She pulled down her shirt. "I'd better go before I really have to whup your ass."

She'd almost made it to the door when he caught her and turned her.

"I didn't get my kiss." He bent down, touched his mouth to hers, rubbing her lips with his in a sweet, soothing motion. "That was beautiful, watching you come for me."

"That was primitive, animalistic, and fucking scary as hell." She kissed him back with the same soft tenderness. "And beautiful, feeling you come under me."

He rubbed a hand over her curls. "You tired?"

She'd never felt more awake or alive. "Why?"

"I want that kiss." He stepped back and held out his hand. "Stay with me, Rowan."

PART FOUR

Maison

September 29, 2004
Nice, France

The chef tested the fragment emulsion three times, lapping it from the wooden spoon with all the enthusiasm of a Pekingese being fed medication. He set down the implement, closed his eyes, and exhaled slowly before looking up. "It is acceptable for the salmon tonight, I suppose."

"Thank you, Chef." After spending two years learning the hierarchy of the kitchen, over which Renaud Giusti ruled with an ungloved iron fist, Nathan Frame knew better than to smile. "Would you consider having Gisele prepare *tarte à la crème vaudoise* to finish?"

Few junior chefs had the nerve to suggest anything to Giusti, but the invocation of his daughter's name pulled a small, sour smile from the old master's face. "Ah, now I know. Giradet cooked for you when you were in Féchy. No one prepares *saumon sauvage juste tiéde* like the Pope of Crissier."

"No one," Nathan echoed dutifully. His was better, and they both knew it, but to say so would be the same as spitting on the retired chef, widely considered to be the grand master of traditional French cuisine.

Giusti frowned. "I am not sure. There is only so much wild salmon in the case." He glared at Nathan. "You cannot make it with anything else, *Anglais*. It would be a crime against Nature."

"Papa. Nathan." Gisele stepped between her American husband and her French father and planted her hands on her hips. "Will you argue about fish and sauce until the bistro opens?"

"They are men," her mother said from the chopping table, where she was packing split leeks with bouquet garni. "Of course they will."

"What would you have me serve, Marie? Cassoulet and black peasant bread? Hmph." Giusti's black eyes softened as he rumpled her light brown hair with a big, callused hand. "Your husband must learn these things, *ma douce*, if he is to be a true French chef someday."

"Someday?" Her dimples appeared. "Surely it will not take so long to teach him everything you know, Papa."

Giusti grunted. "Once I thought it would be eternity. Now . . ." He shrugged before regarding his son-in-law. "Nathan, you will go to the market to buy more fennel tops for the salmon emulsion." He hesitated. "Also I am thinking Gisele will need more unsalted butter for *les tartes*."

"As you say, Chef."

An hour later Nathan made his way through the crowded outdoor markets along the Cours Saleya. He didn't bother to hurry; the locals and tourists crowding around the striped tents, cafés, and boutiques wouldn't allow it. Coming to the market was an almost daily chore, one Giusti probably enjoyed sticking him with, but Nathan didn't mind. If not for the handwritten signs and the voices chattering in French, he might have stepped through time to one of the turn-of-the-century open-air markets in old New York City.

Nathan had been careful since leaving Italy. He'd moved around for almost two years, assuming and discarding identities as he slowly erased all clues to his past. He'd known when he'd left the Order that his mentors would come after him; he'd been brought to Rome to finish his education and engage in their holy war against the *maledicti*, and he could not be allowed to roam freely with the knowledge he had. They had never anticipated his defection, of course; the Order had raised him from birth to serve them.

The day was warm; too warm for the long-sleeved shirt Nathan wore. He never went out bare armed in public, however. Someday soon he would have to have removed the twin dragon tattoos on his forearms. Whatever ability the double taijitu marked, it had never manifested. Now they were little more than slave brands his former masters could use to identify him.

Even now Nathan wasn't sure why he'd turned his back on the men who had created and raised him to fight for their cause. Trained from birth to think of the Order as his only family, Nathan had felt the fire of conviction. Surrendering himself to his masters' will had not caused him a moment of doubt. He had been convinced he was one of the Brethren up until his final test, when he had been pitted against one of the captive demons so that he would know the reality of their cause.

The Darkyn male had been deliberately weakened, both by starvation and torture, and had offered little resistance. Toward the end he had seemed almost happy to be delivered to his death. But when the time came to make the killing blow, all of the fire and hatred had drained out of Nathan. He found himself standing over the pathetic remains of his opponent, his blade hanging at his side, his eyes locked on the ruin of the once-beautiful face.

The evil one had smiled up at him. "I forgive you, boy. I forgive you."

Nathan had backed out of the cell, suddenly awake as if after a lifetime of sleepwalking, completely horrified. He had been whipped for his cowardice, and sent back to training, where he had been beaten and tormented for his failure. Something changed inside him as he endured the pain and deprivation. He had done everything they asked of him, waiting, watching, and when the chance came, he had slipped silently out of the catacombs and through the city, not knowing where he would go, only that he would die before he returned.

He did not deserve his life, or Gisele, but now they were his. He would never spend another night praying on his knees to a God who permitted things like the Order and the *maledicti* to exist among the innocent. If that damned him to hell, he would gladly burn for it for all eternity.

"Nathan." A heavy hand pounded his shoulder from behind, making Nathan jump, and he turned to see a short, bald man holding a brace of *rascasse* in his hand. "You are early today, good. Jacques just came with a fresh shipment from Lympia. You see?" He shook the scorpion fish in emphasis. "Beautiful, no?"

"Beautiful, yes, Henri." Already he could taste the bouillabaisse he would make with them. "How much?"

The fishmonger beamed. "For you, I make the best of deals. Come, see the monkfish I just put out. They are—" He made a kissing sound.

Before Nathan could reply, someone called out, "Excuse me. Are you American? Excuse me." Nathan looked around until he spotted another man dressed like a tourist waving and walking toward him. The stranger wore a straw hat and carried a hot pink plastic tote filled with even tackier souvenirs.

"Henri, go back to your stall," Nathan said softly as he reached into his back pocket.

The fishmonger scowled. "But *mon ami*—"

"Now, please." He took out the butterfly blade he always carried but kept it concealed in his palm. "I'll be along shortly."

Henri grumbled as he trudged off, leaving Nathan to face Straw Hat alone.

"It's awfully good of you to wait," the man gushed as he wove around a couple of Spaniards before stopping a few feet away. The jacket covering his free hand effectively disguised the gun he had pointed at Nathan's chest, but he made sure Nathan got a good look at it. "I don't meet too many Americans around these parts. Could I ask you to step over here and have a private conversation with me? I could use some advice." He shuffled closer. "And we wouldn't want anyone else to become . . . involved . . . in this conversation."

Four years of his life crumbled before Nathan's eyes, but he didn't bother to put on an act of ignorance. The one thing about himself he had not altered was his face, and the man pretending to be a tourist had been one of his trainers in the catacombs. He was also one of the best of their human hunters. "How did you find me?"

"Your pretty wife's doctor. After her last checkup, he was quite concerned. He sent a consult to Paris." The man moved the jacket to the left. "If you want to know more, you'll walk quietly to the parking lot. We don't want to cause a scene, Mr. *Nathan Frame*." He chuckled. "Such pedestrian names you have been using, Dancer. What do they call you? Nathan?"

"I'm not Dancer anymore, and I'm not going back with you."

"Of course you are, my son." The man smiled broadly. "You forget, you are in France, not America. We control the authorities here." His mouth flattened. "And you belong to us, Dancer."

He'd cut his own throat before he voluntarily went back to the Order or used that name again.

"All right. I don't want any trouble," Nathan lied. He headed for the parking lot. As the man followed him, he looked ahead for some private spot where he could deal with the hunter.

The crowd thinned and then disappeared as Nathan made his way down a short side street between two boutiques. There he saw a mound of empty shipping boxes stacked neatly by the wall, high enough to provide cover. He stopped beside them, gathering himself for the strike.

"If you are thinking you will disarm me, drag me over there, and break my neck," Straw Hat said just behind him, "there is something you should first know."

Nathan turned, kicking away the hunter's weapon before he hauled him behind the boxes and slammed him into the building's brick wall. He flipped the blade open and held it under the man's sagging chin. "What?"

"Gisele will be joining us, too." The hunter smiled. "My

men have just arrived at your father-in-law's restaurant."
He glanced at his watch. "By now they should have her in
custody."

Nathan's blood turned to frost. "She has nothing to do
with this or me. She is an innocent."

"Didn't Gisele tell you the reason she saw the doctor?
No? Ah, perhaps she meant it to be a surprise, for your
wedding anniversary next week." The hunter chuckled.
"Your wife is pregnant, Dancer. Good job."

"You're lying." He had taken every precaution with
Gisele to be sure he didn't impregnate her.

"We retested her blood in our Paris facility, just to be
sure." The hunter grinned. "She's already developing a
lovely and quite unique set of antibodies to share with your
son. If she retains them, we may even breed her again. Not
with you, of course. You will have to—"

Nathan slammed his head into the brick until the man
lost consciousness. Then he ran. He ran as he had never
run, with all his strength, through the markets and the
crowds, knocking over bags of grain and people and bins
of fruit, leaving a wide wake of shouting, furious merchants
and frightened shoppers. He ran beyond thought, beyond
breath, and as he reached Giusti's he hurled himself at the
locked front door, breaking it down.

"Gisele."

He found the old man first, sitting on the floor beside
the freezer chest, a bloody butcher knife still clutched in his
fist. The hunter's men had shot him in the chest six times.

Nathan whipped his head around to see a work-worn
hand, still holding a tied leek, on the floor.

"Marie. Oh, God."

He hurried over to discover his mother-in-law, shot once
through the forehead, staring up at him with wide, lifeless
eyes. Nathan felt bile rise in his throat before he stumbled
away through the kitchen door and blundered over the
body of a man dressed entirely in black. From the look of
his wounds, Renaud must have stabbed him with the butcher's knife several times before he'd died.

"Nathan," his wife screamed.

He saw her at the end of the road, being dragged by one man toward a waiting van. He bent to take the gun from the dead man and went after them.

His wife fought desperately, scratching her attacker's face and kicking him as she shrieked Nathan's name. He reached the van just as the man had shoved her inside. A tray of glass vials fell out of the van's side door, shattering and spilling the blood and tissue in them all over the ground. Nathan felt something burn across the side of his head.

"Get in the van with her," the man behind the wheel snarled, cocking the hammer on the pistol as he adjusted his aim. "Or this time I will blow your br—"

The rest of what he said was lost in a gush of blood. The gun fell from his hand as he tried to pull Nathan's knife from his neck, and then slumped over the wheel. The van began rolling forward as Nathan lunged at the second man.

"You bastard." Nathan knocked him to the ground, driving his knee into his solar plexus before the other man shoved the heel of his hand into his nose. Bone and cartilage crunched, but Nathan stayed on top of him, battering him with his fists over and over, shattering his jaw, his teeth, his eye sockets. Only when the man went limp did he stagger to his feet and turn to get his wife.

The van was halfway down the sloping street, gathering speed as it hurtled out of control, striking the back wall of the restaurant before careening in the opposite direction, directly toward a busy intersection.

"God, no." Nathan ran toward the back of the van, where he could see his wife's pale, blood-streaked face staring out at him. "Gisele, jump out," he shouted. *"Jump!"*

The driver of the tractor-trailer passed by the traffic light and then hit his brakes just as the van entered the intersection from the opposite direction. The squeal of grinding metal shattered the air as the massive vehicle swerved, but the trailer jackknifed, slamming into the van, which crumpled like a cheap tin toy.

Screams and shouts erupted around Nathan, and then the truck's gas tank exploded. Windows all around the square shattered simultaneously as a huge fireball expanded outward, enveloping the truck and the van and several other cars.

"Monsieur," someone cried out, and hands clawed at Nathan. *"Monsieur*, get back!"

He shook off the tearing fingers and ran into the fire, just in time to take the full brunt of the blast as the van's tank exploded.

"He has not spoken?" a strange voice asked in French.

"Not a word since they brought him in," another replied in the same language. "I do not think he will before he dies."

Nathan could open his eyes a little, but as before he saw only a swath of black-and-red-stained gauze in front of them. He knew from other awakenings that bandages covered his head and most of his body. He felt no pain, only an absence of feeling and an inability to move, as if his body were dead and only his mind were alive.

"It has been two weeks since they brought him in," the first voice pointed out. "He may live."

Two weeks, here, like this. Nathan tried to understand it. The last thing he remembered was walking through the market to buy herbs and butter. He'd spoken to Henri, the fishmonger. Then . . . nothing. Nothing but opening his eyes now and then and seeing through the slits of his swollen eyelids the stained bandages.

"He has third-degree burns over most of his body, and an infection we cannot identify has taken hold. It will only be a few hours, I think." The second man sighed. "But he cannot be the one who did this thing, Inspector. He ran into the fire. He did this to himself trying to save them."

"Save them, Doctor?" The cop laughed. "All of the witnesses who saw the accident agreed that no one could have survived that explosion. So why would he run into it, to save people who were already dead?"

An explosion? Dead people? A fragment of Nathan's memory emerged, vague and disjointed, bringing with it terrible sounds and burning light, but no faces. No people.

"I do not believe he murdered the Giustis," the doctor said firmly. "No man who murdered two people could do this to himself trying to save others a few minutes later."

"He was seen running after the van involved in the accident," the inspector said. "We know Giusti's daughter was inside; we were able to identify her remains with her dental records. Perhaps she saw everything and was escaping him. He could have been pursuing her. He may have even caused the accident himself to kill her."

"And then, in a fit of instantaneous remorse, he hurled himself into the explosion?" The doctor made a disgusted sound. "Inspector, you have spent too much time with killers. You suspect everyone, even a man like this poor fool."

"As you say. But when it is over, I want his body autopsied. I want to know exactly who this poor fool is."

Nathan heard the men leave the room, but only distantly, as if his mind had been swaddled in the same numb paralysis as his body. The light glowing beyond his bandages dimmed by slow degrees as he tried to make sense of it all. Gisele was dead; her parents murdered. And he was dying.

His vision blurred and darkened, and Nathan fell away from himself into the void, where there was nothing, no color or sound, no scent or sensation. Later, on some level, he sensed the doctor and the nurses working on him, their frantic efforts to preserve his life. He felt sorry for them, but he didn't resist the darkness. His time was done, and he was ready to go, to be where she was.

Non, mon frère. Two vivid blue lights flared to life in the center of the nothingness, like blazing eyes opened for the very first time. *Tonight you do not die. Tonight, we live.*

Chapter 16

Rowan slept on Meriden's chest as if she'd never made her bed anywhere else. She didn't move except to breathe, although after what they'd done over the last five hours she was entitled. He only resisted the satisfied exhaustion that wanted to drag him off into the dark so he could watch her and think.

He'd never hear or say the word "kiss" without smiling again. And he was going to have that fucking chair bronzed.

Meriden hadn't really expected her to stay, not after the tornado of lust they'd generated between them. She'd been on her feet all night, it was late, and he knew it was asking too much. When she'd taken his hand, he'd almost promised to keep it G-rated and simply sleep with her.

Until he'd guided her into his bedroom, and she'd turned those big, beautiful eyes on him.

Her smile had changed from sleepy to feral. "I get to go first."

She'd gone off on him, peeling away his clothes and running her hands all over him. He knew his size was unsettling to some women, but Rowan felt him up like a greedy kid in the backseat of a car, unable to decide what to touch first. Then she started using her tongue, and dimly recalling that he wasn't squeaky clean for her, he'd muttered something about jumping in the shower.

"Later," she purred as she pushed him back on his bed. "Maybe."

His body clenched as the images kept rolling through his head. He'd held himself back to let her have her fun first, and he'd paid for it. Overtime. By the time she'd stripped him bare he'd had to grab the head rail to keep from ripping off her clothes. Then she'd draped herself over him, licking at his mouth and his neck and his nipples, her body insinuating itself between his thighs, her belly rubbing the straining column of his cock until the head rail began to make ominous cracking sounds.

She'd lifted her head away from his navel to enjoy his expression. "Don't let go, or I'll stop."

"No," he promised her, not knowing if he meant letting go or her stopping.

She made a humming sound as she inched lower, nuzzling him. "You smell good."

He smelled like come, and her, and had to agree through his teeth. Then she cupped him, caressing him with her cheek a few times, her fingers stroking the knot his balls were tying themselves into before she slid her tongue along his shaft in a long, slow, wet glide from root to head.

He'd never been a man to beg. "Kiss it." Shit, he was begging.

She pursed her lips and touched them to the hot, tight skin stretched over his cockhead. "Like that?"

"Put me in your mouth," he told her. "Suck on me."

Her lips parted over the wet, seeping eye and slid down to engulf him, and she sucked lightly, teasing him with little flicks of her tongue until his hips arched off the bed. She moved her head with him, just keeping the tip of his penis in her mouth, and he groaned his frustration.

She released him but kept her lips against him so he felt every word she whispered. "Want a little more, Farm Boy?"

"All of it," he muttered, looking into her glowing eyes. "Give me everything."

She gripped him at the base and then took him in, pushing him deep, sucking harder as she worked her head over his, up and down lower, up and even lower, until he felt the tip of her nose graze his body hair and the hot slick drag of her mouth enveloped him. She held his hips with her hands as she sucked his cock, keeping him from thrusting hard as she kept it slow and deep. He swelled over the soft abrasion of her tongue, and cursed as she scored him gently with the blunt edges of her teeth. It wasn't a kiss, she was eating him up from the inside out, and when he couldn't take another second of it without coming he let go of the head rail and reached for her.

Meriden had fully intended to keep his promises about kissing her, but his dick had other priorities, like getting inside her as fast and deep as it could. He rolled her under him, scooting her up the bed as he wedged himself between her legs and rooted against her.

"You're getting warm," she whispered, smiling as she felt his searching cock bumping into her mound. "Warmer." Slyly she shifted, preventing him from breaching her folds. "Colder."

Meriden reached down between them, seized his penis and pushed her folds apart with the head.

"Very warm." Her eyes narrowed as he found the small niche at her core and squeezed the aching bulb inside it. "Hot." She groaned as he jerked his hips, driving another inch past the muscles and into the tight flutter of her inner tissues. "Oh, hell."

Meriden cradled her head and pressed her face against his shoulder. The need to plow into her until he flooded her sweet little cunt to overflowing was so strong he wasn't sure he could make it pleasurable for her. "Hold on to me, okay?"

"I'm holding, I'm—" She lost the rest as he thrust straight in, as far as he could go, and then dug her fingers into the sides of his arms. *"Sean."*

The viselike restriction of her body, the shock in her

eyes, and the way she said his name settled everything for him. *She hasn't been with anyone, not in a long time.* And if he was an ass for taking pleasure in that discovery, so be it.

She'd chosen him.

Somehow the wildness became entangled with tenderness, and Meriden nestled, relishing the relief of being clasped inside her as much as the reassurance of having her body all to himself.

"Right here, baby." He kissed the top and bottom of the O that her lips formed, and caught her gasp as he worked a fraction deeper. "Don't let go."

Meriden recoiled and pressed back in, making the stroke an almost continuous motion that slid into the second breach of her body and then the third. Penetrating her was as darkly satisfying as feeling her nails bite into him. She was drawing blood by the time he brought her to the edge, but it only stoked him more. When she stiffened under him and went over, he fucked her harder, driving into that quivering clench of slick muscle and convulsing nerves without mercy. The sounds that spilled from her were as beautiful as the astonishment in her eyes as he held back and kept stroking.

Sean made it good for her even as his own pleasure built, past erotic, past anything he'd ever felt. Having sex had never been much more than relieving a need and blowing off his frustrations. Fucking Rowan was like wallowing in pleasure, soaking it up until he felt it pouring out of him in waves of heat and sweat and sensation, raining all over her long, sinewy body, and then he was lost in her, his mind gone, and there was nothing more in the world than his cock and her pussy, and planting himself inside her, giving her all that he was, all he would ever be. . . .

As the morning light crept in to gild her curls, Meriden remembered something she'd done after the last time, when he'd started drifting off. She'd gotten out of bed, he assumed to do the girl thing and clean up, but then she'd come back almost right away. She'd knelt beside the bed, holding his hand. When he'd opened his eye to see why she was on the floor—he had some ideas, but he wasn't sure he could give her anything else to play with for a couple of hours—he caught the glint of something shiny.

"What's that?"

"Nothing." She sounded odd, and when she climbed in next to him she was shaking. "Hold me, will you?"

He'd held her then, but this morning he gently eased her away, smiling a little as she grumbled something and rolled over onto her back. He sat over her, looking at each small, beautifully shaped breast until he had to lean down to brush his mouth over each soft areola. They beaded for him, silently pleading to be sucked, but he drew the covers back and exposed the rest of her, his eyes intent on the dark curly triangle beneath her navel.

He slid around her, moving down until he hung halfway off the end of the bed, and nudged her legs apart until he had enough room to lie between them. Her sex was dark pink and faintly swollen, the black curls still damp from the last time he'd filled her up. He wasn't sure how many times he'd done that, only guessing she was probably too sore now to take him again.

He'd settle for a kiss.

Wherever Rowan was, something strong and warm wrapped around her, holding her there. She could feel cool air trying to get at her, tickling the damp peaks of her breasts, but the warmth spreading up from her hips flushed throughout her torso, tingling across her nerves and tightening in her chest. Whatever had her was doing something wet and wicked down there, a sweet, moist stroking between those sensitive lips and the almost painful throb of her clit.

By the time she opened her eyes she was hot, her breasts swelling and her hands fisting, and she saw the head and shoulders of the man who had his open mouth pressed between her legs. He slid his hands up to cup her breasts and squeeze them, and then she saw that he was watching her, too, his eyes burning like her skin as he laved his tongue up and down. He rubbed her clit as if it were a piece of candy to be licked before sliding down and pressing inside the tender ellipse of her body, extending his tongue in long jabs as he fucked her with it.

He'd started doing this a while ago, she thought, dazed by the force of the surging heat forged by his mouth. He'd been kissing her pussy while she slept.

The erotic knowledge made her moan while his mouth coaxed her out of an unremembered dream and into the rush of sensation. She put her hands over his, helping him massage her breasts as she surrendered to it. As she'd learned last night, with Sean resistance was futile.

Rowan spiraled out of control, and then she was free-falling through some intense, dark cascade of joy framed in bliss. Another man might have pushed her past the point of pleasure and into pain, but God, Sean seemed to sense exactly how much she could take, even after hours and hours of endless, mindless sex.

He kissed her down there as she drifted back to reality, a chaste brush of his lips before his tongue swept out to give her pulsing clit one final caress. That last zing made her curl against him after he crawled up her body and rolled onto his side to hold her against him.

"Trying to kill me?" she asked his collarbone.

"No one dies from a kiss." He sounded smug, and idly caressed her shoulder and arm. "And it was my turn."

She lifted her head. "No second thoughts? No postcoital regrets?"

"Nah," he said, shifting her a little closer. "I don't do the girl thing." He tucked in his chin to have a look at her. "You were something last night. Did you like me?"

Did she *like* him? After her little experiment with her hand mirror, she knew she was in love with him. "You were good."

His eyebrows rose. "Just good?"

"All right," she sighed. "You suck. I totally had to fake it. All nine hundred and seventy-five times." She giggled when his arm around her tightened. "Okay, okay, maybe I enjoyed number nine hundred and seventy-four a little."

He pretended to think. "Was that the time you were screaming my name, or promising to have it tattooed with 'Forever' on your keister?"

"Johnny Depp did that before he broke up with Winona," she warned him. "He had to get the tattoo fixed to say 'Wino Forever.'"

"These are something else." He traced the coiling spiral of the dragon on her forearm. "What made you pick dragons?"

"Something I read in a book once." She stared up at the ceiling. "This thing about dragons being princesses in disguise. I liked it." She eyed his arm. "So what's your excuse?"

He examined the S-shaped red dragon wrapped in a circle of its own tail. "Seemed like a good idea at the time."

"Very decent ink job." She touched the sapphire eyes, which had been rendered so realistically they seemed to glitter. "I've seen this before."

"It's a taijitu."

"God bless you," she teased. "You get it done somewhere local?"

He shook his head. "When I was over in Italy. I knocked around Europe for a couple years after school."

"I'd love to do that." She felt sleepy. "So, you ever think about"—she yawned—"moonlighting as an alarm clock?"

"You said you needed one." He pulled the covers up over her. "It's okay, it's still early. Go back to sleep, baby."

Like a light, she was already out.

"The latest test results are back, Mr. King," the physician told him. "There is no change. It would be best for you to consider making your final preparations."

Gerald King took the chart from the oncologist and studied the lab slips clipped to his chart. The numbers, dismal as they were, were holding. He still had a few more days. "You can go."

"Mr. King—"

He threw the chart at the doctor and roared, "Get out."

The oncologist retreated from the suite, leaving King to fume in solitude. He knew he could not allow the situation to continue longer than a day or two; the painkillers were no longer having any effect and soon his nervous system would begin to fail. Once he fell into the final, inevitable coma he would be as good as dead. At best he had forty-eight hours left to find her.

"Mr. King?" his assistant said. "Ms. Carroll is calling on the private line for you."

King could no longer leave his bed, so he summoned his nurse to wheel the secured phone over to him. After she departed, he answered the call.

"You were supposed to report in hours ago," he told his operative.

"Ms. Carroll will no longer be reporting to you, Mr. King," a man with a deep, rather unnerving voice said.

He frowned. "Genaro? Is that you?"

"Listen carefully."

The man spoke at length about GenHance, their transerum, and the hunt for Kyndred. While King was tempted to interrupt several times, the authority in the man's voice seemed to command his attention. Sometime later he realized that the annoying hum in his ear was a dial tone, and that whoever had called him had hung up.

King frowned. He couldn't remember the entire conversation, but two things came back to him: Nella Hoff was dead, killed in a tragic car accident on her way to work, and there was no longer any need to replace her with another operative. Naturally he wouldn't waste his resources by planting another informant inside GenHance, not when his daughter was coming home.

If she came home.

King dialed another number. "Mr. Meriden," he said as soon as the other man answered. "Have you found my daughter?"

"I have some new leads," the bounty hunter replied. "I'm going out this morning to follow up. The rest you'll get in my report tonight."

"I'm afraid your term of employment is coming to an end more rapidly than I had anticipated. You will deliver Alana to me in forty-eight hours, or your contract will be terminated."

Meriden uttered an ugly laugh. "Then kill me now, King, because I haven't found her."

"Perhaps you need some additional motivation." He picked up the latest surveillance report and scanned through it quickly. "Did you enjoy your evening with Ms. Dietrich? I could make you the last man she ever invites into her bed."

His voice turned to stone. "You leave her out of this."

"Then find Alana, Mr. Meriden," he snapped. "You have two days left, and then Ms. Dietrich dies."

Rowan woke up to find herself alone, and frowned as she sat up and looked around the room. She was back in her apartment and there was no sign of Sean. He hadn't even bothered to leave her a note.

"You don't call, you don't write . . ." she sighed as she got up, limping a little as she went out to the kitchen, where she found a small bag of powdered-sugar-covered doughnuts, a Coke, and a pile of folded clothes. The clothes turned out to be every stitch she had been wearing when she'd gone over to Sean's apartment last night.

"I love this man." She grinned as she tore open the bag and helped herself to one of the minidoughnuts that were among her favorite secret pleasures. "And I think he *is* psychic."

Feeling a little sore from last night's frolicking—and this morning's, she reminded herself—Rowan retreated to the shower, where she stood for a good thirty minutes under a hot spray. It was ridiculous, how good feeling sore felt. She had whisker burns all over her breasts, finger bruises blooming on each hip, and something that felt like a bite mark on her right shoulder. Her limbs weren't stiff, but loose, with that faint, satisfying ache left over from sex.

If she could call what they'd done to each other mere

sex, she thought as she dried off, and saw in the mirror some other marks he'd left on her. She'd bet good money he had a nice set of matching scratches running along either side of his spine, and a couple of nip marks inside his thighs and along the curve of his jaw. It was silly, but for the first time in her life she couldn't remember exactly how many orgasms she'd had. From the stupid smile that seemed to be permanently plastered on her mug, she was sure it was somewhere in the double digits.

Of course, part of it was because she hadn't shifted last night.

Rowan had known it was wrong to pry into his brain, but after their last bout of lovemaking she simply had to know. She'd gotten up to get the hand mirror she carried in her bag and then had come back to Sean, kneeling down and holding his wrist while she looked into the hand mirror and shifted.

Only she hadn't shifted.

For the first time in her life, the dreamveil hadn't fallen over her. Her body had simply refused to shift. She stayed in her own form, not a single muscle popping or bone stretching. And there was only one reason that would happen.

She was Sean Meriden's ideal woman, and he was in love with her. Her, Rowan Dietrich. Not someone else she'd become with the dreamveil.

Tonight, after her shift, she'd have to do something special for her guy to show her appreciation. Maybe throw together a midnight feast for the two of them after closing. Sean might think he was happiest with pizza and beer, but he'd never tasted what she could do with lamb and white beans.

The thought of cooking for Sean made her own belly rumble, but the only fruit she had on hand were some plums, which she devoured in a couple of bites. Seeing that she didn't have time for much else, she made a quick sandwich and carried it downstairs.

Lonzo was already in the kitchen, standing and inspecting her station. He eyed her sandwich with a frown.

"You're the sous-chef in the best French restaurant in the city, and you're eating PB and J?" He sniffed.

"Best PB and BB in the city." Rowan held out one half, which he took and cautiously examined before taking a bite.

"Not bad." He chewed. "What's this BB?"

"Banana-pecan butter," she said, finishing her last bite. "I make it myself. The ground pecans give it more texture."

"I'll have to try it on my wife," he said. "She's a nut for the PB." He handed her an apron before tying on his own. "Kind of sudden, him moving you up like this. I know Danz; he thinks you're ready 'cause I taught you good. Me?" He waffled his hand.

"I didn't poison anyone last night," she felt she had to point out. "It wasn't my idea, Chef. I'd have been happy with helper."

"Lonzo," he corrected. "You're not our *tournant* anymore, Trick."

Rowan was surprised at the welling of affection she felt toward the older man. "Don't give up the search for a new sous-chef. I'm not going to be around much longer." And suddenly her night with Sean didn't seem quite as wonderful and amazing as it had a few minutes ago.

When she left New York, she'd have to leave him, too.

"You know what you can do here?" Lonzo was asking her. "The name you can make for yourself?"

"Yeah, I know. But this"—she gestured around them— "this was never meant for me. Maybe in my next life."

"Dansant ain't gonna like it," he warned.

And there was her other problem. "He knew I'd be moving on someday. Someday's just got here sooner than later."

"Listen, you want to come and bunk at my place for a couple weeks, we got a spare room," Lonzo said awkwardly. "You know. If things get tight or Dansant gives you the business."

She could have kissed him, and nearly did. "I just heard from a friend of mine," she confided. "He's going to help me out. But I appreciate the offer." She winked. "Chef."

It was a little harder for her to be so lighthearted when Dansant arrived at the restaurant that night. He was very late; coming in just as they'd plated the first orders, he came directly to her station to check her prep. She was working skate sautéed in clarified butter, arranging it like a fan with ribbon-shaped scrolls of wilted, sesame-seed-studded spinach and her own fruit-vegetable salsa.

"Another interesting variation," he said, looking over her shoulder. "Vigato at the Apicius in Paris uses green apples and bell peppers in his recipe."

"Vigato uses ketchup and soaks his spinach in vinaigrette." She wiped the edge of the plate with her hand towel to remove some drippings from the transfer of the skate from the pan. "I'm not doing his sherry vinegar reduction, either. Cider vinegar works better, and even when it's reduced it doesn't stomp the taste of the skate."

"It doesn't, Chef," Lonzo said as he passed them carrying a pan of chopped, quivering golden aspic.

Rowan handed the plates she'd finished to the expediter and turned to him. "Can I have a minute with you in your office?"

Dansant checked the line, nodded, and followed her back. As soon as they were alone, she looked at him squarely.

"I am having my chef's table tomorrow night," Dansant said before she could open her mouth. "I would like you to share the cooking and the meal with me and my friends."

He was not going to make this easy at all. "I don't think the line can spare me." Rowan tucked her thumbs in her pockets. "I need to tell you something. I spent last night with Sean. The guy who lives upstairs," she added, since they hadn't met.

His face lost all expression. "Did you."

"It just happened." She forced a smile, which didn't last longer than a few seconds. "Anyway, I'm involved with him now. After what happened between us in the kitchen, I thought I should tell you."

"You could uninvolve yourself," he suggested.

"No point. I heard from a friend who owes me some money," she lied. "He's going to lend me enough to cover what I owe you, and then I'm leaving. I don't know when, exactly, but I'll give you as much notice as I can."

He studied her face. "It does not matter."

"Dansant." She felt frustrated. "I'm sorry. After last night, I know you had some, ah, expectations. It's just you and me . . . we would never work out. This guy, Sean, he's more my type. Don't be pissed, okay?"

He smiled then, a warm and beautiful smile. "I am not angry, Rowan. I am happy for you." He took her hand in his. "You deserve to be loved. If not by me, then by someone who can care for you as I would have."

"Sean's a good guy," she agreed, feeling a little uneasy, "but it's just for now. You know, no big thing. You, on the other hand, are going meet a great girl someday." Suddenly she knew what to do, and encircled his wrist with her fingers.

The dreamveil always changed her into the woman most loved by the person she touched. But occasionally she used it on men who hadn't met that woman yet, and when her body shifted she took on the form of the woman they would love most in the future. It freaked her out a little, and made her question just how random love really was, but at least if Dansant hadn't fallen in love before now, she could give him a preview of who was waiting for him in the future.

She pulled from him, and that was when things went bizarre. She not only got nothing; her body wouldn't change.

"I have met her." He brushed his fingers against her cheek and left.

Rowan's legs buckled, and she groped until she found the edge of the desk and clung to it. Her ability hadn't failed her since the night it had first manifested. She'd been able to shift into any woman who had been most loved by the person she touched. The dreamveil had never failed her once. Now, in the space of a single day, it had failed her twice.

How does someone like me know if any guy really cares? She'd asked Drew that just before they'd said good-bye, that last night in Savannah.

He'd grinned. *That's easy. When he holds your hand, you won't change into Angelina Jolie.*

She hadn't changed into Angelina when she'd touched Sean Meriden last night. She hadn't changed into anyone. She hadn't because she discovered that she was the great love of Meriden's life.

Just as she now knew she was Jean-Marc Dansant's.

Chapter 17

Rowan got through the rest of her shift. Somehow. She spent a lot of time silently arguing with the knowledge that not one but two men were in love with her. Theoretically it was possible; plenty of people fell in love more than once in their lives. What was to prevent two men from taking the fall for her?

Maybe it's stopped working, she thought, and felt a kind of panic she'd never expected. Her ability had caused all kinds of damage to her ego, but it had always been useful, especially in some hairy situations. Finally she threw down her towel, called to Enrique, and pulled him out the back door of the kitchen.

"*Sí*, Mees Trick? I mean, Chef?"

"Stand right there." She positioned him so that his back was to the kitchen and her dim reflection showed in one of the windows. "Give me your hand."

Enrique did, and she pulled on him, and her body began to shift. A few moments later a dusky, gorgeous African-American girl stared back at her from the surface of the window. And lo and behold, she was suddenly the proud owner of a rack that would make a strong man weep.

"Takeisha?" Enrique murmured, his eyes wide.

"You really like me?" she asked him in a low, musical voice. "You should tell me, *amigo*."

"*Sí*, I should." He looked dazed.

Rowan stopped pulling on him, and her body resumed

its normal dimensions. As she shifted back, his expression cleared, along with the memory from his mind of what she had just done—another odd but routine aftereffect of the dreamveil.

"Chef?" He frowned. "You need me haul trash?"

"No, Enrique." She patted his shoulder. "I thought I saw a dead rat out here. It's gone. Go back inside."

She was about to follow him in when she heard a shuffling sound behind her. She turned and saw the homeless kid stepping into the light.

"I know what you are," she said. "I saw what you did."

Rowan swore under her breath. "It's just a magic trick."

The girl shook her head, and then held out her arm, yanking back her sleeve and stepping further into the pool of light. She had an old tattoo of a blue ram on her arm, one that had a faint iridescent glow to it.

"Where did you get that?" she asked the girl.

"I don't know." The sleeve went back down. "I've always had it. There's one on my other arm just like it." She jerked her chin toward Rowan's sleeve. "Like yours."

There was something maddeningly familiar about her voice, Rowan thought, but she was far too young to be Takyn. The only other one of their kind who was younger than Rowan was Judith, and she was twenty. "You can't be a . . ."

"What? What am I?" the girl demanded. "Who made me like this? Why can't I stop it?"

Her anger bewildered Rowan. "Stop what? What's happening to you?"

"Nothing." Two wet streaks cleared a path on either side of her dirty face. "Why can't I be like you are?"

"Do you remember what happened to make you like this?" Eager now, Rowan took hold of her arm. "Where were you raised? Was it a lab? Did you run away? Do you know where it was?"

The girl wrenched away. "There was no lab. I'm not a freak." Disgust filled her expression. "You don't know anything about me." She spun and took off.

Shit, she'd spooked her.

This time Rowan had no intention of letting the kid vanish. She ran after her, moving as silently as she could, avoiding the obstacle-course-style escape route the girl followed. The kid was fast, but she was upset, and she never looked back. That allowed Rowan to follow her up to an abandoned hotel, where the girl went to the boarded-up front door, moving two boards to open a hole. After she climbed in, the boards creaked back into place.

She started to go across the street, and then stopped in her tracks. The old hotel was probably where the girl hid out and slept, and if she went in after her the runaway would no longer consider it safe to stay. If she ran from here, she'd never come back.

Retreating a safe distance from the hotel, Rowan took out her cheap mobile and dialed the number Paracelsus had sent her. It went to voice mail, which meant he wasn't in a place where he could speak to her freely.

She'd have to word the message carefully in the event someone else picked up his phone. "This is Dee from Aphrodite Dry Cleaning. We have two orders ready for immediate pickup. Would you call back at your earliest convenience, sir? Thank you."

She ended the call and headed back to the restaurant, where she found Dansant standing in the alley.

"Hi." She'd taken off at the busiest time of night, she realized. "I had to, um, take a walk. Get some fresh air."

He looked her over. "You're covered in snow."

That she was. She shook out her hair, brushed off her clothes, and smiled. "Better."

He gave her another long look before he went back inside.

The entire line was working furiously to make up for her absence, but Rowan knew better than to babble excuses or try to make apologies when they were in the weeds. She washed her hands and went back to her station, trying not to feel the angry glares at her back as she worked.

It took the better part of an hour to catch up with the

orders, but Dansant took out some gratis appetizers and amuse-bouches to placate the waiting diners. Rowan didn't take another break for the rest of the night, and kept working by finishing the cleanup while the other line cooks ate together and rested.

Lonzo stayed behind to vent his spleen, and Rowan stood silently and took it as her due. When he was finished calling her seven kinds of a lazy broad who didn't know her ass from any sort of depression in the ground, and offered his opinion of her state of mind, her value to the restaurant, and the dismal potential of any future offspring she might produce, he told her to report an hour early the next day to make close, personal acquaintance with the next delivery of squid. Then he let her make her official apology, accepted it against his better judgment, and went home whistling.

Dansant had his turn next. "You did not deserve that."

"Not all of it. Maybe seventy-five percent." She recalled she was speaking to the owner of the restaurant that, according to Lonzo, she might as well have set fire to. "I am sorry that I was so inconsiderate tonight, Chef."

"Why did you leave?" he asked. "Where did you go?"

"I had a run-in with that homeless kid who hangs around the alley." She blew out a breath. "She's in trouble, and I thought I could help. But she rabbited on me, and I went after her."

His eyes narrowed. "You pursued this child in the snow, in the streets, in the middle of the night?"

"It wasn't the middle of the night. It was ten o'clock." Oh, that made all the difference. "I'm fine. Nothing happened."

"You cannot run about the streets by yourself at night," he told her. "As we both well know, it is not safe."

"What are you, my mother?" She didn't know why she was so angry, and tried to clamp down on her temper. "I appreciate the concern, but I can take care of myself, Dansant."

"I disagree."

"I'm not afraid of the streets. I used to live on them,

remember?" She turned her back on him. "Just let it go. I'll clean squid until everyone feels better about me."

"You are like a child." He spun her around, and he wasn't Dansant anymore; he was some dark, furious stranger with rough hands that dragged her up off her toes. "You run about as if all the world were blind to you. They *see* you, Rowan. They see how lovely and young and vulnerable you are, and they know they will never have someone like you. It drives them mad. It makes it easy for them to give in to their urges. When you don't think of these things, when you run off like that, *you* make it easy for them."

"You think I ever had a choice?" There went her temper, right out the window. "When I was a kid, my mother went crazy. One night she just snapped and came after me with a knife. She almost killed me, and then she went and took a bath to wash off the blood, and slit her wrists. My father blamed me, and became a drunk, and I had to . . ." No, she wasn't going to think about that. "I ran away a year after she died. Since then I've been on my own, and no matter what you think, I don't make it easy for anyone. I can't." She swallowed against the break in her voice. "Least of all me."

He brought her face to his and kissed her, hard and fast. By the time she went rigid with shock he had wrenched his mouth from hers.

Dear God. That kiss had lasted all of ten seconds, but in that time he had taken her from furious to aching. All of her nerves were jangled, her ears buzzing, and she had her hands on him. She wanted him, right here, on the floor if need be. And that desire, that soul-shredding wanting, was as strong with him as it had been with Meriden.

Dansant swore in French and set her down. "You've made your choice. I cannot stay."

Without another word he left her there to stand and stare after him, her heart pounding, her hands knotted at her sides.

Rowan knew then why she had become so angry with

him. Why she bitterly resented everything she'd said to him in the office, and every moment since. Dansant was wrong; she hadn't made a choice. No woman would choose this.

For the second time in twenty-four hours, she'd fallen in love.

"Paracelsus?" The counterfeiter squinted through his thick glasses at the business card. "What kind of name is that?"

"One you will not forget, my friend." Taske collected the small stack of plastic cards, folded documents, and a brand-new passport. "Thank you for your excellent work."

"The identity won't hold up under a microscope," the man warned as he accepted an envelope of cash and thumbed through the edges of the bills. "It's only good for public use and to fool the cops. Your girl messes with the FBI or another agency, they'll rip it to shreds." He took another folder from his bag and handed it over. "The originals you gave me. I don't keep 'em or dispose of 'em."

"A wise policy." He held out his gloved hand. "Until we meet again."

"Yeah, hopefully not in the joint." The man shook his hand and left.

Taske placed the keys to the motel room on the table before exiting himself. When he reached his car, which was parked two blocks from the motel, his driver met him at the back passenger door to open it for him.

"There was a call for you, Mr. Taske." He handed him his mobile. "They left a voice mail."

He checked the number on the missed calls list. "Thank you, Findley. Take me back to the hotel, if you would."

As they drove from New Jersey back to New York, Taske listened to the voice mail Rowan had left for him. He was not aware of any other Takyn residing in New York, so her request for him to pick up two "orders" perplexed him. He called her back at once.

"Thanks for getting back to me," Rowan said. "The situation has changed. I've found a kid who may be Takyn. I'm not sure what happened to her, but for the moment she's homeless and pretty desperate."

"How old is this child?" he asked.

"Maybe sixteen. I know, she's too young," she said before he could speak, "but she has the tattoos on her forearms."

"I won't remind you how many people in this country voluntarily have their forearms tattooed." He didn't care for the way her voice sounded. "And she is far too young to be one of us."

"What if there were others after us?" she asked. "They could have started the experiments again somewhere else."

"There is always a remote possibility of that," he conceded, "but what makes you believe this child is Takyn? Did she demonstrate some ability?"

"No," Rowan admitted. "She saw me shift, though, and she didn't freak out. She doesn't seem to know anything about us, but I didn't scare her. She asked me some really strange questions, too. You remember, the kind I used to ask you when we first met online."

"'Who did this to me, where can I find them, how hard is it to kill someone, where can I buy a gun?'" He chuckled. "Yes, my dear, I do remember. But until we can verify that this child is one of us, we must proceed with caution."

"I know where she's squatting, and I think with some backup I can coax her out of there and talk her into coming with us." She hesitated. "If I'm wrong, then we can take her someplace safe, get her the help she needs."

"You have a compassionate heart, Aphrodite."

"When it's not being schizophrenic," she muttered. "How much more time do I have here?"

"I purchased traveling identification for you tonight. Jessa will have something more permanent prepared by the end of the week. I expect you should begin packing up your things tomorrow, and if all goes well we will arrange our rendezvous for the next day."

"So soon." She sounded startled. "Okay. Besides the kid,

there's only one problem left. I haven't a fucking clue what you look like, P."

Taske laughed. "I'm rather hard to miss. Does that phone of yours accept photo images?"

"Too cheap for that."

"Well, then, you should be on the lookout for the tallest man in the immediate vicinity with silver-blond hair, a full beard of the same shade, dark Asian eyes, and a very inconvenient limp which requires him to employ a mahogany cane bearing the head of silver lion."

"Wow. He sounds gorgeous."

He eyed his gloves. "He would gladly trade it all to be a short, dumpy accountant from Cleveland, I assure you." A tingling sensation in the base of his spine made him reach forward and tap on the divider glass. Findley nodded and pulled off to park the limo in front of a busy nightclub. "I must attend to something else now, my dear. Keep your phone at hand, and I will see you soon."

He handed the phone to his driver, gritting his teeth as the tingling sensation intensified to small spikes of pain. He hadn't endured an episode in months, but he hadn't been immersed in so much humanity in years.

"Do you wish me to accompany you, Mr. Taske?" Findley, a veteran of such episodes, watched him carefully.

"Not this time, I think, Findley." A serpent of heat had coiled itself around his spine, but as much as it hurt, it also strengthened him. Only when it began to fade did he know he had arrived too late to take matters in hand. "This should not take too long. Stay with the car."

Taske climbed out, removing his coat and placing it on the seat before he limped forward. The bouncer attending the velvet rope glanced at the car and then Taske's face before coming around to meet him.

"Welcome to Club Soleil, sir," the young man said, ignoring the groans and catcalls from the long line of people waiting along the sidewalk.

"Good evening." An image formed in Taske's mind. "I'm

looking for a friend. Has a young lady in a red-and-silver evening dress arrived recently?"

"Yes, sir. I let her through a few minutes ago."

Taske pressed a hundred-dollar bill in the bouncer's hand, holding on to it briefly. "Call nine-one-one and report an assault in progress. Quickly, my boy."

The bouncer, whose eyes had taken on a glazed look, nodded slowly.

Taske entered the club and wasted no time looking for the woman. He could feel her heartbeat in his head, strong and steady, and used it as a guide. The rest of the club's patrons faded to shades of black and white as he limped through them.

"Where are you?" he muttered, turning his head from side to side. His attention became focused on a series of doors at the back of the place; the club's private rooms.

The pain snarling his spine flared as the heartbeat in his ears increased its rhythm to a frantic pace. It was happening, right now, and it pushed him along until he reached the center door, which was being guarded by a man in a suit.

The suit held up his hand. "You can't come in here, sir."

Taske didn't have time to negotiate, so he delivered a short, brutal blow to the suit's diaphragm, which knocked the air out of his lungs and drove him to his knees. Taske nudged him aside and went in.

The man on top of the girl was well dressed, beautifully groomed, and had paid handsomely to reserve the room for himself and his guests. In it he had raped and killed six women in as many months. He had his hands around the throat of the one he intended to make the seventh.

Taske grabbed him by the back of the collar and lifted him into the air.

"Hey, what—let go of me!" The man struggled, swiping at Taske, who snapped his arm, tossing the man over the table and into the wall beyond. The man fell to the floor and lifted his head, then collapsed.

"It's all right . . . Jessica." Now that he had her name, he bent to help her to her feet. Her pretty red-and-silver dress was torn down the front, and she was rigid with terror, but her attacker had not had enough time to do more. "The police have been notified. They will arrive shortly."

"How . . ." She coughed, pressing a hand to her bruised throat. "How did you know?" she finished in a hoarse whisper.

A question he wished he could answer, he thought as he led her out of the curtained room and off to the back hall where the club's offices were located. There he told her what he told all of them.

"It was not your time." The pain in his back had eased, but it had been so ferocious that he had to look. He stripped off his right glove, and took her hand in his. As soon as he touched her, he saw the bright thread of her life, stretching out far into the future.

No wonder he had been compelled to find her. Her timeline would affect millions of others.

"You will not meet him in places like these. He will find you at a museum. In front of . . . a Picasso." He smiled a little. "His name is Harry, and he is an artist, like you."

"Like me," Jessica repeated softly, her gaze riveted to his face.

"You and Harry will have a good life together." He caught a glimpse of an event further along her timeline, the event that would change all the others connected to it. "As will your daughter and her husband, and their son."

He could tell her that her grandson would someday discover a treatment for a deadly disease that would save millions of lives, but she would never remember it. He could only plant the suggestion deep in her mind that would navigate her life toward the event.

"When your grandson Charlie is ten years old, you should persuade his mother to give him the microscope for Christmas." That was the event that would propel the boy along his destined timeline, the single most important act Jessica would ever perform in her life.

"Charlie. Microscope." She nodded thoughtfully, and

when he released her hand, she blinked. "I'm sorry, mister, what did you say?"

"I must leave you now. When the police arrive, tell them you fought off your attacker." He smiled down at her. "Farewell, Jessica."

Taske took the back exit out of the club, and by the time he limped back to the car, a squad car with flashing lights was parked at the entrance to the nightclub.

Findley stood waiting by the door. "I trust everything went well, sir."

"This time, yes." There had been other episodes when circumstances prevented his interventions, and an important life had been lost. When that happened reality shifted in subtle ways, and Taske's limp would grow a little worse for several weeks as he endured the pain of the loss.

Every person had a meaning and purpose to their lives, but some, like Jessica, had enormous impact on the future. If she had been murdered tonight, her loss—and by extension, the loss of her future grandson—would have altered the course of human history.

As he went to get in, Taske's bare hand touched the upholstered seat back, and the other half of his ability flooded over him. He blocked it as he sat down, took out his phone, and dialed Vulcan's number.

"David White."

"Can you talk, my friend?" Taske winced as two naked and too-familiar bodies appeared writhing on the seat across from him.

A faint buzz came over the line. "I can now."

"We have a minor complication, Drew," he told him, ignoring the litany of obscenities being exchanged by the couple having sex in his car. "Our young friend Rowan believes she has found another member of our extended family."

"That's always good news."

"This new discovery is sixteen years old."

"That's . . . definitely not right," Drew said on a chuckle. "Minimum age for the Takyn is twenty. Rowan knows that."

"So it would seem. Drew, I need you to do some checking on the acquisition of new properties by the Catholic Church within the last twenty years. Look for purchases of large parcels in remote, difficult-to-access areas where there are few roads and no local residents."

All the humor went out of Drew's voice. "You think they've restarted the experiments."

"I think it is a remote possibility." He realized the images he was seeing were because he had forgotten to cover his bare hand, and after tucking the phone between his jaw and shoulder he pulled on his glove. "Let me know what you find out as soon as you can." He ended the call, and then said to his driver, "Would you mind terribly if I ride in the front with you, Findley?"

"Not at all, sir." Once Taske had moved to the front seat and they were back on their way, Findley asked, "Is something wrong, Mr. Taske?"

"It seems our gardener has been making use of the car for personal encounters with his amour. Most energetic use." He sighed. "A deserted island in the South Pacific becomes more attractive by the day, Findley. What do you think? Should we relocate?"

"The fishing would probably be wonderful, sir," Findley said, "but I can't imagine you living in a grass hut."

"Agreed." And now he would have to have a word with the damned gardener about his work ethic and poor choice of spots for his romantic rendezvous. "We'll have to be content with whatever the future may bring for me and the Takyn."

The driver gave him a quick glance. "Do the others know, sir?"

"That I can sometimes envision the future as well as the past?" He shook his head. "The temptation to use me as an oracle would be too great." He sighed. "Although I must say, you've adapted to my eccentricities rather well."

"You saved my life, sir," Findley reminded him. "If not for you, I would have been blown to bits along with that mob boss who hired me from the car service in Chicago. That's all I ever needed to know."

Taske had never looked along his driver's timeline, but after that particular intervention he had glimpsed it stretching steadily alongside his own for many years to come. It was the reason he had confided in his driver so freely. "I appreciate that, Findley. And if you have time tomorrow, please do me a favor." He glanced at the rearview mirror. "Arrange for a new car."

Chapter 18

While Rowan waited for Sean to get home, she went into the bathroom, faced the mirror, and rehearsed everything she was going to say to him. She couldn't stay, but she wouldn't vanish from his life without giving him some sort of explanation; he deserved better than that. She also knew it had to be short, sweet, and convince him to forget about her.

She stared into her own eyes. "I'm married, and I'm going back to my husband." That was a good one, but she didn't wear a ring, and last night he had to know it had been a long time since she'd gotten busy with anyone.

Rowan tried again. "I've got this disease and in a few weeks I'll be dead, so I'm going into the hospital." That didn't even work on soap operas. "I've met someone else and I'm moving in with him." That made her into an instant slut; effective but not to her taste. "I've fallen in love with Dansant." At least that was half of the truth.

Despair settled over her as she braced her hands against the edge of the sink. No matter what kind of lie or truth she thought would work, she wasn't going to be able to say it, not to his face. It was too hard. She'd have to leave D'Anges today, find the kid, and hunker down somewhere else until it was time to move.

A clean break, no calls, no face time. There was only one way to do that.

Back in her apartment, Rowan grabbed a pen and

some notepaper, sat down at the dinette, and began writing.

Hey,

Sorry I won't be around to tell you this in person, but I'm leaving. I messed up last night and got into it with Dansant, and now I think I'm in love with both of you.

Rowan gnawed at the end of the pen. She should cross out *I think*; she knew she was in love with both of them. *Jesus, just get on with it.*

I don't want to hurt either of you, and I can't pick. I don't think you guys are up for a ménage, either. So I'm taking off with a friend. I'm sorry, Farm Boy. Sell my bike when it's fixed and use the money to cover the repair bills. Take care and have a good life.

Love,

Cupcake

She read it over three times, resisting the urge to tear it into a thousand pieces. It sounded stupid and wimpy and utterly inadequate, but it would have to do. She folded it and walked out to stick it under his door, then swore, stuck the note between her teeth, reached up over his door frame, and felt around until her fingers found the spare key.

She wouldn't take anything important, she thought as she let herself in. Just something small that he wouldn't miss; something she could have to remember him on all the lonely nights to come. Maybe one of his flannel shirts, one he hadn't washed yet that still smelled of him. Then she'd go downstairs and steal one of Dansant's jackets so that she'd have that, too.

I keep falling in love, people are going to think I'm a cross-dresser.

Rowan went to his bedroom, sat on the bed, and drew the tangled sheets up to her face. His scent was all over them, just as hers was. They smelled good together, she thought, and then she felt the tears coming on and jumped off the bed. She couldn't sit in here crying for what would never be. She had to pack, and she had to get the hell out before he came home.

She'd seen one of his shirts hanging on the back of the chair by his desk, and after carefully placing the note on his pillow, she went out to retrieve it. As she put it on over her own shirt, she noticed a photo sitting on his desk beside a file folder. It was the picture of a little girl with blond hair and blue eyes.

Rowan's hand shook as she picked up the photo, holding it the same way she might a grenade. She turned it over to check for a date mark, and saw the faintest series of marks along the edge. The photo had been cropped, so only the bottom half of the numbers showed, but Rowan already knew what they were.

11-7-1997.

Slowly she opened the file folder, and read the top page, a missing persons report filed in 2008 for a runaway teenager named Alana King. She was reported as being sixteen years old. As soon as she saw the girl's age, she picked up the file and began flipping through it, reading everything: the medical records, the police reports, the witness statements. Alana King had been undergoing psychiatric treatment. She'd also had several elective surgeries.

"You sick bastard," Rowan whispered, throwing the file down on the desk as if it were covered with maggots.

Meriden had told her he moonlighted as a bounty hunter. The old man must have hired him to look for Alana. *He doesn't know*, Rowan thought. *If he did he would never have taken the job.*

She saw the blinking light on his phone, and picked it up to access his voice mail.

"Mr. Meriden," a wheezing, querulous voice said. "I trust by now you are close to locating Alana. I thought I would remind you of the stakes involved. If you are entertaining some notion of going to the police, you should know that I am keeping Ms. Dietrich under constant surveillance. Deliver Alana to me by tomorrow morning, or I will have your lady friend killed before I deal with you."

Rowan switched off the phone. She had always known

there would be consequences for what she had done eleven years ago. She just never imagined he would do this. And now she had to finish it.

She switched on the phone and dialed 411.

"What city and state?" the automated voice asked her.

"Manhattan, New York." Rowan closed her eyes. "Gerald King, three-seven-one Riverside Drive."

"One moment, please." A moment later the automated voice recited a number, and offered to dial it for her for a small charge.

Rowan hung up and dialed it herself.

The voice that answered was female, pleasant but professional. "King residence, Selah Baker speaking."

"Ms. Baker, I have a message for Gerald King. Listen carefully." Rowan told her everything she needed to know, and hung up before the woman could reply. Then she called Paracelsus's number and left a modified version of the same message without giving him names or details.

"Don't try to come after me," she told her friend. "The old man's place is like a military stockade. His policy is to shoot first and ask questions later." She hesitated, and then added, "It's time I faced him. I guess I always knew I would in the end. So let me do this by myself, okay? People I love are going to die if I don't."

Outside the open door of Sean's apartment, the stairs creaked. Rowan went over to the door, expecting to see him climbing up, but no one was there. She did hear the back kitchen door, and wondered if he'd been standing outside, listening to her give the message to Ms. Baker.

He wouldn't have left if he had, she thought as she went to her apartment.

She ignored the bag she had been packing and instead took all the cash she had and stuffed it into her pocket. By the time she walked downstairs and out to the end of the alley, the cab she'd called for was waiting for her.

"Where to, hon?" the cabbie asked her.

The old man had waited all this time; he could go another couple of hours. Before she faced him, she would go and see the sisters, the only real family she'd ever had. "Riverpark Cemetery."

The long ride across the city took less time than she expected. She paid the cabbie, asked him to wait, and bribed him with a twenty to overcome his reluctance to keep the meter running. Then she walked into the little cemetery, past the modest headstones and plaques to a quiet spot back in the corner.

The headstone was, like everything in the sisters' lives, shared between the two of them. Rowan crouched down to trace the letters of Annette's name, and then Deborah's, which were wreathed by flowers. She'd paid the stone company to chisel in the extra line on the stone: *Beloved mother and aunt of Rowan.*

"I know last time I was here I said I wouldn't be back," she told the stone as she brushed a couple of dead leaves from the edge. "But shit—" She paused, imagining Deborah's frown. "I mean, stuff, happens."

She sat down beside the stone and leaned against it, looking out at the other graves. "I did pretty good after I left. I made friends, helped take care of some other people. Fell for the wrong guy, of course, but even that was okay. I didn't think it would happen for me, you know? And now, believe it or not, I'm in love again. You were right, Deborah. There was someone out there for me. Just turned out to be two of them."

She reached down and rested her hand against the grass. "I wanted you to know that I was happy, like you wanted me to be. I'm going to stop running now. It's time. If things don't go okay, well, then I'll be seeing you sooner than later. That's why I'm not going to say good-bye."

A bird flew down to perch on the headstone, cocking its head to stare at her. It chirped twice.

Rowan smiled. "Don't try to talk me out of it, either, Mom."

The bird flew off as she got to her feet, gave the headstone a final touch, and took out her phone to make one final call.

"Skylight Farm; this is Annabelle," Jessa answered.

"Annabelle?" Rowan laughed. "You have got to be kidding me."

"Di, my God, where are you? Are you all right? We've been so worried." She took a sharp breath. "I'm sorry, Di— I mean, Rowan. I'm all hormones this month."

"Honestly, I liked it better when we were Di and Jez." She didn't want to do this, but she couldn't go, not until she cleared her conscience. "Listen, I need to tell you something important."

"Paracelsus said he was getting you out of the city," Jessa said. "You can come to the farm now. Wait 'til you get here."

"This can't wait." She tightened her grip on the phone. "Matthias had me infiltrate the Takyn group so we could identify the members. It's the reason I pretended to be your friend. To make you trust me enough to bring me into the group and start gathering information about you and all the others. I used you, Jessa."

"Oh." She was silent for a moment. "He didn't tell me that."

"I stopped after a while—you remember, that night in the chat room when we started talking about our families." Aka the worst and best night of her life. "I didn't lie when I told you about my mother, and how she tried to kill me before she committed suicide."

Jessa made a soft sound. "Rowan, it wasn't your fault. You were just a little girl, and she was a very sick woman who didn't understand what we are."

"I know." Rowan smiled sadly. "Even though I was still gathering info, well, that was the night I stopped pretending to be your friend and became the real thing." She bit her lip. "Jessa, what happened after we took you from Atlanta . . . I thought I was in love with Matthias. That's why I used my ability on him, and I turned into you. And then when I saw you for the first time, and you were everything he wanted, the woman I knew he would love . . ." she sighed. "That's why I was so hateful to you in Savannah, and why I didn't tell you who I was. I know I'm a liar and a bitch and I used you, but can you forgive me for all of that?"

Jessa's voice came over the line like soft, sweet music. "Rowan, you're my best friend. I love you, honey. I'd forgive you anything."

"Thank you." She released a slow, shaky breath. "I've got to go and take care of some old business. If I don't get a chance to see you again, I just wanted you to know that I love you, and I'm happy for you and Matt. And please, God, make him change your name to something besides Annabelle."

"Rowan—"

She switched off the phone and pocketed it before walking back to the cab. The peace she felt settled over her, as warm as the sun, as tough as armour. She was ready.

"That was quick," the driver said. "Where you wanna go now?"

She didn't want to go, but she had to. "Riverside and a Hundred and ninth," she told him. "The King estate."

Meriden opened his eyes shortly before dawn and found himself staring at the Bitch Madonna. "Hello, sweetheart. Miss me?"

The painting glared at him, probably because he was completely naked. He went to the front closet, took out the duffel bag he kept there, and pulled out some clothes. No doubt Dansant had left him a note on the message board in the kitchen—the asshole always did whenever he came to the apartment—but when Meriden went to check it he found it empty.

There was, however, shattered glass and splashes of red wine all over the kitchen floor.

"Looks like someone had a party last night." He didn't have time to worry about whatever had pissed off Dansant; he had to track down Alana King. If he didn't find her by that afternoon, he'd stop looking and focus on getting Rowan out of harm's way. He wasn't sure yet how he'd smuggle her out without tipping off King's surveillance team, but whether he had to stuff her in a garbage bag or roll her up in a carpet, he was getting her out of the city.

Sean spent the day following up with every witness who had seen Alana King, but no one had remembered any new information. His canvass of the surrounding area also turned up nothing. He spent hours showing the age-progressed photo of Alana to everyone who worked around the coffee shop where she had been spotted, and it was then that he struck gold.

"Yeah, I know this kid," the owner of a small electronics store said. "She don't come out during the day much, but at night I seen her plenty. Skittish as hell. She flops over at that hotel they boarded up. You know, the one with the family that's suing each other over ownership. Greedy bastards."

Sean wasn't convinced. "If she's so skittish, how did you get close enough to see her face?"

The shopkeeper smiled and hefted a complicated-looking pair of goggles. "Night vision lenses. I use them when I do nighttime shoots. Keeps me from running into trouble in dark alleys."

He wondered just what sort of photos the man was shooting. "Did you happen to take any pictures of her?"

The man shook his head. "I post mine online for my, ah, Web site. You can't put up any of people unless you get a signed release from them." He winked. "Unless you blur their faces."

Sean would have gone to the hotel to check out the man's claim, but he was running out of daylight. He drove instead to the restaurant, and called his answering service on the way to check in.

"Hey, Sean," Rita greeted him happily. "How's it going? You got the best messages tonight. We're all talking about them."

"They're that good, huh?" He slowed down to stop at a red light. "So read them to me."

"First one's from Mr. Dansant, and it's a scorcha. He made me write it all down, exactly like he said. He sounded really pissed off."

Sean grinned. "So what did he say?"

"The message is, 'I know you slept with Rowan, and now she believes that she is in love with you. If you agree, tonight I will tell her everything, Miami.' Oh, wait. Diane wrote that wrong. It's '*mon ami.*'" Rita sighed. "I know I'm not supposed to ask, Sean, but are you in love with this girl, or is this just a fling?"

He spoke without thinking. "I'm in love."

"Oh, jeez, that's so romantic." Rita sounded as if she was on the verge of an orgasm. "You are the best guy in the city, I swear to God. Is she gorgeous? Are you buying her a ring? Can we meet her? Speaking of which, when are we going to meet you?"

"Let's hold off on planning the wedding until I get the rest of my messages," he told her drily. "What's next?"

"This one said her name was Taire," Rita said, her voice a little more stern. She spelled the name out. "You say it like it's short for Theresa or something. Anyway, she wants to meet you at the restaurant. She says she knows where the girl you're looking for is. I hope you're not keeping a honey on the side, Sean. Not a good idea if you want things to work out with Rowan, you know?"

"She's just business." Although he couldn't recall speaking to anyone named Taire since he'd taken the King case. "Anything else?"

"Someone called from your home number, but they hung up without saying anything. We just logged the call-in number a couple of hours ago." Rita sounded disappointed. "Maybe it was Rowan." She caught her breath. "You don't think she knows about you meeting this girl Taire, do you?"

"I don't know." He pulled into the alley behind the restaurant. "I've got to go, Rita. Hold my calls for today."

"What if Mr. Dansant calls again?"

He grunted. "Tell him I said he can fuck off."

Rita chuckled. "Sean, I could get like so fired for saying that."

"All right. Tell him Rowan is my business now." He saw a young girl waiting by the back door of the restaurant.

"Talk to you later, sweetheart." He climbed out of the car, and when he drew close to the girl he saw she matched the description Rowan had given him of the homeless girl. "Is your name Taire?"

She nodded. "You're the guy who lives upstairs, right?"

"Yeah. How did you get my number?"

"A girl gave me this." She produced one of his business cards. "She said you're looking for Alana King."

"You know where she is?"

"No, but that girl who works here, Rowan, she knows," Taire said. "She was just in your apartment for a while before she left." She glanced at the windows. "I saw her up there."

Sean was tempted to run upstairs, but he had to find Rowan and get her stashed someplace safe. "Which way did she go?"

She shrugged. "She probably went down to this place where she goes by the river."

"What's the address?"

"I don't know, but she walks down there a lot," Taire said. "I followed her a couple times." She gave his car a hopeful look. "If you drive I can show you where."

"All right." He went to the car and unlocked the passenger door. "Get in."

As he drove toward the river, Sean glanced at the girl, who had flipped down the visor to look in the mirror while she brushed out her tangled curls and fluffed her bangs. "You're sure Rowan walked toward the river?"

Taire nodded as she searched in her bag and retrieved a lipstick. "She probably went to meet Alana. They're friends, you know."

"Are they?" Sean recognized the lipstick; it was one Rowan left on the shelf in the bathroom they shared. The brush belonged to her, too. "How did Rowan become friends with someone like Alana King?"

"She used to live in her house." She pouted at the mirror before turning and smiling at him. "Do you think this is too red for me?"

"It makes you look very grown-up." Sean recalled the age progression he'd done on Alana King's childish face. Taire bore a faint resemblance to what Alana would have looked like as a teenager, but there was something off about her features. Her nose was a fraction too short, and her eyes weren't the exact same shape. "Do you know Alana King?"

"No, but I've seen pictures of her." She smoothed back her curls, revealing a long, faint scar running just along the curve of her jawline. "She was the most beautiful woman in the world."

He saw the dark roots at the base of her blond hair that she was trying to disguise by fluffing it. "Was she."

Taire nodded. "She was perfect. I mean, she is."

"Who showed you the pictures?" he asked carefully.

She sighed as she tucked away the lipstick. "Father did. He wanted me to grow up to be just like her. That's why he had them dye my hair blond, and do all the operations. My face and my body, they weren't good enough." She turned to him. "Do you know Rowan doesn't even need operations? She can just change into Alana anytime she wants."

The girl was obviously unbalanced, and Sean's mind raced as he tried to decide what next to do. "Taire, maybe I should take you back to the restaurant. You could wait there while I find Rowan."

"She loves you," Taire said, sounding forlorn. "That's why I need you. To make her do it for Father."

Sean felt something slam him back into the driver's seat, an unseen force that held him pinned even as it took over controlling the wheel and the accelerator. "What are you doing?" he said, trying to free himself.

She turned to look through the windshield. "I'm going home."

Chapter 19

Rowan heard the security camera swiveling on its base as she walked up to the side door. As she stood waiting, she noted three others performing sweeps of the side street, the river, and traffic passing by. She knew Gerald King's elaborate security system was even now zooming in to snap pictures of her hands, her face, and her clothes.

Some things never changed.

A thin, older man dressed in a dark suit opened the door a moment later. "Welcome, miss," he said as he stepped back.

She walked past him into the long hall. The air inside was warmer but smelled sterile, as if she'd just stepped into a void. Hepa-filters in every duct, she guessed, along with electronic dust-zappers and God only knew what else. A speck of dirt wouldn't survive long within these walls.

"May I take your jacket?" the butler was asking.

"No."

"As you wish. Mr. King is in the master suite." He gestured toward the hall to the right. When she didn't move, he added, "He's expecting you, miss."

"Thanks." She shoved her hands in her pockets and strode down the hall, which ended at the double steel doors of a private lift. That took her up five flights to the top floor, where she stepped out into one of the most beautiful rooms in Manhattan.

The antiques dated back to the turn of the century, but

the art hanging on the polished cherry wall panels was much older. She eyed the brooding masterful Renoir hung between a complicated da Vinci sketch and a serene Raphael Madonna before walking across priceless Syrian rugs to the open arch leading into the next chamber.

With all the pricey, impressive stuff displayed in the receiving room, the master suite seemed almost bare. A plain four-poster bed stood against one wall, and a complicated computer system neatly arranged on an extended black worktable took up most of another. There were no chairs, tables, or other furnishings; the only other objects in the room were various bits of portable medical equipment crowded against both sides of the bed.

The old man lay under the plain white linens, his balding head and thin face the color of ash. A few tufts of white hair stuck out over his ears, and the white bristles of an uneven beard tried to cover his lantern jaw and the lower half of his hollowed cheeks. Although his labored breathing rasped audibly, his chest barely moved. Only his eyes, two little espresso beans floating in bloodshot whites, showed any signs of real life.

Rowan walked up to the end of the bed but didn't touch it. "I'm here, old man."

"So you are." The corners of his mouth tried to dig into his jowls. "I never thought I would see you again."

"I thought you'd be dead by now." She studied the equipment keeping him alive. "Maybe if I hang around for dinner."

"I regret that I've disappointed you." He lifted a hand with effort, and gestured toward the heart monitor. "As you've guessed, I don't have much time left. It's an aggressive form of brain cancer, if you are interested."

"I'm not." She shoved her hands in her pockets. "What do you want?"

"My dear." His smile was a ghastly thing, a skull's grin. "What have I always wanted? Only your happiness, and my own."

She produced the photograph she'd taken from Sean's

apartment. "You didn't waste any time in looking for me, or in replacing me."

"No one could ever take your place in my heart," he countered. "You know that."

Nothing he said would move her. "I'm sure you got my phone message, but in case I wasn't clear enough, here's the deal. You call your guns off Sean Meriden, and I'll do whatever you want."

"That's a very generous offer." He inspected her face. "Seeing as you don't know what I want."

"Oh, I know, old man." She would have all the time in the world to puke over it later, when he was in the ground. "But I'm not doing it until I know that Sean is safe."

The old man pushed aside the linens and rose from the bed. The difficulty of the task seemed beyond him, and his face blanched as he placed his feet on the floor. He rested for a minute before straightening, and held on to the bedpost while he gasped in air.

Rowan didn't move a muscle. If he dropped dead on her now, she'd ring down for champagne.

"As you've surmised, I stopped searching for you several years ago," Gerald told her as he shuffled around the end of the bed. "I had resigned myself to the situation and, with some alternative arrangements, made the best of it."

Rowan wanted to hit him. "I know all about your 'alternative arrangements.' How could you do all that to another kid? She could never be what you wanted, and you knew it."

"I had hoped she would prove a reasonable substitute. Besides," he chided, "it wasn't as if she had any sort of future. Her birth mother abandoned the girl a few hours after her birth. She would have spent her childhood in foster care. I gave her the life children only dream of having."

"While you hacked up her face and tried to make her into a dead woman." Now she *was* going to puke. "If you found someone else to play Alana, why did you come after me?"

"I discovered—much to my consternation—that while

some things can be altered, others cannot." He propped himself against the end of the bed. "Such as the cancer my physician discovered growing in my brain. It was only after I was diagnosed as terminally ill that I realized what a mistake I had made by giving up the search for you."

"You thought I'd come back here and hold your hand? Stay with you to the end? Are you out of your fucking mind?"

"I see your language has suffered immensely since leaving my care." He sighed. "The fact of the matter is that I did not appreciate the other gifts you possess. There is no one like you, my dear, and there never will be again."

The sick smell rolling off him—a stomach-twisting blend of chemicals and rot—didn't make her step back. The greed in his eyes did. "Where is the kid?"

"I haven't the slightest notion." His upper lip curled back from teeth pasty with plaque. "She doesn't matter anymore. You're home again, my princess. You can give me what I want and need."

Princess. If he touched her, she was going to scream, and she wasn't sure she would ever stop. "I want to hear you make the calls to pull your men off Sean. Now."

He nodded. "Of course I will. Just as soon as the nurse arrives and begins the procedure."

She glanced over her shoulder. "What are you talking about? What procedure?"

"A very simple blood transfusion," he told her. "It shouldn't take long. Thirty minutes or so."

Rowan looked at the medical equipment again, and saw the two long tubes that hadn't yet been used, and the tray of needles, swabs, and tape. "You want my blood?"

"I want to live," he corrected, "and your blood is the only thing that can save me now."

Drew kept his footsteps light as he passed the novelist's room, but before he could reach his own the door opened and a head appeared.

"Mr. White." Brian Cantwell stepped out into the hall, his arm filled with a thick stack of pages. "I thought that might be you. Do you have a minute?"

"I really need to get back to work." Drew silently cursed himself for ever speaking to the would-be author in the first place. "My thesis isn't going to write itself."

"You may find this of great value to your own writing," Cantwell said. "I've just discovered the most marvelous blog about writing. You'll never guess what the title is."

" 'Words R Us'?"

"Paperback Writer," the other man said, beaming. "Exactly like the Beatles' song. I've always considered that my personal anthem, you know. I think it's an omen, Mr. White."

"It probably is," Drew said. Now he'd have the damn song stuck in his head all night. "I'll look it up when I have a chance."

"Be sure to leave a comment on one of the giveaway posts when you do." Cantwell held up a paperback book with the naked, wet torso of a man on the cover. "I did and I won a free copy of her latest novel. She even signed it for me."

Drew smiled, nodded, and began backing away toward his door.

"And do come by whenever you take your next writing break," the novelist called after him. "You can read the first draft of chapter thirty-seven. The Orcs have just surrounded my paladin and his band of elven warriors."

"Sounds amazing." He was almost there.

"They have a spell battle, and accidentally transform the Orcs into dragons—"

"Okay." Drew unlocked his door and darted inside, leaning back against it with a sigh. "Next time, I swear, I'm posing as an illiterate migrant worker."

He chuckled at his own joke as he went over to the computer and booted it up. There were several messages from Jessa and Matthias, no doubt with details on Rowan's identity makeover and relocation. Another e-mail caught his eye; it was from Paracelsus. The e-mail itself contained a terse suggestion he play the lottery immediately.

He took out his mobile and muttered as he saw ten voice mail messages from Paracelsus waiting. He didn't bother to listen to them but called his friend immediately.

"It's Aphrodite," Paracelsus said. "She's decided to go home and give herself over to her demons."

Drew knew a little about Rowan's background. As a kid she'd run away from a wealthy, abusive father, and although she'd never gone into details, she'd always made it clear that she would rather kill herself than see him again. "Maybe she needs to do this."

"Do you know what he did to her?"

"Not exactly."

"He forced her to become the image of his dead wife," Paracelsus said. "The same religious fanatic of a wife who thought Aphrodite was possessed by a demon, and who tried to kill her when she was nine years old."

Drew closed his eyes briefly. "Why is she doing this?"

"Her father has made some very effective threats against Rowan's lover and her friends, which he is fully capable of carrying out." The other man sighed. "She never gave me her father's name, so she could be anywhere. I had hoped she had told you something."

"I know she grew up in New York, but we've never used real names, either." Drew thought for a minute. "Jezebel might know." He logged onto his system and tried to IM Jessa Bellamy, who fortunately was also online. "I've got her. Hold on." Quickly he typed out the situation and asked if she knew who Rowan's father could be.

J: *She never told me his name, but once she mentioned that she had lived in a mansion. A very old one, in Manhattan I think. She said there were only two of them left in the city.*

There are more than two mansions in New York, Drew typed back.

J: *There was something else about it. Now I remember.*

Freestanding. Her father's home is one of only two freestanding privately owned mansions left in Manhattan.

Drew sent her his thanks and promised to keep her updated before he logged off from the session. Over the phone, he related what Jessa had told him.

"I know both of them," Paracelsus said. "One is being converted into a hotel. That leaves the King mansion. Rowan's adoptive father must be Gerald King."

Drew frowned. "Didn't Gerald King die a few years ago?"

"Evidently not. I am going over there, but if it is as fortified as Rowan claimed, I will need some technical support."

Drew was already opening the highly illegal program he used to hack into other systems. "Consider me your personal assistant."

Taire guided the car into the garage. Driving it—and raising the garage door—had forced her to break the rules, but now that Rowan was here, Father would understand.

"I'm going to ease up on you and let you out," she told Sean Meriden. "You have to go upstairs with me. If you try to run away, I'll squeeze you harder," she warned. "I can break all the bones in your body if I want. All I have to do is think it."

"I know you can," he gasped. "But you don't have to do this to me. I promise, I won't try to hurt you. Let me go."

"I can't. Maybe after I talk to her and explain things. I don't know." Taire pushed open the driver's-side door with a flick of her thoughts and then pulled back some of the force she had wrapped around Sean.

Some of her father's men came out into the garage with guns in their hands, but Taire made the bullets fall down to the floor and pushed the men aside like rag dolls. She had Sean walk in back of her as she went in, and after knocking out six more guards she led him to the elevator.

"This is my house," she explained as the lift took them to the top floor. "I grew up here."

"You're Gerald King's daughter?"

She shook her head. "I don't have any parents. I just call him Father because he said to when we're around other people. When we're alone I call him Gerald, just like she did." She watched the numbers light up: 2, 3, 4, 5. "I hope he's home. Sometimes Father goes on business trips."

"Taire, you don't have to do this."

She frowned at him. "I told you, this is my house. I live here. I don't have anyplace else. Father is all I've got."

"Then why were you living on the streets?" he asked as she made him walk out into the hall.

"I made a mistake, and Father got angry. He said I had to leave. Then I hurt one of his men and I ruined his car. I couldn't come back until I fixed things." She guided Sean toward her father's suite. "All he ever wanted was to see Alana again."

"Taire, is Rowan his daughter? Is Rowan Alana King?"

She stared at him in surprise. "No, of course she's not. Rowan's like me. She was just the first. When she went away, Father got me to take her place."

Taire stopped outside the doors to her father's suite. She had never entered his rooms without an escort, and for the first time since she'd left home, she felt uncertain.

She gnawed at her bottom lip. "Maybe I should knock."

"Let me go in," Sean suggested.

"That would be stupid. Father has lots of guns. He would just shoot you." After politely knocking on the door, she opened it and crept inside, pulling Sean along after her.

The nurse who came out of Father's bedroom saw Taire and dropped the tray she was carrying. "Who are you? How did you get in here?"

Taire was confused, too. "What are you doing in my father's room?"

"Mr. King is very ill," the nurse said. "I'm sorry, but he can't have any visitors now. You'll have to go."

"Rowan?" Sean shouted.

"In here," Rowan called from the bedroom.

"Stop yelling." Taire opened the closet door on the other side of the room and pushed the nurse across the floor into it. She slammed the door shut and fixed the knob so the woman pounding on the inside couldn't get out. "I can't believe Father is sick." She dragged Sean with her into the bedroom.

Rowan sat in a chair beside the bed. Father, who was in the bed, looked thin and ashen and didn't move. Taire forgot about everything as she rushed to his side and took his frail hand in hers. He looked as if he'd aged fifty years since she'd run away.

"Father? What's wrong with you?" When he didn't answer, she stared at Rowan. "What did you do to him?"

"He was like this when I got here." She glanced at Sean before she reached down and pulled out a needle port that had been taped to the inside of her arm.

Gerald King opened his eyes and looked at Taire. "Why are you here?"

"I found Alana for you, Father." She looked over at Rowan. "You have to take his hand now and change for him. Do it."

"I'm not Alana, kid, and neither are you. My mother's been dead for a long time." She stood up and turned to Sean. "We need to get out of here."

Gerald grabbed Taire's arm suddenly, and dragged her onto the bed. "You're not leaving me to die," he told Rowan. "Give me the transfusion."

"My blood won't save you, old man," Rowan said. "Nothing will."

"Father, please, don't get mad," Taire pleaded, at the same time trying to free herself from his bony grip.

"Shut up," he told her. As she stopped fighting, he turned his head to Rowan. "My physicians think differently." He reached under the covers, and took out a gun. Taire's eyes widened as he pressed it to her temple. "Put that needle back in your arm and start the transfusion, or I will shoot her in the head."

Taire went still. "You don't want to hurt me. You love me. I'm your princess. You said when I got old enough you were going to marry me. Like the first Alana."

King spat in her face. "You're nothing like Alana. Why would I want you when I can have her?"

Taire felt something blaze up inside her, a cold fire that devoured everything she felt. She looked at Rowan, who could have everything but didn't want it. She looked at Father, who had everything but didn't want Taire.

The walls began to shake.

Chapter 20

Rowan reached out to the walls, losing her footing when the floor began to vibrate. Sean's arm came around her, dragging her back away from the bed.

"What the hell?" She looked around wildly, trying to find the source. "Earthquake?"

"It's the kid," he said as he steadied her. "She's telekinetic."

Gerald King started rising out of his bed, the tubes feeding into his body snapping and the sheets falling away. He looked down at the runaway girl, his face contorted.

"Stop this at once," he said, trying to hold the gun in his hand steady. "You can't do this to me, Alana. I won't permit it. Do you hear me?"

"I'm not Alana. I'll never be Alana." The girl straightened, watching the gun as it flew out of his hand and embedded itself in the door. "I'm Taire."

Several men armed with rifles burst through the door. Sean rammed into one who tried to knock down Rowan, and tossed him into the computer array. Sparks exploded from the ruined equipment as the man went down, but when Sean turned three of the men tackled him.

"Make her stop this," Gerald hissed at Rowan. "Before she kills us all."

"You're her father," she snapped as she dodged a swing from one of the men. "*You* stop her."

The second swing connected, and Rowan went down

beside Sean. She heard panels cracking overhead, showering down chunks of plaster and several glass globes, which burst like bombs all around her. She covered her head, and then felt the same push she'd felt the night of the accident, which this time shoved her out of the way as the bodies of King's men went flying out through the doors.

"Rowan." Sean crawled over to her, lunging at the last minute to cover her with his body as noise filled the air and the ceiling collapsed on top of them. Dust and smoke choked her as she struggled to push away a beam that had Sean's still body pinned on top of hers.

"Sean? God damn it, Sean." She shook him, but he didn't move, and when she grabbed the back of his neck her hand came away wet with blood. "Oh, no. No."

Rowan struggled to her knees, squinting to see through the cloudy air. She saw the outline of the girl's form and called to her.

"Please, kid, that's enough." She curled over Sean as a wall buckled. "You've got to stop now. The whole place is coming apart."

"No." She turned toward the windows, which exploded outward. "He doesn't want me. He doesn't love you. There's nothing left."

Rowan saw Gerald King's body hovering just beneath the hole in the ceiling. He was unconscious, possibly dead. Beyond him the sky was turning purple.

An ominous rumbling started beneath them, deeper and lower, as if the mansion's foundation was beginning to shift and come apart.

"You don't have to live here," Rowan shouted over the noise. "You don't need him. You've got me."

The girl glanced at her. "You don't even know my name."

Rowan struggled to her feet, staggering toward her with her hand outstretched. "I know who you are. I was just like you. He did the same thing to me."

The girl shook her head. "You ran away. I never wanted to leave."

"Didn't you?" Rowan got to her, and rested her hands

on the girl's shoulders. "He only loved Alana. We were just substitutes for her. He's a sick man, honey. He shouldn't have done those things to us."

The girl looked up at her. "You don't understand. You don't know how it was. How hard I tried to make him happy." Her voice broke. "You don't know anything."

"I know who you are," Rowan insisted. "You're my sister. My little sister." Going with her instincts, she wrapped her arms around the girl and hugged her tightly.

The rumbling gradually died away, and the mansion stopped shaking. And then the only sound came from the girl as she clung to Rowan and wept.

"Shhh." She stroked the tangled curls. "It'll be okay, kiddo. I'm here. I'm not going anywhere."

A gun fired, and her little sister jerked. She looked up at Rowan and tried to smile before her eyes closed and she crumpled against her.

"You son of a bitch." That came from Sean, who was struggling to his feet.

Rowan eased her down to the floor and looked into the dying eyes of Gerald King, who held the gun leveled at Sean's head now. "No."

She didn't have to touch her father to shift; her body still remembered the sick, obsessive love he had felt for his wife, and drew on it to change back into the image of her one last time.

As Rowan had hoped, it completely distracted him. "Alana," he whispered, his mouth wet.

"You're a monster, Gerald," she said calmly. "Just as I was. Now you're going to die."

The old man bared his teeth. "Not without you, Alana," he rasped.

"Put down the gun." Sean stepped in front of her, shielding her and the girl. "It's over."

"No." Gerald tried to get up, and looked down at his useless body. He struck a fist against his motionless legs. "I'm not ready. I'm not . . ." He glared up at Sean. "You can't have her. She's mine."

Sean bared his teeth. "She's not a fucking possession."

Rowan heard the change in his voice, and saw her lover's back make a strange ripple. The smell of jacqueminot flooded the dusty air, and it seemed to be coming from him.

"Sean?" Her eyes widened as his body began to change, his shoulders lifting, his torso narrowing. The close-cropped blond hair on his skull erupted into a curtain of black that hung down to his shoulders. When he looked back at her, the chiseled angles of his tough face began to soften and flow, changing into more refined, elegant planes and hollows. The midnight black of his eyes gradually lightened until they were the light blue of heaven.

"Forgive me, *ma mûre*," Sean said with Dansant's mouth, in Dansant's voice. And then he was Dansant, Sean's clothes hanging like curtains from his leaner frame, and when he moved over to Gerald King the old man fired directly at him.

"No!" Rowan ran to him, but skidded to a stop as she saw a smashed bullet fall at his feet. She reached out and touched the hole in his shirt, and then tore it aside to look at his unmarked chest.

She touched the place where there should have been a ragged, bloody hole, and then looked up into his angel eyes. "What are you?"

"We have never been sure," he said gently. "But I cannot be killed by bullets." He looked down at King, who had fallen unconscious, and bent to take the gun from his hand. "Or madmen."

A very tall, broad man struggled his way into the room. He had a full head of silver-blond hair and a full beard of the same. His eyes were narrow and flat black, with a distinct Asian slant to them, and his skin was neither Caucasian nor African-American but something in between. He used a cane to pick his way across the floor.

"Paracelsus," Rowan breathed.

"I see I've arrived late. Hello, Rowan. It's lovely to meet you at last." He nodded politely to Dansant as he knelt beside the girl and checked her pulse. "This child is still alive. My car is waiting downstairs, and I know a surgeon in the city who can help us."

"I will carry her," Dansant said, bending down to carefully lift the girl into his arms.

Although debris littered the floors, and the elevator had locked down, they were able to make their way to the first floor by way of the emergency stairs. Paracelsus's limo was parked just outside, and when the driver came around to help them in, Rowan did a double take.

"Do I know. . . ." She studied his face for a moment and then slowly smiled. "I'll be damned. Jimmy Findley."

Findley tipped his hat and grinned. "Happy to help bust you out of here again, miss."

Paracelsus's surgeon friend arranged to admit Taire to the hospital under an assumed name and personally operated on her to remove the bullet lodged in her back. The surgery took several hours, which Rowan spent pacing the breadth and length of the waiting room a hundred times. Dansant disappeared with Paracelsus, while Findley brought her snacks and coffee from the vending machines and kept her company.

Eventually she ran out of steam and nerves and sat down beside him. "Jimmy Findley." She shook her head. "I can't believe it, after all these years."

"It's been a long time." He smiled at her. "I took your advice and showed my mother those bruises, and she never let me go back there. She also wouldn't let my dad see me again until he quit working for Mr. King."

"I never would have gotten out of there without your help," she said seriously. "Not now, and certainly not when I was a kid."

He shrugged. "You'd have found your way. You were always strong. My employer is going to have a few words with you later about your reckless and foolhardy actions, by the way."

"Yeah, I imagine he is." She stared at the door. "I've got to have a little talk with someone myself."

Rowan was working on her fourth coffee and seventh package of peanut butter crackers when the surgeon came in to talk to her.

"She came through the procedure just fine," he told her. "She lost a lot of blood, of course, but fortunately the bullet just missed her kidney. She'll be in recovery for a while, and then we're going to move her to the pediatric surgical ward. Because of her unusual . . . condition, I'm going to keep her sedated for twenty-four hours. You should go home, get some rest."

Rowan thanked him, and went with Findley to find Paracelsus and Dansant. The two men stood deep in conversation at the other end of the hall, but as soon as Dansant saw Rowan he broke off and came to her.

"She's going to be okay." She related what the doctor had told her to both men, and added, "I want to be back here tomorrow when she wakes up."

"Findley and I will go back to the hotel to make some additional arrangements," Paracelsus said. "I have the entire floor, so you're welcome to join us."

"Rowan will be staying with me," Dansant said, and took her arm. "You have my contact information, Samuel. Call if you need anything."

When Paracelsus and Findley left, Rowan turned to Dansant. "Samuel?"

He led her to the elevator. "That is his name."

She waited until they were inside the elevator before she asked, "What's yours?"

"Mine was lost to me," Dansant admitted, "and Sean does not remember his birth name."

"Speaking of Sean," she said, folding her arms, "does he know you're a shape-shifter, and you've been pretending to be him?"

"I *am* Sean, Rowan."

"You do a flawless impression of him," she conceded, "but you forget, I've watched you change."

"I did not change myself into Sean Meriden's form."

The elevator opened. "Sean Meriden and I are the same man. Or, rather, we share the same body."

"Oh, no, you don't." She folded her arms. "I'm a shifter, Dansant. I know how it works. You're good, maybe as good as I am, but there is no way in hell both of you share one body. It doesn't even look like the same body."

He muttered something in French and waved for a cab. "I will tell you after we go to my apartment. It is a long story."

"Honey, it always is." She climbed in the cab.

Dansant's apartment was like something out of an architect's wet dream, all clean lines and avant-garde style, and would have seemed almost sterile if not for the paintings on the walls.

"Friends of yours?" she asked as she eyed one portrait of a blond fallen-angel with vivid green eyes.

"I don't know. I dream of their faces, and I paint what I remember." He brought her a glass of wine and gestured for her to sit on the squiggle of cushions that served as his couch. "I don't remember my life before Sean, Rowan, so I probably have as many questions as you do."

She hmphed. "I doubt that."

He glanced at the windows. "I have only an hour left before I change places with him. We have no memory of each other's activities, so it would be best if you stayed close, so you could reassure him." At her blank look, he added, "The last thing Sean will remember is being in King's suite and your father pointing a gun at him."

"Oh. Yeah." She took a swallow of her wine before she felt ridiculous again. "How can you be two different men?"

Dansant tugged back her sleeve to reveal part of the dragon tattoo on her forearm. "I do not know for sure, but I think in much the same way you can be any woman." He pulled back his left sleeve, and revealed on the inside of his forearm a mirror image of the S-shaped dragon tat Sean had. The only difference was that Dansant's dragon was inked in blue with red eyes.

"Just because you both have this yin-yang dragon tat on your arms doesn't make you Dr. Jekyll and Mr. Hyde," she argued. "It's not even on the same arm."

"Nonetheless, Sean and I bear identical marks, just as we share the same form." He spread his hands. "For this part of every night, that is me."

"Shifting doesn't work like that. I know. I pull the thoughts from someone and use it to create the dreamveil," she said. "I know you're not Sean Meriden pretending to be an executive chef. You're a completely different person. A separate person."

Dansant nodded.

Rowan had seen a lot of weird things in her life, but nothing like this. "So how could you and Sean end up sharing the same body?"

"I have only theories, not facts," he admitted, "but over the years Sean and I have come to some logical conclusions. It begins in Nice, with a man named Nathan Frame, who was married to the daughter of a chef."

Dansant told her the story of the accident, and the few fragments of memory Sean had retained of Nathan's past before he had come to France.

"When Gisele was taken, she was put in a van filled with test tubes and biological samples. These were things taken from other people these men tortured. When the accident happened, Nathan ran into the fire to try to save Gisele. Then the van exploded and he was very badly burned. That must have been when one of the specimens entered his body, through his wounds, for pieces of the test tubes were found embedded in them. After two weeks in the hospital, he died of his injuries."

Her throat tightened. "No, he didn't."

Dansant nodded. "In the moments after his death, I came to consciousness in his body. At the same time, his body spontaneously healed and changed shape into mine. I was not hurt or burned, and I knew I could not stay in the hospital and be discovered as I was, so I escaped and hid myself. Then, sometime after midnight, I lost consciousness.

My body shifted again, this time into Sean's form, with his mind and personality."

"So Sean is Nathan."

Dansant shook his head. "Neither of us is Nathan Frame, although we both have some of his knowledge and characteristics. I acquired his cooking skills and love for fine cuisine. Sean inherited his mechanical talents and his fighting abilities. We both have some skill with weapons."

"Was Sean burned when you changed into him?"

"Fortunately, no. The first shift had healed him as well." He sighed. "I am not Sean, and I am not aware of him. Upon my second awakening, when the sun set the next night, I woke to find myself standing on the docks looking at a boat. I was thirty miles from where I had gone to my rest and I could not remember how I had come to be there. My clothes were torn at the seams, as if a larger man had tried to wear them. Fortunately that portion of the docks was deserted at the time, and no one saw us change."

"So sunset triggers the change from Sean to you, and you don't change back until after midnight," she said, to be sure she had it straight. "You have no memory of what he does while he controls the body, and it's the same for him. When you're awake, he's asleep."

He nodded. "We seem to have divided the best of Nathan Frame between the two of us, although physically neither of us bears any resemblance to him. Sean has a few fragments of his memory, but I have none at all. What we do have of Nathan's original form are these." He touched the tat on his arm. "According to his medical file, Nathan also had a taijitu on each arm. One scarlet, one blue. Those, too, were divided between us."

She considered how a man's life and experiences could be split in half, and how much grief the division must have caused Meriden and Dansant. "How do you know all this about each other? If your minds are separated, and you're never aware of each other, how can you communicate at all?"

He smiled a little. "At first we tried to leave messages

with other people, but over time we have learned that they sometimes changed the message or even forgot them. Then we wrote notes and left them in our pockets, but *mon frère* does not always have the patience to write. When we came to America, Sean hired a twenty-four-hour answering service for his garage. It was my idea to call it and leave messages for him, and set up an account for myself so he could do the same. We have to be guarded in what we say, of course, but it has proven to be most effective."

Rowan chuckled. "You should really try e-mail." Her smile faded as she studied his face. "You really don't remember who you were before all this happened to you and Sean?"

"I wish I did, but no. My memory begins the night I woke in the hospital." He grimaced. "There are some clues about the sort of man I was. I speak many languages, some that are very old and no longer used, but French is the most familiar. I know how to handle weapons, especially blades, very well. As you have seen, I paint portraits and landscapes. They are people and places I have never seen, but still I know them." He touched his chest. "Here, inside, I feel them."

"Do you remember dying?"

"*Non*. I only remember waking. I had thought perhaps my first body must have been destroyed by the men who took Nathan's wife, but then that woman came to me, the night you and I went to the opera. She called me Michael and kissed me." He gave her a troubled look. "I was looking for you, so I did not pay much attention to her." He nodded toward the portrait. "That is the same woman."

"Michael is a pretty common name, but at least we know what he looks like," Rowan pointed out. "When it's Sean's turn to have the body, he can start hunting him down for you."

"*Non, ma mûre*. If the man I was lives, I have no wish to meet him."

"Why not?"

"He cannot know he was born again in another body.

He has his life and his woman." He ran his hand over her curls. "I have mine."

"For eight hours a day." Now she shook her head. "How can you live like this? You didn't even get half days."

He gave her a wry look. "Regrettably I was never consulted. But it is not so bad as you think. You sleep every night, and you do not resent the hours away from the world. When Meriden takes my body, it is much the same for me."

"Jesus, that's another thing." She twined her fingers in his. "Neither of you really ever sleeps, do you?"

"Sean does." He shrugged. "I do not seem to require it."

She tucked a long strand of his hair behind his ear. "Aren't you afraid when he takes over that you might not come back the next night?"

He considered that for a moment. "I have always felt that it is Sean's body, not mine. I am grateful for my life, but I live it through his flesh." He sighed. "After the accident, neither of us could accept it at first. Sean was too damaged in spirit, and I could not bear the thought that I had only existed as bits of skin and blood and bone. We still struggle with it, and we often resent each other. For example, he will not like that I was the one to tell you about us."

"I'm not afraid of Sean." She kept hold of his hand. "I'm in love with him."

His mouth tightened. "I know."

"I'm also in love with you." As he stared at her, she leaned in and brushed her lips against his. "Whatever problems you have with each other, you're both going to have to deal with that."

He looked stunned and pleased, and threaded his fingers through her curls. "You would choose both of us?"

"You might be two different guys, but you have the same heart. Literally and metaphorically speaking." She pulled him over on top of her. "I don't care if you change into one man or two or nine. I want you. I want Sean. I want us."

Dansant braced himself on his forearms. "Do you." He

settled himself between her legs, rocking his hips a little so that his erection stroked her gently. "I've wanted you since the first moment I saw you."

"Same here." She reached down in between them, un-zipping his fly and pushing her hand inside.

"Rowan." He caught his breath. "Sean is your lover. He may not accept this. I love you, but I do not want him hurt. He is my brother."

It touched her that he was so concerned about his other half. "We'll be okay. Just let me do the talking."

"In that, I have no choice." He tried to lift himself away from her, and when she held on he frowned. "I will change in a few moments. I cannot be with you when he emerges. It is too dangerous for you."

"I'm tougher than you think, Jean-Marc." She palmed him, enclosing him in her fingers and guiding him to where she was already wet and pulsing with the ache of empti-ness. "This is the best way to tell him, you know. And when you wake up tomorrow night, we'll pick up where we left off. I promise." She lifted a little to seat him between her folds, and then tightened her muscles to draw him in. "And if Sean doesn't cooperate, I'll just handcuff him to the bed and ravish him until he changes."

Dansant swore softly and shook as he sank into her another inch. "Do you understand what happens? I will change while I'm inside you."

She smiled. "I don't think it'll hurt. And this way, I get to have both of you inside me."

He stroked into her, groaning as she clasped him with her body. As the sky outside turned dark gray, he began fucking her, driving himself in and out as she held on to his shoulders and cradled him with her legs. When his eyes began to darken from heavenly blue to midnight black he bent his head and kissed her, pressing in as deep as he could, and she came around him, her body arching as he pushed her over the edge of pleasure and into the darkness with him.

His body shifted in a wave that had no beginning or

end but just swept out in all directions, like water swelling and spilling from a winter thaw. It was beautiful to see and feel.

Dansant's long, sinewy muscles broadened over stretching bones, and his weight went from delicious to maddening as he twisted against her, his cock jetting inside her with frantic jerks. His long black hair receded to a pale blond stubble, his jaw lengthened, and his brows shifted from a sweep of wings to a menacing arch. As his hair lightened, the luscious scent of jacqueminot from his skin darkened, changing into something deeper and spicier. His expression went from taut delight to dazed confusion, and then he was Sean, his big hands pinning her down as he shoved himself deep.

"Hi, there." She gasped as he tangled a hand in her hair and brought her mouth to his. The kiss took what was left of her breath away, and when he lifted his head to look into her eyes, she curled an arm around his neck. "In case you were wondering, King is dead, the kid is in the hospital but okay, and we're fine."

"Yeah." He looked down at their bodies. "I can see that. But how did I . . ." His expression darkened, and he lifted up. "Shit. Sorry I interrupted."

"Oh, no." She put the other arm around his neck. "You're not going anywhere."

"If you want to fuck him, Cupcake," he said through gritted teeth, "I'm afraid you'll have to wait another sixteen hours."

"I was waiting for you."

Sean cupped her face with his hand. "You think I want to share you with him? Is that what this is all about?"

"You already share a body with him," she pointed out calmly. "What's one more?"

He turned his head, his jaw working. "You're not just a body to me."

"Neither are you. Neither is he." She sighed. "Of course, if we can't work this out, I can call it a draw and walk away. There are plenty of one-dimensional guys out there. I'm sure you'll meet someone else someday who will understand that you turn into a were-chef every night."

Now he looked at her. "I was the chef. He was a bunch of fucking test tubes." He looked at her mouth. "What does he say about this?"

"He's worried about you," she said, kissing his chin. "Like me."

He made a disgusted sound. "Sure he is. He was so worried he changed while he was fucking you."

"I asked him to do it, so you'd know." She ran a hand over his short hair. "He also said he'd step aside if you want." When he stared she nodded. "He knows it's your body, Sean. You've got the final word here."

"Yeah." His expression thawed a little, and he rolled over onto his back, bringing her along to straddle him. "Between the two of us, you're not going to get a whole lot of sleep, Cupcake."

"I like where I am." She worked herself down on him until their body hair tangled. "And who the hell needs sleep?"

Epilogue

"Losing Hoff in that car accident was unfortunate, Elliot," Genaro said, "but Delaporte positively identified the remains, and brought back a DNA sample from the morgue to confirm. She's dead, as is Gerald King. Their deaths have closed the matter."

Kirchner wasn't satisfied. "What about the heir to King's estate?"

"She's sixteen years old," Genaro said. "Too young to be Kyndred. Once she recovers from her injuries, she'll be shipped off to prep school and spend her summers with her uncle in Martha's Vineyard. I doubt she even knows how to spell transgenic."

"I don't like it." The geneticist looked at Delaporte. "You should have brought in Hoff the night our team disappeared in New York."

The security chief shrugged. "Mr. Genaro wanted her taken here, in the building. I can only do what I'm told, Doctor."

The doctor's face darkened. "Yet somehow you still manage to screw it up."

"Would you excuse us, please, Chief?" Genaro waited until Delaporte left the conference room before he continued. "Don Delaporte has been in charge of GenHance security for the last twenty-two years, Elliot. His loyalty to the company—to me—is unquestionable."

"He was the last person to see Nella Hoff alive," Kirch-

ner said. "He permitted Bradford Lawson free access to the
building, which resulted in Lawson's theft of the transerum
and the progenote. He also failed to detect or capture Andrew Riordan when he was spying on us. He's completely
incompetent."

"I disagree."

"That is your prerogative," Kirchner said. "But how
many more mistakes does Delaporte have to make before
you see that he's a liability?"

"I think you're becoming paranoid, Elliot." Genaro rose
from the conference table. "Why don't you take the rest
of the week off, and spend some time with your family?
Maybe that will put things in perspective for you."

Delaporte was waiting for Genaro in the analysis lab.
"Dr. Kirchner seemed upset."

"He is. He cannot reconstruct Nella Hoff's experiments.
Apparently she removed some of her notes, or destroyed
them." The chairman watched the simulation looping on
the terminal screen. "He's decided that you are to blame
for his lack of progress."

Delaporte nodded, unperturbed. "The doctor doesn't
accept failure well."

"Neither do I, Don." Genaro regarded him. "We've been
together a long time. I would consider it a personal as well
as a professional loss if I had to terminate you."

"Then I'll make it my business never to give you a reason to, sir," Delaporte said.

Several weeks after that meeting, Delaporte drove up to
his cabin in the mountains to spend the weekend hunting.
He invited Genaro to go with him, but the chairman had
a prior commitment, and refused. The security chief spent
the next two days tramping happily through the cold, un-
welcoming woods and bringing down two bucks, which he
skinned and butchered himself. He then invited a woman
friend from a nearby town to stop in for a late dinner and a
friendly romp in his sheets. He enjoyed the sex as much as
the fresh venison.

On the drive back to Atlanta, Delaporte easily shook off the men who had been tailing him for the better part of a month before he stopped at a public rest area, and walked out to the picnic area to eat the lunch he'd packed for himself. After he finished his meal, he took the phone taped to the underside of the table and carried it with him into the woods, where he found a spot where he could watch the road while placing the call.

"I was followed up into the mountains, my lord," he told his master. "I was able to elude them briefly, but I will be unable to report on a regular basis until the surveillance stops." He listened to the instructions he was given, and memorized an address and phone number. After that he made his only request. "May I speak with her?"

"Hello, Don," Nella said a short time later. "How are things in the States?"

"Lonely," he said simply.

"I've been writing letters to you. I can't send them, so I'm boxing them." There was a hitch in her voice as she said, "I expect the next time we meet, I'll have quite a stack."

"Every night I think of you," he told his lover. "I remember how you smell. The sounds you make."

"How long will it be before I see you again?"

He saw a familiar car pull into the rest area parking lot. "Maybe years. Don't wait, baby. Enjoy yourself. And stay safe."

"You, too, love. Bye."

Delaporte switched off the phone, removed the battery and the sim card, and wiped it down before dropping it inside a hollow tree. The battery he dropped on his walk out of the woods. The sim card he mangled slowly inside his pocket; he wouldn't discard it until he reached home and could drop it in a container of acid he kept in his garage.

The men following him made a pretense of using the vending machines as they watched him make his way back to his car. He dumped his trash and stowed his cooler in his trunk before getting back onto the road.

He eyed in his rearview mirror the men hurrying back

to their car to follow him, and allowed himself to feel a small amount of satisfaction. "Amateur cocksuckers."

Taske found his driver working out behind the garage, waxing the limo in the shade of one of the estate's massive oak trees. "Findley, can you spare a moment?"

"Yes, sir." The driver put down his buffing rag and came around the car to join Taske and his new employee.

"This is Neville Morehouse," he said. "Neville, James Findley." He waited until the two men shook hands. "Morehouse will be taking over as house manager, as Mrs. Wallace and Mr. Rodriguez have decided to relocate to Miami."

Findley didn't comment on the sudden departures of the housekeeper and gardener. "If I may be of assistance during the transition, Mr. Morehouse, or at any time, please let me know."

"I appreciate the offer, Mr. Findley." Morehouse's smile was faint but genuine. "Perhaps you could assist me this afternoon in picking up my belongings from the club."

"An excellent idea," Taske said. "Well, gentlemen, I have several dozen calls to return. Morehouse, I will see you tomorrow morning at six a.m. Findley." He nodded and limped back toward the big house.

Once Taske was back in his home office, he checked over the documents he had brought back from New York before placing them in his safe. Along with favors called in from many of his associates in New York, Taske had once more employed his newest vendor in the forgery business, who had successfully seen to every document he had required to take over Gerald King's estate and assume guardianship of young Taire.

Rowan had insisted on remaining behind in New York to look after the girl during her recovery and make arrangements to reside in the city permanently.

"I know you don't think it's safe for me to stay," she had argued, "but this is going to work. If it doesn't, I will personally pack up everyone and relocate them myself."

Taske was more troubled about her involvement with

the shifter who had stolen her heart—twice. He was not convinced that a relationship between three people, two of whom shared the same body, could last. He'd even been tempted to try to see how the three timelines converged. But in the end he had to admit that both of her lovers were decent men who cared deeply for her, and would provide her with the additional bonus of round-the-clock protection. So he had capitulated to her wishes, obtaining in return a promise to call on him if she was ever in trouble.

He placed his first call to Drew, who had decided to stay in Halagan until spring, after which he would head north. Until then he was going to research the circumstances surrounding Sean Meriden's accident, and trace the ownership of the van that had been carrying the biological specimens. Taske had a feeling that it would not belong to GenHance.

"I need to learn French," Drew complained. "Most of the records aren't in English, and the online translators just turn it into babble."

"Be careful to cover your tracks, my friend," Taske warned. "Whoever tried to take Nathan Frame did not hesitate to murder his entire family. They won't take kindly to being identified."

"So far all I have is a registration to some Italian doctor who disappeared in Nice on the same day the accident happened," Drew admitted. "But I'll be cautious. Whoever these guys are, evidently they'll cross any line to get what they want. So where are you off to now?"

"I think I might spend the holidays in France," Taske said, looking at his gloves.

"Does Mr. Taske always rise quite so early?" Morehouse asked casually.

"Always," Findley said. "The first thing I bought when I started here was a very loud alarm clock." He gestured toward the second-story living quarters above the garage. "Can I offer you a cup of tea?"

"If you would allow me to make it," Morehouse said. "No offense, but it is my country's national drink."

"None taken, as long as you never try to make me coffee."

The two men went upstairs to Findley's apartment, which Morehouse admired as much as his new quarters in the house. While the house manager prepared the kettle, Findley went to into the small bathroom to clean up. By the time he returned Morehouse had the table set and the tea ready.

"How long have you been living in the States?" Findley asked as he sat down.

"About four years now." Morehouse poured and added a spoonful of sugar to his cup. "I hadn't set my sights quite so high as this, but when Mr. Taske opened the door, I ran through it."

"He's a good man. I've never worked for better." Findley gave him a measuring look. "Don't carry a torch for him. He's straight as an arrow."

Morehouse smiled a little to acknowledge the perceptive remark. "I'm not in the market for a wealthy lover."

Findley grinned. "I hope not. Mrs. Wallace's scones will be greatly missed."

After Findley cleared the table efficiently, he accepted Morehouse's help at the sink.

"Is there anything I should know about the household?" Morehouse asked.

"Mr. Taske is considered eccentric," Findley said carefully. "He travels quite a bit, often without giving much notice to the staff. He's meticulous, punctual, particular about details, and very generous."

"How long have you been carrying a torch for him?" the house manager asked gently.

"Since he saved my life." Findley turned off the taps. "I guess I always will, at least in my heart."

"You're young." Morehouse covered his hand briefly. "You should leave room for another flame."

Findley glanced at him. "Should I?"

"One never knows what the future will hold." More-house frowned. "Did I say something funny?"

Rowan opened the door to the hospital room with her hip. "Incoming overpriced floral arrangements," she announced as she peeked over the vases of wildflowers, roses, and orchids in her arms. "I need major table space here, Terry. Clear the deck."

Taire grabbed her water pitcher and cup from the rolling table, and flicked a thought at a vase that was about to tip over. "Jeez, Trick, what did you do? Knock over a couple of gift shops?"

She managed to set everything down without dousing the patient. "I'm playing delivery girl. The orchids are from Samuel, the roses are from Jean-Marc, and the wildflowers are from the large grumpy man stalking me."

"I wanted to carry some of the flowers," Sean told Taire as he started piling gift bags on the end of her bed. "She said she didn't need any help." He glanced over his shoulder before taking a grease-stained cardboard box out of one of the bags. "Medium-thin-crust pepperoni and sausage, extra cheese," he murmured. "Should still be hot."

Taire yelped with joy and tore open the box, ripping out a slice and sinking her teeth into it. She closed her eyes and groaned with pleasure.

Rowan gave him a dirty look. "You brought her pizza? For breakfast?"

He leaned back against the wall. "I'd bring her a beer, too, if she was old enough to drink one."

"Well, at least I was thinking about her nutritional requirements." Rowan took a can of Coke out of her jacket pocket, which she opened and set beside the pizza box. "Tah-dah."

Taire swallowed, took a drink from the soda, and then looked from Rowan to Sean. "What, no Snickers bar?"

"Shit. Be right back." Sean disappeared.

"I love watching his butt when he runs." Rowan came around the bed, and when Taire scooted over climbed in beside her. "So I talked to the doc on the way in, and he says I can maybe bust you out of here on Friday." Before Taire could say anything, she held up a finger. "As long as you don't pop any stitches, refuse to do your therapy, or give the nurses any grief."

"I'll do extra therapy," Taire promised. Some of the happiness left her expression. "Where am I going to live now, though?"

The King mansion had been declared unsafe for further occupancy, and since the heir to Gerald King's estate had decided to donate the land to a free medical clinic for underprivileged children, it was slated for demolition in the spring.

"Well, Sean and I were just talking about that." She took hold of the younger girl's hand. "You know that you inherited like a million trillion dollars from Gerald, and with that you could build yourself a couple hundred new mansions—"

"No," Taire said flatly.

"I didn't think so, either." She squeezed her hand. "Door number two is Samuel, your legal guardian thanks to all those papers we forged, who would love to have you come up and stay with him in Martha's Vineyard, where you would be waited on hand-and-foot style and get to hang out at the country club and date very rich boys and dress way better than me."

"I like Samuel a lot, but Martha's Vineyard?" Taire looked doubtful.

"Which brings us to door number three. I really wanted you to live with me, but I also thought you might like to have your own place. I'm moving in with Sean, so my apartment is going to be empty. What do you think about moving in across the hall from us at D'Anges?"

Her chin dropped. "Really? You mean it?"

"Absolutely. Of course, it's pretty small and basic, but we can redecorate and stuff. You'd still have to share the bathroom with us," she tacked on.

Taire leveled a look at her. "Trick, I haven't had *any* bathroom for like months now."

"Okay, but sometimes Sean hogs the hot water," Rowan warned. "And he's a neat freak. Seriously. He folds the towels so much they're like origami. I have to keep drying my hands on a swooping crane."

Taire giggled. "You love him and you know it."

If only the kid knew. "We're working on it, but yeah. I do."

"What about you and Jean-Marc?"

Rowan had explained her romantic triangle with Sean and Jean-Marc to Taire, who had accepted the ménage without a quibble. "I'll also be spending some of my nights off over at Jean-Marc's place," she admitted. "He, ah, wants to paint me."

"Oh, he wants to do a lot more than that," her sister said, rolling her eyes.

"Stop talking about the damn Frenchman," Sean said as he breezed in, and presented Taire with a Snickers bar. "Your dessert, Sweet Pea."

Taire wrinkled her nose at Rowan. "He's going to call me that forever, isn't he?"

"It's better than Cupcake," Rowan grumbled.

They stayed with Taire until morning visiting hours were over. By that time she had fallen asleep, and Rowan used a tissue to wipe a betraying smudge of pizza sauce from her chin before tiptoeing out of the room with Sean.

"So who did she pick?" Sean asked on the way down to the parking garage.

"Us." She laughed as he picked her up and twirled her around. "I told you she would."

"Samuel is a tough act to follow." He kissed her. "I can't believe I'm this happy." He frowned. "She's sixteen. We've just inherited a teenager."

"Who is a multimillionaire," Rowan reminded him, "and who can tear down a building with the power of her thoughts."

"I don't feel so good." He pressed her against him. "I think I need to lie down."

"Wait 'til we get home," she said, patting his cheek. "Then I'll tuck you in and rub your tummy."

Sean reached out and hit the stop button on the elevator. "Why don't you rub it now?"

Author's Note

I would not have been able to write this book without inspiration and guidance from many other writers, chefs, and other expert sources on French cuisine. Although I generally don't write acknowledgments because I suck at them, this time around I would like to tip my chapeau to Peter Mayle, author of *A Year in Provence* and *Encore Provence*; Anthony Bourdain, author of *Kitchen Confidential* and *The Nasty Bits*; and innumerable amazing articles and recipes published by the staff and writers of *Cooking Light*, *Food & Wine*, *Gourmet*, and *Saveur* magazines. My thanks to you all for keeping me barefoot, flour-powdered, and in the kitchen.

I do love to cook, and have spent many happy years entrenched in the kitchen and preparing several of the dishes mentioned in this novel. I also count among my friends several people who work in the food industry and who generously answered my endless questions no matter what the hour, so my thanks to Marlisa, Jean-Pierre, Renee, and Sandre. The next time we're all together, I am truffling chicken for everyone.

The reader should be advised that despite the brilliance of my consultants and the fount of information provided by my resources, I am not by any means a trained chef or an expert on French cuisine. Any mistakes found herein should be attributed solely to me.

French-English Glossary

Aïoli: a type of garlic mayonnaise from Provence traditionally served as a dip or to accompany seafood stews

Anglais: English

Bonsoir: Good evening

Brigade de cuisine: the hierarchy or pecking order of a restaurant or large kitchen staff

Ça ne va pas, non: What's the matter with you?

Charcuterie: preparation or cooking of prepared or preserved meats

Chasse: hunt, pursuit

Chez soi: home place

Courgettes à la niçoise: sautéed zucchini and tomatoes, Nice style

Cuisses de canard au chou: roast duck legs with cabbage

Douce: sweet

Écrase: shut up

Enfant trouvé: a deserted or abandoned child of unknown origins

Filet de boeuf au vin: filet of beef with wine

Garde-manger: the pantry supervisor, or the chef responsible for preparing charcuterie, salads, cold dishes, and buffets

Jamais dans ma vie: Never in my life

Je m'en fiche: I don't care

Je suis désolé: I'm sorry

La marche en avant: a principle of French restaurant kitchen work design that ensures that food moves through the kitchen efficiently and that clean items never cross the path of unclean items (literally: "the move forward")

Le bébé: the baby

Loup de mer rôti aux herbes: whole sea bass roasted with herbs

Maison: home

Mise en place: a line cook's setup at his workstation, where he maintains the various oils, seasonings, and other supplies he needs for cooking. Also known as *meez*.

Moules farcies gratinées: mussels with green garlic butter

Mûre: blackberry

Naturellement: naturally

Non: no

Oeufs à la neige: Floating Island (literally: "eggs in snow")

Onglet aux échalottes et aux frites: steak with shallot sauce and french fries

Oui: yes

Parties: a group of chefs

Pâtissier: the pastry cook, or the chef in charge of pastry making, desserts, and sweet dishes; in smaller restaurants can double as the chef in charge of pasta making, bread making and all baked dishes

Petits pois aux morilles: ragoût of peas and morels

Plongeur: dishwasher

Pot-au-feu de fruits de mer: seafood stew (literally: "pot on the fire with fruits of the sea")

Poulet demi-deuil: truffled chicken (literally: "chicken in half mourning")

Ratatouille: thick vegetable stew

Rôtisseur: the roast cook, or the chef in charge of preparing fried, grilled, or roasted foods

Saucier: the sauce maker, or the chef, who is in charge of preparing sauces and finishing meat dishes, and who also prepares warm appetizers; often the most respected chef in a restaurant kitchen

Saumon sauvage juste tiède: warm wild salmon filets

Tarte à la crème vaudoise: a type of Swiss cream tart

Trinxat: cabbage and potatoes (literally: "chopped")

Tournant: kitchen helper, chef's assistant

Très bien: very good

Trouvaille: discovery

Trufflieres: truffle hunters (origin: Italian)

Vous êtes tout excusé: it's quite all right

Please read on for an excerpt from

Frostfire

A Novel of the Kyndred
by Lynn Viehl
Coming soon

A jolt brought Lilah out of the darkness and somewhat awake; she felt so sleepy she almost slipped back at once. Something held down her chest and legs—the weight of an arm and a leg. Someone was beside her, in her bed. Then she felt the hard, cold surface under her and wondered how she'd ended up on the floor.

Opening her eyes took a very long time, and when she did pry her lids apart, they felt gummy, as if they'd been sealed with inferior glue. Blinking to clear her blurred vision, she began to register other things. Blue plastic over her. Something metal around her right wrist. The sense of being exposed came from her body; she was naked. Her right arm had gone numb under a long stretch of heavy, hard warmth.

A body.

She squinted in the dimness, trying to see who it was, where she was. Short black bristles of hair no more than a quarter inch covered a scalp, curved over an ear. She shifted her gaze down, and saw part of a cheekbone, the tapered end of a wide black brow, the jut of a hard jaw.

A man was on top of her arm. A strange, unconscious man.

A *naked* man.

Lilah swallowed against her dry throat, her head swimming with sensory overload. "Help." It came out like a cough, short and wheezing. She tried again. "Help. Me."

The head next to her face turned slowly, exposing more of his face. He opened his eye slowly, only partway, and stared at her. From the one she could see he had dark eyes, framed by lashes beaded with drops of water. Sweat streaked his skin and collected in little pools by the bridge of his nose and the corner of his mouth. He tried to pull back, only to go still. A muscle throbbed in his cheek as his jaw shifted.

"Drugged," he breathed out, his voice more air than sound. "Taken."

"Me?" She watched his head move in a small nod. "You?" Another nod. "God, no."

The man didn't say anything, but she felt something move against her neck. His fingers, stiff and clumsy. He was trying to reassure her.

Lilah didn't dare close her eyes again. "Where? Who?"

"Truck." The lines beside his mouth deepened as he tried again to move, and managed to slide a little of his weight over her right arm. "Men. Two."

Lilah went still, listening. Now she felt the motion of the truck beneath them, heard the hum of the engine. The truck traveled at a steady speed, but she didn't hear any signs that there were men around them. She didn't dare move until she knew for sure.

She gazed at the man beside her and swallowed against the dryness until it receded. "GenHance?" He nodded again, confirming her worst fears. "Where are the men?"

He shifted his eyes up toward the sound of the engine.

Lilah felt his rigid body tremble, and saw pain in his eyes before he shut them tightly. He was in worse shape than she was, perhaps having some reaction to the drugs he'd been given. She moved the lead-weight of her left arm until she felt the back of his arm under her hand and held on as he shook.

"Easy," she said, over and over.

Gradually the convulsive movements slowed and then stopped, and he released a breath against her cheek. A moment later his left hand moved from her neck, his fingers sliding up until he cupped her cheek.

He opened his eyes, blinking away the beads of sweat that trickled down from his hairline. "Must. Escape."

Her heart constricted. "You're too sick."

Now he moved his head slightly from side to side. "Better. Stronger. Soon."

Lilah understood the string of words. He wasn't convulsing, he was fighting the drugs—or they were wearing off. She watched him as he rested, although like her he kept his eyes open and on her face. She tested her limbs, grimacing as her right arm began to wake with a wave of pins and needles. She managed to ease it out from under him and flexed her hand, touching his fingers in the process and making a new discovery.

"They handcuffed us together."

He nodded slowly.

"Damn them." She tried to touch his fingers with hers, but could only rub the back of hers against his knuckles. He had huge hands.

"My name is Lilah," she whispered. She glanced down at his neck where the only thing he wore, a length of chain with two metal tags, lay against his skin. She could read one of them. "Walker Kimball. U.S. Marine Corps." She looked into his eyes. "You're a soldier."

His expression turned curiously impassive, as if he were waiting for some negative reaction. From the beginning the war had never been popular, but Lilah knew the troops who were sent over to fight in the Middle East were never consulted as to whether they thought it was worthwhile or not. They were sent there to fight, many of them to die, in a conflict that probably made as little sense to them as it did to the rest of the world.

"Were you home on leave?" Lilah asked.

"No." He struggled to get the next word out. "Afghanistan."

"They took you from there?" He nodded, and Lilah felt sick. "How?"

"Wounded. Dying." And then he said one last word that chilled her to the bottom of her heart. "Sold."

Aphrodite and her other Takyn friends had told Lilah about GenHance's plans to harvest their DNA and use it to create a superhuman vaccine, one they intended to sell to factions and governments for use on their covert operatives and soldiers. Walker must have been purchased for use as a test subject—who better to experiment on than a real soldier who had been left for dead? No one would ever know what had really happened to him. The military would simply list him as one of the missing in action.

"We have to get out of here," she told him, gripping his arm. "Now."

"Too weak. Rest." He moved his hand to stroke his palm over her hair. "Soon we will go." He gave her a small, grim smile. "Very soon."

The truck's brakes squealed as it slowed down and came to a stop. Lilah listened to opening and slamming doors, and the fainter sound of two male voices arguing. They were too muffled to make out the words, but they drifted around the truck toward Lilah's feet.

"Coming," Walker said at once. "Check us. Quiet. Don't move."

She nodded, closing her eyes and holding still. The sound of the truck door being raised made her heart quake, but Walker turned his hand and pushed his stiff fingers through hers, holding them tight.

"See?" a young male voice said. "They ain't moved. I told you."

The truck bed dipped as someone climbed in. Lilah held her breath as she heard footsteps thump across the floor and the light over them was blotted out. Something prodded the plastic, a jabbing finger. It struck the knob of her elbow, which she instinctively held in a rigid position.

"It's like nine degrees back here," the young voice said. "They're ice cubes now, man."

"Yeah, I guess," the man standing over her said in a deeper, disgusted voice. "I coulda sworn I heard voices, though." A hand scraped against the plastic and then took a handful of it.

"You're just tired, Bob," the younger man said. "Let me drive for a while. You can catch some zees."

Silence stretched out as the man hovered. Lilah didn't dare breathe, and her lungs felt as if they were going to burst. Finally he released the plastic and moved away.

"You better wake me before we cross into Mississippi," Bob said as he climbed out of the truck. "If we're gonna get there before this storm hits, we've gotta head north and take seventy."

The truck's sliding door slammed down, and Lilah exhaled, tears of terror and relief flooding her eyes.

"Don't cry."

He had shifted his head so that his lips brushed the edge of her ear, the words breathed without voice. If she had woken up alone, Lilah realized, she would have called out loud for help until the men had stopped and come for her. They'd already stripped her out of her clothes and had done God only knew what to her while she was unconscious. She didn't want to think of what they'd want to do to her if they'd found her awake.

His hand was moving again, brushing over the hair at her temple, not as awkward now. She had never understood exactly what it meant to be trapped, to be helpless in the face of indifference and cruelty. The men who had drugged and abducted and stripped her had no mercy. To them she wasn't even a person. Her feelings, her needs didn't matter. They had denied her even the most basic decency, the right to die with some dignity.

It had to be worse for Walker. Left for dead while serving his country, alone and suffering, perhaps making his peace with the brevity of his life, only to have his body stolen and sold like a piece of meat . . . it was too much.

"Lilah."

She hadn't realized that she was silently weeping until she opened her eyes and looked through the shimmer of her tears. They softened his stern features, and for the first time she realized how handsome he was, like some dark angel, the light in his eyes glowing in two slivers, as if reflecting some flaming sword.

"Sorry." She gulped back a sob, aware that she had to guard against making any sound that might be overheard again. "Where are they taking us?"

"Denver."

From what the older man had said she guessed they were somewhere in Alabama. She'd driven straight from Lake Gem to Tupelo, Mississippi, once, and that had taken her twelve hours with two short rest stops. Since drugs rarely affected her as strongly as normal people, she guessed she had been unconscious for six, maybe eight hours. That put them in the center of the state. With roughly fifteen hundred miles between them and Denver, they had maybe twenty-four hours left.

In another hour or two Lilah felt sure the drugs would wear off completely, and she'd be able to attempt an escape. Walker wasn't Takyn like her, however, so he would need more time to recover. She might be able to free herself from the cuffs, but abandoning him was not an option. Everything depended on how fast he could shake off the drugs they'd used on him.

"Soon," he murmured, as if he were reading her mind.

He flexed his fingers between hers, and she bent her arm, bringing up their bound hands between them so she could see the cuffs. They were police-issue, and had been cinched too tight to work off. She couldn't even hold their hands up longer than a minute before her muscles began to tremble.

"I'm afraid," she whispered to him.

"I know." He shifted his arm down so that he was holding her in a half-embrace. "I will save us. Protect you."

He could barely move, and she was still so listless she could barely think straight. "How?"

"The door." His gaze shifted toward her feet. "They forgot. To lock it."

New York Times bestselling author

LYNN VIEHL

Shadowlight
The first novel of the Kyndred

With just one touch, Jessa Bellamy can see
anyone's darkest secrets, thanks to whoever
tampered with her genes. What she doesn't know
is that a biotech company has discovered her talent
and intends to kill her and harvest her
priceless DNA...

Gaven Matthias is forced to abduct Jessa himself
so he can protect her, but Jessa has a hard time
believing the one man whose secrets she can't
read. As a monstrous assassin closes in and forces
them to run, Jessa will have to find another way
to discover if Matthias is her greatest ally—or her
deadliest enemy.

**"Lynn Viehl sure knows how to tell a
hell of a story."**
—Romance Reviews Today

Available wherever books are sold or at
penguin.com